I0565868

THE LA PROJECT
A novel by Alfred Cool

ISBN: 978-1-7752501-3-5

Copywrite © 2020 Alfred Cool

Table of Contents:

1. The Thumb Drive

Chain-smoking and scowling at his cellphone, pensive nuclear chemist Ivan Sobriev exhaled smoke from his nose in the European fashion. He kicked backward at the wall beneath blaring, urgent flight announcements thirty feet from the airport Departure doors. The pounding rain mixed with heavy traffic and the bustling stream of people hurrying into the building through the summertime Seattle morning.

Ivan hid behind his hour-inappropriate sunglasses, warily scanning the changing faces in the crowd, naively thinking that if they were coming for him, he would see them before they took him. He pocketed his cellphone, tossed his half-finished cigarette and then went into his pants pocket again to pull out the thumb drive. It held both a curious fascination and disgust for Ivan. He held it over the garbage can, still undecided about it. Finally, he closed a determined fist and pocketed the drive.

Ivan started another cigarette as his cellphone vibrated. The message warned him he was late for check-in. He dropped the cigarette, juggled his phone, briefcase, and suitcase, and joined the mad rush into the terminal. A Red Cap approached, but Ivan waved him off and hurried to the entrance.

Nearby, a woman pulled her Volvo into a space vacated by a taxi, where she peered urgently through the rain. Her eyes followed Ivan. She turned off the ignition, grabbed the keys, and ran through the crowd and into the building.

Inside, the vast terminal teemed with wet, jostling passengers shaking off raindrops. Everyone was in everyone else's way, forming lines, dissolving lines, people mobbing ticket counters, coffee shops and food kiosks. Tired airport security guards yawned beneath the steady downpour of elevator music colliding with indecipherable announcements.

Ivan stepped up his pace. Despite juggling his luggage through the surging crowd, he also managed to speed dial a number on his cellphone.

*

At the TWA security gates, a vaguely sinister couple scanned the faces approaching the security portal. The woman, wrapped in a long leather coat, was taller than the man beside her. He was olive-skinned and slim and a victim of deplorable style, so he appeared greasy in a shiny black suit and thin tie.

*

Ivan spoke into the phone, his eyes tracking left and right, his voice straining, "I've been calling... They're onto me. They broke into our house last night. They got my cellphone and laptop, but I still have the thumb drive. Bosun must've scared them off with her barking." The woman chasing Ivan began running, urgently shoving through the packed crowd. The voice over the public address system announced, "Would international passenger Mr. Ivan Sobriev please report immediately to TWA's passenger portal inside the Departures terminal."

"Why the fuck are they paging me?" Ivan swore into the phone. The announcement spurred him on, and he fell into an awkward jog, leaving the intense woman chasing him farther behind. She fumbled for something in her coat pocket. "They know," said Ivan, huffing into the phone. "Mason, would it kill you to pick up once in a while?"

The woman gunslinger in ambush at the TWA security portal spotted Ivan and shifted her eyes slightly. Her partner caught her cue and rolled his eyes in the same direction. He flexed his right hand, cracking his knuckles.

Ivan, still on his cellphone, unknowingly closed in on the two killers. "The cops came this morning… I need your help, but don't even think about calling my old cell number." Ivan joined the end of the short lineup at the security portal. Another passenger fell into line right behind him. Ivan huffed into the phone, "I hope you can decode the files, or whatever you computer geeks do. Send them to me at CERN. I can get these bastards, but don't tell Lena. Don't tell anyone." Ivan was next in line at the security gate. "I gotta go... This is, you know, new."

The hitman stepped in front of Ivan before he had time to end the call. The hitman opened his suit jacket slightly, showing Ivan the gun tucked in his shoulder holster. "Outside," he said.

Ivan searched for his tickets with his phone in his hand, so he failed to see the gun. "Excuse me?" said Ivan.

The screening agent sent the passenger in front of the hitman through. The agent spoke to the back of the hitman's head. "May I see your tickets and boarding pass, please, sir? And you'll have to remove your shoes." She rolled her eyes at the nearby, uninterested security guard, sipping a coffee.

Ivan juggled his phone; the hitman closed his jacket and stepped out of line. Ivan dropped his briefcase, reached for it, bumped the impatient traveller in line behind him, then again on his way back up. He piled his briefcase and suitcase on the luggage belt for the agent. Flustered, Ivan patted his jacket pockets. "Shit... I don't seem to have..."

A woman's hand on Ivan's shoulder spun him around. "Honey," said Lena, laughing and waving his passport and online tickets, "besides making me run after you and not kissing me goodbye, did you forget something this morning?"

Lena's mild amusement drew a thin smile from the bored security guard, but her apparent cutting in outraged the frustrated passenger behind Ivan. Out of patience and holding both his shoes and tickets, he said, "C'mon, buddy, we all have a plane to catch."

"Please, Lena," said Ivan, ignoring the other passenger, "I'm Skyping Mason."

"They've been calling for you," said Lena. She gently took the phone from Ivan so he could remove his shoes. She said, "Mason will be here when you get back. When was he ever not wired into his computer?" Lena gave Ivan his passport and tickets, then spoke into the cellphone camera. "Hi Mason, bye, Mason. Ivan has to go be brilliant now." She looked at Ivan, who kissed her cheek. "Run, now, hon," she said, "I'm not the only one looking for you."

2. Conspiracy

Thirty-six hours before Ivan boarded his flight, Renton Hawke, the head of Nuclear Energy World Corporation's D.C. Security Division, sat at his desk and shook a nearly full prescription bottle, and smiled. Overhead, on an expansive wall monitor, a GNN talking head millionaire droned on denigrating as "socialists" a lengthy list of POTUS critics. Hawke dreamily contemplated the crystal tumbler half full of quality scotch, turning it slowly in one hand. A long-time addict, Hawke anticipated the superlative scotch and the Oxycodone's comforting relief until the cellphone buzzing on his desk interrupted him.

Hawke frowned and quickly exchanged the pill bottle for the cellphone, answering the vibrating equivalent of a jerk on a choke chain around his neck. His division was in crisis, and the timing of this one, in particular, had generated waves at the highest corporate level. When riled, CEO Delaci was a ruthless dictator infamous for conducting humiliating terminations, or worse, for anyone who threatened the LA project timetable. Delaci's first text, which had demanded action and information, arrived six full minutes before Hawke ingested the narcotic. Hawke's team had discovered the hacker, but that would not be enough for Delaci. As NEWCorp's security dragon, Hawke breathed hellfire over the department and all transgressors for his CEO, but this hack was the kind of incident that placed even powerful men working for Delaci at risk. For the second time that day, Hawke reacted to a Delaci text. He slammed his fist down on his intercom, bouncing the T.V.'s remote control and accidentally opening a CCTV channel, splitting the images on the screen. Not noticing, Hawke said aloud, "The last thing I need is that godamned Delaci getting his grubby fingers in this."

On the screen, an analyst sitting at her workstation in a row of six similar, low and backlit workstations flashed her eyes upwards at the red light on the micro-camera aimed at her station. An open window on her screen played a video of the break-in, clearly showing Ivan's face as he climbs out from under the desk. She deleted the video.

She began typing furiously. "Sir?" The woman's voice

6

drowned out the GNN talking head, filling Hawke's office when she spoke into her headset microphone. "Our firewall integrity procedure is finished. I have control of the hacker's laptop and cellphone."

Hawke disabled the two-way video to hide his surveillance. He began to drift off in the warm haze, so he pushed back against the drugs. He muted the GNN feed to concentrate on the woman who filled his monitor, watching her confer with others on her team. Above the clatter of her keyboard keys, her voice enticed him as she collated the details of both the security breach and the hacker. Studying her, Hawke saw she was young and gorgeous. "Level? Data? Last name? First? Birthplace?" she inquired, her voice a monotone. "Address? Age? Single, married? Banks? Income? Ethnicity? Occupation?" Within seconds NEWCorp owned all the hacker's personal information. Her soft southern lilt transfixed Hawke. Her breath across the microphone sobered him briefly when she asked a co-worker, "What did he get?"

Hawke said, his voice husky, "Would you like to share that information?"

She stared into her camera. Her voice was quiet but definitive, "We have a mole."

Hawke's eyes narrowed. Her inflections and her personal, ready response made him want her. "What did he see?"

"Level two. He downloaded three documents, but the contents are not sensitive."

Hawke's team screened inbound data for bots, viruses, and trojan attacks every nanosecond of every day. Most of the unsuccessful efforts to pierce their firewall were from competitors, but some were from the gutter—the Tor hackers. These had been partially successful in the past and had paid dearly for their actions when Hawke's crews showed up at their doors. The other hackers came at them through the dark web and were stopped. Still, occasionally a hacker with more skills breached NEWCorp's sophisticated security software. So Hawke's technicians set up and disguised digital access ports as traps, or blind alleys, to appear vulnerable to outside probing or from casual, or malicious, interest from inside the perimeter. Delaci had insisted security expand to monitoring any attempts made through unauthorized access by employees or moles clever enough to earn a rap on their knuckles.

"Who is this fucking traitor?"

The sudden and explosive intensity of his voice set her back. Her face turned passive on his screen, but her eyes were wide and looking right into the camera. "Ivan Sobriev, one of our nuclear consultants, just a curious amateur."

Hawke, still struggling to minimize the encompassing effects of his mid-morning highball, continued to over-react. "You're not paid to make assumptions." Hawke's eyes bulged at his screen, his voice menacing. The analyst looked away.

NEWCorp hand-picked their security staff. Each was a specialist. Most were ex-military personnel trained to man their stations and report swiftly, but above all else, execute orders professionally, efficiently, and without question—thinking was a management-only prerogative. She looked back at the camera. Hawke zoomed in on her face; the auto-focus clarified her image.

"Yes, sir."

He reached for the bottle of Oxycodone. "What's he done?" He gulped down another pill.

"He is copying files to a removable thumb drive. I've hijacked control of the drive and scrambled its contents. He can't delete or transmit, but he'll think he has normal access until we recover the devices. We own his eyes."

"Tear out his fucking eyes. What's in those files?"

"Only a trail of crumbs."

Frustration flared in Hawke's voice. "Tell me."

"They refer to the LA Project."

"God damn it."

*

Corrupt Senator Albert Victor, snake-eyed, alpha male in the swarming D.C. pool of predatory political sharks, sat in a high-backed chair at the polished, antique, and exquisite NEWCorp boardroom table. He watched another Senator, Smith, stop to arrange one of the other chairs slightly out of place until it aligned perfectly with its neighbours. Smith took the chair across the table from Victor, who said, "Now that we're all here…"

Smith nodded slightly, arranging his paper pad perpendicular to the table edge, moving his phone to the pad, then moved it to the table, put it back on the pad but in line with the edges of the pad. He then checked his tie and finally intertwined the fingers of both hands to wait. Victor sighed heavily. Smith responded to the audible but subtle rebuke. "I like order."

Smith followed Victor's gaze when he turned to the widescreen monitor mounted among superlative oil portraits of George Washington, Samuel Adams, and Abraham Lincoln. Hawke's prescription sticker was clearly legible on the T.V. monitor until Victor zoomed out, and Hawke's face filled the screen. "You should take it easy on the oxy, Renton, or your doctor may cut you off the scotch."

Hawke glared back at Victor from the split screen—the immaculately preened senator turned his nose up at him, replacing the analyst's frame. Hawke scooped the pill bottle off his desk, put it in his drawer, and then sneered at Victor. "Senator," snapped Hawke, "kissed any babies lately?"

Victor reacted immediately. "You insolent toad. If any details concerning the project get out..." Hawke's red-ringed eyes became vengeful slits. Exploiting his advantage, Victor calmed his voice, then continued, "We want to know what you are doing about this data theft?"

Hawke back-pedalled quickly. "Take it easy. I have the thief—he's one of our hires." He pinched his leg under the table, punishing himself for his blatant admission.

Victor frowned. "Yes... but what about the data?"

"We scrambled it. I'll have that equipment here within twenty minutes." Hawke's mouth remained open.

"No, let him go for the rest of the day. Let's see what he plans to do with our information first."

"As you like, then I'll crush him like a fly."

"Is that your guarantee?" said Smith.

Hawke sneered at the camera and nodded once, his mouth still agape.

"This spy got through your security screening. Don't forget about our hole in the desert. It's our option to retire you there if you fail us. Don't let it happen again."

"You're threatening me?"

Senator Victor ended the call. He slid his eyes sideways, but he faltered as if kneeling before his hooded executioner. Victor's eyes quickly shifted to the window where the sun highlighted the Capitol Dome. A chair scraped. Victor turned back slowly to the room and met Smith's eyes. The third man in the boardroom, Delaci, his voice quiet and yet menacing, spoke from the shadows, "Smith. Have a chat with Hawke in Washington." The two senators turned simultaneously to watch the heavy mahogany door close behind Delaci. Smith said, "How long has Hawke been a mouth breather?"

*

Hawke stood, kicked his chair hard against the back wall of his office, cursed aloud, then slammed both palms flat on the desk. He stabbed his console buttons to bring his analyst back to full screen and leaned over his intercom. "I want that thumb drive."

"Sir," said the analyst, tucking her phone under her clipboard again.

Hawke exhaled. "I want a background briefing on this bastard right now: his family, friends, associates, his goddamn dog's name if he has one. Deploy a team to watch him; by that, I mean... What's your name?"

"Amelia, Captain, Marines, Combat Information Specialist, sir."

"You're new?"

"I've been with NEWCorp for five months."

"I've never seen you before." Hawke looked baffled.

"No, sir."

"So impress me. We assume Sobriev has a handler or media contact. We keep him on a short leash until we have that information. This stays between us—you and I go dark on this together." He stared at the screen to watch her reaction. Hawke craned his neck, yawned off the insistent Oxy, and rolled his shoulders to twist out the tension, but he kept his eyes on Amelia.

She looked directly into the camera. "There's more. Sobriev is flying to Europe the day after tomorrow... his destination is CERN, in Geneva. I recommend a passive device extraction before he leaves Seattle."

"We don't specialize in second chances or passivity, Captain. Deploy a recovery team to Sobriev's house. He won't leave his bedroom, let alone the continent with that drive."

Her fingers flew across the keyboard for mere

seconds. "It's done. But..."

"And there is still more...?" Hawke felt the Oxycodone coming on, demanding his surrender. He closed his eyes and released a slow, deep sigh before he mustered more control.

"After the theft, Sobriev made several calls from his cellphone to a Mason Stone, primary occupation: writer and a taxi driver. He has a podcast show too. Sobriev never made contact, so..."

"... so that's where he's dumping the information."

"Negative. I traced Stone's background. There are no previous threads that lead to him, no history of subversion." The video playing on her computer screen was a recent protest at the decommissioned but still troubled Hanford nuclear facility. The camera zeroed in on Ivan Sobriev and a young, angry man beside him, both chanting anti-nuke slogans with the crowd. She deleted the video. "We could deploy surveillance..."

"Surveillance is in our rear-view mirror. Order up a second team and authorize it to deal with this writer. Authorize extreme prejudice."

"I can't do that, sir."

"No? This happened on your watch. I'm holding you responsible. That's why we pay you. Got that?"

"Yes, sir."

"Good... the alternative was going to be bad for you. Now, nothing about the LA Project gets past you and me, not even the name. Activate another team to meet the scientist before he leaves for Switzerland." Amelia stared at her camera. Hawke barked at her, "Bring that briefing to my office. You have ten minutes." He terminated the video call and disabled the channel feed, pressing the silence button with a manicured index finger. He opened his desk drawer and stared at the bottle.

Minutes after he finished three more ounces of scotch, his intercom buzzed. Renton Hawke, sitting at his desk, his elbows on the chair armrests, tapped his fingertips together, watching his steel pocket door slide open. "Amelia. Good." She stopped at attention inside his door. He waved a gracious hand to invite her further inside. The pocket door whispered shut behind her. Hawke said, "No brief?"

"No."

"I see... Maybe we got off on the wrong foot today."

He appraised her athletic figure as she crossed the room to stand at ease in front of his desk. He poured out his version of charm. "I might as well conduct your performance review right now—unless you'd prefer a scotch?"

"Performance review? I've never agreed to any..."

"At attention." Amelia responded to his order. Hawke stood and slowly circled her. His voice was little more than a hoarse whisper. "NEWCorp has expectations. I have expectations, and when I give an order, I want it executed." Hawke raised his voice to a powerful command, "Without question." Standing close and behind her, his acrid breath on her neck, he softened his approach. "I'll be blunt—you've impressed me." When he touched Amelia's elbow, she tensed visibly. He slid his hand up to her shoulder. "You could do well with us if you learn to follow orders." He clamped his hand on Amelia's throat, pulling her into him. She resisted, balanced and rigid in her stance. Hawke grunted into her ear, "I can wipe your military record, your pension, write you up as a traitor... I have powerful friends you can't even imagine exist. Give me what I want."

Amelia lowered her center of gravity, threw the dissipated man over her shoulder, and body-slammed him hard onto his desk. The collision caused the remote to activate the monitor, and the GNN talking heads reappeared. Hawke gasped for air after her violent move had emptied his lungs. She held the pen in her fist half an inch over one of his eyes and spoke through gritted teeth, "Wonderful offer, but I just broke up with a guy, and I'm not quite ready to date again. So, if you'll excuse me, I have a job to do."

3. Early Warning System

At 4:45 a.m., Mason Stone, a stubborn idealist, woke to the song *I Don't Like Mondays* playing on his smart home device. He ran his tongue over his swollen upper lip. *Shit. I caught one yesterday.* Brooke, his desperate Lab-Rottweiler cross, ran into his bedroom and licked his hand. When Mason opened his eyes, he looked at her and said, "I told you last night, buddy, that was one too many dog cookies."

Brooke wiggled in needy anticipation, bumping the bedside table, knocking the cellphone onto the floor where it tumbled under the bed, face down. Mason ignored the phone but kept the song playing on the external speaker. He stood and stretched. Mason was fit and of moderate height. He padded in bare feet and white boxer shorts past his kitchen and the inspiring coffee aroma coming from the pre-set coffee maker, past his den jammed with computer and video recording equipment, to the patio door where he let Brooke outside. He looked for a moment at the rain pouring down into the dreary West Coast darkness, breathing in deeply. Mason, who had to be at work by five-thirty, slid the door closed. He backtracked into the kitchen to fix a cup of coffee, then went to shower. He was unaware when an incoming call interrupted the song on his phone. Ivan's airport video call finished under his bed in a blur of images and Lena's laughing. When the clip ended, the phone resumed playing his 'Greatest Hits' list.

Feeling revived after his shower, Mason refilled his coffee cup and leaned against the kitchen counter, a towel wrapped around his waist. Brooke smeared a muddy paw across the sliding glass door, so he let her in but made her wait on the mud rug. Mason dressed, looked for his cellphone, found it under the bed, saw no messages, and put it in his pocket. After pouring the last coffee into his worn Space Needle travel mug, he put on his rain jacket and took Brooke outside for her proper pre-work walk.

He opened the outside door and stopped short. He pulled his hoodie over his head to fend off the chill of the monsoon and subtly scoped the black SUV parked down and across the street. Cop cars stood out and drew everyone's attention in his neighbourhood. *Interesting.* Mason called Brooke back to start her in the direction of the cops. The SUV's engine turned over, the headlights came on, and the driver cruised toward them.

Mason blocked his face and profile with his hoodie, but his side-glance caught two faces locked on him. Raindrops and swiping windshield wiper streaks blurred most of their details, but he saw a woman in the passenger seat beside the driver, a smaller man with black, slicked-back hair. Shadowy, authoritative figures inside unmarked SUVs made ordinary people paranoid. They fueled rumours that outside-the-law private firms ran squads, armed to the teeth, patrolling the streets for people of colour, snatching them, stripping them of their rights, and leaving them to rot in for-profit prisons. At least, that was the opinion of his hardcore, loyal listeners and callers, the group he sometimes felt guilty about tagging as the *lunatic fringe*. One listener commented, "Americans spying on Americans…that has to stop."

When he had started live podcasting, Mason considered those suspicions were at best urban legends and scoffed at the idea that ever happened in America. He had always demanded a high standard of proof from his callers on all conspiracy theories. However, lately, winning the debate by countering circumstantial or hard evidence with only his personal doubts had moved him from a cynical dismissive jerk to a citizen troubled with concerns. The SUV driver continued driving slowly down the street until he turned the corner.

*

Months ago, Mason did something unpredictable, even risky. He climbed the ten-meter tower of his life and dove a perfect, imaginary jack-knife into the deep end of the conspiracy podcasting pool. He did that because of the unchanging view from his roomy, dumpy Seattle apartment. (His landlord described the space as "almost heritage" to squeeze an extra hundred out of the rent.) Mason gazed out his window every day from near the top of Seattle's Queen Anne district, searching for meaning. He looked through the spindly tops of Christmas tree evergreens lining his section of the fence, down and past the mottled mosaic of roofs descending and blending into the sprawling city and the uneven blue of the harbour. The world roiled in conflict and beauty and discovery, but his life was inert. He was on the doorstep of an ordinary future that would produce the anemic answer, "Because," to the big question in his life, "Why bother?"

When he told Peabody, his good friend and pragmatic editor, Mason sat in his repurposed den, about to end their video call. Mason looked at the pictures in a double frame standing on his table. On one side was Brooke with his ex-wife, Julie; the other photograph was a wedding shot. He looked up and frowned at both his wall posters in the thrown-together studio. The largest poster portrayed crazy hair Einstein. The second was a blow-up of the cover of his slow-selling novel, *The Hottest Place on Earth*. Mason, a little too much doubt in his voice, said, "I'm set up now to podcast, you know, to sell more books."

Peabody's frown and heavily-lidded eyes forewarned Mason to expect one of his patented heavy sighs. "Didn't we go over this idea? But, sure, tell me again, a podcast about what, exactly?"

A fire had always burned in Mason's belly, so he did bother. He needed to try *something* to jump-start his life again after his divorce, find meaning, and make everything matter. If he had to make drastic changes to pursue his destiny, despite Peabody's mocking him, then he would do that too. "God damn it," he said, lashing out more against his stalled future than Peabody's tone. "Did you even read my book? Does 'NEWCorp uranium miners exposed to radiation' ring a bell?"

"That's alleged exposure."

"There was nothing *alleged* about any of it. I was there." He looked at Einstein's poster again, searching for empathy in the eyes but found only folly at his presumption. Mason was testy when he looked back at his phone screen. "Tell me, how'd you survive high school with that name and that attitude?"

"I had a friend who was a boxer."

"*Is* a boxer. Maybe try gettin' behind him as support?"

Peabody relented when he saw Mason had dug in. "Okay, okay, we've been friends a long time, and you chased the high school bullies away. I owe you…"

"You and Ivan owe me."

"What a scary backup we were."

"That boxer became a writer, don't forget."

"If I may interject a word? If you decide to go after NEWCorp, get big fast, or that giant might step all over you. That's what giants do to us little people." Peabody mellowed.

"You never should have dropped out of college. You would have been a system analyst by now; instead, you drive a taxi."

"That sounds like something Julie would say." Mason shook his head to clear the thought that followed his words. "I still dabble, but I had to write my book."

"It cost you your marriage."

"I'm a realist—we weren't going to make it anyway."

That was half of the truth. Within a year of the marriage, Julie changed, drowning Mason in her plans, needing him to fit into her life in a certain way, and Mason tried. But in the end, her vision was all too calculated and intellectual for him; he wanted substance before anything else.

"Realists don't do conspiracy podcasts. Julie's okay."

"I hear she's still single."

"I hear she's off the market. But why so sensitive today? It's been a while since she dumped you."

Mason slipped Brooke an organic cookie while pleading his case to Einstein again. However, his eyes were still full of cheery irony. "No one dumped anyone," said Mason. "It was our mutual decision. I kept the place, and I have Brooke—she got our stuff. I came out way ahead."

"How is Brooke doing?" Peabody only tolerated dogs, so the change of topic was his way of saying he wanted to end the call.

"Better than my love life."

Before signing off, Peabody said, "If the podcast works, let's do another book."

*

Mason and Brooke returned to the apartment. He hung his dripping wet hoodie in the shower to dry and gave her a dog cookie, which she took to the couch. After locking his door on his way out, he turned and saw his insomniac, widowed neighbour, Rosemary, had cracked her door to spy on him. He lifted his travel cup in her direction and said, "Good morning, Rose." Like a turtle receding into her shell, she quickly and silently closed her door. Rosemary brought Mason strawberry butter tarts occasionally, so they were friendly. He had to hurry; he was late for work.

*

In the parking lot outside the dispatch office, Mason radioed from his taxi. "Car sixty-three, good morning, Jeanie." The fifty-something, bleach-blonde, trans-gender graveyard dispatcher famous for smoking three packs a shift croaked back, "Good morning, sixty-three." She called him right back on his cellphone. "Lucky you, there's a personal waiting at the Haida lobby. She wouldn't give a name." Mason drove toward the men's hostel, a rundown rummy version of its former heydays a block from the docks. "

Mason left tire tracks through the garish neon reflected off shiny early morning streets until he stopped the car in the entrance tunnel. Many of the marquee bulbs were out or flickered sporadically. Minutes passed, but no one came out. Mason reported the "no load" to Jeanie. "All right, sixty-three, chill there; something else will come up," she said, her voice husky from inhaling years of self-abuse. Minutes later, she phoned Mason. "Did you win a lottery or somethin'? Suddenly you're popular. She's waitin' at the Jackpot." The convenience store was across Queen Anne, so Mason booted it.

The hotel owner insisted all taxis exit through a narrow, poorly lit alley, where a badly placed cluster of four power poles made the exit a tight turn. Mason pulled away slowly. He double-checked for dumpster-divers and cars moving behind the adjacent Gentleman's Club—flooring the accelerator and cranking a desperate left turn a split second before the vehicle appearing out of nowhere slammed into his taxi. Behind him, the SUV smashed into the power poles.

Mason stopped at the end of the alley and lowered his window, but he stayed in his taxi. The front end of the black Ford SUV had wrapped around the pole. Its windshield was flung across the hood, and both front door windows shattered from the violence of the crash. Oddly, the SUV motor still raced wildly. Thick blue tire smoke drifted down the alley from the rotating rear tires screeching on the pavement. The driver hung over the wheel, one arm moving, his bloody hand grabbing at the air and then his chest.

Then he focused on Mason.

The driver forced his door open. He fell to all fours in a spreading runnel of rainwater spewing from a downpipe. Mason saw he was the same smarmy-looking bastard with greasy, slicked-back hair from earlier that morning in the SUV. He aimed a massive handgun at Mason. At that moment, the SUV backfired. In an awkward jerking motion, the man ducked down, dropped his weapon, and spun around, grabbing his right shoulder.

Mason sped off toward his waiting fare. By driving off, he avoided filing the incident and police reports he'd have to fill out if he mentioned the gun to Jeanie. That would take hours, and Mason needed the money more than he cared about that guy's arrest. *It's not like the guy was trying to rob me.* Still, his heart thumped in his chest. Then his mind slowly formed the statement; *he tried to ram me.* Mason kept his voice even when he talked to Jeanie on his cellphone. "I saw a single-car accident in the alley behind the Haida. The drunk driver looks injured. I wasn't involved."

Go ahead, pull a gun on me, whoever you are, you fuck.

*

An irritating tailgater followed Mason through Queen Anne to the Jackpot. His phone vibrated, and because the caller might be his dispatcher, he looked at its screen. The display showed a gorgeous young woman's image. A pink shock of ribbon controlled her platinum blonde, cock-eyed ponytail, and her V-cut top plunged under a tight, black leather jacket. Mason rolled his eyes to glance in the rear-view mirror, made his decision, and tapped the Skype window to accept the invitation.

Amelia drove while she speed-talked, furtively glancing in the mirror. "Mason, your life is in danger—you don't have much time." Her voice had a Southern inflection. "I know this sounds crazy, but your book, your podcast…"

Mason snatched looks at the phone while he drove. This was nothing new; his podcasts attracted listeners who were way out there on crazy street. *This one doesn't come off as the lunatic fringe, not totally.* "This is a private number; please don't bother me again." He hesitated, then added, "I'm at work."

"I know. I'm right behind you."

His eyes shot to the rear-view mirror. The headlights flashed twice to high beams. Mason ended the call and stomped on the accelerator, managing to keep the taxi on the road in a tight corner while blocking her number. He checked the rear-view mirror and saw the headlights had disappeared. Relieved, Mason tuned into a favourite golden oldie station. Pagliaro's upbeat chords to *Lovin' You Ain't So Easy*, so he cranked the volume to clear the air and his thoughts. *What would she know about my book?* The distraction rebooted his roller-coaster morning as he drove the last few blocks to his next fare.

Mason pulled into the 24-hour convenience store parking lot, coasting slowly toward a pretty-enough but thin woman. She wore a full-length, black leather coat, black, mid-thigh leather boots, and an outdated, leopard-skin mini skirt. Her unbuttoned coat exposed a busty black bra, and her cropped, purple hair stopped an inch below her ears. Mason had to admit she rocked the Uma Thurman *Pulp Fiction* bangs, but the *femme fatale* vampire type was uninspiring and cliché.

He stopped several feet outside the store's awning, turned his stereo off, and lowered his window. He never picked fares up in an alley or at night before deciding they were safe. She exhaled a thick plume of smoke. When she dropped her cigarillo, the glowing red coal hissed on the wet pavement. She slipped on a pair of black, wrap-around sunglasses, stepped off the curb, flashed another smile and the second glimpse of her cleavage.

He parked the car. "Would you mind if I ran inside to buy a coffee?"

"The last wish of the condemned?" She had a distinct Brooklyn accent, which was a perfect fit for her urban leather.

"Sorry?" he asked. His guts turned over. Every experienced cabbie had the same self-defence alarm mechanism, and those still living paid strict attention to it.

"Just a private joke… Is it okay if I sit in your cab? It's cold."

"The door's unlocked." Inside the store. Ranjit, the full-time, young night clerk, stood behind the glassed-in counter, his grin wide. "Oh, Mr. Mason, I wish I had your job."

"It's always available, Ranjit." He poured a coffee into a tall go cup. The President gave another of his famous GNN-televised chopper-talk sound bites before heading out to the golf course. "…and we see this bill, this nuclear waste, it's bad stuff, very bad, you don't want it in your back yard. I'm the only president to do something about it. We're working with good people who want to clean it up. It's the best deal ever, really good. We'll sign the contract, July fourth…" Mason rolled his eyes away from the screen. "Hey Ranjit, I wonder which of his billionaire friends will get this contract?"

Mason paid for the coffee. Ranjit said, "Mr. Mason, that girl…"

"She's not my type, Ranjit. See you tomorrow." Mason hurried out of the store.

Ranjit's worried gaze followed Mason after he left. He said aloud, "Mr. Mason, she has…"

*

A handgun, its silencer an inch from his face, froze Mason's blood when he slipped back behind the wheel and looked into her deadly, cold eyes.

4. Girl Trouble

"Guys like you... I bet you think there ain't no substitute for experience, am I right?" Her garish perfume mixed with tobacco to fill the cab. Mason fixated on her gun. She looked disappointed. "Forget it. Take me to that Kiwanis Ravine." The expansive community park was a local favourite at the top of the Commodore Heights greenbelt. Mason knew the area well. He ran the isolated trails with Brooke after most shifts to get in his roadwork. No one came to the park before dawn on rainy Seattle mornings.

Mason saw his reflection in her alien-eyes sunglasses. "Please, be careful with that thing."

"If you play nice and do as I say... move the car."

Mason silently cursed the taxi company for not installing in-car cameras, then said, "Not a chance. Besides, I've hit the taxi alarm—the cops are coming."

"You're a terrible liar. We do this my way." She punctuated her command by jabbing his ribs with her gun. She produced a slim steel case from an inside coat pocket, snapped it open, and placed a cigarillo between her lips. She looked straight ahead while she tucked the case back into her coat pocket. "Light me up."

"I don't smoke." Ranjit stared out the window at them.

"Right. That's my mistake. That's in your dossier."

"My what?"

"Never mind." She flipped her lighter into his lap. "You're going to call and tell your dispatcher you're busy for a while. Then you're going to be a gentleman and light up a lady." She jabbed the silencer into his ribs again. "With a calm voice, okay, babe? And no codes and no funny stuff."

He waited for a break in the cabbie chatter, then reported himself "away" on a long trip. Jeanie answered and asked him to check in every twenty minutes, which was standard protocol.

"Now, give me a light." Mason reached over to hold the flame for her, but his hand would not stop shaking. He felt her strength when she grabbed his wrist to steady the flame. The hooker raised her eyebrows but otherwise remained statuesque. When she exhaled, she released his arm but kept the gun jabbed in his ribs. He snapped the lighter closed, and the flame extinguished.

"You owe that clerk large…" Mason turned to see Ranjit glaring at him through the window. The hooker jabbed Mason in the ribs again to make him turn toward her. "Look, don't piss me off. Drive. Maybe later, after you help me trap a rat, if you're a good boy, we'll have some fun before you go on your merry way. Turn off your dispatch radio. I won't ask twice."

Mason switched off the CB. Alone in the world, he felt like a serial killer squeezed his throat with icy fingers. He put the cab in reverse and slammed on the gas.

"Easy," she said, "this thing could go off."

He slowed to a crawl and drove off the lot onto Commodore Way. Half a block from the store, a car pulled away from the curb and followed them. The hooker adjusted her side mirror and glanced into it. She said aloud, "She's close. Good."

When Mason turned onto Gillman Street, the drizzle turned to a persistent downpour. Huge raindrops reflected like pearls in his headlights, shattering and bouncing off the wet blacktop as he drove up the hill on the isolated, tree-lined road. The car behind them made the same turn. The hooker glanced in her mirror again.

"I don't know who you are or what you want," said Mason, frantic, "but I never screwed anyone over. Ever. This is some kind of mistake."

"Not if you're Mason Stone and I'm Hawke's insurance, it's not."

"Hawke? Who…?" He flared angrily. "How do you know my name?"

"Too many questions." She hit him in the mouth with the gun barrel. The pain caused him to accelerate. "Drive slower. We want to keep her close. That bitch shot my boyfriend today."

Mason tasted the blood from his upper lip, but she stopped short of breaking his teeth. "You're a *bona fide* psycho."

"Language. I shot the balls off the last guy who talked to me like that."

"Alright, alright… I'm driving. Please, tell me what I did; I can fix it…"

Her voice was thoughtful. "You know, when I see

blood, it turns me on. Too bad time's runnin' out."

"Are… are you coming on to me?"

She flicked her cigarillo out her half-open window. The hooker reached over and wiped Mason's lips with her middle finger, watching his reaction when she licked the blood clean. "Yeah, disappointing…" Her voice changed to a command. "Take the second entrance to the lower lot."

Mason followed her orders with a growing dread that buying time no longer worked in his favour. "Is it my podcasts?" She motioned with her gun for him to keep driving across the vacant parking lot, back to the draping Weeping willow branches.

"Stop here. Turn off the car. Get out." She kept her gun trained on Mason when she came around to his side of the taxi. When she raised the muzzle to aim at his eyes, raindrops splashed off the gun barrel.

The gun flew out of her mangled fingers. She cursed then shrieked in agony. Her gun fired when it hit the pavement, and a small hole appeared in the taxi's rear panel. The hooker screamed and lunged at Mason, stabbing with the knife she held in her good hand. Her face exploded in a mash of bones, flesh, and blood. Already dead, she dropped at his feet.

He stared, shocked.

The shooter approached. She slipped on black, movie-star sunglasses and then pulled off her platinum wig to shake out long, brunette curls. Her arm at her side, her fingers wrapped around the pistol grip, the index finger still on the trigger, she stood over the hooker, straddling her. She kept her eyes on the hooker. "Shit," she said. "You and I, Mason, were never supposed to meet, but here we are." Amelia tossed her wig into the open taxi door. "I would have taken her at the store, but I saw the clerk watching. We have to go now."

"Go?"

"It'll be dawn soon."

"We're going to the police?"

"If you want Death Row, sure. But I have to get out of this rain, or my hair's going to go crazy frizzy."

5. A Woman and Her Gun

Mason's world disconnected from his reality. He stared, wide-eyed and disbelieving, at his hand moving in slow motion to his chest. He pulled it back and saw the gore as if through a stranger's eyes, more purple than red under the parking lot lights. Then the distance between his shock and the moment snapped tight, and the impact dropped him to one knee. "I don't want to die; I don't..." He fell back to sit on the wet pavement, leaning against the car, both hands in his lap.

She glanced over her shoulder at him. "What's wrong? Did she get a round off?"

Amelia's voice dragged him back from his smothering, growing hysteria. He held out his bloody palm looking for an explanation from the woman with the Southern Belle accent. His voice sounded far off and unfamiliar when he said, "I thought you were a blonde."

She glanced at him, knelt quickly, then placed two fingers on the hooker's neck. After confirming both shots had hit her target, she tucked her gun inside her belt at her back. She studied Mason. "Do you like me more as a blonde? I've thought about it." She frisked the dead woman until she found her cellphone, then stood up. She removed the SIM card, broke it in two and threw the pieces and the phone into the back seat. She stood over Mason. "Stand." Mason stood on shaky legs, letting her frisk him, then she looked hard at him again. He stared at her lips. In a quiet voice, she said, "That's her blood. You're lucky. She had a rep for leaving a mess in her wake."

"Are you in insurance too? She said she was..."

"Insurance? No. Neither of us. But she was a damn good shot, just not good enough." Amelia was thoughtful. "I don't talk badly about the departed, but if I did, I'd say she was a skank." Amelia studied him briefly. "Your pupils are dilated." She slapped his face hard. "Snap out of it."

"Please don't do that. Are you a cop?"

She removed her sunglasses. Her eyes were interested while she matter-of-factly evaluated Mason. "You were the bait. She made it personal. She wanted my ex."

"She was going to shoot me."

"Because you know too much."

"I do?"

"Ivan sealed that deal when he called you. After I get you off their radar, I'm going to help him."

"You know Ivan?"

"Not like you do. That's the second time I saved you today."

"What? When?"

"In the alley… the car accident. I took out the driver—he was my ex." Mason looked at her, not comprehending. "That's enough chitchat for now. We have to get with the program. I'll grab the body, steal your taxi, disappear, and you take your chances with the cops. How does that sound?"

"Like American Psycho on steroids." Mason stood up. "And that sounds like death row to me."

"You can pin everything on me."

Mason had landed back in the world. He had blood on his hands and a body of a dead hooker at his feet. He knew he should run as fast as possible in the opposite direction. But this woman was magnetic, so whatever compulsion had come over him was powerful and immediate. *We killed a woman, right here, right now.*

"What'll it be, Mason?"

"I'll drive." He sat in the driver's seat, his hands shaking on the wheel.

Amelia leaned into the car, close to his face, looked deep into his eyes; her hair tumbled about her shoulders. "Brave," she said, impressed, "or missing a few gears. If you come with me, there's no turning back. There will be consequences." He reached up, reacting to her proximity, her eyes, to slide his fingers through her curls, inhaling sweet jasmine. "Good choice," she said, "they would have crucified you anyway. Let's take a ride." She stabbed a pin into the fleshy part of his thumb.

"Damnit. What the hell was that?" Mason rubbed his hand over the blood spot.

"Something to calm you down. I need you lucid."

"I am lucid, very lucid. I'm..." Mesmerized. His eyes went round, his furrowed brow relaxed, the tension in his shoulders released, and his hands folded into his lap. His anxiety dissolved; a physical warmth consumed his body. His head fell slightly to one side when he looked at her with a gentle, blissful smile.

She left him and went to the back of the car to open the hatchback. She was snappy, working through options, her voice clipped. "That blood stain's a problem. We'll ditch your car. And her. Did your dispatcher know you were coming here?"

"I told her I was on call."

"Call and tell her you have a flat on Mercer Island."

Mason called Jeanie on the CB, unable to keep his voice steady. "Hi Jeanie, it's sixty-three. I have a flat tire on Mercer island, just over the bridge."

Jeanie hesitated, then said, "When it doesn't rain… Sorry to hear that, sixty-three. Does your passenger still need a taxi?"

Drowsy, Mason watched in his rear-view mirror as Amelia folded the dead hooker into the hatchback. "No, she's gone."

Jeanie hesitated again at the change in his voice. "My GPS shows you in Commodore Heights."

"Nope. I'm on Mercer Island."

"Very good. Watch for the tow truck." She said, "Call me on my cell." The request proved she had sensed something was off.

Mason said, "Roger," ending the call. He tried twice to replace the mic on the hook then dropped it on the floor. Jeanie sent a distress message to all taxis, which flashed on the meter's video display: car 63 in distress at Kiwanis Ravine.

Amelia appeared at the open driver's door and saw the message. "Well, that sucks. I need your credit card. And your phone." She looked at Mason disapprovingly.

Shaking his head, he said, "I wish I could trust you."

"C'mon now," said Amelia, "I'm the one you *can* trust."

"I trust Jeanie, and I trust Brooke, but not you."

"There's nobody named Brooke in your file." She slid her hand across his chest and into his jacket pocket to commandeer his cellphone. He offered no resistance. "New girlfriend?"

"No," he said, giggling.

"Give me your credit card." This time it was an order, not a request. Without hesitation, Mason fumbled for his wallet through euphoric surges. Amelia took the SIM card from Mason's phone and was about to break it but hesitated, keeping the card and the phone but in separate jacket pockets. Amelia stopped his writhing, putting her hand on his arm. "You hardly know me, I shot someone, and you were about to give me your credit card. I'm no shrink, but I'd say your anxiety is under control." She reached across him to cut the CB mic cable with the hooker's knife, then tossed the microphone and knife into the back seat. "I'll drive."

Mason had lost all control. "You smell like jasmine."

"Maybe not so good at handling the drugs thing. Slide over. We don't need your taxi buddies showing up here."

Mason was clumsy, scrambling into the passenger seat, where he watched Amelia move like a leopard into the car. "You're really beautiful."

"Sure, honey, but that's what all the boys say." She put the car in gear, crushing the hooker's phone into plastic and carbon fibre splinters under the wheel. Amelia stopped at her car, returning with a small cooler and a stuffed black athletic bag. She placed both items on the floor in the back.

'What's that?"

"Insurance." Amelia looked him in the eyes. "Now," she turned on the car stereo, "how about some music?"

"She said she was in insurance, and birds, too." Mason rolled his head sideways to look at Amelia.

She studied him briefly, then drove away. "Birds of prey, maybe. Sit back, try to relax; I could never hurt you. On the scale of good or bad, I'm a good girl. Please believe me. We have to get to the Tacoma Narrows airport."

Mason could not relax more, but he followed her suggestion, leaning his head back against the headrest. She reached across him to set his seat into the almost-prone position. He held her arm, trying to nuzzle her neck. She let him for a moment; then, she gently unravelled his fingers on her arm. "Sorry, lover, there's no time..." She said it like *luv-uh*. He drifted off with the music, each song on the stereo sounding to him like the syrupy *Seasons in the Sun*.

*

Mason raised his seat when they stopped at the airport. Amelia turned off the radio. Private hangars were on their right, and the main terminal was on their left. Amelia turned right, drove to the end of the pavement, to the last building, and stopped the taxi where the road turned to gravel. It was still early on a grey, misty weekend, so most parking spaces were empty.

"Wait here." She took the ignition fob with her. She moved to the end of the hangar, took a quick look around the corner of the building, and then returned. "They're here, but there's only one guard. There's a lane up ahead where we can wait in some good cover. We can leave the taxi there."

Mason grabbed her arm in protest. Even in his delicious fog, he resisted the idea of dumping the taxi with a dead woman in the trunk, but his grip was weak.

Amelia gently removed his hand. "I know this is going fast for you. I promise I can explain everything."

They accelerated toward the partially overgrown lane, then backed in until they were stuck. Low hanging limbs and leafy green ferns hid them from the road, while the thick green canopy shielded them from above. She turned off the car. Large raindrops plopped and splattered on the sunroof.

Mason looked past the last hangar, spotting the helicopter's black tail rotor.

Amelia said, "I figure we've got less than an hour before my ex shows up. After I clean up here, I'll get us a rental."

"What about the hooker?"

"Did she try to bang you?"

"Hey, how'd you know about that?"

Scanning the road, Amelia muttered under her breath, "Skank."

"You're clairvoyant?" He slurred through the multi-syllables.

"Us good girls are chock-full of surprises."

6. **Breakin' Up is Hard to Take**

Amelia set the windshield wipers to intermittent before turning back to Mason. "How are you feeling?"

"Like millions of tiny fingers are massaging me with this music."

She turned the radio on but at a low volume. "I might need to adjust the dosage..."

"Why do I want to tell you everything?"

"It's the drugs. They're a combination of Dr. Feel Good and Mr. Tell-The-Truth. I didn't have time to dry interrogate you. It lasts about forty minutes."

"Why did you have to kill her?"

"She was about to kill you."

"She wasn't so bad..."

"Definitely adjust that dosage down. Mason, a nice girl won't point an automatic revolver at your face—and pull the trigger." Amelia looked at Mason curiously. "Do you believe in destiny? Like it was our destiny to meet on a wet run?"

"Yes. I didn't want to tell you that." He struggled to push his question through his euphoria. "Do you kill your ex when you break up?"

"Not every time. Why did you write your novel about the uranium industry, but in your podcasts, you're hard on your listeners who hate nuclear power?"

"Uranium poisons the earth for, like, 700 million years, but people who believe in conspiracies ask for it."

"Not buying that. Why do you challenge and deliberately embarrass people who try to change the world?"

"Do I do that?"

She frowned at him. "Do you like me?"

"You smell like a Jamaican beach at sunset. But you kill people..."

"When we get you and your dog to a safe place, you'll never see me again."

"I scare you, don't I?"

She flashed a quick, poignant look at herself in the rear-view mirror. "No, it's just... you remind me of someone I used to know a long time ago... here we go." She pointed toward the hangar.

As much as he wanted to process her intentions, his attention span was still at her command. He followed her eyes, unable at first to focus through the boughs across the windshield. The blurred impression of a man in a black suit ran across the gravel road. He approached the fence with one arm across his chest, tucked inside his jacket. He scaled the seven-foot chain link fence instantly, barrel-rolling over the top and landing on his feet on the far side.

Amelia reached into the back seat for the cooler, taking out two gadgets that looked like small desk clocks. She plugged coloured wires into two separate grey gum-like blocks attached with black electrical tape to each clock's bottom and set the time on both.

"Are those presents?"

"Going away presents." She smiled at Mason and got out of the car, turning to close the door without making any noise. She tucked one of the clocks inside her jacket and waved a finger in front of her pursed lips, warning him to stay silent.

The peculiar high, whistling whine of an amped-out helicopter turbine motor ruptured the silence. Amelia crossed the road, easily scaled the fence, and dropped inside the private field. The main rotors circled lazily, then faster, and soon buzzed at full speed, cutting through the air. Amelia pulled her gun from her belt. The tail rotor spun in a blur as the turbine's pitch settled back down from ignition to liftoff speed. She approached the near side of the helicopter, holding one of the clocks in her other hand. She reached out to the fuselage, near the bottom, halfway along the tail, then again farther down the length of the chopper, reaching higher up on the fuselage.

In a blur of motion from under the far side of the chopper, her ex scissor-kicked Amelia to the ground and then pounced on her. But she was ready for him, flipping him off. She held her gun pointed at his head, but he kicked upwards, striking her elbow in a lightning-fast attack that sent her backwards. She threw herself to the ground before the deadly tail rotor cut her to shreds. He regained his feet and pulled his gun, but Amelia had rolled, jumped up, and aimed her firearm. They held each other at gunpoint in the howling rotor downdraft.

Amelia shouted something; he nodded, then they holstered their guns at the same time. She kicked her ex between the legs hard enough to lift him off the ground. The man doubled over and took a knee. She kicked his weapon from his hand, recovered it, emptied the clip and the shell in the chamber, and threw the gun beyond the tail rotor. Amelia backed away, her gun in her hand, and effortlessly renegotiated the fence before turning to watch him from the gravel road.

He was laughing, waving the clock he had removed from the fuselage. He threw it over the fence toward Amelia before disappearing behind the chopper. She tucked her gun in her belt, retrieved the explosives, and disarmed the bomb. The turbine roared, and the black Bell Kiowa Warrior lifted off, ascending on a southerly bearing below the ceiling of low, grey clouds. A thunderous crack initiated the sustained rumble of the explosion. The ignited fuel enveloped the chopper in an orange-yellow fireball as flaming wreckage fell out of the thick, black smoke trail. She turned around once, then looked back at Mason deadpan, shrugging her shoulders. When she sat back in the taxi, she said, "So much for sweet goodbyes."

Mason was outraged but unable to show emotion. "Why do you keep killing people?"

"They were here to kill you, and he would have finished the job." She reset the clock on the lethal bomb. She flicked her head over her shoulder. "Two of your immediate problems are solved, and I bought us some time. Fifteen minutes, to be exact." She turned the device over in her hands. "You can thank me later."

"He was leaving... he wanted you, not me."

She became thoughtful. "It was fast... That's a win in our business." She placed the bomb under her seat. "We're burning time we don't have." She flipped a pair of handcuffs off her belt, snagged his left wrist, and latched him to the steering wheel. "If you think you might want to run, you need to listen to what I have to say first." She showed him the handcuffs key. "I can help you." Mason looked at her with doleful eyes and tugged weakly on the bindings. She looked at him, momentarily doubtful. "We talked about consequences."

She left the taxi, walking briskly toward the terminal. Mason watched emergency vehicles with sirens blaring and lights flashing race across the runway toward the helicopter wreckage. Scant minutes later, Amelia stopped a new burgundy Buick on the gravel road and got out. She smiled when she freed him.

Inside the Buick, Mason noticed several coloured wires inside the removed cover of the steering column. "You like?" said Amelia, stuffing the black bag into the floor behind the driver's seat. She sat behind the wheel. "I can't believe they had an Enclave on the lot. It has a kick-ass stereo, and these things haul ass on the highway." She nodded toward the commotion across the runway. She backed the Buick to turn around when she looked at him. "Let's go get Brooke."

*

They drove away from the airport as if they were the last car in a funeral procession. Behind them, an explosion caused a fireball to rise above the treetops in the overgrown lane. Their second murder scene was relatively clean, even if it was easy enough to locate. When they pulled onto Interstate 5 to head north, Amelia cranked the stereo and buried the accelerator, backing off after entering Seattle's city limits.

By the time they arrived at Mason's apartment, most of the drugs' effects had worn off, replaced by powerful, mounting anxiety, which crippled his sense of well-being. Mason was out of the car before they came to a full stop. "Mason, wait," she said, but he ignored her, hurrying in a sullen mood to the front door and inside. Her voice trailed off inside the car, "I have to check your apartment first."

Amelia quickly scanned the street before she skipped down the stairs. Mason's neighbour, Rosemary, closed her door as Amelia followed Mason into his apartment. Inside, Amelia immediately closed and locked the door. Brooke had never experienced the mix of human blood, explosives, and jasmine before, so she sniffed at Amelia before wagging her approval. Mason watched her kneel to make friends with Brooke, saying, "Hi, beautiful." She looked up at Mason as he closed and locked the bathroom door.

*

He looked in the mirror, knowing his life had flipped upside down. He hardly recognized the horrific image of the dried blood caked on his face and neck. He was determined to get that lunatic away from his dog, out of his apartment, and out of his life—forever. Then he'd go to the cops.

*

Hawke looked at the caller ID before he took the call on his cellphone. "We're done here." He waved his hand to dismiss the managers from the meeting. "Make sure your reports are on my desk by four this afternoon." When his office door closed behind the last man, Hawke said, "Go."

"Sir, Romeo and Juliet got away. The bird is down. We think our actors are off the stage." The nervous-sounding analyst communicated in cellphone patois.

Hawke frowned. "What about the second troupe?"

"They're staged."

"Tell them they're the final act but give BK the lead role. And tell him I want the theatre cleared."

"Cleared, sir?"

Hawke's voice was icy with malice. "Would you prefer working some mid-west fair as a security guard by, say, later tonight?"

"Cleared, right, sir."

"Don't bother me again until the final curtain falls."

The analyst activated BK by sending him a text, then forwarded the activation codes, as required, to Delaci and the second squad.

*

BK, a lithe Latino as smooth and deadly as liquid mercury, deleted the text. NEWCorp's on-call assassin holstered his gun and knives before slipping out of his Seattle hotel room.

7. Debrief Me, Baby

"You can't hide in there forever." Amelia had one of Mason's clean shirts in her hand when she twisted the knob on the bathroom door. She frowned when she found the door still locked. She waited, but Mason did not answer. "You need to face reality; we don't have time for pouting." She banged on the door again. "I have a clean shirt for you. Mason?"

Inside, Mason had removed his blood-stained shirt and scrubbed off the dried body parts stuck on his face and neck. He was angry when he opened the door and reluctantly took the shirt from her. "You dope me up, then demand I face reality?" She stood her ground. He closed the door and locked it, pissed off that the dregs from Mr. Tell-The-Truth were still active. The next time he opened the door, Amelia held two mugs of fresh-brewed coffee, one fixed with heavy coffee cream. He ignored her. She watched him go into the bedroom, muttering, "You know I take cream too?"

"The container in the fridge said Coffee Cream."

Mason came out buttoning a different clean shirt from the one Amelia had picked. She followed him to his podcasting den, where he quickly flipped the wedding picture on its face before they squeezed into chairs at his cluttered desk. Amelia took the guest's chair, sitting sideways to the window, then placed his coffee cup in front of him.

"Talk about keeping a candle in the window… that's sad," she said. Mason frowned and blushed. "C'mon, give me a chance… I read your book. I bet she didn't."

"She wanted me to finish it…for the full impact." Brooke curled up between them, settling at their feet. "Anyway, by my count, that makes me, my editor, and you who've read it."

"You can add a few NEWCorp eyes to that list too." She raised her eyebrows at him, then said, "I liked the idea you set the mine in Canada. They pretend they're so nuclear clean. And publishing under a pseudo name was smart."

"To avoid a lawsuit." He begrudgingly took a sip of coffee, not looking at her. The hot drink was delicious.

"Not much sex in it."

"You don't go to a mining camp in the sub-Arctic to score. Are you here to critique my book?" With attitude, he said this to the sexiest woman, the first woman in his life since his divorce. He took a thoughtful sip of coffee, challenging her over the brim of the mug. He put the coffee down and twiddled a pen on the desk, rolling his eyes to his Einstein poster.

She leaned inward and placed a hand on his. He looked at her. "You ruffled some powerful feathers. A trail of bodies leads to us now. The airport means the local cops and the FAA will be involved. The truth can set you free, for sure, but it can also get you killed—or charged."

Mason let her hold his hand for a moment, then took it away. He looked at her with questioning, vulnerable eyes. "This is you saving me?" He sipped his coffee and sighed deeply. "It's all too crazy. How can I believe you?"

Amelia placed a small case and her gun on the table, and then she pushed the weapon across the table to him. He scoffed at it. "What does that prove?" he asked. She opened the case, took out a pin, and passed it to him. She laid her forearm palm up on the table. "Do it. I have nothing to hide."

"Maybe I should tie you up, so you don't act on your first instinct and shoot me."

She cocked her head sideways, flirting. "That's not in your file." He pricked her with the pin. She did not flinch—she patted Brooke. "You know what this did for you," she said. "When I say so, you go ahead and ask me anything you like." They both sipped their coffee and held eye contact. Seconds passed, then Amelia stopped patting Brooke and said, "I'm ready."

"Are you here to kill me?"

"No. I've never been an assassin; I'm about information."

"How do you know about Ivan?"

"If I tell you..." She stopped her warning tone abruptly, exhaled, made a decision, then started again, "NEWCorp didn't hire me so much as I infiltrated them."

"You know a lot about NEWCorp."

"We've had them on our radar."

"You don't work alone?"

"I couldn't let them kill you and Ivan, so I blew my cover to come here."

"You don't strike me as the sentimental type. You killed

two people for cheating on you. Most people split up, have a good cry, drink too much, and revenge screw the first acceptable thing that walks in the bar."

She looked at him reprovingly. "Is that what you did?"

"That's my business."

"I didn't think so. You're not shallow." Amelia snatched the photos off the table and sat back in her chair. She rolled her eyes to his wedding photograph, seemed thoughtful for a moment, looked at him again, and said, "She's pretty enough, I guess." She tossed the photo back on the table. "Is your attitude about Julie dumping you? Because if it is, that surprises me."

"She has nothing to do with anything."

"Did she ever?" Mason blanched at Amelia's blunt review of his marriage. Amelia said, "I guess that was embarrassing, even a little emasculating...?"

"Can we get on with my questions, please?"

"Sure," she said, "but that must suck large." She flipped the wedding picture, face-up, across the table at him and muttered, "The dumped one is always so defensive."

He flipped the photo over on the table. "There was no emasculating. And I'm not defensive," he said defensively. "Didn't you ever get dumped?"

"Me?" She laughed.

His cheeks flushed again. "Your heart must be a block of ice."

She turned to him again. "If that were true, would I be here now?"

He thought about that. "I'm not afraid to follow my emotions."

"That's a luxury we can't afford." She reached for his hand again. "But, there are alternatives."

He blinked hard, brushed her hand away from his, and wiped his face with both hands. The effects of his dose had worn off. When he looked at Amelia again, he said, "Your boss. Who are you working for?"

"I—we're freelance." She patted Brooke under the table.

"Please don't do that."

She took her hand away from Brooke. "I just took out two of their agents for you."

"Call me a hard sell. Who the hell is this guy Hawke?"

"NEWCorp's chief of security. He controls their muscle and shelters the senators and lobbyists on the payroll. They sell hard to promote NEWCorp inside government channels. By promoting, I mean ramming it down their throats. We noticed."

"You're telling me this is about powerful people in D.C.?"

"They have something big planned, the LA Project, and it's coming up fast. That's why Hawke put the hit out."

"Hawke probably expects you to go back to D.C. to shoot him."

"I do know where they bury the bodies." She took a dog cookie from a bowl on the desk and raised questioning eyes at Mason. He frowned. She faked a pout but put the treat back.

"How many of those bodies are yours? Don't you ever just wing anyone?"

A breeze whispered through the Evergreen boughs along the fence. Amelia scanned the yard, poised but on high alert. "Let's move into the kitchen." She stood up, keeping her body between Mason and the window. "Now."

"Why?" His alarm escalated to Brooke—she began pacing. "Did you see something?"

"Do you want to end up in an incinerator or rotting in a clandestine prison in any one of several backward-ass countries? Now, c'mon, move."

Mason stood; Brooke trotted before them into the living room, where she stopped and stared at the patio doors. "Those secret prisons exist?" asked Mason, looking at Brooke.

"On a few continents," she whispered. "Didn't you watch *The Daily Show*? Where have you been?"

"In denial, I guess. Let me think about this."

"Leave everything except Brooke. Move."

"Stop…stop…stop." Mason raised his hands as if under arrest. "I can't do this. You're delusional. I'm out. I'm calling the cops."

Disbelieving, Amelia said, "But…"

"It's insane. This is America. Take your pins and your gun and your conspiracy with you. Please, leave." He took her by the elbow and walked her to the door. "Go. And stay away forever."

Amelia looked at Mason. "You won't leave here alive." She pulled her elbow free, kneeled, and spoke kindly to Brooke. "Your daddy is making a big mistake. Try to talk some sense into him, okay?" Brooke wagged her tail.

"You're talking to a dog."

"Like you don't?"

Mason bolted the door behind her, done with Amelia forever.

8. **Breaking Reality**

Brooke followed Mason back to the podcast den. He leaned against the door frame and fed her a cookie. "That's the end of that, isn't it, Brooke." A series of cracks in the living room sounded like someone had thrown a handful of gravel at the patio door. Then slabs of glass fell out of place onto the carpet. The curtain wafted into the living room and then floated back into place. A man's outline blocked the den window, which imploded, spraying glass across his desk. His computer monitor exploded into fragments, as did his podcast camera and microphone. Like a black pearl necklace, a string of holes appeared across his book poster and Einstein's forehead. An instantaneous scatter plot of holes formed on the interior wall, causing a billowing cloud of sheetrock dust. Mason could not connect the crash of explosions and shattering glass, Brooke's barking, and the patterns forming on his wall. Someone kicked in his front door. He turned, terrified.

"Hit the deck." Amelia crouched in his doorway, her pistol drawn and trained on him.

Disbelieving his eyes, Mason shouted, "What's going on?"

She lunged across his apartment. "I mean now." Amelia took her own advice to heart. In a blur, she scissor-kicked Mason's feet out from under him and threw herself over his sprawled body. She reached up and grabbed Brooke by the collar to pull her down beside them. Glass shards showered them as a low line of black holes formed across the wall over their heads.

She spoke with throaty intensity. "We have to work on you doing what I say when I say it." She looked down, hovering over Mason's face, the calm in the centre of the hurricane, and said with empathetic urgency, "They're coming in now. You and Brooke need to leave. Crawl."

Mason snapped into action, crawling with Brooke across the carpet and into the hallway. Rosemary opened her door and came out wearing a bright yellow Smiley Face polka dot robe. She looked down at Mason and Brooke from under a colourful headdress of pink curlers and blue-tinged hair. Then looked at his demolished door. "Is that girl pestering you?" she said conspiratorially.

Mason jumped up to lead her back to her apartment. "It's okay, Rosemary. We're playing a new computer game."

She seemed intrigued. "It's very realistic." Nodding, Mason closed her door and returned to his apartment door.

The hallway silence rang echoes in his ears now that the action in his apartment was muted. Amelia slipped out his door and huddled face-to-face with him. She snatched a look up at the building's front door and whispered, "Yell and duck if anyone comes through the front door."

"You mean there are more of them?"

"Stay here, so I know where you are." Amelia turned off the hall light, then went back into Mason's apartment. Seconds later, he heard two loud snaps, a groan, and a thump from inside. Mason shoved the door open a crack and saw a motionless, camouflaged lump crumpled and bleeding on his carpet. Amelia's hand covered his, so they whispered, again, face-to-face.

"Is he...?"

"A figment of my imagination?"

"I might have over-reacted."

"That was supposed to be you and Brooke bleeding out in there. Am I registering any credibility with you yet?" He tried to go into his apartment. "Un-uh," she said, "front door." Before she slid past him, she jabbed a finger at his chest. "You owe me." He nodded. She turned back to business and scoped the main stairwell up to the door. "There's still one more; I'll go first."

"That's your plan?"

"Unless you have a better one?"

"Can I get the door for you?"

She rolled her eyes at him, ascending the stairs, then nudged the front door open an inch with her shoulder to peek outside. She closed the door and whispered, "I don't think he'd be in the trees beside the dumpster... the limbs would obscure his line-of-sight. Across the road, do any dogs live there, behind that fence?"

"Rowdy, a yappy terrier. He's always outside, and he barks at anything."

"He's not barking now," Amelia said, her voice ominous. "Just in case, I want you to know I faked taking the drugs."

"See?" he whispered, popping his eyes wide. "That's why I can't trust you."

Amelia shushed him and focused her attention outside before glancing back at him once. She shook her head and muttered, "Delusional..." then exploded into action, shoving the door open wide, leaping out, twisting in mid-air, and firing two quick shots down toward Mason's bedroom window well.

A man grunted. "You shot me."

Amelia fired again while prone on the walkway. "And you shot a hole in my jacket. This *Gucci* cost four grand, okay? Mason, we're probably clear."

Mason leapt up the stairs to pop his head out the door. Brooke ran past him. "Is 'probably clear' in your assassin manual?"

"Where's your passport?"

"In the cupboard over the fridge."

"Get in the car. Stay low. I'll cover you."

Whoever Amelia was, she was on his side, and his side needed her. He followed Brooke, running in a crouch together to the Enclave. Brooke jumped into the back seat when Mason opened the passenger door, which he quickly closed when he was inside and scrunching down in the front seat. He kept his eyes on Amelia until she went back into the building. She opened his blinds, slid his bedroom window open, and pulled the second dead assassin inside, leaving a blood smear on the sill. She closed the window and the blinds. Seconds later, Amelia was behind the wheel, her demeanour one of remarkable composure. She flipped Mason his passport. "You'll need this for one more day." She sparked two wires beneath the steering column to start the car.

"You did that faster than I could find a set of keys in my pocket," he said.

She took out her cellphone and began texting, her thumbs blinding fast.

"Shouldn't we be getting away?"

Amelia turned a quick, questioning look at him as if to ask, *You still think I don't have this?* She touched his lower arm, and he relaxed and soaked up her calm demeanour.

"Cleaner?" Impressed, she looked at him. "I saw Pulp Fiction twice," he said.

"You learn fast. That's a good survival skill," Amelia

said with that infuriating dismissive distraction people have while engrossed with their phones.

"How did you... Do you have cleaners in every city?"

"This guy was flown in special."

When she drove them away from their third murder scene, he was part of Amelia's world forever, so Mason said goodbye to his own. He looked at his passport, then at her. She looked in the rearview mirror, then threw an arm over his shoulder, twisting in her seat to back up, and, looking him in the eyes, said, "You've never been to Mexico, right?"

*

She stuck to the speed limit, travelling north toward I-5. "I'm sorry you had to see so much today."

"I had no idea my novel... That last guy, is he dead?"

"It was him or us."

Mason was quiet and thoughtful until they entered I-5. "Where are we *really* going?"

"Survival is about innovation. There's no way NEWCorp sanctioned Hawke's operation. It will take him a few hours to produce our fake criminal profiles, so we should set up our smokescreen. But let's ask Peabody to take care of Brooke for you first."

Hearing his editor's name shocked Mason. "How do you know about Peabody?"

"Lots of people know a lot about you."

"Comforting. But come on? Fake criminal profiles? As in federal databases?"

"After this morning, maybe not so fake."

"That was them or us."

"The self-defence defence... you do learn fast."

They merged with the increased traffic flow. Thousands of Saturday morning families, soccer moms, golfing dads, shoppers doing the usual weekend stuff were undeterred by rain, crowds, or prices. Brooke slept stretched out on the back seat; she loved any car ride.

"Cat got your tongue?" asked Amelia.

"There are four dead people in my life. I've destroyed a car, my apartment, lost my job, and been high as a kite. It's not even noon yet."

"Some first date, hunh?"

Mason looked at her thoughtfully. "I forgot to say

thank you for killing those people and saving my life, didn't I?"

"Don't mention it. I mean that—don't mention it."

He shook his head, perplexed by his sly smile. "What else is in that bag?"

"Open it."

He got on his knees on the seat to reach into the back to unzip the bag. He found bundles of US hundred-dollar bills. He took a bundle out and held it up. "This *is* turning into a pretty cool first date."

"The money gets 'em every time," she said to no one in particular. "I intercepted a cash drop in New York before I flew here. That's why Hawke is pissed at me, one of the reasons anyway."

"At the risk of sounding crass, how much is here?"

"Four hundred grand. We can travel on that after we drop Brooke."

He tossed the bundle of cash into the back and zipped up the bag. When he belted in again, he said, "You never told me how you know about Peabody."

"Same way I know where you live, that you're single, twenty-five, a Dragon-Libra, that you're hetero, where you work, sorry, worked, that you take cream in your coffee, even the last time you got laid, and that you're a fighter..."

"Boxer, please."

"Have you ever heard of *the Pursuit*?" He shook his head. Amelia drove through moderate traffic, signalling to change lanes, neither tailgating nor speeding, driving to avoid anyone noticing them. "That's the way they like it." She was thoughtful. "Have you ever woken up one day to find the world is a different place?"

"Recently, actually, yes."

She looked at him approvingly. "Right. After we got Saddam, I wondered, well, we all did, about private corporations making billions on the battlefield sidelines, sometimes on both sides simultaneously, and why we were still there, why there were no WMDs—anywhere. I rotated out of the military. I wanted all the way out, but it's not as easy as simply walking away. Asshole," she said when a kid in a pickup cut her off. "I knew after they killed you, Ivan was next, and then probably his wife, maybe Peabody too. It wasn't going to stop." She sighed. "How much did you involve Ivan in your research?"

"We studied the radioactive waste leaking into the Columbia River at Hanford; the rest was on my computer, sometimes we Skyped."

"You did more than that at Hanford; I saw a clip of both of you at that protest."

"Someone has a clip? Did it also show you that our military left millions of gallons of radioactive poison there, that we are nuking ourselves?"

She ignored Mason's vitriol. "Was Ivan ever with the government?"

"Never. Ivan's a consultant."

"Do you know who he consults with?"

"He said he couldn't tell me because it was part of his NDA."

Amelia took his phone and sim chip out of her pocket and handed him the pieces. "Check your phone for messages."

"I didn't have any this morning."

"Look again."

Mason searched his viewed messages, found Ivan's video, and played it. When it finished, Mason looked up at Amelia and said, deadly serious, "Who else has seen this?"

*

They pulled into a busy truck stop outside of Everett. "If you want to walk Brooke," Amelia said, "I'll get us a bite to eat and more coffee. Can I have your phone?"

Mason watched Amelia from the dog stretch area when she tossed his phone onto a loaded car hauler pulling out. Then she went into the restaurant. When she came back to the Enclave, she said, "We're still ahead of them. There was a TV blurb about the explosion at the airport. Here, Brooke." She fed Brooke the roast beef from a sandwich.

"How'd you know where that truck was going?"

"I didn't, but does it matter, as long as he's not going to Peabody's house?" Amelia picked at her small salad with her fingers. "Right," said Mason, inspecting his sandwich. "Tuna. Lucky guess?"

"It's wasn't a guess."

"You know, it's a little weird that I'm an open book to you, but all I know about you is you can handle a gun and can kick the hell out of guys."

Amelia poured water into a large paper cup and held it steady while Brooke slurped her fill. "You know I love your dog."

*

They approached the long driveway entrance at Peabody's rural farm on Mt. Vernon's outskirts. "It's still not too late," she said, patting Brooke, "we can turn back, maybe fix this..."

"Park beside that red car. Do you mind waiting? Come on, Brooke."

Maintenance of the abandoned, weather-worn horse barns stopped years ago, so the walls and roofs sagged with neglect. Tall, green grass swayed with the breeze filtered through Evergreens and tall Cottonwoods lining the northern fence.

Peabody came out to the porch to greet Mason, where they finished talking about Brooke's arrangements at the open front door.

"So you'll take care of Brooke for a few days?"

Peabody fidgeted with his pipe but avoided looking directly at Mason. "Consider it done." Peabody checked out Amelia, waiting at the Enclave parked next to Julie's red Echo. Inside the house, Julie padded in bare feet down the shadowed hall to the kitchen.

"How long has this been going on?" asked Mason, petulant, but his voice steady.

"We waited 'til long after you two broke up."

"So, the goddamn sheets were still warm?" he said loud enough for his voice to reach the kitchen. Mason shook his head. He looked around the porch for an answer, but there was none. He sighed deeply. "Maybe you'll have better luck. Sorry about the short notice. We should be back from our research in New Mexico in a week." To make his lie less painful, he gave Peabody ten crisp hundred-dollar bills. "For Brooke—just in case." He knelt to say goodbye to her. "See you soon, girl," said Mason.

Peabody took a long look at Amelia. "Is she your research?"

"We're writing associates. Tell Julie I don't drive a taxi anymore."

"She'll be happy to have Brooke again—for a while."

Mason walked back to the Enclave. Amelia said, "I was

going to tell you…"

He took her in his arms and kissed her passionately, knowing full well they were watched. She did not resist when he pulled her into his body, arching her back slightly in the dramatic pose. When they broke, she let one hand linger on his stomach, slowly drawing it across when she moved away. He sat in the passenger seat. When Amelia sat in the driver's seat, she had a wry smile. "I've been missing that in my life, but next time you do that, give me a little warning, okay?"

"No more secrets. Deal?"

"Deal."

From the passenger door window, before they sped away, Mason yelled, "I forgot to tell you, my old phone number won't work anymore."

9. Running

Mason switched to the driver's seat at the Bellingham Airport and waited while Amelia went inside to buy their tickets. A persistent airport security guard bared down on him for the second time just as Amelia returned. She fanned three ticket pouches at Mason from the passenger seat as he drove away. "We might throw them off the scent for an hour or two with these. They'll have to check to see if we actually flew out of Bellingham. Hawke bought us first-class tickets for Rio, Stockholm, and Hong Kong." Tearing all the tickets in half, she said, "I raised a few eyebrows in there. We're heading south to Los Angeles. Are you still up for this?"

"I'm fine. My fatalistic resignation has subsided into nihilism and shock, despite your best efforts, so, what the hell, let's go."

"Keepin' it light. That's the spirit. Pull into long-term parking."

They left the stolen Enclave at the airport and took a cab to the rundown section of downtown Bellingham, across the street from a rowdy biker bar. Amelia slipped into the front seat of a customized black pickup. The Harley-Davidson patch on the rear window was a warning, not a car alarm, so they had no trouble jacking the truck. "These guys don't report stolen vehicles," said Amelia, as six bikers emerged from the bar yelling and waving fists, rushing the truck. Laughing at the nearest incensed goon pounding his fists on the driver's window, she laid down thirty feet of rubber and an impressive smoke show. Mason looked at her reprovingly. "What?" she said. "I wanted to know what's under the hood."

They retraced their route on I-5, heading south and passing through Seattle again, setting their sights on Portland and LA. Forty minutes later, at a spaghetti junction of ramps and interconnecting highways, Amelia exited to the I-90 in Tacoma. Mason said, "LA is still in southern California, isn't it?"

"Change of plans. We're not going there—yet; we're going to Salt Lake City. But I have to make a call first."

He was mildly irritated. "You don't ask me? Why Utah?"

"Sorry, saving your life here. We're looking for a large

metropolitan airport away from the coast. They'll clue in we weren't on any of those flights, but I doubt they'll look for us in Mormon country. Especially after I make a call from Tacoma."

"Are you calling Ivan? We have to warn him—and Lena."

Amelia glanced at him. "We can't. Calling either of them will put them both in more danger. Right now, the bright lights at CERN are Ivan's best ally."

"But what about Lena? Maybe they'll kidnap her, torture her…"

"They won't go for her." She tried to soothe him, but Mason was incredulous and doubtful. Amelia added, "They still believe they can get their data back."

"You don't know that."

"I do, especially if we stay on NEWCorp's radar. They'll come after me and you first."

*

They drove without speaking. The mood in the truck had changed. Amelia said, "I wanted to know more about you, so I read your book on the plane. Hawke wanted me to take you out of the picture. I'm so glad that never happened."

"People died today," he said gloomily.

"Mercenaries and their pilot. And they fired their guns at you first."

Mason shrugged and stared out the passenger window. "How the hell do you expect me to believe anything you say if you keep changing plans on me? And where the hell is your compassion?"

She rolled her eyes, put on her sunglasses, and said, "There's a time and place for everything." He glared at her. She muttered, "And I'm all out of *Dr. Feel Good.*"

*

Amelia exited the interstate into Tacoma's west side ghetto. Cruising through blocks of neighbourhoods struggling through tough economic times until she pulled into the parking lot beside the small, down-and-out Lucky Dice lounge. Several seedy, tired hookers hovered around a skinny pimp dressed in a tan, velvet pantsuit and matching, wide-brimmed hat. He hung half-out of the driver's door of an older model Cadillac convertible with its top down. Amelia dialled a number on her cellphone, putting the Skype call into speaker mode, and pointing the camera at the front of the bar.

The male voice said, "Go."

"It's me." Amelia mouthed the name *Hawke* to Mason.

"Where's my money?"

"I'm spending it now. When I'm ready, the rest goes to charity."

"Why don't you come in? We can work this out. You know I like you."

"Is that why you sent those four killers after us?"

"Tell the writer he made a bad choice teaming up with you. He should know it won't be long before this is over, and it's going to end badly if you make us come to you."

"Who knows, maybe you and I will see each other first. Mason, throw out a handful of those hundreds."

Mason waved the bills out the window and said, "Hey, buddy, look, free money."

The pimp watched the bills flutter to the pavement. "You crazy, man?" He shoved one of the women out of his way in his rush to scoop up the cash. His bouncy gaggle of hookers followed him.

Amelia held the phone up, "Say thank you to the man."

"Say what? Rich folks sure as shit be crazy." The pimp retreated to his car with the cash. The shrieking bevy flocked after him, mobbing the pimp.

Amelia enjoyed the moment. "So, Hawke, did you like that?"

"One word of advice, big boys play in my sandbox."

"Now you're playing hard to get? Tell you what, how about we meet early in July in Washington? That's the big day, isn't it?"

"Tell lover boy his prospects with you aren't so good—because you're already dead." Hawke disconnected the call.

*

"Tell me you got them," Hawke said, his voice an icy, implied threat.

"Yes, sir. On screen three." The analyst sounded nervous.

"Pipe it through to me and keep it live."

"Coming through now, sir." A satellite shot of the black truck in a long line of traffic appeared on Hawke's wall screen.

"We've been on them since Everett," said the analyst. "The writer's phone is stationary at the Canadian border, but we stayed on our targets. They switched vehicles to that black pickup, center screen."

"Hello, Amelia," said Hawke, his voice colder still. "Where's BK now?"

*

Amelia took a long, sober look at Mason. "That should draw some fire. It won't take long before they zero in on us, but that should draw the heat off Ivan." Before Amelia circled the Cadillac, she flung another two hundred-dollar bills out the truck window. When the pimp scrambled after the money, Amelia tossed her cellphone into the back seat of his caddy. She called to the pimp, "Hey, buddy, you're doing all right, so why not give the ladies the rest of the night off?" When they drove away, she said, "We'll backtrack to I-84 out of Yakima, then to Salt Lake City."

"How do you know all these roads?"

"NEWCorp has a piece of Bluffdale. I got up here a few times, but we always flew out of Salt Lake City."

"What's Bluffdale?"

"Really? Billions of dollars going to NSA data centers? You don't know? That's how Hawke will track our GPS position to good time Charlie back there."

"Americans spying on Americans isn't a conspiracy theory? It's for real?"

"Snowden's marathon should be proof enough good ol' *Big Brother* is always keeping an eye on us, and he doesn't like anyone catching him at it."

10. **D.C. Games**

NEWCorp CEO Delaci, a vibrant, trim, ruthless man, sat alone, having coffee at the boardroom table. His eyes were dull and yet penetrating. Everything about Delaci said efficiency, control, power. He fixated on the magnificent, miniature alabaster centrepiece carving of the world in front of him. He reached out to take the globe, stopped, and then did a fantastic thing: he gripped the edge of the table, pulled himself out of his chair with his arms, and rolled into a full handstand on the table before lowering himself back into his chair. After completing the gymnastic move, he cupped the globe in both strong hands, testing its weight. His thin smile was a revealing testament to his inner thoughts. "You see," he said, speaking to the globe, "I am worthy." He replaced the globe, sensually sliding one hand over its surface as if patting a favourite pet, then picked up his cellphone. Delaci placed a speed dial call, absent-mindedly rotating the skull and crossbones ring with the thumb. When the man with the faint Latino accent answered, Delaci said, "I need to double down on this one. It has to look natural."

"That will take a few days to arrange."

"I want it to hurt."

"I double my usual fee for custom requests."

"Half is in your account. Do it."

Delaci ended the call, and another, a Skype call, came in. "Cessily, wonderful. I wondered if I still had a daughter. How is Baltimore?" The woman on the screen appeared bright and young, but her eyes were troubled, accusatory. She sat at a table at an outdoor coffee shop. She did not answer. Delaci said, "Cess, now that you've graduated, I want you to join me in Washington... to launch your career with us, I mean... it's time to start learning how to become the next world leader. What do you think?"

"I think you're despicable." Her lips tight, she waved a single page of writing paper at the screen. Her eyes were full of tears, and her face was red with rage. "I found this letter from mother—my dead mother—taped in a hidden compartment in her jewelry box, the one she left me for when I graduated. You know what you did to her, and now I know. I always knew, but now I have proof. Don't ever talk to me again. Murderer." She began sobbing.

Her accusation rocked Delaci. "Darling," he said, "how can you think that? No—no. I did nothing. Your mother wasn't stable—at the end."

A male voice said, "Cessily, hang up."

The Skype window closed.

Not this, thought Delaci. *I will not let this happen.*

*

Hawke's hands shook when he put the pill on his tongue. He followed it with a neat scotch, then made a cellphone call. "Meet me now… at the usual place." He left his office, walking briskly through the data center, a grim look of determination on his face.

Hawke walked beside the shade trees bordering the cement walkway, then through the immaculate green grass and brilliant white tombstones deep inside the Arlington Cemetery. Within view of the eternal flame, he wondered if it was like this in Dealey Plaza when the loudest crossfire of shots heard in history took out JFK. Most days, this stroll engendered in him a sense of power, an oasis of control inside the oppressive city din, far from NEWCorp's unrelenting demands. Although it was mid-June, the infamous summer humidity smothered everything under a dome of thick, indistinct clouds.

He sat on the park bench most distant from the others, under the shade trees. He watched a group of slovenly young men in droopy shorts and oversized tank tops walk through the trees. Every day, they invaded the park to sell dime bags of crack to a constant flow of nervous mix of middle-class and ghetto urbanites willing to smoke away their futures. The drug dealers ignored Hawke after jeering at him as a suit, not a cop.

A thin, olive-skinned man, wearing large, very dark sunglasses and a National's baseball cap and team jacket, arrived unseen from behind Hawke, sliding onto the same bench. Neither man looked at the other.

Hawke said, "You know what has to happen. It's urgent now. I need our problems terminated."

Jairo replied, "That is my intention." He adjusted his hand on the lethal injection needle he hid in one jacket pocket, ready to strike.

"I'll double your fee."

Jairo hesitated. "You will make the deposit today?"
"Yes."

Jairo seemed satisfied and released his grip on the needle. "It will happen soon."

"Excellent," said Hawke, standing up and smiling nervously. "Call me when it's done."

"You'll be the first to know." Jairo stayed behind, lit a cigarette, and watched Hawke disappear among the gravestones.

*

Red and blue lights strobed across the Lucky Dice parking lot, crowded now with cop cars, an ambulance, busy detectives and watchful cops. One cop directed a curious, serious man to the dumpy female detective. The serious man flashed his ID. She said, "Why is a Fed here for a greasy, gunshot pimp?" The man recorded a video of the Tacoma murder scene and the investigators. BK was in play.

The Asian medical examiner directed the police photographer to take snapshots of the dead man's body. He wore a tan suit and was sprawled across the front seat of the Cadillac, his head hanging at an impossible angle. Swarming one of the police cruisers, his bevy of hookers was in varying stages of hysteria, sobbing, angry, pleading with a young policewoman. She tried to settle them down and interview them. "So, ladies, do you have anything else for me?"

"They shot him."

"Killed him in his car."

"Poor, poor Willy."

The policewoman held her hand up to stop their all jumping in at once. That did not work, and they all started in again. "Yeah, he was a saint. Has anyone got anything else? No? Okay, wait here. No one leaves." The policewoman approached the lead detective, who was searching the car for cartridges. "Detective, I have some information. It's weird."

The lead detective looked at her. "Oh yeah?"

"It seems a man and woman were here about an hour ago throwing hundred-dollar bills out their window."

"That explains where Willy got so much cash."

"Two of the women recalled them leaving in a black pickup. No one saw the shooting; they were working inside the tavern."

The medical examiner joined them. He asked the bored detective, "Why'd they break his neck if they were going to shoot him?"

The detective responded, "My guess? It's local—a turf war. Whoever it was wanted Willy dead and to send a message. We'll let our guys know; we want that truck."

*

Texting while walking, BK returned to his metallic grey Mercedes Coup CL600. He sent Hawke the video and followed it with the text: we have a runner

*

Mason and Amelia crossed the Washington-Idaho border before they topped off the tank and bought water, coffees, and more plastic gas station food. Two hours later, Amelia pulled over. "I need some sleep. Tomorrow will be a big day. Give me what you can." They swapped places without getting out of the truck. When he slid under her, she dropped in his lap. "Oh, sorry," she said, giggling. She kicked off her shoes in the passenger seat. "I'll spell you later. No matter what, don't stop." She curled up in the passenger seat, placing her feet in his lap. "Is that okay?"

"If it's what you need...."

"G'night. Mason, you're amazing."

"I bet you say that to all the boys." Amelia smiled, then fell asleep.

He drove through violent rainstorms, then under clear, starry skies in the mountains. Wildfires still raged in drought-stricken valleys farther south, but he never saw any flames.

Cool first date, alright.

*

It was quiet in the truck, so Mason's thoughts drifted until he remembered Amelia's comment. *Snowden's in jail.* He found the man intriguing but had trouble with him. Snowden revealed American agencies and the FBI were illegally mining personal information on the internet. When they were outed, they actively tried to cover it up by smearing Snowden. But it wasn't like Mason could remain cynical when researching other theories too. He believed the phenomenon exists because all theories share one common trait: the suspicion of manipulation by powerful forces. Vetting his research meticulously, everything he learned about Snowden undermined his trust, not

54

in Democracy and free speech, but the status quo. But vigilantes solving social problems with gunfire was pure anarchy—that's where his rubber hit the road. Some of his listeners went crazy over Snowden, either passionately defending him as a freedom fighter for Democracy or attacking and condemning him as a traitor. But he did bring the truth forward. If that's the criteria, everything else is a talking point, a distraction counterfeiting the legal issue that someone in the government contravened the constitution and federal laws. Common sense says that Snowden is a hero and should be a free man. But whistleblowers like Snowden or Ivan, thought Mason, wear a target on their backs in this terrorized and paranoid America.

*

Three hours from Salt Lake City, Mason woke Amelia. "Thanks for the sleep, baby." She shook her hair out and looked instantly awake, beautiful, and refreshed. "Let's switch places." Without stopping the truck, Amelia planked over top of Mason and slipped behind the wheel. Mason tried to stay awake and talk but fell asleep, exhausted beyond caring—for the moment—about dead assassins, corrupt corporations, armed militia groups, and scumbag politicians.

11. Stuck Here in Lehi

Mason woke with a start. His limbs were stiff; his eyes squinted into the brilliant, blinding desert sun as he stretched out the tightness in his neck and back. He was alone in the truck, parked outside the office of a third-rate motel. The lettering peeling off the front door said, 'Welcome to Utah.'

He wrenched out a deep and demanding yawn, watching Amelia talking to a man behind the counter inside the office. He was a skinny, older, black man with a white goatee who kept his eyes on Amelia. She finished filling in the registration card, pushed it across the counter, and then handed him cash. The manager started to make change, but Amelia waved him off, speaking to him briefly before leaving. He smiled a wide, toothless grin watching her walk back to their truck.

"I signed us in as Mr. and Ms. A. Christie. An extra hundred transformed our truck into a yellow Volkswagen on the registration card."

"Cute, Agatha. Fun fact… do you know that your namesake disappeared in 1926 for eleven days? Ms. Christie claimed she didn't know where she had been, but most of her readership think she was spying for the government."

Amelia laughed brightly. "I did not know that. This is fun travelling with a writer."

"Where are we, anyway?"

"You slept through Salt Lake. We're in a bedroom 'burb I know, Lehi. The airport, our way out of here, is back there too. Anyone looking for us, and they will be, will have to search dozens of city hotels and motels before they get here."

"You think they're still on our trail?"

"They're coming, but we have time, and I need a shower."

"I've been told I'm a magician with a luffa."

She flicked her eyes at him, then drove through the lot to park at the end of the building, where the truck would be less visible from the highway.

Mason scanned the strip mall, the car lot down the street, and the Starbucks. "I'll get us coffees. What room are we in?"

"207. I'll check it out." Amelia hoisted the duffel bag

over her shoulder, lugged it up the outdoor steps, unlocked the door, and went inside. She reappeared a minute later, scrunched the room key in a hundred dollar bill, then dropped the small bundle over the balcony rail to Mason. "Pick me up a burner phone, too, would ya'?" she said when he caught the package.

He crossed the highway, entering the mini-mall drugstore first. Next, he bought two expensive, identical travel mugs in the coffee shop where he had the barista fill each with French roast and espresso shots. The slogan on the cups was "Visit Utah for the snow, stay for the lifestyle." Amelia was still showering when he returned to their motel room. He knocked and called out her name before placing her coffee and the drugstore items on the bathroom counter. He returned to the main room; the air was stuffy from Amelia's long shower. He fiddled with the air conditioning buttons. The fan made a horrible grinding noise when it started working, but he left it running anyway.

Inside the cramped bathroom, the atmosphere was even thicker with steam. "Do you mind if I turn the fan on?" He didn't wait for her answer and flicked the switch. Nothing happened. "No fan. We'll have to deal with the London fog."

"I'll be out in a minute." Amelia poked her head out from behind the transparent shower curtain. He handed her the shampoo, then the bar of scented soap. "Jasmine. How interesting." She winked at him.

"The weather conditions in here are brutal, so I'm either joining you or leaving." Amelia tilted her head sideways, moved the curtain slightly to expose an enticing invitation.

"I thought we were in a hurry," he said, pulling the bathroom door shut on his way out.

Mason turned on the TV using the remote, adjusting the volume to low, sipping his coffee. Ellen was defending her friendship with a former president. He muted the volume. The air in the room was less stuffy, so he turned off the noisy air conditioner. The stairs outside the room creaked, setting off his internal "cabbie" alarm. He went to the window to look through a crack in the musty curtains. He sipped his coffee, scanning the second-floor walkway. A cleaning woman pushed a cart past the window. He closed the gap in the curtains and paced the room while Amelia finished her shower. He locked his gaze on the phone on the bedside table. Sitting on the bed, he made a call.

"Hello?"

"It's Mason."

"I thought my call display was wonky. I don't know anyone in Mormon country. Brooke is fine." Peabody always saw right through him. "She's sleeping on the couch. She ate a ton yesterday and has put the feral cats on the run. I thought you were going to New Mexico?"

"Final stop."

"I hope you took your date out for dinner before..."

"I told you, we're not in that kind of relationship."

"Always the last to know."

"Gotta go now. I just wanted to hear how Brooke was making out."

Peabody said, "Go take care of your travel buddy and don't do anything I would."

Mason ended the call and said aloud to himself, "It's not like you aren't."

"Who the hell was that?" Amelia stood wrapped in a towel, holding another in her hands at the open bathroom door. She threw her hair over her head as she bent forward to towel off. When she stood up again, she was radiant, sexy, and livid.

"I was checking on Brooke."

"Did you talk for more than forty seconds?"

"I thought we had some time..."

"Not now, we don't. You do recall that people are trying to kill us, right?" She took a step toward him. The intoxicating scent of moist jasmine reached him in a humid wave.

"Sorry."

"Sorry? We have to assume they tapped Peabody's phone."

"Then I better get in that shower..."

*

At the same moment Amelia was furious with Mason, Hawke ordered his analyst to send the text message to both BK's and Delaci's cellphones: Lehi Utah motel 6 go

Hawke exhaled with relief.

BK texted back: on it no backup reqd eta minutes

*

58

When Mason came out of the bathroom, Amelia was dressed and texting on the new burner phone with her Glock on the bed beside her. "I thought that was forbidden."

"I know this guy—his number is clean."

"You treat your ex-boyfriends like that, and you still have friends? Interesting crowd you run with."

"You keep forgetting the ex tried to kill me first."

Mason winced. "I deserved that."

"Our cover is blown anyway, so now our choice is between information and running. We need intel." While he dressed, Amelia let him read over her shoulder.

you have powerful enemies

how close who

15 min tops get out bk coming

Mason said, "BK? I guess we drew their fire."

Amelia kept texting.

where next drop

forget it suicide

where when

private equity 1600 thursday

need a plane TTYL

She turned off the cellphone.

"BK's a long-range specialist; he's good with a knife too. He gave himself that nickname because he trained to work almost exclusively as a night crawler. You know, black knight—BK?"

"I'm afraid to ask, but what's a night crawler?"

"A very effective asset in another military outfit I worked with you'll never hear about. My intel supported him on missions. He completed every assignment."

"And Hawke put this guy on us." She shot a look of cold reprove at him. "I put this guy on us."

"All these assholes after us, and you want to beat yourself up some more? Go ahead, but first things first," Amelia said. Stripping the sim card from the phone, she took it into the bathroom to flush it.

*

When she was in the bathroom, the blaring TV filled the suite. Amelia called out, "Do we need the TV that loud?" She threw the bathroom door open and froze. BK muted the TV and dropped the remote but squeezed Mason's larynx in his vice-like grip. Using Mason as a shield, the assassin put a gun fixed with a silencer to Mason's temple.

Amelia lied to both men. "I wasn't expecting you so soon. Let the citizen go. You want me? I'm right here."

"I have two missions."

Starved for oxygen, the agony plain on his crimson face, Mason's knees buckled. His shifting weight momentarily distracted BK, giving Amelia the opening to lunge for her Glock and fire twice from the bed. The first bullet grazed BK's left temple; the next hit his hand holding the gun. He shrieked in pain, dropping both the weapon and Mason like bricks. Mason jumped up, gagging for air, blocking her clear shot, so BK pounced on her, twisting the Glock from Amelia's fingers. They fought viciously, rolling onto the floor. BK rammed Amelia into the cramped corner, choking her with one hand, pinning her arms in the confined space. He looped the bedside lamp cord around her neck with the other bleeding hand.

Mason leapt at the bed, kneeling on the remote and unmuting the T.V. The room filled with Ellen's giveaway portion of the show. Mason grabbed the landline telephone from the bedside table and clobbered BK; the bell inside the phone rang loudly from the impact. Twisting sideways, BK reached for Amelia's pistol on the bed. Amelia took advantage of her momentary release and smashed her palm upward into BK's nose, jamming the cartilage inward. BK screamed in pain. Mason slammed BK's head harder with the telephone. "It's for you," he yelled. Then hit him again. Bemused, BK paused, then his eyes rolled back in their sockets, and he slumped onto Amelia. She shrugged the assassin off and onto the floor, heaving in deep gulps of air, shaking off the exertion.

Amelia said, "You sure can't do that with a cellphone."

Mason put the phone down. "Is he...?"

"I wish. Can we please turn down the TV?"

Mason muted the TV and checked that the door was locked. Amelia went back into the bathroom to rinse a facecloth and wipe BK's blood from her face and neck. Mason stood in the door frame, watching her. "You should be watching him and the money, not me," but she smiled. She spoke calmly to his reflection in the mirror. "Before we stopped, I saw a totally cool green Camaro at that dealership down the street." She gathered up the money bag and the room key. "We have to follow the New York money, but there's one more small thing I have to do first." He was ready to leave, but she stopped him at the door. "Isn't there something you're forgetting?"

"You mean the body?"

"Our coffee mugs? That's the first present you bought me, and I'm not leaving without it." She tossed him the truck keys and the money bag. "Maybe wait in the truck until I buy a new phone."

"Super, I can update my trip diary. This morning's entry will be 'I'm adjusting to fighting to the death before lunch.'"

"I'll leave first, but I'm sure he was working alone."

Mason flipped the door hanger to 'Do Not Disturb' when they left.

12.   Test Drive

When she returned from the strip mall, Amelia went straight back to their hotel room. She reappeared in seconds and descended the stairs crooking her finger at Mason, calling him over. They met at the bottom stair. "I sent an Instagram to Hawke," she said. "Do you want to see?"

"The j-peg of a dead man? No, thanks."

"Relax… We just *winged* him. He'll be out for a while, but that nose…" She grimaced briefly, then destroyed the SIM card and tossed it and the broken phone into the motel dumpster. "Here, I'll take that." She slipped the money bag straps over her shoulder, and they left.

They dashed across the highway and hurried down the block to the Chevrolet dealership, where shiny new cars waited to trap buyers into years of high-interest payments. Beneath cross-hatched strings of multi-coloured triangle flags, his red tie flapping over his shoulder, a young eager-beaver salesman ran over to them. "Hello, folks, can I help you today?"

Amelia said, "I was wondering if we might take that green Camaro for a test drive? Can we do that? I've finally talked Lux into buying a new car."

Mason flashed a questioning glance at Amelia. The gushing salesman said, "Yes, ma'am. Unless you're interested in a family-sized van?" He extended his arm, trying to hand out a business card, but Mason ignored the offer. "We sell a lot of them. They're great on gas, you know," said the salesman, less brightly after Mason's refusal, "to get the kids around."

"Sonny, I would never put Lux into a castration machine." The salesman blushed. Mason rolled his eyes at Amelia. "Yes, ma'am, I mean, no ma'am," said the salesman. "I'll go get the keys." He ran off toward the showroom, shouting over his shoulder, "I can get you a great deal on rust protection."

Mason said, "You were kind of tough on the kid."

"So, shoot me."

"No can do… I'm not shooting anyone else before noon." He shook his head and looked away, sighing heavily. "That joke wasn't in my lexicon yesterday."

The salesman ran back and hung the dealer plate from

the Camaro's trunk while Mason squeezed into the back seat with the bag full of cash. The salesman sat in the passenger seat. Amelia drove.

"Not much gas."

"No, ma'am. Can I ask you folks to please take care with your coffees in the car? My manager pitches a fit if the cars come back with even a flyspeck on the windshield. I can't imagine what it would do to him if someone spilled coffee."

"We'll use the cup holders." Amelia lowered all the car windows, then caught Mason's eyes in the rear-view mirror and mouthed the word: *seatbelt*. He belted in. Amelia beamed her supermodel runway smile at the salesman, belted herself in, adjusted her sunglasses, then she roared the engine. She smoked the rear tires in reverse out of the parking slot before idling them through the lot. "Frisky," she said to the shocked salesman. Amelia stopped at the sidewalk as thick clouds of tire smoke caught up and billowed around them. Lanes of moderate traffic flowed in both directions. The salesman pleaded with Amelia, "You'll want to feather the gas peddle."

Amelia pumped the pedal twice; the powerful motor growled and rumbled back to a vibrating idle of pent-up torque. She asked in a sweet voice, "This *is* the ZL1, 580 horsepower, zero to sixty in 3.9 seconds model, isn't it?"

"Yes, ma'am. I'll tell you when my side is clear."

"You go ahead and do that." Amelia punched the gas, sinking Mason deep into his seat as if they were launching an F-18 off the Nimitz, shooting them into traffic and laying down another impressive smoke show. The salesman's eyes bulged. He yelled something short but indecipherable, drowned out by the roaring engine and peeling tires.

Several hundred blindingly fast yards later, Amelia said, "You're right," dicing the performance monster between cars and trucks, "it has more pep than a family van. Wouldn't this be fun to drive to the parent-teacher meetings?"

"Eighty-five. Eighty-five. You're driving a little fast." The salesman's voice cracked. "This is a twenty-five zone, ma'am." Amelia cut over the center double line to speed past a semi-trailer truck. "Can we please stay in our lane?"

She looked in the rear-view mirror for Mason's eyes, flicking her shoulder and lifting her eyebrows. Mason turned and saw BK driving the Mercedes, holding his bloody nose with one hand, coming up fast behind them. "By the way, what's your name again?" Amelia asked the frightened salesman.

"Brigham," he squawked out, shooting recriminating eyes at Mason, "it's on my card."

"Popular name in this state. Brigham, not a seatbelt fan?"

She changed lanes again, cracking the salesman's head against the passenger window while he frantically scrambled for his seatbelt. Amelia punched the gas pedal to crank the muscle car around the next corner. In the acute, drifting turn, their screeching tires ground inside the wheel wells as they drifted onto the next street. "Spongy rear suspension," she said, shooting a condescending look at Brigham. Amelia cut through cross-traffic, forcing other drivers into sliding, screeching stops. Behind them, a slow-to-react driver clipped the Mercedes with his minivan, causing BK's car to fishtail wildly, but he stayed with them.

They raced toward a red light and stopped traffic. Amelia slung the Camaro into the oncoming lane. "Wrong side. Whoa. Wrong side." shouted Brigham. They peeled through the intersection and around the corner, darted into an alley, and sped down the tight gauntlet. BK followed her every move. A surprised man wearing kitchen whites emptying a garbage can jumped out of their way at the last second. They hit the garbage can, which flipped over the hood, clipped their windshield, turned half of it into a frosted web, and rolled off the back of the Camaro. The dented garbage can, wedged under BK's front fender, sparked dangerously, but he kept coming. Amelia raced across a mall parking lot. They upset empty outdoor tables, umbrellas, and chairs in front of a restaurant at the exit, mixing in a spray of cardboard boxes and plastic garbage cans. Brigham sustained a high-pitched squeal, and Mason's heart was in his throat too, but Amelia, in her element, kept the gas floored— the grey Mercedes was still tight on their tail.

"Brigham," she said calmly, "which way to the highway?"

Brigham strained his voice to reply above the engine roar, "The I-89 or the fifteen?"

An outrage of horns blared at them, and more tires screeched at the exit of the mall parking lot when they cut through two lanes of traffic, accelerating to near one hundred miles an hour. "It doesn't really matter, dear, as long as we get there soon."

"Um, um, make a right, then go past the furniture store."

Heeling them over again, Amelia slid the car onto an industrial access road, swerving dangerously around a loaded forklift backing out from the long, hectic loading dock. Mason checked; BK was gaining on them again. "We still have company," he yelled.

Amelia looked at Brigham. "Which direction now, Brigs?" They sped up to another intersection. Traffic was heavy and stopped for equally congested suburban cross-traffic. Amelia pulled onto the narrow apron, blitzing them past the waiting lines of vehicles, creating a spray of sparks as they ground along the containment wall.

Brigham yelled over the car's deafening dual exhaust, "Ma'am, please slow down. I don't want to die." They were fast approaching a red light, racing toward moderate cross traffic.

"Straight through this red light, then?"

"Go right, go right. It's the bypass." Brigham called out through his hands held over his face.

The distance narrowed between the line of vehicles waiting for the light to change and the cement barriers on the outside of the apron. Amelia raced into the gap slamming the sides of three cars behind the semitrailer truck idling at the light. The impact tore off the Camaro's front fender, flattened its passenger side panels, and blew off both side mirrors. Thirty feet from the corner, they raked the base of a light standard on the passenger side while scraping along the full length of the semitrailer truck. The torturous squeeze of metal and tires squared both sides of the Camaro and ripped off its rear bumper. Mason followed its arc through the air. BK's Mercedes, which took the same punishment through the gauntlet of honking vehicles and cement, drove over their dismembered bumper, flipped it into the line of cars. The bumper impaled a Smart car, the impact knocking it off its wheels and onto its side. Seconds later, Amelia punched them through to the highway interchange, turning toward the airport.

Brigham seemed to have transported mentally to a parallel, safer world where he was not racing down the highway, smashing a supercharged Camaro driven by a demon vixen from Demolition Derby Hell. Far too calmly, he began his incongruous, rehearsed sales pitch. "So, if you think you'll buy the car, I can get you half off on the undercoating. You know, like in the movie Fargo."

Mason caught Amelia's eyes in the mirror and sent her a questioning look. Amelia did a double-take at Brigs, then snapped her fingers at Mason. "Brigham," she said with a sugary tone, "do you mind if Lux drives?"

The young salesman brightened, smiled warmly, but only mustered a stutter, "Th-that would be fine."

Space between the vehicles on the bypass highway allowed BK to catch up and ram them, violently jolting the Camaro with enough force to accordion their trunk. Amelia was able to keep them on the road. Brigham yelped at the collision. "If you slow down, I'll try to get his tag number. My manager is going to go insane." Amelia punched the gas pedal, and the red speedometer needle flew past 130 miles an hour. She put the car into cruise mode, then accidentally-on-purpose doubled Brigham over when she drove her elbow into his solar plexus.

With Brigham bent forward and gasping for air, Mason had enough room to swing his legs across the space between the front bucket seats. Grabbing for the wheel with his left hand, he used it to pull himself forward, but the jerking motion put the Camaro into a dangerous lane-to-lane slide. Amelia took back control and steadied them. "Careful, Lux," she said in a calm voice, her hand on his, "we don't have triple-A."

This time, Mason tried again with a lighter touch, planking from the dash to the driver's seat while managing to keep his eyes on the road. Amelia had enough room to slip into the back seat. BK was close to ramming them again when Mason slid behind the wheel and punched the gas.

The corners of the shattered windshield partially peeled away from the glue and moulding. Alarmed, Mason yelled, "Do something and do it now." Brigham raised both knees, holding his hands in front of his face, but peeked between his fingers. Mason kept one eye on the road and one on the rear-view mirror while he weaved from lane to lane. BK fired three shots from his driver's window. Glass shards blew into the Camaro, spraying Amelia and spider-webbing the last of the windshield when bullets ripped through it.

Brigham yelled into his hands, "Oh my fucking God."

BK's intentions seemed to be to park on their trunk. Amelia yelled, "Hold it steady." She pivoted on the back seat to kick the rest of the rear window out of the car, rolled back, took careful aim, then pumped two rapid-fire shots, shattering BK's windshield. She fired again, taking off a large chunk of BK's left ear—one of his hands grabbed at the gory wound. "Did you shoot him?" Mason yelled at her reprovingly. "Yes. But I just winged him—again," she yelled back. Her next shot blew BK's other hand off the steering wheel, splattering bloody fingers, skin, and bone into the maniac's face, snapping his head back and to the left. The Mercedes lurched sideways, flipped twice, scattering other vehicles, spun on end, then slid, spinning on its roof, until it came to a stop. A semitrailer truck jackknifed behind BK, bashing into several cars, anti-climatically nicked the Mercedes and broke one of its taillights. The semi and the wrecks it collected during its slide blocked the highway's lanes after the pileup had finally ground to a stop. Mason slowed the Camaro. BK's car had not burst into flames.

"Now there's truth in advertising," said Mason. "They claim it's a very safe car in an accident."

Dumbstruck, Brigham stared back through the blown-out rear window. They approached a busy truck stop on their right. Amelia said, "Lux, I could stand another coffee."

Mason coasted out of gas into a neat parking job on the truck stop's backlot, where they exited the destroyed Camaro. Amelia slipped on her sunglasses and then retrieved the money bag and both mugs. She handed the mugs to Mason but slung the bag over one shoulder. "Try not to chip them," she said. Brigham stood beside Mason, wobbling on unsteady legs, shocked at the damage.

Amelia asked him, "Can I borrow your cellphone?" Mason wrinkled his forehead and raised an eyebrow at her. Brigham, the ever-placating salesman, mutely surrendered his iPhone to Amelia. She pulled the SIM card, dropped the phone on the ground, stepped on it, then ground her heel into the display. He looked down at his broken phone. "Of course," he said, unable to raise more than that mild protest that Amelia had destroyed his lifeline back to his world.

Amelia counted fourteen hundred-dollar bills from the duffel bag and gave Brigham the cash and the SIM card. "Buy yourself a new phone and a couple of months of use on us."

Brigham took the cash. "Thank you, ma'am." His gaze drew theirs to the Camaro. "About the car..."

"Yeah, the car. It's a great car, hon, " they all looked doubtfully at the wreck, "but the colour is wrong."

"So, no sale?"

Amelia shook her head. Mason patted Brigham on the back and said, "Sorry about the spilled coffee, but, for the record, you had me sold on the rust protection." The shaken young man nodded, then staggered away toward the payphone outside the restaurant side door.

Mason and Amelia hurried through the truck stop parking lot. "Lux?" he said. "That's the best you could come up with? A name that sounds like a porno set hand lotion?"

Amelia said, "You're the writer, not me." She indicated the coffee mugs. "Why don't you get those filled? I'll pick you up at the front door?"

When Mason exited the restaurant, he was incredulous to see Amelia had chosen a minivan. She pushed the passenger door open, and he got in. They drove away, merging smoothly and at the speed limit into the traffic heading toward Salt Lake City. "After all that, you steal us a castration machine?"

"Finding a single minivan in Middle America, stolen or not," Amelia said, "is like looking for a needle in a stack of needles."

After skirting the city via the I-85 bypass, they flew out of Tooele Valley Airport forty-five minutes later on the private jet waiting for them. Before takeoff, Amelia changed their destination again; they were flying to Newark. Mason accepted the change of plans without protesting—New York was just too obvious.

13. History Repeats, Again

They sat on a white leather couch in the posh interior of their Lear rental jet. After their lung-crushing ascent to 31,000 feet, Mason said, "How much is this going to cost?"

Amelia kicked off her shoes. "Fifteen thousand," she said. "We'll reimburse Alacrán when we see him. We're good for it."

"Does this Alacrán know we're playing with Hawke's money?"

"Of course."

"In that case, the drive to the airport made me thirsty. We have hours to relax. Fancy a martini?"

"Three olives, please."

The jet hit an air pocket. Mason had to steady himself to pour. "And look, they're shaken, not stirred." She smiled at him.

Mason busied himself raiding the galley mini-bar and fridge. Amelia fiddled with the TV, landing on a classic rock music station. He poured half a bottle of Canadian glacier water vodka into a cocktail shaker half-filled with ice, then liberated a bottle of Vermouth, an ice bucket, elegant glasses, and olives and onions. He brought everything with him on a serving tray to their side table. Mason poured under her approving eye—he took onions and Amelia olives, but their tastes overlapped in their appreciation of a drop of Vermouth. Amelia held Mason's gaze, tasted her drink, and said, "Delicious." He smiled. "Good choice on the music," he said and left abruptly, returning in seconds from the galley fridge with a veggie-cheese tray.

"Oh, God, yes. Food." He sat beside her. She draped one playful leg over his. They both made discreet choices from the hors d'oeuvres tray. "Don't you think we make a great... team," she said, her tone upbeat, "even if we are olives and onions?"

Disarmed, he said, "I don't mind olives on my pizza."

"Anchovies?" she asked, probing his tastes, her eyes wide.

"Never..."

Amelia sipped her martini. "That's perfect."

"There's always more if you'd like..."

She took her leg back and became quiet, munching a slice of English cucumber, peering out the window at the brown foothills and pastures thousands of feet below. Mason kicked off his shoes and scrunched the deep carpet between his toes.

"At the motel," he said, "I should have known better."

She leaned back on the money bag, turned to him, and gently laid the tips of her fingers on his arm. "I haven't lied to you, not once. Do you believe me?"

"Let's have all of it first."

"Okay, short version... Dad was a Navy SEAL, so it's in my DNA. I always wanted to be a SEAL but ran up against the West Point glass ceiling, so I entered specialist training in the military. I had explosives and warfare technology training in the Pursuit."

"I was more interested in this guy Hawke. He was your boss, right?"

"At NEWCorp, he thought he was. I read a lot of documents while I was inside. Anything nuclear the US has, NEWCorp makes it theirs. But we think the LA Project is bigger than that."

"If we get Hawke off my case, can this end?"

"The guy controlling Hawke is our key."

"There's someone else?"

"A lot of people want us dead." Her words hit Mason like 9 MM rounds. "I—I'm sorry. I'm looking for a way to get you out—safely." Amelia spoke faster now. "We don't have a lock on it yet, but there's that July fourth NEWCorp photo op with the president, for starters. Both inner circles must want that, but we—I can't let that happen."

He said, "To stop it, *we* have to track down whoever jerks Hawke's chain."

Amelia caught the nuance and placed her hand on his arm. She said, almost in a whisper, "You worked in that mine, and you're a boxer. You've survived lots of dangerous stuff before."

"This is different."

"But survival is survival. Tell me why you wrote your book."

"Your turn to explain everything sure ended fast." She punched his shoulder. "Okay," he laughed, "that's simple. I

70

want to leave a fair shot at a good life for the next generations."

"A knight in shining armour… rare. But you were going to die in a car accident, or from a slip in the shower, or a heart attack, or shot dead in your apartment during a botched break-in. They find ways. I thought that was unfair."

"So it is." A teasing smile creased Mason's face. "I suppose we'll have to get married."

"Married?" Amelia was genuinely shocked.

"Then they can't make us testify against each other."

"Oh, right."

They stopped talking when Amelia placed her hand on his because the cockpit door opened enough to catch one of the unsmiling pilots studying them. He smiled when Amelia twiddled her fingers at him. Embarrassed, the younger, tall copilot came into the cabin. He stooped as he approached. His eyes flicked to the black duffel bag before he formed a broader, phonier smile.

"Hi, folks. How's the flight so far?"

Amelia sat up to put her glass on the table, subtly putting half her weight on the balls of her feet. "Good, thank you. We're good."

"Great. Great. Can I arrange transportation for you in New Jersey?"

"We've made arrangements."

"Very good. Some of our customers want their pictures taken when they fly with us." Without waiting for approval, he snapped the quick shot on his Smartphone. "Thanks." He looked at the digital photo. "You're a great-looking couple." His smile was wide and forced.

Amelia tensed her hand on Mason's, so he watched her. "Say, sugar, may I see?" At first, the copilot hesitated but then said, "Of course," and passed Amelia his phone. She released Mason's hand, reached for the phone, but it slipped out of her hand and dropped into the ice bucket half filled with melted ice water. Amelia pushed the camera through the ice and into the meltwater, fishing for it before giving it back to the copilot. "I'm so sorry. I hope I didn't…"

Amelia passed him the phone. He said, "No worries, ma'am. This phone is waterproof." His smile thin now, he added, "Enjoy the rest of your flight." At the cockpit door, the copilot snuck a quick, unsmiling look back at them before closing the door.

"He made us." She retrieved her Glock from the moneybag, and, as determined as a Sumatra leopard closing on an unwary meerkat, she was up and moving forward.

"But who's going to fly the plane?" There was no time for Mason's protest—Amelia had opened the cockpit door and stepped inside.

*

Amelia signalled to the copilot to be silent. She showed the startled captain her Glock and whispered briefly to him. He looked at her, then sideways at his terrified copilot, then the gun, then back at their serious passenger. Amelia nudged the captain in the ribs with her gun. The autopilot system flew the jet at high altitudes, so they responded to her gun by unbuckling their seat belts and following Amelia when she backed out of the cockpit. She waved her gun toward the couch across from where Mason waited and sat beside him, her gun trained on the pilot's kneecaps, shaking her head at them.

"Don't blame us." She nodded at the copilot. "You brought this on yourself."

"Miss, please be extremely careful with that gun," said the captain.

"Mister Copilot, tell your captain what you did."

"I took their picture..."

"And?" said Amelia.

"...and I sent it to someone."

"Tell him the rest."

"For money."

The captain was outraged. "You'll get yourself fired for doing that."

"He might get himself dead for doing that." Amelia addressed the copilot, "You and I know where that picture went, don't we?" The co-pilot nodded, defeated.

"You should both know I'm qualified on carrier night landings for Night Hawks and F-15s, which means if I have to shoot you two, and if my partner and I kept all this money, we would still get to live happy, long lives spending it." She smiled matter-of-factly at them both and said, "But you two would be dead." She menaced the copilot with a single look. "How much is the bounty?"

The copilot began begging, "Please, ma'am, I have a

wife with a baby on the way."

"How much?"

"Twenty thousand."

The captain exploded, "You put my life in jeopardy for that?"

Amelia's voice was polite when she said, "Captain, shut up." He sat back in his chair and looked at her. Amelia unzipped the bag, showcased the cash, then zipped it back up, "This is Sinaloa cartel money for Matty Indurito's Manhattan outfit and import services rendered."

The pilot's eyes popped wide, his voice desperate, "Oh, sweet Jesus…"

"It gets worse for you," said Amelia. "Matty Indurito, the *capo* of the organization and our long-time business associate, has no sense of humour. Three of Matty's men are waiting for us in Jersey. They're old-school, stone-cold killers. I say the word, and you two and your families are history after the upcoming airport war this idiot started." She flicked the Glock toward the flinching copilot. "When that war shoots itself out, everyone will know you've tripped up a CIA-Mafia money mule." She let that sink in. "So, what do you plan to do about that? I mean, besides sitting there filling your shorts."

Both men sat mute and small and stared straight down the barrel at the end of their lives.

"Right. Captain, you'll drop my friend and me at a private airstrip, and then you will continue to Newark. Or you can jump now, and I take over in the cockpit." From the looks on their faces, Amelia's proposition resonated with them when she said, "What's it going to be?"

14. **Meet the Parents**

The pilot landed the jet on what appeared to be an abandoned Cold War airstrip in western Pennsylvania. The narrow river valley was flush with trees and a river that cut geological features into the uncultivated back-country terrain. Near the end of the cement runway, they taxied toward the bulging outline of an immense, half-interred Quonset-shaped hangar. It was more impressive as they approached its gaping maw beneath leafy camouflage.

Amelia leaned forward over the pilot's shoulder to remind him she was close and had a gun. "Keep going, Captain, right to the back of the hangar," she said. "There's enough room at the bottom of that ramp to turn a B-52 around."

As they rolled under the cement arch, Mason whispered to Amelia, "Matty Indurito in Manhattan? That's rich."

She flicked her eyes at him. "Yeah," she said, under her breath.

"Yeah?"

"Yes," said both pilots and Amelia in unison, looking at Mason. Amelia rolled her eyes at him, her brow furrowed.

"Oh," he said sheepishly.

Against the back wall, one of a massive set of interior doors slid partially open. A male figure holding an unmistakable gun in one hand was silhouetted in the light. His oblong shadow formed in the slice of white light that gashed a blazing streak across the vast cement floor. "This will do. Stop here. Kill the engines." The pilot followed Amelia's orders. In the background, the engines wound down. She turned to Mason. "I hope you're ready for this. And you two," said Amelia to the pilots, "let's meet the welcoming committee."

She held the pilot at gunpoint. The copilot opened the door, dropped the stairs, and they deplaned. Amelia stopped them at the foot of the steps. Four armed men exited through the interior doors in double file behind the man still standing in silhouette. Two of the men ran up the ramp. Two others took positions at the foot of the steps, behind the pilots and Mason and Amelia. At the top of the ramp, the men used chains to unravel a giant camouflage tarpaulin suspended from the ceiling across the hangar's gaping maw. The two guards covering them had drawn their pistols.

The background lighting made it difficult for Mason to discern details of the last man, who appeared to be their leader. He strode toward them, rigid in his upper body, tight in his movement. He kept his face in shadow until he stood at ease six feet away, chest out, his arms folded behind him. Mason had the distinct feeling this mystery man evaluated him. When the man spoke, his voice was resonant, gravelly, and accusatory, "We expect our visitors to knock before they come barging in."

Amelia said, "We had an in-flight emergency..."

The anxious pilot interrupted, "Get her gun. We've been kidnapped..."

"I'll get to you later." The man in charge approached Amelia. Mason struggled to connect the man's deep, bold voice and his slim build. "What kind of emergency?" said the leader.

"The unnecessary kind, but it's handled now." Both mute pilots looked confused and afraid to speak up.

"I see," said the leader, pausing for a moment before addressing the pilots. "Well, if you won't stay for a beer," cold menace laced his slow speech, "can you forget this airfield exists. Will that be a problem?"

"No, sir," said both pilots in unison.

The leader said, "Then you'll want to be on your way."

The intimidated pilots turned tail and scampered back up the steps and into the jet, where the copilot pulled the door closed. The leader spoke into his tactical portable radio mic, and the two men operating the tarpaulin chains raised the camouflage tarp. The leader turned and walked toward the open door, and Mason and Amelia followed him with the silent guards. They stopped in front of a huge wall-mounted monitor to watch the jet leave. Its engines roared until the two men operating the tarp caught up and closed the hangar door. The air and noise blast from the jet battered the walls but subsided quickly after the plane exited the hangar.

When Mason turned from watching the jet depart, he saw Amelia rush at the leader. Mason steeled himself for the fight, but Amelia threw her arms around the thin man and laid her head on his chest. "Daddy, I want you to meet my friend, Mason Stone."

Despite surviving the past two days, Mason suffered jagged angst witnessing Amelia's conflicting change from a confident warrior to a sensitive daughter. The throes of meeting *parents* shook him as the most abnormal of so many recent events.

"Little girl, you owe me some money." Amelia's father stuck his hand out to Mason, so he shook it. Mason saw the black scorpion tattoo drawn across the rope-like muscles along his forearm while his hand met the man's firm grip. "Pleased to meet you, Mason. Call me Alacrán. Let's get back inside."

Mason shot Amelia his best revenge look, but she smiled and looped her arm in Alacrán's before entering the facility as a group. The sliding inner door slammed shut behind them with a metallic boom. They walked through a cavernous machine shop, farther into the cement bunker, along an unadorned hallway. They entered an ante-room and gathered around the consul of an enormous radar screen surrounded by an array of high-tech electrical equipment. They watched the jet blip disappear toward the northeast.

Under his green camo tank top, Alacrán was close to Mason's height, but not more than one sixty-five, Mason's weight when he was twenty-one. Alacrán's face was weather-beaten and bronzed into a deep tan beneath a gray, unkempt beard. The man showed his vintage, but lean muscles still rippled on his bare arms and across his chest. "Let's have a beer," he said.

Mason and Amelia followed Alacrán to another room set up as a clubhouse. They took a separate table for privacy, apart from the couches and the massive TV monitor in the lounging area adjacent to the modern kitchen. An American flag and several photographs of heavily armed men in jungles, deserts, and bombed-out cityscapes adorned the walls. Alacrán's crew, the armed guards, relaxed on couches where they became engrossed in the televised basketball game.

While Alacrán retrieved beers from one of the fridges, Amelia said to Mason, "I was going to tell you about all this."

"It *was* still your turn."

She took the coffee cups from the money bag and placed them on the table. "These stay here."

Alacrán arrived with the refreshments. "Dad, I want you to know Mason has been courageous. He saved my life twice in the last forty-eight hours."

"Sir, I'm no hero."

"Get used to it if you plan on hanging around with this one." Handing Mason a cold beer, Alacrán was proud of his daughter. "Now that you're unemployed, what are your plans, Ames?" His use of a family pet name caused Mason to smile, which he shared briefly with Amelia.

She looked back at Alacrán. "We can talk shop later. What's for supper?"

Alacrán wrapped an arm around Amelia's shoulders, hugged her, and said, "That's my kid—always hungry. Steak barbecue in two hours."

Amelia went to the beer fridge and took out a six-pack. "C'mon, Mason, let's go let off some steam."

*

Concise in her moves, Amelia slipped on safety glasses and ear protection, then aimed her Glock at a target seventy feet down the firing line. She fired nine rapid shots. She flipped the safety on, placed the smoking Glock down on the shelf, and removed her ear protection,

Mason slid one side of his ear protection off and asked, "How much of that stuff did you make up to scare the pilots?"

"I can't fly an F-15, certainly not at night onto a carrier." She pushed a green button on the wall. A line pulled the paper target back to her, stopping at the shelf. Mason was impressed—every bullet had hit the centre of her target. She attached a new target and pushed a red button on the wall to send the target back to the same position. She snapped a full clip into the gun and handed it to Mason. "Safety is on."

He held Amelia's hand with the Glock in his, staring her straight in the eyes. "Considering we were flying five hundred miles an hour at thirty thousand feet, that was a hell of a bluff." He released her. Mason raised and lowered his shooting hand. "This thing is heavy." He adjusted his ear protection, then slowly aimed the weapon, carefully turned off the safety, and pulled the trigger once. The gun kicked hard. Mason's shot hit the back wall ten feet left of his target. He frowned and then removed his ear protection. "I got this," he said.

With a look of doubtful concern on her face, Amelia raised her eyebrows. "Not all of it was fantasy; the mafia part was true." She straightened his arms. "Lock your elbows. Squeeze, as they say in the movies, don't pull." She positioned his legs from a boxer's stance to a shooter's position. "Matty Indurito is a long-time friend of the family. We've partnered with him before. Sweetheart of a guy if you don't cross him."

"The mafia?"

"You don't get the *bad* bad guys unless you're tight with a few *good* bad guys."

After some practice, Mason still never threatened the black circles but hit the paper target at forty feet three times out of a full clip, but he took time between each shot. She was philosophical. "If we ever have to shoot our way out of a scrape, I hope the anti-NRA slogan is right."

"About what?"

"That it *is* the guns that kill people."

*

The man, a caricature of a 1936 lower-East Side mobster-thug, took the landline call in the back booth of the dank pizza restaurant on Mulberry Street. His thick accent dominated his gruff voice, battered by years of cigars and heavy drinking. "Go."

Delaci said, "I want their hides."

"She's almost family. We don't do that work for no one—except us."

"I have three million cash if you'll make an exception."

Matteo Indurito, the boss of the New York crime family, stared with lifeless eyes.

"So," said Delaci, "will it be *almost* family or money?"

*

The black limousine stopped near the patio tables outside the trendy Baltimore café, Java Shooters. Delaci looked up from his cellphone, took in his surroundings, and scoffed. "This is on her mother. I should have insisted on Yale. What do you think, Herbert?" he said to the burly driver.

"Yes, sir, Yale's the best," the driver responded.

"I mean," said Delaci, exasperated, "what future could Towson University possibly promise my daughter? Arts and culture? Bullshit. And now she thinks she can shut me out of her life." The driver looked in his rearview mirror at Delaci again. "I suppose I can only do my best," he continued. "I can tell you, Herbert, single parenting in the modern era is no picnic. Let's get on with it."

"Yes, sir." Herbert exited the car and held the door for Delaci.

Standing up, Delaci asked Herbert, "You're sure about this?"

"Her GPS shows her here. Do you want me inside?"

"That won't be necessary."

Delaci walked into the busy cafe. He saw her immediately. She was thin and pale, neither attractive nor unattractive, her eyes sensitive, intelligent, and troubled. He watched her for a moment, writing on a pad of paper, occasionally stopping and absent-mindedly tapping her tiny ruby nose stud with a pen. A dishevelled man, his mop of bright red hair covering half his face, brought two mugs of coffee to the table and sat down. When he kissed Cessily on the lips, Delaci's demeanour soured dramatically.

"Hello, Cessily," said Delaci, "I've missed you."

"How'd you find me?" she asked, a flicker of fear tainting her surprised eyes.

"That's not important."

"It is to me. My GPS is off," she said, then the realization crossed her face. "You hacked my phone. Figures." Cessily looked away.

"Hey, Cess," said the boy with a sneer, flicking his mop away from his eyes, squaring his body on his stool to face Delaci, "do you know this guy?" Delaci ignored the blatant challenge from the young man.

Cessily watched her father. "Just how far is far enough away from you?" she said.

Despite her acidic greeting, Delaci took a chair. "I've been worried sick."

The boy stood up and said, "Private table, man. Cess? I'm calling the cops."

"Yes, let's do," said Delaci, staring at the boy, "and find out whose life matters."

Cessily shook her head at the boy. "Bad idea; he owns the cops."

"Manners, Cessily," said Delaci, his icy voice alerting her, "you didn't introduce us."

"No, don't," said Cessily, but the boy was determined to interfere. "It's Ruben. Yeah, your daughter lives with a black man. Does that bother you?"

Delaci ignored Ruben and instead implored his daughter, "Please come home, Cessily, it's time. And you know I can give you everything you want."

"I asked if that bothers you," said Ruben aggressively.

Delaci lashed out, striking Ruben with a vicious chop to the throat. "You're interrupting."

Cessily screamed, her notes scattered off the table as Ruben gagged, his eyes rolled back in his head, and he tumbled to the floor when his knees buckled. Other patrons jumped up from their chairs. Several of them took their cellphones out. One man said, "I'm recording this. Leave now, buddy, or I call the cops."

"Cessily, I..." stuttered Delaci.

She knelt to help Ruben. She looked up at Delaci. "Get away from me." With panic in her voice, she yelled, "Someone call a doctor, my friend, he's hurt."

The man with the cellphone warned, "Leave right now, man; the cops are on their way."

When Delaci sat back in his limousine, his face was a mask of determined rage.

"Do you want me to go inside and straighten this out?" asked his chauffeur.

"Again, not necessary," said Delaci, for the last time.

*

The crew fired verbal jabs over steaks, beers, and sports while Mason, Amelia and Alacrán sat apart from them, talking over their next moves. Mason looked at Amelia sharply when she told Alacrán, "I'm going to New York. I need to borrow your ride."

"Is that a good idea? I can send two of the guys instead."

"I clean up my own mess. The plan is to follow the money, find out who's paying Hawke, especially now that we're his problem. Maybe I can stop this before it gets crazy."

Mason shot a look of unbridled disbelief at Amelia.

Alacrán kept his steely eyes on her. "I don't like it," he said. "Lay low here for a while. Rest up. Decide after that. We might need extra manpower."

"What have you heard?"

"It's big, just like we thought. I'm still waiting on details, but it's something about Kazakhstan. NEWCorp has been calling in markers, and the big guy is signing a bill in D.C. on July fourth."

"Two weeks from now doesn't give us much time," said Amelia.

"Our Italian friend is pissed off too. You disrespected his business the last time you were in Manhattan. It is messy, but let it go; you have your pride back. I can cover what you had to use and send Matty the cash and a nice bonus to smooth things over."

"I..." Amelia looked at Mason; he nodded. "*We're* meeting the next cash drop."

"You're taking Mason? But he seems like a nice guy."

Mason weighed in, "I'm going with Amelia."

"See? I told you he was a keeper." Amelia let a line of doubt crease her brow for an instant. "I can talk to Matty."

Despite the edginess in their conversation, Mason struggled to stay awake. The few beers, the jet lag and the turmoil of the last days and nights had caught up with him. Amelia noticed him flagging. "Okay, then. Mason, I'll show you where to sleep. G'night, Dad. I love you." She hugged her father with a long embrace. He held her close for an instant longer.

One of the boisterous crew hollered over to her, "Hey Amelia, we're playing cards tonight. We can save a seat at the table for you and your bag of cash."

She slid out of Alacrán's hug. "We're runnin' and gunnin' at first light, Yuri. I'll have to take your money next time." The crew tossed around a few good-natured barbs, teasing her about curfew.

Minutes later, Mason fell sound asleep beside Amelia on a double bed in a private cement dorm deeper in the cavern, mumbling, "Kazakhstan is all about uranium."

15. **Firefight**

Mason opened his eyes when Alacrán, tense and on point, threw their door open, switched on the overhead lights, and took a photograph with his cell phone. Mason pulled a sheet over his naked bare chest. He was surprised Amelia was still beside him, but she was instantly wide awake. "We're under fire," said Alacrán, intense but not panicked. "They're in the hangar. Take Tulip. Go now. I'll activate Redbird too."

Mason, half-dressed, released himself daintily from Amelia's embracing arm. He stood up and pulled on his shirt and runners, leery of how miffed the man holding the Uzi was at the guy in bed with his daughter.

Amelia, wearing a T-shirt and panties, reacted too, scooping a bundle of hundreds out of the moneybag onto the bed. "Have this, in case Redbird catches one on our way out."

Alacrán turned toward the faint crackle of automatic gunfire. "Keep it," he said, his voice tense.

Amelia pulled on a pair of jeans and an olive-green tank top before slipping on knee-high, black boots. "Dad, please." But Alacrán was gone. She slung the moneybag, now twenty-five thousand dollars lighter, over her shoulder. "This way," she ordered, and Mason followed.

They ran at a crisp pace along the hallway, their strides falling into sync, in the opposite direction from Alacrán. Motion sensors activated strings of overhead lights ahead of them, then turned the same lights off behind them. "That was weird. Why'd your dad take a picture of us?" Mason's shirt was soaked with sweat when they stopped in front of a steel door.

"Future reference." She pulled the heavy door open, then slammed it closed behind them. The air inside the new chamber was stagnant and faintly damp. The crackle of gunfire coming from somewhere close above them echoed in the room. A dim blue light radiated from an illuminated digital keypad mounted on the wall beside the door. Amelia activated the overhead lights when her fingers flashed over the keypad. Sixty-foot ceilings dwarfed them in the cold war cavern. A steep ramp led up and out of the garage along the far wall. Two black humvees and a camouflage four-by-four nearly filled the floor space.

"If your dad is paying for parking, he should get his

money back from the landlord," he said, wiping the sweat off his forehead.

"What? Why?"

"Because his garage is in the next county."

Amelia flashed a smile at him. The calculated, lethal, and impressive poise she possessed while in her special zone mesmerized him. She walked past the larger vehicles and stood in front of a dark green electric car parked at the bottom of the ramp.

"This is Redbird? Really?" The walls echoed his disappointment.

"This is Tulip. Let's go."

"I must be nuts."

"C'mon, it's electric," she said, throwing the bag of stolen Mafia money into the back seat and placing her loaded Glock on the dashboard. "How much trouble could we possibly get into?"

They fishtailed onto the bottom of the ramp in Tulip as Mason scrambled to buckle his seat belt. Amelia lowered her window and, halfway up the ramp, punched a red mushroom button mounted on the wall, then floored the accelerator pedal. They raced toward the closed garage door at the top of the ramp, which lifted open seconds before they slammed into it. They exited into blinding daylight, gaining speed. Two hundred feet across the creeper-strewn runway, Amelia stopped inside the fringe of the tree line. Mason lowered his window to listen. A firefight raged on the airfield's far side, where a black helicopter ascended into the sky.

"That's Redbird," said Amelia proudly.

The minute the chopper cleared the tree line, a smoke trail formed out of the foliage on the far side of the runway. "And that's a Patriot," Amelia said, her voice monotone, "surface-to-air missile." Both horrified and mystified, Mason watched the zigzag haze become straight as an arrow when the missile guidance system locked onto its target. An orange and black ball of fire enveloped the helicopter when target and missile converged, creating a resonating thunderclap over the valley. Flaming fragments of metal and plastic burst outwards and then spiraled back to earth, propelled by the violence of the explosion.

"Still think I'm deranged?" said Amelia, her voice had a

hint of 'I told you so' in it. Redbird's mangled remains crashed mere yards from them; a plume of thick, black smoke swirled upwards from the unrecognizable burning wreckage.

"Not anymore, but I'm thinking I might be."

"Whoever fired that missile thought we were in that chopper. Dad converted Redbird to a drone last year. That's going to piss him right off." She punched Tulip's accelerator and raced across the runway. One of the unseen attackers took a bead on them. A line of bullet holes fired from an automatic weapon formed behind them before they bumped into the cover on a dirt lane cut through the dense forest.

"Your father and the guys, will they be okay?"

"Dad will disarm the ones he can. He brings them in to cool off and will make one of them send the right code for completion to Hawke. He ships the hard asses out in a container on a slow boat to China."

"A slow boat... you expect me to believe that?"

Amelia questioned him with her eyes. He stopped laughing. She said, "They get out after a week or so at sea..."

"I wonder what he'll do to me—you know, for hanging out with his daughter?"

"The same, but with half-rations—and no call."

"You're joking, right?" She flashed a deadpan look at him, making him blanch as they bumped along the rough country lane beneath the full canopy of leafy Oak and Maple trees. "Aren't there satellites up there? Can't they see us?"

"They can't see much through this cover. Besides, Tulip's heat signature is almost invisible. Why don't you crank us some tunes? Life's good today, isn't it?"

"We did escape certain death in a firefight, so it could be worse."

A text arrived on Amelia's cellphone. "It's from Dad... everything worked out. It's over."

Mason found and cranked up Chilliwack's *Fly At Night* on Tulip's stereo

16. **Senator Smith in D.C.**

Senator Smith had demanded this meeting. Now he flaunted his authority, which was solely based on his servility to Delaci, mocking his fealty to his nation and his voters. Hawke clenched and released his jaw repeatedly, unaware he was doing the same with his hands. His eyes darted from the exquisitely framed copy of the U.S. Constitution to Smith, the object of his intense hatred. The infuriating, methodical Senator guided a young male Page by properly setting the glistening silver tea set on the elegant side table. Hawke's oxy was in his pocket, but he dared not self-medicate with Smith in the room, so his unrequited addiction fanned the flames of his wrath.

The tea service had interrupted their meeting in the space where opulence rioted with arrogance. A simple glance at Hawke's crimson face proved his disdain for the Senator and other country-club leeches like him whose sole purpose was to recruit monied interests into the LA Project. Hawke moved to stand in front of the window, away from Smith's rebuking, sidelong glances. The full view of the Congress Dome under another unbearably humid, overcast sky failed to inspire him. He turned his back on the foundation of American Democracy. Smith had finally finished the Page's tutoring. "There's no need to record this visit," Senator Smith said to the young man. The page nodded in deference, excused himself and silently closed the door as the two men eyed each other across the void of strained silence.

Hawke would never let the snide, entitled prick dress him down. "It was your mule who messed up the last cash drop," said Hawke on the offensive. "Then that fucking Amelia intervened... You created this mess. I take no responsibility for that."

The Senator replied, "You're right to assume many people are upset. You had her in your office but failed to solve the problem. We need clarifications."

Hawke doubled down. "How do you know about that? Are you spying in my..." One look from Smith confirmed that, of course, they monitored him. "Your New York situation, that's the threat to the LA Project. I've taken measures to solve *mine*, Senator."

"So?"

"As of 5:00 a.m. this morning," said Hawke. "I'm waiting for the report from the team I deployed last night. I don't whisper behind doors like your type does; I get things done in the real world."

"And here it is 9:00 a.m. You bait me, but we're still speculating on a favourable outcome?"

"Tell your D.C. vultures they can stop circling," said Hawke. He scorned Smith and the other blood-sucking messengers like him operating in the shadowy back hallways of Congress and the Senate. "We both know I don't have the luxury of any other kind of resolution," said Hawke.

"No, you don't." Senator Smith pressed a green button on the small electronic gadget he placed on the desk. His voice dropped into a whisper, and his words were slow and articulate. "This device emits an electro-magnetic pulse that incapacitates listening devices," said Senator Smith. "Now, I get to talk freely."

Despite his contempt for the politician, there was no mistaking Smith's words were a distinct threat. Scrutinizing eyes from an oil painting of the Founding Fathers watched both self-serving men. Hawke stepped into the centre of the room, where the diffused light from the expansive bulletproof window infused the gloom with a pallid, sombre mood.

"Senator Smith," said Hawke, placatory and back-pedalling in anticipation, "I'm sure you know NEWCorp values your molding a malleable senate is a vital key to our LA Project."

Senator Smith shot back with a menacing sneer. His vicious contempt, made worse by its silence, weaved into the implied dignity of the exquisite, hand-woven Persian carpets, the rich, hand-crafted cherry wood historical motif of Washington crossing the Delaware River, the law books and senatorial records on the expertly-inlaid dark teak bookshelves, and the priceless post-Revolution works of art. Withering under Senator Smith's critical scrutiny, Hawke craved his Oxycodone. But pulling it now would indicate weakness, serving to incite even more of Smith's inexhaustible supply of arrogance. Hawke turned his gaze to the tea set. "Do you have anything to make that Irish?"

Senator Smith ignored him. He tested the scrambling device. A small indicator on the device's colour meter glowed steadily in the green. Smith looked up, sat on the corner of the desk, and said, "Sit." Hawke obeyed, sliding and sinking into the ironic and rather uncomfortable William Morris chair. "We're concerned about two lingering issues that could still prove detrimental to pending contracts."

"I expect that report at any time."

Senator Smith stood up and yelled, "Shut your claptrap and listen, you dissipated fool." The violence of his outburst landed on Hawke like a broadside blow. He shrunk into the chair. Baleful eyes from a life-size, masterpiece oil painting of Thomas Jefferson peered at Senator Smith from over Hawke's shoulder. Smith was undaunted as he dictated his demands. "Your incompetence has thrown off our schedule. Our bill must pass this vote, and the president must agree to sign the document into law by July 3rd. Our schedule is everything. You failed to solve the problem in New York. Why?"

Hawke responded with numbed subservience, knowing that beneath the customary veneer of the velvet glove was the iron fist of brazen, relentless greed. "The situation is under control."

"So you say," responded the senator with palpable, staccato arrogance. "You will be successful today, or we will employ others who can facilitate..." Hawke nodded, so Senator Smith toned down his vitriol. "We compensate you well. You alone are responsible for the security deliverables of this project. I was unable to collect the last package. There was a robbery. Why?"

"We're working on that," bleated Hawke, a polar opposite from his earlier accusation the problem was Smith's. "I expect to have that money back, and the problem of the scientist rectified today. These are small missteps."

Senator Smith pounced on Hawke's response. "Allowing the scientist to leave the country is not a *small misstep*. Your incompetence is astounding." Senator Smith glared at Hawke, then breathed in deeply and sighed. "You know he doesn't tolerate failure; I don't know what I can do for you. He expects these two problems solved and the money returned within twenty-four hours. The *LA Project* will survive, but you..." Senator Smith adjusted his tie and shrugged himself comfortably into his suit jacket. "Consider yourself dismissed from this meeting and from serving this corporation in the

future if you do not produce—today—what you guarantee."
He reached out and clicked the green button on the scrambling
device once the digital metre faded to black, and then Smith
placed it in his desk drawer.

Hawke did not look back before leaving.

*

Hawke sat mortified behind the wheel of his Suburban in the
underground parkade, staring at his buzzing cellphone. He
answered, and Victor said, "Is our problem still a problem?"

"I spoke with Smith. I have that covered. She got lucky
in Utah, that's all. Then the pilots gave us away. Otherwise, it
would be over."

"And what about the pilots?" said Victor.

"They died during an attempted robbery when they
arrived at Newark."

"This must end today." Hawke breathed deeply. "New
York," continued Victor, "was messy. People are nervous. We
want that cash returned. Show us you can protect the bagman.
Now, what about the girl and the writer?"

Glancing at his watch, Hawke said, "Like I said, they're
dead," and ended the call. He took two pills, then texted an
unlisted number—still no response. "Where the fuck is my
report?" he yelled, pounding the steering wheel. Hawke scowled
and exhaled, waiting for his nervous tension to dissolve into
narcotic relief. When that happened, he slumped, asleep, until
forty minutes later, when his buzzing cellphone woke him.

The text read: mission successful returning to base

Relief relaxing his face, Hawke speed-dialled Victor's
number, unconcerned about slurring, "The accounts are
closed," he said and blacked out again.

*

Delaci looked out the side window in the stretch limousine,
flexing his fingers in the leather gloves. He told the driver,
"You know where I'm going."

An hour later, the chauffeur parked the limousine on a
narrow side street near Towson University. Recent, trendy
refurbishing had failed to change the neighbourhood's
bohemian character. The status and disrepair of the nineteenth-
century brick apartment buildings lining both sides of the street
remained the same, but the facelift tripled the rent.

"Where is she now?" Delaci asked his driver.

88

He checked his cellphone and said, "She left the university, and it looks like she's on her way here, but there's still time."

"I won't be long…"

After 5:00 p.m., the sidewalks were busy with people arriving home from classes or day jobs. When Delaci exited the limousine, he entered the older, barely affordable buildings so popular with students. He climbed the stairs without effort or haste to the third floor, stopping outside '3F'. The door paint was checked and peeling. Inside, he heard rock music played at an apartment-acceptable volume; the discreet aroma of Italian sauce filled the hallway. Delaci knocked on the door.

Footsteps approached. Ruben opened the door, saying, "I hope you're ready for the best sauce ever." His face turned to fear. "What do you want?"

Delaci raised an eyebrow. Ruben tried to slam the door, but Delaci forced himself inside, stepping into the surprised boyfriend to silence him with a vicious jab to his larynx. Delaci kicked the door shut. The wooden spoon dropped from Ruben's hand as he grabbed his neck, unable to breathe. Delaci grabbed the terrified victim by his shoulders, pushing him back, staring in his eyes, and holding him up and off-balance. "Your sauce… not bad," said Delaci, "perhaps even amusing." Ruben pawed harmlessly at his assailant until, with a final shove, Delaci thrust Ruben backwards through the open window. Ruben's skull came apart on impact after plummeting three stories to the sidewalk, shocking strollers in the trendy street.

Screams and screeching tires rose from the street. Delaci calmly scanned the apartment; it would take the authorities time to connect the incident with the open window. He was about to leave the apartment but returned to the stove and picked a clean spoon from the dish rack to taste the sauce. "My daughter likes hers with a tablespoon of butter, you buffoon."

*

Cessily dropped her groceries when she saw the crowd gathered around the stairs to her building. She watched the departing limousine with darkened windows cruise slowly past. She pushed into the crowd. A whispering onlooker said, "Jumper." When she saw the body, she spoke quietly, "You bastard, you Godamn bastard." A uniformed policewoman heard Cessily and said, "Do you know this man, miss? Can I help you?"

Cessily's stared down at the dead boy on the street, then answered, "I don't need your fucking help."

17. **Dirty Money**

The Fifth Avenue skyscraper hotel provided a row of hookups for electric cars, so, after taking rooms, Mason and Amelia risked using Tulip for the rest of the day. They parked on Houston Street, across from the deli where New Yorkers said 'Good mawning' and haggled over the Mets and the Yankees or the bagels' quality.

A black Mercedes pulled onto the lot and parked. Mason and Amelia watched as a short, twenty-pounds-past-pudgy man scaring the hell out of his thirtieth birthday got out and went into the deli. "That's our bagman, Normy," said Amelia, "and it looks like he's still an ultra-geek."

Norman Garfinkle grew up in St. Albans on Long Island. In this community, most vote for law and order because they believe authority controls the hordes and tempers the would-be socialists and fascists. Leery of new social ideas as harbingers of unrest, the community was ultra-conservative. Normy was one of their favourite sons.

"You knew him?"

"We met at NYU. He was brilliant back then. He won an award for a project he did in actuarial forecasting. High-end stuff. But he's really let himself go."

The rest of Norman's story was in Alacrán's files. Three months after graduation, a Wall Street firm, Diedrich Brothers, lured Normy to the dark side. After ten months of running for coffee and suffering body shame humiliation from the brokers, Normy graduated to a desk and phone.

Until the crash of 2008, Normy's contribution to Wall Street was earning extortionate transaction fees for Diedrich Brothers and sponging his living from them. It was a counterfeit life, void of family and love unless you factor in a doting, social-climbing mother and cynical, timid father. But Normy's rewards were a life of extravagant consumption. When the crash was inevitable, Mr. Diedrich ordered his brokers to short the market but continue to lie to their thousands of investors that their money was safe. Their investors ended up swindled out of their life savings, but Diedrich and his brokers continued to roll like barnyard swine in obscene profits. After the crash, the geek from NYU saved his job with Diedrich when he showed them how to wring the very last dime from the rest of the frightened investors "in too deep" to quit. He applied the cruel, immoral skimming off what remained in the crippled economy through derivative trading. Normy positioned himself as a pet of the Wall Street elite while the financial world crumbled around him. He scooped up huge bonuses, bought a new Mercedes, acquired a haberdasher, mortgaged a lower-floor Manhattan apartment in a glass icon skyscraper on 5th Avenue, and ate exclusively at the best restaurants with the highest visibility in the business community. But every Tuesday, he still lunched at Katz's Deli.

"A few years after the crash," Amelia told Mason, "I bumped into him here. He came on to me, asked me to join him at his booth, but I flipped him off. That messed him up. He started speed talking, telling me about his car, his job, the money he made. I told him, 'I know a few people who lost everything because of you creeps.'"

"We all do," said Mason, "and it will keep happening."

"He jumped ship to Meister-Fleisher-Fuchs, the biggest Investment Bank on Wall Street. Interesting fact—they're also NEWCorp's cash flow spigot. Every Tuesday, Normy delivers a briefcase full of party cash to a senator so clients can wine and dine without it costing the corp. And it's all tax-deductible, of course. That caught Dad's attention."

"Who's the creep senator?"

"His name's Smith."

"I doubt much on Wall Street happens by chance," said Mason. "A few anonymous, colluding fat cats control over $34 trillion market dollars every year. There's nothing 'free market' about much of it, except for the dumb-ass investors. I guess the Normy's down here fall into line for the cash. He's lucky."

"Lucky?"

"Isn't he the boyfriend you dumped without using a bullet?"

"We only dated twice."

"Knew it." He grimaced at her. "So, even after being robbed last week, Tuesdays and lunch at Katz's are part of Normy's *black bag* day?"

"People like routine."

"They don't know the fun of firefights before breakfast."

"Look at that cocky bugger… he's strutting." Amelia scanned the immediate area. "Matty's guys have to be here—they wouldn't let this happen twice."

"Dad's guys followed Normy for a while—to learn his routine. But last week, it all went wrong. I caught him on the neck. Usually, you don't get second chances with these guys."

"Who? The Mafia?"

"Them too, but no, I meant Wall Street embezzlers. Normy has to have powerful people higher up the food chain protecting him."

"This is torture, flat out torture."

"I know it."

"I don't see why I can't go in and order a couple of sandwiches to go. Normy doesn't know me."

"No, but they might." Amelia nodded her head toward a black Mercedes E 63S with tinted windows. The driver was not visible, but Mason watched it park down from the front of the deli. "We'll rain check on that sandwich and chill—stick to the plan."

"Are they mafia? Or cops, maybe?"

"That's a spook car."

Minutes later, Normy exited the restaurant wiping his mouth and jowls with a white paper napkin. He dropped it before getting into his Mercedes. "Litterbug," said Mason, "I don't like him." They watched Normy drive off the lot, looking straight ahead, appearing unconcerned. A Crown Vic pulled into traffic several cars behind Normy's Mercedes. Both men in the front seat were beefy and serious. "Now, that's a mafia car," said Amelia, with emphasis.

Mason said, "At least we know they're not following us. Shouldn't we move? We don't want to lose them."

"Patience."

As if on cue, a yellow, late model Jeep drove off the deli parking lot, half a block behind Normy's Mercedes. The driver was wearing movie-star sunglasses. "Look who's following the people following Normy. That guy driving the Jeep… that's Smith," said Amelia. "He came into work once to meet with Hawke. He's one of NEWCorp's nasty errand boys, and he's our Pied Piper." Amelia started Tulip and fell in line when the Jeep passed them, staying a few cars back.

Mason was exhilarated and flushing with chase

adrenaline. "What about the Mercedes?"

"We can't wait around." Amelia looked him in the eyes and curled her lips into a wry smile. "It's exciting, right?"

Unwitting, Normy led the convoy to lower Manhattan, down LaFayette to Chambers. He parked at Washington Market Park. The mafia car took two spaces, being obvious, keeping the vehicle running, watching, cigar smoke filling the car's interior. The Jeep driver, Smith, pulled in two slots away from Normy but stayed in his vehicle. Amelia drove past all of them and parked across the lot. She adjusted the rear-view mirror to watch Normy; Mason watched through the rear window, pretending to talk to Amelia. Normy exited his car, reached inside to retrieve the black briefcase, then leaned against the car, holding the briefcase in both hands, high on his chest.

Amelia said, "So far, this is normal." Senator Smith was still behind the wheel in the Jeep. His window opened. He said something to Normy neither Mason nor Amelia heard. Normy snapped his head around before cautiously approaching Smith's car. Before Normy got to the Jeep, their heated exchange escalated, but he kept moving closer until they were face-to-face.

"I lost the Crown Vic. Do you see it?"

Mason scanned the parking lot. "They moved."

"Keep an eye out for them. I'll be right back." She got out of Tulip and crossed the lot, drawing her gun.

The sky was like a cloud-filled globe of static trees and miniatures of Manhattan skyscrapers. The park was silent and still except for two strollers crossing the green. The moment seemed as lifeless as an empty theatre stage. Smith and Normy's argument grew louder. Amelia entered stage left, her Glock held at her side, approaching the two discordant actors arguing at the Jeep. Five roller-skaters dressed in brash Spandex outfits rolled on the sidewalk from stage right toward the argument at center stage. They interrupted Smith and Normy spewing mutual abuse before Amelia could get there. Smith grabbed the briefcase, but Normy pulled back. Smith exited the Jeep. Amelia, holding her Glock behind her back now, yelled at the two men. Simultaneously, the two strollers scattered off the green's wide service road when the black Mercedes sped from under the trees bordering the far side of the green and accelerated toward the parking lot exchange. The Mercedes, its driver window down, drifted into a long, lazy arc, bearing down on Amelia, Normy, and Smith. Behind a spray of grass and dirt, the driver aimed a handgun held in a black-gloved hand, its muzzle flashing several times. The skaters fell to the sidewalk, tangled into a heap of screaming rag dolls as Smith crumpled to the sidewalk, gagging. The dark red blood poured from his carotid artery. The Mercedes was coming back for more. Amelia dragged shocked Normy down with her to take cover behind his Mercedes. Using the car as an armrest, she returned several accurate, rapid shots. Bullet holes appeared in the front door panel of the Mercedes. She fired another cluster. The driver's mirror blew off. His rear window shattered in a spray of glass. He sped away, leaving deep brown ruts cut into the grass.

The skaters screamed because a bullet had found the upper thigh of one of them. Senator Smith lay dead, his eyes open and dull, forming a trickling stream of blood on its path of least resistance into the sewer.

Amelia grabbed Normy's arm, but he yelled, "No," and fought her off. When he pulled free, he ran to his Mercedes, retrieved a black case identical to the one Smith died for, and ran with her to Tulip.

"Get in the back." Normy hesitated. Amelia showed him her Glock.

"Jesus. Okay." Normy climbed in from her side, folding awkwardly into the small back seat.

He shouted. "Who was that guy? What the fuck was that for?"

"Get the money, Mason. And search him."

Mason moved on Normy, but he was defiant and clutched onto the briefcase. "You're not frisking me."

Backing out of their parking space, Amelia raised her right hand in a single fluid motion and placed the Glock's business end against Normy's cheek. She mashed the accelerator pedal to the floor. "It's your choice, but make it fast. I'm a little busy, Normy."

"Okay, okay, Jesus. I don't have a gun. Here," he said, turning his coat inside out, "see?"

She turned back to driving and staying in front of the Crown Vic, hot on their tail. "Get the briefcase."

Mason pulled the briefcase out of Normy's grasp. He threw the case to the floorboards, then tried to frisk Normy, who squirmed at Mason's invasive hands. Mason gave it up. He turned to Amelia, "This guy's a creampuff. Did you shoot Smith?"

"I wish… they must have been NEWCorp. He shot Smith, and I shot at him. What's the combo, Normy?"

"Six six six."

"Cute. Check it for a taser." Amelia slowed to the speed limit and turned toward the Hudson River, keeping one eye on the thugs in the Mafia car filling their rear-view mirror.

Mason rolled up the combination and opened the briefcase. It was full of cash. "How long have you had this knack of large sums of money falling into your lap?"

Amelia handed Mason the Glock. "This feels familiar and yet odd," said Mason, putting the Glock on the floor. With Amelia driving, he zeroed in on buckling his seatbelt. She flicked warm eyes at Mason, and they shared slight smiles before she turned icy. "How much, Normy?"

"The same. Four hundred grand." He sounded defeated. "It's always the same."

The Crown Vic pulled up tight behind them. Amelia ducked into an alley to shake them, but her dodge didn't work. "That's $800,000 in two weeks." She talked fast. "You're a dead man. You know that, right? You pretended it was business as usual, except you switched the briefcase with an identical one filled with, what, newspapers you bought at the deli? I hope you had an amazing escape plan, 'cause those guys behind us seem a little pissed."

Normy snapped his head around, said, "Oh shit," and turned back, alarmed.

"You were going to disappear, maybe try to blend in for a couple of years in Mexico or Canada, call mom once a week?"

Mason said, "Pretty sure they don't want you, either."

Amelia pressed, "How am I doin' so far?"

Normy pouted. "I was going to live in Israel." He crossed his arms and shrugged his shoulders. "Who's this *schmuck*?"

Mason yelled, "Watch out." The Mercedes slid toward them at high speed from a side street, cutting between the Crown Vic and Tulip, sending the Crown Vic swerving into a lamppost.

"One down, one to go." Amelia cranked the wheel. Tulip held onto the corner; they raced back toward the park. "Normy, Mason. Mason, Normy. If you want, I can drop you right now, Normy? The guy behind us probably wants to talk to you, too." Both Normy and Mason looked. The black Mercedes was coming on fast, but Tulip had reasonable acceleration speed. "Or can you play nice?"

Mason said, "Is that BK again?"

She shook her head, drifted Tulip around another corner, then sped them alongside the park, dodging through light traffic, past an ambulance and an NYPD prowler. She cut hard into an alley. The Mercedes driver missed the turn, slammed on his brakes, peeled rubber backing up, then followed them. The police joined the chase, their siren wailing and lights flashing. Both lead cars swerved around dumpsters and power poles at breakneck speeds through the narrow brick canyon, with the cops hot in pursuit. Amelia raced through the next cross street. At the end of that block, she pulled another sharp left toward the Hudson River. The centrifugal force of the turn threw both Normy and Mason against the doors. Tulip's tires screeched in protest, but she kept her grip on the pavement.

"What's this guy got to do with any of this anyway?" Normy yelled at Amelia.

"He's the writer your boss wants dead."

Normy yelled over the wind blowing in the open windows and peeling tires, "He's killing writers now? This new guy behind us must be the heavy hitter I heard they put on you two. You don't stand a chance."

The Mercedes rammed them hard from behind, shoving them through a temporary roadwork barrier. A giant hole appeared in the street right in front of them. Amelia hit Tulip's accelerator, using their spinning momentum, cutting a hard right into a pile of sand at the curb. She jumped Tulip's passenger-side wheels onto the sidewalk. The gaping hole swallowed the Mercedes and then the cop car.

Mason said, "Remind me later to send a thank you postcard to the New York sewer utility."

They narrowly avoided plowing into half a dozen trendy and very relieved customers lounging at tables in front of a café before Amelia slowed down, dropping all four wheels back onto the street at the end of the construction zone. They drove along West Street then turned onto Hubert to avoid tunnel traffic, winding through a maze of city blocks and alleys, hiding in the heavy traffic on the Avenue of the Americas. Finally, they parked a few blocks farther along on Houston. Amelia said, "Taxes, death, and traffic in the city, all guarantees in life."

Mason handed the Glock and the briefcase to Amelia. She turned to the back seat, tapped the barrel of the gun on the briefcase to focus Normy's attention, then said in a playful lilt, "So, Normy Garfinkle, how are things?"

"I'll give you fifty grand if you let me go."

"It's not that simple anymore. Your contact is dead, and that roller skater catching a bullet implicates you in a deadly shoot-out. That could mean hard time for life if you even make it to court." She let that sink in. "The guy in the Mercedes? I know him. We used him in Iraq until he went psycho... Jairo. Him killing Smith means something else is going on."

"I just drop the money off. That's all I do."

Mason said, "There's a psycho on us too?"

Amelia glanced quickly at Mason. "Hopefully, you'll never meet him. Normy, I know that. I saw that last week. How's the neck?"

Normy sat back. "You! What more do you want from me?"

"A meeting."

"Oh no, no. You go ahead and shoot me now." Amelia cocked the gun and pointed it at Normy's face. "They'll kill me."

"Doubt it. They're second in line."

"Okay, okay, don't take me so literally. If I do this, will you let me go?"

"Hook us up, and then we'll talk. Let me see your hands."

Normy tentatively held his hands up. Amelia reached into the back seat and took his soft, chunky left wrist in her firm grip. Normy resisted, then relaxed when she smiled at him. Amelia pulled his arm toward her and stuck the pin into the fleshy part of his thumb.

"Ow." He pulled his hand back. "What'd you do that for?"

Mason looked at Amelia with a quizzical expression. She said, "I picked up a little more at Dad's. Lunch is over. Can you bring the briefcase? Let's grab a taxi," said Amelia, heaving the money bag over her shoulder, "and head uptown."

18. **Glass Houses**

Amelia asked the cabbie to stop at a lock-box storage facility while she stealthily transferred most of the cash in the briefcase to the moneybag. Outside the U-Lock storage facility, she left with the money bag and came back empty-handed minutes later. When she returned, Mason rolled his eyes at her, "You have an admirer."

Normy slobbered at her. "Ames," he said, lolling across the back seat of the taxi. "I love you." Grabbing at Amelia's thigh with limp-noodle arms, she rebuffed him by lifting and removing his hand with the Glock barrel. Amelia directed the taxi driver along a circuitous route. She and Mason watched for anyone tailing them, but they were alone among millions of strangers.

Amelia slipped her Glock inside the briefcase before they exited the taxi. They crossed the plaza crowded with tourists taking pictures of the charging bull statue, paying homage to greedy, bloated financial systems manipulating and fleecing Futures markets investors and corporations inflating their value prices by buying back their stock. The Meister-Fleisher-Fuchs building leered over the city as a similarly vulgar statement in glass and steel, rising seventy stories above the square.

Mason said, "Glass houses."

Amelia said, "*Bulletproof* glass houses."

From deep in his bliss, Normy asked, "Would you date me, Ames?"

"Let's concentrate, Normy. Do you have your ID?"

Normy performed an intoxicated pantomime, patting several pockets until he found his wallet. "Someone's going to have to help me. I feel like I had champagne for lunch."

"If it gets us into the building..." Amelia took Normy's hand, steadying and leading him down the ramp to underground parking. When they passed the ticket booth, Normy waved at the slim Puerto Rican attendant. He nodded once, in recognition, not familiarity.

In the cooler shades, their echoing footsteps gradually outlasted the receding din of the unrelenting traffic. It was well after lunch, so the car park was full of gleaming, over-powered sporty imports and avant-gauche, domestic luxury cars. Normy led them to a solid, gray steel door. He pressed his thumb on the fingerprint reader and looked up to the camera. The red light on the reader turned green, the door lock buzzed, and the latch snapped open. Amelia kept hold of the briefcase. Mason held the heavy door open for Normy and Amelia.

An armed security guard had been watching them on his CCTV monitors from a cramped alcove across from a bank of three elevator doors. "Good afternoon, Mr. Garfinkle. Your elevator is here." The thumbprint device had delivered an express, high-speed elevator to the no-frills foyer.

In the elevator, Amelia said, "Good, Normy. How are you feeling now?"

"I wanna have sex on my desk."

Amelia looked at Mason, mouthing the words, "Dr. Feel Good." Turning to Normy, she said, "You go right ahead and do that, but let's meet your boss before you start."

The elevator doors opened. The business chic lure camouflaged the fatal financial barbs within. A lavish reception area was soft with oblique lighting and a bursting expanse of palm trees. Stacked Redwood Cedar garden boxes stuffed with imported ornamental Bonsai trees and expansive ferns, a thick red carpet, and a glass wall water feature including the statue of two onyx black, beautifully carved leaping dolphins accentuated the design.

Normy's administrative assistant worked alone. She was thin, fifty-ish and as orderly as a tray of ice cubes. She offered them any one of several possible eating disorders, pinched-face smiles and calculating eyes from behind her immaculate faux-mahogany desk. "Good afternoon, Mr. Garfinkle," her voice cloaked with indifference. "How was your lunch?"

"Ducky."

"I see… Shall I bring in the coffee service?"

"You bet, Bev. And no calls."

Bev gave up the slightest hint of judgement. "Of course, Mr. Garfinkle."

Aside, Normy said to Mason, "I can never tell if she's mocking me."

Mason raised his eyebrows in confirmation, whispering back, "There was mocking."

They hurried Normy into his expansive office. His post-modern art collection shattered the obscenely expensive boredom of immaculate, dark walnut walls. A large window above a full-length, white leather couch framed a slice of the Manhattan skyline's top thirty floors. A luxurious black carpet suffocated the floor but was a welcome relief from the foyer. A compact wet bar and a small private bathroom door broke the continuity on the farthest wall.

Normy plopped into the high-backed leather chair behind his desk, rocking back and forth. Humming an abbreviated Shania Twain soundtrack loop, he was one very stoned executive who appeared quite capable of having sex at his desk.

Mason picked up a vase from the bar and flipped it upside down, looking for the label. "That's worth sixty grand," said Normy, giggling, "you break it, you buy it." Gingerly, Mason placed it down on Normy's desk.

Amelia placed the briefcase on the desk, dialled its unlocking code, and opened it. She chilled Normy's mood by tapping his desk with the Glock barrel. "Time to sober up. I need you to call your boss. Tell him there was a problem with the money. You'll come to his office, but don't say anything else. Can you do that?"

"Quick as a wink." He picked up his handset, tapping a speed dial button on his desk phone. After a brief pause, he said, "Sir, there's been a snag... over the exchange. I need to come up." Another break, then, "Fine." Normy hung up the phone. "He lives on Staten Island. I think he's mafia."

Amelia said, "Shocking."

Bev knocked on the door once, then it swung open. Amelia slipped the gun back in the briefcase and closed the top. Bev pushed a coffee cart into the office. She began arranging the service on the bar. "Can I offer..."

Amelia said to Normy, "We can come back."

He looked at Bev with half-lidded eyes, "We're going into a meeting."

Bev seemed perturbed and distracted by the vase, then moved it back to its original position on the bar. "If that will be all then..." she said, obviously miffed. She left, closing the door behind her.

Normy checked with Mason, "Mocking?"

Mason nodded, "Served with a side order of petulance."

Amelia checked the clip in her Glock, put it back in the

briefcase, locked it, took it, and then said, "Let's get this done."

When they walked past Bev, her head stayed bowed to her keyboard. They entered the executive elevator after Normy thumb-printed the door open. Inside, he printed the button for floor sixty-eight. Amelia snapped open one of the briefcase clips. Mason nudged her and looked up at the CCTV camera. She flicked her eyes at him to acknowledge that cameras were at every cross-section of the offices, hallways, and elevators.

The doors whispered open to heightened opulence, inviting them out of the elevator. Normy strode like a stiff-legged marionette. The smoking, stylish receptionist, a Bev clone, waved them on without smiling or saying a word. Subtlety, she reached under her desk, pushed a button, and the latch on the bulletproof glass door protecting the offices inside swung open.

Normy brought them through to another wall of curtained glass and a closed, solid wood door. He knocked once and then walked in. Amelia snapped open the second latch on the briefcase. A silky-friendly male voice, as slick as his hair lotion, encouraged them from inside. "Come in. Norm, you should have told me you were bringing clients."

Amelia jabbed Normy in the middle of his back with the Glock, urging him farther into the office, right up to the Manager's desk. Mason shut the door behind them. "You, Trader Dick," said Amelia to the dubious manager, stepping out from behind Normy, still holding the briefcase but showing the executive her gun, "stand up and call your CEO. Normy, you sit on the couch."

The manager stayed seated. "Not a chance." He shot a glare at Normy, "You fucked up again?"

"You need to stand up, shut up, and listen," said Amelia, menace in her tone. "This Glock says you have five seconds before I blow a hole in your right elbow. Thirty seconds after that, I'll take out the left. Don't test me. I'm a good shot."

The manager focused on Mason. "You're with her, is that right?"

"That's right—she's an excellent shot." Dick looked back at Amelia.

She said, "Now, what's your real name?"

He sneered at her. "Call me Trader Dick; I like that."

"You know," she said thoughtfully, "you're more a dickhead." He seemed unimpressed with the serious woman aiming her Glock at him, although the reflection off the thin veneer of sweat forming below his hairline counterfeited his bravado. Amelia said, "You're not dialling. Three...two..."

Dick grabbed his phone. "So I call him, then what?"

"Tell him you have some bad news about today's lunchtime transaction. Get him down here."

"Little lady, I don't think you know who you're playing with here."

"Right back at you." Amelia fired the gun.

"Fuck." Dick grabbed the fleshy gore dangling from one ear. Blood poured between his fingers, staining his pearl-white silk shirt.

"Quit whining. A family of four could live for a year off what you paid for plastic surgery on that nose. You can afford a little more." Stepping closer to him, she pistol-whipped him in the mouth, bursting his lips. Amelia looked at Mason quickly and said, "I asked once nice... Keep an eye on the door." Then she looked hard at the bleeding executive. "Just so you and I are square, I hit what I aim at," she let the muzzle fall to his crotch. "You took one for the team... ready for another?"

"Okay, okay, the phone... can I get a fuckin' towel?"

"Normy, pass your boss a bar towel."

Normy snapped to attention and fetched a white, monogrammed hand towel for his boss, made googly eyes at the horrific wound and said, "She *is* a good shot," then flopped back down on the couch. Dick pressed the towel against his bleeding ear while he talked to his CEO. "We have a new situation in my office. It's about the delivery. I need you here." He listened intensely. "Right away? Good." He hung up. "Can we all calm down now?"

"Call your receptionist. Tell her we want copies of everything you have on Kazakhstan. We'll pick up the files from Bev on our way out." Dick punched a button on his desk phone. "I'll need the Kazakhstan folders copied for my clients. No need to bring them in. Deliver them to Mr. Garfinkle's receptionist." When he hung up, Amelia motioned the bleeding executive onto the couch beside Normy.

The next silent seconds passed like hours.

19. **Cameras Don't Lie, Right?**

The door opened, and the meticulously groomed CEO of Meister-Fleisher-Fuchs took two steps inside. His blue eyes were bright, amused even, until he surveyed the office. He halted, holding the door handle, looking at his bleeding manager and the woman with the gun. Mason, standing behind the door, shoved it closed with the CEO inside. The tension in the room crackled like stylus static on a scratched record. Still, Amelia ruled, waving him away from the door with her gun.

The CEO's eyes looked from Amelia's weapon to Mason, then back to Amelia, then at Dick. The CEO said, "Rough day down here in the trenches..." Dick offered the blood-soaked towel as silent confirmation.

Amelia said, "You know who we are. What do we call you?"

"Daniels. Yes, I know you're a serial murderer on the run from the US Government, the FBI, and Homeland Security. You're here to extort private corporate information from us. This man behind me is Stone, a mediocre novelist, also your accomplice. I hope you enjoy your brief moment of fame, sir," Daniels scoffed at Mason, "because unless I say otherwise, you're on your way to death row."

Mason was disgusted. "Did you ever make friends with that vocabulary?"

"What vocab—," said Daniels, confused, "death row?"

"Mediocre."

"Waving that gun at me," said Daniels to Amelia, "won't do you any good. You'll leave this building if and when I say so. We expected you..."

"Since we're chatting, give us the short version of NEWCorp and Kazakhstan."

"Right to the point, that's what I've heard about you." He sighed. "Who'd have thought that shit hole would ever be important."

Normy passed in and out of interest on the couch while Daniels spieled off uranium mine production numbers, such as "seventy percent of the world's uranium and profit margins above $3 Billion annually," remaining mostly oblivious to the conversation. But hearing Daniels spout his money fantasy, so putrid with greed, made Mason want to wipe the smirk off the charmer's face.

Mason said, "So they have uranium. So do we…"

Daniels' eyes grew far away, even moistened, before he focused on Mason. "But we want it all before Putin takes it."

"How patriotic of you, and yet not an American flag anywhere in sight."

Amelia waved her gun for attention. "Is Hawke part of this?"

Leaning forward, Dick said, "Don't tell her anything."

"Are you looking for matching ears?" said Amelia, forcing him back into silence. Inching away from the door, Daniels said, "Hawke is nothing more than a security risk, a toad."

"I'll carve that into your gravestone if you move one more time."

Mason stepped in. "What's going on, exactly, in Kazakhstan?"

*

Sixty-eight floors below, the olive-skinned man entered the lobby off West Street. He re-read Daniels' text as he walked through the metal-detecting portal, setting off warning sirens. Unconcerned, he stopped for the young guard brandishing her metal-detecting wand. It repeatedly beeped, flustering the woman. When she reached for her sidearm, her squad commander tapped her on the shoulder, moving her back with a look, and then silently waved the man through. Compelled by deadly purpose, Jairo thumb-printed his way onto the executive-only elevator.

*

"Do you mind if I stand here, dear?" Daniels smiled at Amelia.

"What's the joke?"

"Just that little people like you three have no chance against us. But come back and dispose of these two, and we'll forgive you your…flight of fancy. It's that, or, well, what a waste…"

Amelia's index finger twitched on the Glock's hair-trigger when the office door burst inward, knocking Mason awkwardly against the wall behind the door. Amelia threw herself into cover behind the desk. The shooter fired at her from his silenced automatic. The bullets lodged into the solid teak desk, blasting the briefcase onto the floor and spraying a portfolio of desk papers against the far wall. Paralyzing shock riveted Mason behind the door, rendering him unable to see the person on the other side of the office door, except for the hand and a blazing gun. When Mason looked at Daniels, he was smiling.

Having neutralized Amelia, Mason watched, horrified as the shooter turned his gun on Trader Dick. He fired three rapid shots into Dick's chest, throwing him backwards. Normy screamed, shoving Dick's body onto the floor, where it rolled face up at Mason's feet. The shooter fired toward Amelia again, forcing her to stay down, then he aimed his gun at Daniels. The CEO's face had frozen into a cold, financier's smile.

Another shot shocked the room. In a spray of red, Daniels flew backward onto the couch beside Normy. A wet gore escaped from Daniel's blood-filled mouth, where the bullet entered before separating his spinal cord on exit. Another shot created a concise hole in his forehead, which oozed a single, thick drip of dark red blood. He gurgled, and his dying eyes rolled skyward as if glancing toward the pieces of his skull and brains splattered across the financial reports on the bookshelves. Normy yelped and dove face-forward onto the carpet. The assassin rapid-fired two more shots into Daniels's chest then three more shots at the desk. The violence and blood mixed with the acrid propellant filling the room. Leaving, Jairo closed the door, exposing those left behind to the CCTV camera.

Her Glock trained on the door, Amelia moved quickly but cautiously and placed a hand on Mason's shoulder. "Well, you've met Jairo."

Mason was in shock after the explosive action. "I didn't think... I didn't know..."

"He didn't want us. We have to go. You too, Normy, get up. We can't do anything here." Her voice was the soothing, healing voice of a nurse in an operating triage room. Still holding her Glock, Amelia took Mason by the hand. They walked away from the horrific scene and onto the elevator.

They passed by Bev's workstation in the reception area as if they were three intimidated immigrants crossing an Eastern European border. Mason said, "The files we wanted?" Bev handed him the thick wad of photocopies, raised her eyebrows, then quickly looked toward the elevator. She looked pensively at Normy.

The automatic doors closed behind them, placing an odd, subdued finality on the murders. Amelia, Mason, and Normy exited the elevator silently into the carpark foyer and then the carpark. The security guard kept his eyes glued to his screen, buzzing the door open—no questions asked. Amelia led them through the underground as if they were three ghosts.

*

In the security office, Jairo watched on the CCTV system as they departed the building. He said into his cellphone, "I sent you the video, and I have the disk."

Delaci responded tersely, "You have a green light to finalize the other detail."

*

Delaci, a Bonesman to the core, smiled at the cowed, silent men. He ended his cellphone call, seated below the oil painting of an embellished, flattering, wholly unbelievable portrait of the sitting president. In that opulent room, dreams of would-be emperors gilded the walls. Delaci held one hand up, his slightly curled index finger extended as if waiting for Zeus' touch. He hushed the court waiting in fascination until intimidation scented the air. Seated at the head of the table, flanked by the complicit contingent of NEWCorp board members, Delaci delicately stroked his skull and crossbones ring. The ring connected Delaci to historic, elitist lore, the number "322" carved into the inside of the gold ring. Each member of the inner circle appeared terrified of its bearer. Delaci glanced at them in succession until they all broke eye contact, and only then did he speak.

"Gentlemen, observe." Delaci flourished his hand toward the wall-mounted screen. "Cameras don't lie." The short, raw footage of the Wall Street double murders played out in shocking reality. Delaci was pleased. "A tragedy. Senator Victor," he said, his voice strong and faintly echoing in the large room, "I expect you to assume interim control of our Wall Street operation." Victor, seated to Delaci's right, accepted the promotion with a silent, obeisant nod. "The authorities will receive copies of that film evidence within the hour," said Delaci, "with a few improvements." Almost as one, all eyes looked to Delaci. "GNN will loop the event continuously in the interests of public safety, linking the woman and the man to the

108

Seattle incidents as well. If the authorities fail to hunt down the killers within four hours, NEWCorp will issue a reward for their capture. Thank you, gentlemen, that will be all. Senator Victor—a word?"

Dismissed, the board members filed out silently. Delaci queried Victor, "The key and the code?"

"He has them."

Delaci's mouth spread into a thin, cruel smile.

*

No one intercepted them on the sidewalk—three eyewitnesses leaving a double homicide on Wall Street. It took them twenty minutes to flag a taxi. During the Manhattan rush hour, hailing a cab can be pure murder.

20. **Rabbits**

The waning rush hour traffic was still a heavy slog. Taxis aggressively switched lanes to go nowhere, horns blared, miles of blocks of commuters suffered frustration at red traffic lights. At the same time, waves of pedestrians streamed across claustrophobic intersections. The taxi and driver who eventually stopped for them reeked of pungent marijuana and the car's interior of patchouli oil. The bearded, beat-poet driver was laid back and disengaged from the traffic mania outside. Amelia issued route instructions to their hotel, often checking for anyone following them.

When Normy crashed hard out of his drug euphoria, he showed elevated signs of anxiety. He tried to bolt at a traffic light, but Mason held his arm. "To where?" Mason asked. "They're out there. Where can you go?" Normy shrugged Mason's hand off, pouting like a grounded teenager, and stared out the side window until they got out at the Museum of Modern Art.

Mason kept Normy in tow as they walked the last blocks to a different, upscale Manhattan hotel. They stood off to the side while Amelia paid cash for separate suites on the same floor, producing ID to register as business associates from Pennsylvania. Walking through the garish, cathedral-like lobby beside Mason, she said, "If you're hiding in New York, either go to the Bronx and hole-up in an abandoned car or take rooms in the most expensive hotels, paying for everything with cash. It buys discretion."

A bellhop led them to the elevators. "How did you know Jairo was coming through that door?"

She moved closer to him, slipping her arm inside his. "Daniels knew we wanted the files. How's our date going so far?"

"We're dating?"

That momentarily amused them both. Before entering Amelia's suite, she said, "I'll sort Normy out, then it's you and me, but I have a couple of things to do first. Sit tight."

*

Normy dropped the photocopies on the bed and raided the mini-fridge. He pulled four vodkas out, made himself a double shot, and then slumped onto a Louis XV, peach-coloured chair at the equally ornate writing table. Before the bellhop left, Normy was chugging vodka from tiny bottles and looked as miserable as Mason felt. The interior decor failed to charm Mason while Normy played the role of the glum roomy.

Mason might have thought their view magnificent on any other day, but today, the vertical, cement cliffs and spires rose like impermeable canyon walls to cramped clusters of servants grinding out their nine-to-five, American indentured lives behind a thousand reflecting lifeless glass panes. "Ten million people," said Mason, "and this is the loneliest city in the world."

"Great," said Normy. "I'm stuck in Hell with the master of clichés."

"Sorry, buddy, but that's all I've got left." Mason commandeered the TV remote and sat on the bed to surf listlessly through channels. Normy said, "Put it on five for GNN." Mason indulged him, switching the channel. They stared silently at the screen. Film bites of the murders were overlaid by the red "Breaking News" banner. The voice-overs of scripted panel hosts dishing out lies and accusations successfully scandalized their alarming false narrative. "Man," said Normy, "these guys really want your asses dead." Amelia and Mason were labelled, judged, and condemned as the Wall Street and Seattle murders perpetrators.

*

Hawke, unaware of the latest events of the day, had moved from his SUV to sleep undisturbed on his couch in his Georgetown condominium. He woke in the dark, checked his cellphone, found no NEWCorp phone calls or texts, then rose to surf through the fridge, picking at the remains of a *Cordon Bleu* he had ordered in the previous night. Slowly climbing the stairs to his bathroom, the effort drained the last of his energy. He fumbled through the pill drawer for his bedtime pill, then shuffled into the bedroom. He stripped to his underwear. "Alexa," he said, "I'm going to sleep." The robot turned off his reading lamp, rebolted the front door, turned down the heat, and Hawke succumbed to the soothing, hypnotic diazepam.

*

Mason responded quickly to the knock on the door and swung it open. Amelia came in, slinging the money bag onto the bed.

Still glum, Normy said, "We're going to jail for the rest

111

of our lives."

The camera closeup was on the TV anchor, a young, blonde news media Barbie clone adept at flashing her eyes. As the camera pulled back slowly, she leaned forward slightly, her cleavage expanded, her upper body pressed out and over her desk. She pursed her lips while reading from the teleprompter. "We have confirmed this remarkable video footage of the double murder on Wall Street," she said convincingly. "If you're sensitive, please turn away from our extremely graphic content." The warning always glued their viewers to their screens.

Normy said, "I don't know why they don't do naked news. It's what they're selling anyway."

The edited tape loop showed Mason, Amelia and Normy in the elevator at the Meister-Fleisher-Fuchs building. They, and millions of New Yorkers, saw the cut to Dick's office, a double execution performed by an off-screen shooter, then the zoom to both bloody and dead bodies. The tape showed Mason, Amelia and Normy leaving the office, in the elevator, and then walking through the parkade. Headshots were frozen in the sidebar of each "… perpetrator," said the host, "of this heinous crime. Both victims were family men," she read from the teleprompter. "Gunned down in cold blood. One man we confirmed was the CEO at the Wall Street investment bank of Meister-Fleisher-Fuchs. We cannot release their names in respect to their families."

"Which family?" shouted Normy. "The fuckin' Induritos?"

"For now," said the talking head on GNN, "the perpetrators are unidentified, and their motives unclear. Authorities have yet to confirm this was a terrorist attack. Let's go now to Manhattan's Chief of Police, Thomas Larson…" The feed cut to a live, hectic scrum jostling around the chief in a crowded hallway. A dozen arms held recording devices close to Chief Larson's face. He struggled to remain calm and recite from memory a prepared statement in response to muffled, urgent questions from the reporter's scrum. "The men and the woman we see in the elevator are persons of interest at this time, but we're very interested in speaking with them." The news feed played the murder loop on the split-screen. The media swarmed, yelling more questions at the chief as he turned away from the cameras to escape the gaggle.

Mason muted the sound. "They let us leave so they could finger us and let the cops do their dirty work."

Amelia said, "At least the video is poor quality."

Normy said, "They saw us in the lobby. The bellhop will squeal on us."

"Easy, Normy," said Amelia. "By the time our pictures filter out to the airports and hotels, you'll be long gone to Florida. If you want to try for Mexico after that, it's up to you. We're flying to South America on the first flight we can get out of La Guardia." Mason nodded but said, "That's quite the cliché."

"Go with what you know in times of stress."

*

In Georgetown, the assassin pulled on his black leather gloves before leaving the shadows to cross the elm-lined street. After unlocking the front door with the key, he entered the code to disarm the security system. He paused, listening to the constant, rhythmic snoring coming from upstairs. A magnificent Howard Millar grandfather clock ticked away seconds as Jairo ascended the remaining stairs to the landing. Slipping into the bedroom, his weapon drawn, he placed his steps until he stood beside the bed. Jairo tapped the once-useful man on the fleshy part of his left hand. The tip of the pin hardly piercing the skin would leave no mark. Hawke's hand twitched, but he remained asleep. Jairo used Hawke's cellphone to dial a number, placing the phone on the sleeping man's chest. An efficient voice on the phone asked, "9-1-1. What's your emergency?" Jairo left the bedroom.

From the hallway, the assassin heard the operator's fading voice repeating the same question. He reset the alarm, then closed and locked the front door. He returned to the shadows under the elm trees across the quiet street and waited. He had specific orders about the method: Delaci wanted excruciating pain involved.

*

Amelia unzipped the moneybag, counted out $20,000, and handed the bills to Normy. "Time to go. You should be able to dodge the authorities for a couple of months. Here's something extra, just in case." Amelia tossed Normy another $10,000. "Let's get you onto the train. Normy, do you understand why you can't rat on us?"

"I'm a victim. I didn't do anything wrong. They don't want me. They want you two."

"Are you forgetting the real killer is still out there? So are thousands of New York cops, the FBI, and Homeland Security. They'll put you in jail for a long time if they bother to take you alive."

The anxiety on Normy's face spoke volumes. "I can't go to jail."

Amelia doubled down. "And you copped Matty's cash and embarrassed his bodyguards—twice."

"I'm a dead man."

Amelia coached Normy, "Maybe not if you do what I tell you to do." She took the Kazakhstan photocopies and said to Mason, "Dad gets these." When they left, Normy shuffled after her, a baggy-pants comic without a Vaudeville audience.

*

In his comfortable bedroom, Hawke woke to the shocking agony in his chest. His eyes were wide, and he was hyperventilating. His mind told his arm to reach for the bedside lamp, but he could not move his arm. His face was beet red, and his eyes bulged hideously. The chest pain paralyzed him. "9-1-1 emergency. Hello? Help is coming. Hold on."

The phone slid to the carpeted floor. Then the slow, final asphyxiation, like a king python's coil, began slowly constricting Hawke's lungs.

*

Just miles from CERN, Chief Inspector Emile Descartes, a thinking man's detective, read the bulletin sitting at his desk in the Geneva headquarters for INTERPOL. Descartes was reluctant, unlike the bulletin's creator, to draw conclusions or his gun. He reread the urgent bulletin published from the NSA's international desk, noting it was copied to Homeland Security and his agency. He dwelled on the letterhead. The date and time stamp looked legitimate enough, but the wording was curious:

> Imminent arrival of suspected terrorist Ivan Sobriev (US citizen) at Geneva AP. Do not approach—suspect considered armed and dangerous. Will expedite the necessary extradition after our arrival.

Please notify us as per the contact information below.

The Inspector pressed his intercom button. "Stephan, join me in my office. *Merci.*" The rookie detective came in and stood wide-eyed and at attention in front of Descartes. He ordered Stephan to confirm the origin of the bulletin, then tested him, "Do you see anything in this dispatch that seems odd?"

Stephan read the bulletin Descartes passed to him. "No, *monsieur*, it all seems in order."

"In order, yes. But no copy to their CIA. Why would they be left out of this loop? It's curious, no?" Stephan nodded. Descartes continued, "We never allow Americans to fool us into making mistakes and doing their dirty work. We will be thorough and professional, always, and we will watch this Ivan Sobriev."

*

Alone in the luxury hotel room, Mason was unimpressed. He turned the TV to the channel listings, checking the clock every five minutes. His thoughts were conflicted. *A few days ago, I was an unknown writer doing a conspiracy podcast, living a quiet life. Is this about Ivan? Or me? Or NEWCorp and their damn fraud? Murders, guns, assassins, dead pimps and ex-boyfriends, hookers, car chases and Wall Street executions. Why am I here alone? Where the hell is that woman?*

He stared out the window and then made another drink. Then he stood in a hot shower until the wet heat calmed him. He wrapped a towel around his waist but did not dress. Someone knocked twice. He pounced toward the door, peered through the peephole, and then let Amelia in.

*

Jairo made the cellphone call.

"You're quite sure?" said Victor.

"I watched them wheel the bag out."

"That is excellent news. Are you interested in a recently vacated position?"

"I work freelance."

"They cannot make it to CERN—name your price."

"I will have any assets I need and a full green light."

"Certainly."

"Then, I accept."

"When we confirm their destination, you can follow from Andrews." Victor ended the call.

In the bed next to Victor, his wife spoke through her oxygen breathing mask. "Phone calls? At this hour?"

"I'm sorry, my love. I woke you. It was nothing. Rest now."

She removed the mask. "Who calls in the middle of the night with nothing?"

"Unending duties of office... do you want a sleeping pill?"

His wife conjured up a weak smile. "Yes, please, and some relief from this pain, if you can manage that." She suffered from virulent multiple myeloma bone marrow cancer. After eighteen years of marriage, the intimacy they shared was that nothing more could be done for her; she was in stage four. She asked dreamily, "Do you think they sing in heaven?"

"Like angels," said Victor, placing the pill on her tongue; she sipped the water.

Struggling to swallow, she said, "You're such a good man," then she put on her mask and closed her eyes.

*

Amelia took Mason in her arms. "Kiss me." He responded instantly. They melted into each other's embrace. For Mason, at that instant, the world became simple again. He wanted more, but she pulled back and turned the sound down on the TV.

"Why not?" he asked. "The last wish of a dying man? Oh, shit, your father's not here too, is he?"

"I needed to know if you're still into me or if I had to stash you somewhere safe while I go after these guys."

"One kiss can tell you that?"

"That one did. When we leave this room... They want me more than they want us. You can take the money and..."

"You're not getting off that easily."

She twisted her lips into a smile. "Yeah, you'll do. We can't make mistakes if we want to fix this, but we need to regroup. This will be the fight of your life."

He scoffed at her playfully and boasted, "Have you forgotten I won custody of Brooke in my divorce."

Amelia's eyes twinkled. "I took Normy to Kennedy. He's on a flight to Montreal. I kept fifty grand for us and couriered the rest for Normy to sit on in Montreal. We may need it in a hurry later. NEWCorp won't be happy about Normy on the loose, but they'll be concentrating on us. And they have no idea how much of a problem we're going to be."

"How much time do we have?"

"We should leave now. I..."

Mason kissed Amelia passionately. "Darling, are we waiting to exchange vows?" He ran his hand lightly up and down the tight lines of her back, down to her curvy hips. Amelia reached around and removed his wandering hand.

Amelia was flustered. "Not now... not yet..."

"I had no idea you're a traditionalist. No icing spoon unless I buy the whole cake?"

"That's not it..." Her eyes saddened for a second, then she rebounded. "We have to make our next move now, and that means we disappear, pretty much to the ends of the earth."

"We're going to Rochester?"

"That would almost work, but I have a better idea."

*

Amelia produced sunglasses, and they left the hotel through a side entrance, flagging a cab a few blocks away. They stopped at a hole-in-the-wall restaurant for "... the best ziti in New York." They ate in a back booth, still wearing their sunglasses. They were both starved, and Amelia was right—the ziti was delicious.

After eating, they flagged a taxi to Jackson Heights. Amelia's forger lived a block from the zoo. He opened the bungalow's front door on a city block like a thousand other post-WWII blocks of cookie-cutter houses. The fleshy man could have passed for an assistant manager of a Fat Burger restaurant. The forger left the porch light off.

"Did you bring a cab here?"

Amelia said, "We're not stupid."

"You two are white-hot right now." Wordlessly, they exchanged Amelia's Glock and the $5,000 in the doggy bag they brought from the restaurant for a brown bag. "Don't come back. You don't know me." The forger slipped back inside his door.

They flagged a taxi in front of the lounge on the corner. "That guy looked like a cop."

"You're getting better at this—he's a retired Manhattan detective. Forgery is his sideline now. He did this as a favour to dad." Amelia produced two fake Canadian passports from the brown bag.

Mason looked at his passport. "Some favour—I don't have long black hair or a mustache."

Amelia tapped the brown bag. "You will."

*

They bought two first-class tickets for South Africa at La Guardia Airport before slipping into the cocktail lounge's 'family' bathroom. When they came out, Ms. Arnasen looked sensational as a redhead, punk rocker. Mr. Arnasen sported shoulder-length hair and a bushy Elliott Gould moustache. They each carried $20,000 cash taped under their loose clothing to supplement the legitimate $8,000 in Cook travellers' cheques they purchased. Forty-five minutes later, they boarded the 747.

Mason was overwhelmed by a wave of relief when the plane departed, even though they flew away from their right to *habeas corpus* and the hope of a fair trial before an impartial judge. When Mason said as much to Amelia, she said, "You're forgetting we're 'shoot on sight' fugitives. Besides, Obama suspended habeas corpus years ago."

They fell asleep leaning against each other before the in-flight movie ended as two exhausted, globe-tripping newlyweds.

*

Mason woke when the pilot announced their imminent arrival at *OR Tampo* airport. From there, they would book flights with any airline flying to Jakarta. The stewardess brought dark coffees, which they sipped appreciatively. But when the sensational eggs Benedict and crunchy sesame toast arrived, Mason devoured his and half of Amelia's portion.

"Will they follow us?"

She shrugged her shoulders at his naivety. "That's cute."

"How far ahead of them are we?"

"It's best to keep moving. We'll ditch our disguises in Jakarta and pick up new ID there. I know an MI6 guy."

"You *know a guy* in Jakarta?"

"I was an intelligence officer, remember? Leave getting through customs to me. You should expect a change of plans once in a while, darling. After all, we are honeymooning."

He never blinked an eye at her endearment before saying, "You got it, lover."

*

118

Walking through the long airport exit corridors towards Customs, Amelia unbuttoned her blouse's top three buttons, revealing her ample cleavage.

"Feeling the humidity, Ms. Arnasen?"

"The three-button sell works, Mr. Arnasen."

"How are we going to explain no luggage?"

Before she could answer, they were up to bat. The custom's officer seemed far more impressed with Mason than Amelia. And he wanted to know why they travelled so light, so Amelia flirted with him, explaining they planned on buying locally at their final destination. The officer casually thumbed through their billfold of traveller's cheques. He seemed satisfied they were not entering the country to go on social assistance. He handed the passports back to Mason, staring him in the eyes. "Enjoy your stay with us."

After they cleared customs, Mason said, "I think he was going to hit on me,"

"Why not," said Amelia, "I would have."

They studied the departures monitors, then bought tickets on a Qatar Airways daily, direct flight to Jakarta departing within two hours. Then Amelia bought a burner cellphone and downloaded the Kazakhstan file images Alacran had already converted.

"So he was in New York?" asked Mason.

"He came in after the shooting."

*

Qatar Air treated them like royalty. An ebony-haired woman in an elegant, full-length gown with gold highlights ushered Mason and Amelia through the passenger swarm to the first-class lounge. They cleared customs there as a mere formality. Amelia looked knowingly at Mason through dark sunglasses. "Status," she said, "and money buys privilege. What colour is she wearing, anyway? She's stunning."

"Cerulean."

"Travelling with a writer *is* fun. I would have called it blue."

The staff pandered to them with offers of delicious sweet green teas and outrageous trays of edible delights. Mason enjoyed bites of several delicacies, raving to Amelia about them. At dusk, they departed on the 767 Boeing airliner.

They settled in to watch the trivial comedy and sipped

dark Arabian coffee with heavy cream. Halfway through the film, Mason whispered to her, "I gotta get this off my chest… I really, really want to make love with you."

"So, why didn't you?"

"You mean we could have?"

"Darling, I'm a newlywed, and I've been waiting."

*

When he woke, the Malaysian sun streamed through their window. "Good morning. How did you sleep?" Amelia beamed at him, giving him her most delightful smile. She reignited his desire.

"Ms. Arnasen, you are beautiful. Why are you with me?"

"Awe, c'mon, you know why, sugar… an arranged marriage." She sipped at her cup of coffee.

He laughed, squinting into the sun. "How long 'til we land?"

"Two hours."

"Order me some coffee?" Mason retrieved the travel kit he bought at the OR airport from the overhead compartment and refreshed in the roomy first-class lavatory. A stewardess poured him a steaming cup of black coffee. He added heavy cream into the rich dark liquid, stirring it with a delicate silver spoon before looking Amelia in the eyes over the coffee cup. She smiled at him, a hint of something new in her amusement. "Delicious." Then he said, "So, Jakarta?"

"We'll blend in until I can arrange for new passports. If we read the NEWCorp files now, maybe we'll figure out exactly how Kazakhstan fits in with NEWCorp's plans before we head for CERN." Mason was captivated by her. "Interested?" she asked.

"Intrigued."

21. The Hat

Mason wondered why all 10,000,000 Jakartans were at the airport surrounding him and Amelia trying to flag a taxi. They managed one, finally, although the crowd teemed despite the combination of murderous heat and humidity. The smog was worse than any thick August haze that ever choked the life out of asthmatic Los Angelenos. Jakarta is the beating heart of the mysterious Malaysian archipelago. Mason had flagged one of the dozens of wacky, three-wheel tourist taxis to ferry them across the mad city. Their driver treated them to a crazy ride. Competing with crazier drivers negotiating pulsing mobs of white-shirted bicycle riders, he squeezed into non-existent slots between speedy motorcyclists and impatient, harried car and lorry drivers. Hundreds of taxis and busses outfitted with functional horns repeatedly risked near-death experiences to switch lanes opportunistically and then switch right back when the imagined advantage vanished.

All that chaos disappeared in the cooler shade under their modern hotel's covered entrance that seemed to stretch to both horizons. The eight-story Hotel Indonesia Kempinski was awe-inspiring and a wealthy, weary traveller's relief. Amelia asked Mason, "You like?"

"I hoped for something a little more upscale. Do you think this fleabag joint includes free Wi-Fi?"

"When I worked in Afghanistan identifying potential targets, I smeared myself with goat manure and played dead in ditches. Let's enjoy this…" She took his hand as two efficient bellhops retrieved their luggage. Amelia whispered, "We'll be at CERN soon, I promise." She took his hand in hers. "Try to look rich."

"How the hell am I supposed to do that?"

"I don't know, think arrogant, spoiled and entitled… stroll."

Mason summoned his best Truman Capote by curling his upper lip as if affronted by a strong blue cheese, half-closed his eyelids, tilted his head back, raised an arm for Amelia to take, and tried to peer sardonic and bored down the length of his nose.

Amelia watched his face turn into a monster's and said, "Better idea… go normal."

"I can do that. Keep the stroll?"

"Walk." And they did that, deep into the air conditioning in the lobby. The noise of the city evaporated behind them, melting with it some of Mason's unrest. An expansive tropical garden grew lush in the hotel's foyer, the plants held at bay behind floor-to-ceiling walls of glass. They entered a world of luxurious splendour accessorized with striking, colourful flowers and every shade, size, and shape of exotic green frond imaginable. They booked a mid-size suite for two nights. The receptionist graciously accepted the $5,000 cash deposit without batting an eye, requested their passports, and kept them. She returned a receipt and a beautiful smile, then, with a pricey, single ding on a desk call bell, manifested two bellhops to guide them through the hotel.

The suite layout and furnishings were luxurious and apropos of the hotel entrance and lobby expectations. Through a glass wall, a white cotton tent canopy shaded an inviting deck. The private terrace featured gossamer panels billowing in the soft breeze. Behind these, and uncluttered by the cityscape, was the expansive view promising unparalleled portraits of magnificent ocean sunsets reserved for the wealthy. Tasteful, dark, hardwood furniture was dramatic against the plush white carpets on the sandalwood floors. Stainless steel appliances were available in a small recess should guests travel with their domestic servants. One wall was a modernity statement in glass, complementing the artwork and placed to accent other subtleties of design and cooler shades throughout the suite.

"What," said Mason, "no mini-fridge?"

One bellhop busied himself organizing their suitcases in their closets. The other retrieved the remote from the coffee table, pressed a button, and the glass artwork wall slid sideways on a whisper to reveal a fully stocked, back-lit bar. Amelia pushed the door open to the *en suite* spa facilities. Inside, the immaculate body shower, sparkling glass tiers of body lotions, elegant robes, linens and towels promised more lavish, indulgent pampering. She gave Mason a quick, covert thumbs up, then closed the door behind her.

"When night," the second bellhop said to Mason, emerging from confirming the kitchen was in order, "it bin den lights make dazzle you."

"Until then," said Mason drily, "I suppose we'll have to

linger in opulence," then he over-tipped the bellhops. The minute the door closed, Amelia said, "Now you're just acting the ignorant elite with money to burn."

"That man earned it with his bold prediction. Besides, we're on our honeymoon, and you have overwhelmed me with great sex."

"Have I now?" she said, flirting coyly with him.

"You know you drive me crazy."

"If you promise to get that disguise off your face, when I come back, I'll make our drinks." Amelia left Mason standing alone, wondering if he said something to upset her.

*

Jairo was alone in his Watergate suite, loading cartridges into his Beretta M9 magazines. His phone buzzed, so he lit a smoke, pausing to answer the call. "They're in Jakarta. You can pick up the trail there." A cloudy smoke-pall drifted from between the assassin's teeth. "A military flight departs Andrews through to Guam in one hour," said the caller, "then to Clark Air Base in the Philippines. Our jet will be waiting for you. When you finish in Jakarta, continue to CERN."

"I don't work on speculation." Jairo snapped a full magazine into his Beretta, punctuating his annoyance.

"Half now plus expenses and the rest on completion."

"That's acceptable." The call ended. Jairo controlled his breathing while drawing the army knife's razor-sharp blade along the oiled, Nakato sharpening stone. HIs slow, deliberate purpose also honed him intellectually to his ultimate assignment. Online, he checked his bank account in the Belgian bank and watched the six-figure deposit arrive.

An hour later, the thin man with the olive skin tone walked through the Ambassador Hotel's lobby, as vaguely threatening as any other D.C. rumour.

*

After Mason had showered and exited the bathroom, Amelia handed him an open beer when he joined her on the couch. "You went all out with the drinks."

"Just a reality check. We'll meet my guy tonight, at ten. I hate using hotel phones, but we're in a hurry. I'll book us on a flight to Nursultan tomorrow."

"Ivan isn't in Nursultan."

"It's sort of on the way. I called dad. He's had time to

123

read the photocopies we left in New York. He says something is going on in Kazakhstan that we should make our business."

"Inkai?"

"Yes."

Mason put his beer down and moved closer to Amelia, their thighs touching. Amelia leaned into him, caressing his face with gentle fingertips. He took her hand gently in his. Tears welled in her eyes. She smiled at him then turned away, but he held her and gently turned her face back to his, wiping her tears away with his fingers, kissing her cheeks tenderly. Amelia kissed him softly on the lips. She whispered, "Did you know that the US invested almost $900 million this year in Kazakhstan?"

"Stop—I can't handle all the romance." He said tenderly, struck deeply by her struggle with vulnerability. He sighed and said, "They say uranium paved the Silk Road."

The warm breeze flowing inland from the Java Sea wafted their silk curtains into the suite. "I can't, I'm sorry," said Amelia, "the time's not right."

He nodded and exhaled, peeved but understanding. "I will figure you out one day, but for now, it's the gym."

*

They exercised ferociously despite their jetlag until 7:00 p.m. and then returned to their rooms for showers as the sun set. "The bellhop was right about the lights," said Mason, flaking out on their king-size bed. Bars of dancing multi-coloured reflections shimmered on the walls, infusing the atmosphere in the suite with magic. Amelia joined him, and they fell asleep in each other's arms under the spell of the exotic delights and mysteries of Indonesia, waiting until the right time.

*

After an elegant seafood dinner, Mason and Amelia sat at their dinner table near the outdoor pool near the magnificent Monument Selamat Datang fountains. They enjoyed dark aromatic coffees with liqueur while waiting for Amelia's contact to arrive. The contact was late, so they ordered a second coffee each, biding their time.

Eventually, a short, sour-smelling man slipped out of the shadows, following the waitress to their table. The ex-MI6 man wore filthy cotton shorts, grungy-white knee socks and tired leather sandals, a faded plaid shirt under a soiled, ill-fitting white-linen blazer, and an absurd Chi-Chi Rodriguez-style straw hat. Mason sensed the man was 'too smart for his own good' and decided he was untrustworthy.

When the MI6 man sat down, he removed his hat and placed a plastic go cup on the table. His emasculated, puffy face beneath the failed comb-over turned imperious when their waitress arrived. The Hat barked his order, "Ice. In a bucket. And don't bother running a tab." His accent was working-class British. The waitress nodded deferentially and left, so he explained his rudeness away to Mason by shaking his cup and saying, "My gin is warm." He looked at Amelia. "It's been a while." She did not react. "Chad, wasn't it?" She frowned at him. He whispered, "You two are trouble—someone made you. They'll come here to find you—and me."

"That didn't take long," said Mason.

The Hat glanced at Mason nervously, then went into his inside jacket pocket. Amelia tensed; her hand moved under the table. The Hat looked at her and froze. "I'm not a fool," he said.

"Neither are we."

"Do you want the merchandise or not?" The Hat pulled out two forged British passports and put them on the table. "Where are you off to now, if you don't mind me asking?"

Amelia stared at him. When he wilted, she slid a fat envelope across the table. She considered him. "That's a fool's question—Singapore," she said finally.

"Not America… or Europe?"

Amelia picked up the passports, studied them both, then passed one to Mason, who tucked it inside his dinner jacket pocket. The Hat stood up. "I always liked you, but we're square now. And you," The Hat said to Mason, "should remember that black widow spiders eat their mates."

Their waitress returned with the ice bucket. Before she put down the container, the nasty little Englishman grabbed a handful of ice and plopped it in his plastic cup. "Get out of my way." He shoved past the waitress, but before he scurried into the night, The Hat stopped to look back at Amelia. "I wouldn't stick around; the humidity can be bad for your health." He slunk back into the shadows and the lush foliage.

Mason said, "That guy's deep undercover as a world-class dork."

"He owed me that, from Chad. He was an assassination

target. Gun dealers wanted him dead. Everyone knew he was dirty; some people never change."

"That attitude… maybe he figures someone is listening."

"Let's go," said Amelia, scanning the occupied tables, "we're in the open here."

*

Mason woke up alone the next morning. Opaque light filtered into the room through the curtains. The rhythm of the city drummed in the background. He got out of bed and turned up the air conditioning—another humid scorcher was in full bloom. He found Amelia's brief note on the bar: gone shopping back soon, A.

He plugged in the coffee percolator then slathered himself with aromatic soap in the hot shower, stretching out his sluggishness in the steam. He stepped out of the shower refreshed and caught a glimpse of himself in the mirrors. He approved; he'd lost another ten pounds. He put on his robe, drawn to the compelling aromatic coffee aroma inviting him back to reality.

He filled a mug, turned on the Smart TV, and flipped it over to the internet app to search for 'Wall Street Murders.' Pages of sites listing the Wall Street murder clip popped up. The most popular site had over 3.6 million views and tens of thousands of shares. But what surprised him was that the comments were practically all hostile toward the executives because of the 2008 financial meltdown. *Forgiveness,* he thought, *is one commodity you can't trade on Wall Street.* He put on bathing trunks, and when Amelia returned, he embraced and kissed her cheek, not letting go of her.

She stayed in his hug. "Did you have breakfast?"

"I waited."

"I'll make eggs and toast." Her offer of an ordinary meal delighted Mason. "This is such an amazing city. We're going to have to come back to do some sightseeing. Hawke is dead."

"That never made the internet."

Amelia held up a burner cellphone. "Dad texted me." Amelia pulled out of his arms. "Does this mean the honeymoon's over?"

She waved two plane tickets at him. "It's just starting to

get good."

*

They flew out of Jakarta that afternoon on a 737, sitting in coach. "We have enough cash with us until we get to Montreal and the states."

"What makes you think Normy hasn't spent it? Or maybe it was seized in some random customs inspection?"

"If that happens, we'll go get more."

*

The Hat sat sweating, staring, and smoking in the dark. He hid behind wooden rails and pickets on his tiny balcony, suffering the heavy humidity outside instead of the oppressive humidity inside his dank, dark flat. He had chain-smoked his way deep into the second pack of cigarettes. The low bass beat coming from across the street pounded in rhythm to his heart and into his anxiety, beating into him a refrain of deadly night moves. He took a sloppy gulp of his drink but stayed vigilant, scanning the street for *him*. Competing neon signs coloured the scene alternately between gory red then black and white. The waiting was excruciating, made more so by the turnstile mob clamouring at the front door of the brothel-cabaret across the road. He stubbed out another half-smoked cigarette into the ashtray overflowing on the glass deck table with half-smoked cigarettes, then fumbled another out of the package and lit it. His shaking fingers grabbed the faded wooden railing as if it might provide him with an anchorage.

He threw his hat onto an empty rattan chair; his comb-over was unruly. The ice in his gin and tonic had long since melted. Couples beating the late evening heat on the street mixed with white-shirted workers returning from long hours of serving jobs. The popular brothel also drew the usual middle-aged tourists on sex tours out of their cheap hotel rooms, so the congestion stretched the full length of the street. The ex-MI6 man detested the Indigenous clamour and the scum of Europe and North America mingling with locals. As a *tuan* on this street, he exploited the propensity for polite deference but not for cheap sex. The Hat liked the *feel* of the archaic legacy of white privilege, clinging to his pathetic fallacy of racial and gender superiority. It was so much more rewarding than his beginnings as the poverty-stricken, second son of a lorry driver in West Yorkshire.

The lorry driver's son froze when he felt him near—the ex-American Forces killer filled his balcony door. *Damn it to hell. I'm jittery as a schoolboy about to be caned.* "W-what do I call you?" In brusque swipes, he wiped away the sweat stinging his eyes.

"If you waste my time, I will put a bullet through your skull."

"I… Jesus wept... I had a drink with them. Here, in Jakarta, I mean…"

Jairo stayed still and spoke evenly. "There's no reason to raise your voice. Answer when I ask a question." Jairo's black silk suit rustled slightly. When he unbuttoned his jacket against the humidity, his Beretta never moved from aiming directly at the informant's belly. "You and Amelia," said Jairo, "helped us in Libya with Gaddafi. That was good work."

"I did some of the background work, that's all."

"You were essential—then," said Jairo, his eyes narrowing. "Are you recording us?"

"God, no. If they knew, they'd cut off my pension. Do you want the information?"

"If you don't mind, I have to check your *flat*. Isn't that what you call these apartments in your country?" Jairo's eyes never left the informant's face, the gun as steady as Death's bony fingers squeezing an old man's heart. "It's the little things that ensure we manage the future."

"There's nothing to find."

Jairo kept his eyes locked on The Hat's eyes when he reached across the table and retrieved the micro-camera taped beneath the railing's top bar. He dropped the tiny wireless device on the deck, slowly grinding it under his heel, paralyzing his victim with fear. The assassin ran his fingers over the top sill of the door, pulling a wired device from the cracks in the door jam. Shaking his head, Jairo waved his gun, indicating The Hat was to move inside. Quaking under pressure, the informant collapsed when he tried to stand, landing on all fours on the deck, knocking the table over. In a lightning-quick move, the assassin crossed the balcony, his steely fingers squeezing the man's throat until he dropped flat on the deck, supine and unconscious.

Jairo dragged the limp informant inside, leaving his body sprawled face down on the floor. He closed and locked the sliding glass door to the deck but did not close the blinds.

He waited, listening while he mounted the silencer onto his Beretta, allowing his eyes to adjust to the ambient neon lights strobing through the room. No one on the street raised the alarm.

Jairo worked fast and silently. He followed the wire trail from the sliding balcony door to a black box behind the stereo cabinet. He picked up the compact unit, unplugged the attached electrical and USB cords, and wound them into a ball. Removing the thumb drive, he placed it and the coil of wires in his suit jacket pocket. He put the box on the kitchen counter beside the uncleaned pots and dishes. The Hat groaned, so Jairo filled a dirty bowl in the sink with water and returned to his captive. Jairo used his foot to roll The Hat onto his back, then threw the bowl of water in his face and dropped to one knee, pinning The Hat to the floor.

The Hat stirred with the shock. He was groggy, but his eyes bulged at the gun an inch from his left eye, his hand grabbed at the knee on his chest. Jairo swiped the hand away with his gun. The Hat coughed, his voice pleading, "I was protecting myself. You'd have done the same."

"Perhaps." Jairo searched the man's blazer pockets and retrieved his cellphone.

"What about the reward?"

"You'll get what's coming to you."

"It's Inkai, isn't it? They have British passports. Please. That's all I know. I swear. Please…"

The single retort from the Beretta sounded like a popping champagne cork. The gunshot snatched The Hat's life, splattering his blood and brains across the dirty carpet.

"Betrayal is the eighth deadly sin."

Jairo frisked the body, pocketing the envelope filled with American hundreds. He efficiently removed the hard drive from the dead man's laptop and took a second thumb drive from its USB slot. He retrieved the black box from the counter and left the murder scene. Outside, he calmly blended into the crowd and walked away. He paused in the middle of the ornate, deserted, covered footbridge across the narrow, polluted canal. Jairo dropped the computer components into the muck, where they sank to dead, digital erasure in the deep primordial silt.

He rounded his shoulders to make himself small and disappeared like a spectre into the gloomy Indonesian night.

22. **In Situ Hell**

Their flight path took them high above the Indonesian islands' western-most periphery toward the Indian Ocean's heart. The passenger buzz around them settled into quiet murmuring and the occasional petition to a flight attendant.

Amelia said, "We'll take the first flight from Delhi to Nursultan we can get."

They sipped tepid green tea from disposable plastic cups, hunching together and conspiring like lovers, whispering so no one could hear. Then they chilled and slept almost until they landed in New Delhi.

After clearing customs without a second glance from the agents, they discovered there were regular flights between New Delhi and Kazakhstan. The Indian ticket agent scanned their passports and said, "British... Good. Two months ago, the Kazakhs lifted visa requirements for British and US travellers. We have available seats in coach." Without so much as a security guard glancing in their direction, they boarded the flight to Nursultan. The Custom's authorities at Nursultan were even less visible.

*

A travel bug had attacked Mason during the flight. He flopped on their hotel bed, feverish and weak.

Amelia said, "I'm going to pop out. I'll find something for your stomach." She woke him up when she returned to the room, tossing a pill bottle and two large water bottles onto the bed. "It says to take one every six hours. Let's double that up for you and make it every four hours." He gladly swallowed the pills in a single gulp.

The next morning, Amelia woke Mason when she returned to the room with a batch of warm potato pancakes and more bottled water. "How are you feeling?"

"Better," he said bleakly, "but weak."

"Take more pills and give it a minute. Then I need you to eat these."

Mason waved the food away. "I can't even..."

"Hold it right there. We're in the field. Do you think I never had problems? These pills work. Eat. I may need your help."

She pissed him off. He stood up. "You're a damn

bitch."

"I am not. I'm a *deadly* damn bitch." She softened her tone. "I got us a car. We're driving to Inkai in an hour." She appraised his naked body. "You're losing weight, buffing up… me like."

He was still angry, but a smile curled the ends of his mouth. "That's dirty fighting, disarming me with compliments."

"All's fair…"

To Mason's great relief, the pills and potato pancakes worked.

*

The Vespa came with a bashed-in passenger door, missing rear bumper, and blue smoke pouring from the exhaust. Mason stood beside the car, evaluating the windshield's crazy map of cracks that perfected their disguise. "Who wins the race," asked Mason, "us or a band of Kazakh bandits on three-legged camels?" Mustering a vestige of fortitude from his vastly diminished supply, he added, "Do you think NEWCorp knows we're here?"

"They have eyes in the sky."

They drove across the inspiring, great steppe of central Asia on the Silk Road, linking centuries of East-West wealth, art, culture, and trade. To their south, Uzbekistan was once controlled by Alexander the Great as part of the overland route to China. They drove through towns rich with the enigma of mosques and a cultural collage of historical identities. The breathtaking Pamir Mountains were a natural boundary on the southeast horizon, while the Caspian Sea's eastern shores form part of Kazakhstan's western border. Forbidding Russia dominated the northern, common border, which sliced the seemingly endless plateau's breadth in half, roughly west to east. The Ukraine and Chernobyl were a thousand miles west of the Polygon, the primary Russian nuclear test site deep inside northwest Kazakhstan. Moscow was always safe from Kazakh nuclear pollution. However, the Russian military agenda subjected generations of unsuspecting Kazakh civilians to the fallout from hundreds of nuclear atmospheric tests fueled with Kazakh uranium.

Amelia leaned over to kiss Mason on the mouth, lingering there, allowing the car to drift dangerously toward the deep, roadside ditch. He corrected their direction, holding the kiss until she burst free, laughing, "I hope you know how much I appreciate your company. Now, let's go see what the big deal is in those uranium fields."

*

"Any idea where we are?" asked Mason, tapping his blank cellphone display. Hours had passed, and it was after dark. They were somewhere north of Inkai, approaching a small town. Amelia pulled off the road, giving way to an armoured car leading a NEWCorp truck convoy rumbling past. Two Toyota pickups with machine guns mounted on the back trailed the convoy. "Not sure," said Amelia, "but those guards are wearing Russian uniforms with NEWCorp logos."

"Then we must be on the right road," said Mason, rolling his window down to let in the frigid air. The roar of the convoy had faded behind them when the dust settled. The nighttime highway was desolate and deserted, but the moonless canopy was brilliant with stars and galaxies. "Look at that sky."

Amelia did not look up. "Yeah, nice," she said, pulling a *Yangon PYa* 9 mm out of her shoulder pack.

"Do we need that?"

"We do."

"Where'd you get it, anyway?"

"You were sleeping in, so I went shopping in the black market. If you can't get a Glock, Russian Grachs are the bomb." She tested the bolt action. "I could have bought Afghan heroin from the same junkie, an American flag, and a Chinese RPG-7, with ammo—for three hundred bucks."

"How does a junkie get an RPG to sell?"

"How indeed. That's Shieli ahead of us, then the mine."

*

They pushed on, passing through the ancient, worn-out town seemingly held together with Kazakh mud bricks and sweat fortified by Russian cement and terror. Another convoy of semi-trailer trucks with NEWCorp logos roared past, transporting thousands of tons of yellowcake to still-active factories the Russians owned and protected in Kazakhstan. The windows were dark and shuttered in the drab and crumbling Soviet-ordered cube structures looming like Cold War ghost ships in the dust clouds.

"The Times published articles about this," said Mason. "The Russians control twenty percent of the global nuclear chain after purchasing the mine holdings from that Canadian-Iranian billionaire. They use it for weapons and fuel for nuclear power programs in Iran, Russia, and even the American West. This where they extract that three billion dollars worth of uranium every year—and they take it by fracking."

Amelia put the Vespa in gear and drove. "Zero signs of economic rewards here, considering how much drives by on this road every day."

*

Five hundred yards from the mine gates, Amelia pulled into the desert, away from the highway, parked, and they got out. "Is it me," said Mason across the roof of the Vespa, "or does it seem to you NEWCorp is acting uncharacteristically civil, letting us waltz in?"

"Let's not disappoint them."

Mason took her elbow. "We approach from upwind."

"Not tactical."

"Research. Nothing downwind of that cancer hole blowing out radon gas stays alive for long."

"You win." Amelia knelt and began stuffing her jeans into her socks. "There will be poisonous spiders."

Mason instantly scanned the desert floor around his feet. "Are you shittin' me?"

She snapped a clip into the Yangon and slung it over her shoulder. "I hear they're world-class jumpers too." She started a comfortable jog, then, laughing, turned to call out, "Don't step on anything I wouldn't." Mason stomped his feet, then rifled his fingers through his hair. He was well into his second wind when he caught up to her.

"Novelist, eh?" she said, breathing effortlessly. "How many copies have you sold? Two million, a million, a hundred thousand? How many, Charlie Scribner?"

Mason huffed back at her, "Enough, that's how many. That makes me a published, professional author. Why are you being so damned mean right now?"

"Took your mind off the spiders, didn't it? Are you up for some double time?" They raced to the fence.

*

Twenty minutes later, they had circumnavigated the ten-foot chain-link fence constructed around the perimeter of several mine wellhead buildings. A sign tacked to the front of one building read, "NEWCorp Wells 50 – 74." Overhead, stadium-sized light racks pointed inwards, illuminating several warehouses. Massive forklifts loaded a row of mammoth semi-trailer trucks parked side-by-side inside the compound. Drilling pressure release valves pierced the silence of the otherwise still night.

Amelia whispered, her voice hoarse, "Where exactly is this mine?"

Mason stomped his foot. "Down there." He nodded at the tall aluminum stacks coming out of the ground. "They force water, sand, and chemicals into the rock to pulverize the uranium ore and force it and the radon gas to the surface. They collect the uranium, but that pressure cooker sound is them blowing the cancer gas off for the rest of us to breathe."

"Water? What water?"

"They're draining subterranean aquifers the size of Rhode Island, bigger, maybe, all over the world. Texas does too, to frack oil and minerals out of the earth." Mason scoured the fence.

"Now what are you doing?"

"You're the one who brought up spiders."

The activity inside the compound changed—forklift drivers parked their machines, drivers and swampers closed the trailer doors. A crowd of men exited the building and got onto a bus, which drove them out of the compound. Amelia said, "It looks like the night shift is going off duty. I'll go over first." She handed Mason their Yangon, the chain-link rattled twice, and Amelia looked back at him through the mesh. "Throw me the gun."

He tossed her the weapon, which she caught and tucked in her belt. A flood of spotlights illuminated them. Pickup trucks roared in from several directions. Amelia drew the Grach from her belt, but a distinctly Latin-American voice from behind the lights said, "Drop it right there if you want your boyfriend to live." Amelia froze, the gun still in her hand.

Two armed men approached Mason from either side. Another thug jabbed a rifle barrel into the small of his back. "You move, and I shoot."

"I'm not moving."

Another thug grabbed the Yangon from Amelia's hand, holding his automatic machine gun on her. She stared at

Mason. "I messed up. I'm sorry." Four more guards appeared behind Amelia, three with handguns trained on her. The fourth man raised his rifle, stepped in, and then crashed it down on her neck, driving her to the ground. Mason leapt forward, grabbing the fence before the guard at his back bashed him on the head with his rifle, knocking him out.

*

Mason struggled to revive without vomiting. They lifted him off the ground, rolling him into the back of one of the small pickups. A thug wearing a camo uniform with a garish NEWCorp patch held him down, his boot on Mason's chest.

"You harm her," Mason slurred through his nausea, "and I'll watch you hang from a flagpole."

"*Molchi.*" His thick accent was Russian.

Mason shoved his boot aside and sat up despite his guard's grim sneer. They drove through the main gates, passing a dozen prefabricated Quonset-style buildings. By design, the sanitized camp would reveal nothing if viewed from satellites or with Google Earth. Neither would the site raise alarms if a crusading eco-journalist published photographs.

They drove past the Administration building, stopping at 'Generator Shed 3'. The Toyota pickup transporting Amelia stopped behind them. Three men in NEWCorp uniforms dragged her out, holding her in front of the displeased, balding, middle-aged man waiting for them. He stood tall but at ease at the shed door. Amelia stopped struggling against the goons holding her arms when they brought Mason over to stand beside her.

They faced the man, his jacket resplendent in NEWCorp company logos. His name tag said, "Manager." Then another man moved inside the building, pausing at the door, his frame silhouetted in the backlighting. Mason's guards tightened their grips on his arms. In a pit of lizards and vipers, Mason knew instinctively this man was the drooling, lethal Komodo dragon. He moved forward, and Mason saw the man's eyes levelled at Amelia. A goon handed Amelia's Grach to Lizard Man.

"Keep your gun on him. If she moves, shoot him, but don't kill him; I need him." One of Mason's goons trained his automatic on Mason's left knee.

The manager asked, his accent distinctly Canadian, "Is

that necessary?"

Lizard man said, "NEWCorp pays me to provide security, so let me do my job."

"All they've done is trespass," insisted the Canadian.

"These two murderers are engaging in corporate espionage."

The manager recoiled a half step. Bloody strands of hair across her face, Amelia said, "That's rich, Jairo, you piece of street trash, accusing *us* of murder."

Jairo! Being in the same country with the man sent shivers down Mason's spine, let alone being in the same conversation and at his mercy.

"Corporate espionage in this country," said Jairo, repeating for emphasis, "is a criminal offence punished with years of jail time, but most spies don't ever get to court." He let that sink in. Jairo looked at the manager. "I need statements from both of them. If they cooperate, no harm will come to them." The manager hesitated at his dismissal but departed silently to walk back toward the Administration building. He looked back once, quickly, and doubtfully at Jairo's prisoners.

Jairo scoffed at Amelia. "We both know you're powerless while I have him." He issued an abrasive order to the thugs, "Take them inside."

"Not a word, Mason. Tell them nothing." Amelia fought like a lioness, but her guards held her. Extreme pain shot through Mason's shoulders as if he had suffered a partial dislocation when his guard wrenched his elbows together behind his back. He writhed away from the pain, but the tight handcuffs cut into his wrists.

Jairo seemed mildly amused. He exhaled and said, "Change her restraints. One arm goes behind her back and the other over her shoulder." The guards standing behind Amelia held her in powerful arms while the third changed her handcuffs. "If either of them speaks or struggles again, break her ribs." He smiled thoughtfully at Mason. "I'm curious to learn how much you know."

*

Two massive diesel generators thundered in tandem outside the storage room's plywood walls at the building's rear. The motors' roar, which diminished behind the closed door, served to drown out any noise coming from inside the back room. A single bare light bulb hung from the low rafters above a steel washtub full of stagnant water. There were two wooden chairs in the room. Jairo said, "I know I won't get much out of you, Amelia, but perhaps if I take advantage..."

"Touch him, and I swear I'll..."

A guard punched Amelia in the ribs, knocking the air out of her. Jairo laughed. "Sit her down and tape her mouth shut." He said to Amelia, "We can chat in a minute." Jairo watched her as he rolled up a ball of duct tape.

Three men wrestled Amelia onto a wooden desk chair, forcing duct tape over her mouth. One guard pulled hard on her handcuffs while two others taped her legs to the chair. Mason's guard removed his handcuffs, forced him into the chair next to the tub, and then the two guards taped his wrists and legs to the chair. Jairo gagged Mason with the ball of tape.

Jairo wrinkled his forehead at Amelia, who tried to scream while she writhed at her bindings. "You care, Amelia? That's a professional flaw I've seen occur in others. It's as fatal as betrayal, a lesson I had to teach to our recently deceased, mutual friend in Jakarta." He smiled thinly at her. "His passing was fast and unsatisfying, but I promise you I have the patience to make this last a long, long time." She stopped struggling. Her guard held a fist full of her hair, forcing her to watch.

Mason could breathe, but he was terrified, and the gag stifled all but desperate gasps. Jairo cupped one hand behind Mason's head, and another held his chin up in a soft embrace, their eyes inches apart. "When I finish here, I'm going to CERN," he said in a low voice, "to personally deliver NEWCorp's termination notice to your traitor friend."

Jairo pulled a putrid, soaked heavy wool blanket from the tub. "Let's get started," he said, draping the blanket over Mason's head, twisting its tails tight around Mason's neck. Two thugs lifted and tilted Mason backwards until he was upside down, immersed headfirst in the putrid water. He closed his eyes and held his breath. Someone elbowed him hard in the solar plexus; the spasm made him gulp for air, but they kept him under, and he panicked, twisting his legs against the bindings until he thought his bones might break. When Jairo released the choking blanket, Mason inhaled water, which started to fill his lungs. The pain was an unbearable, black agony. They tipped him back to a sitting position. Mason's heart pounded; he took a horrible, half-drowned gulp of air through the soaked blanket before Jairo twisted it tight around his neck again. Mason choked on his vomit. Jairo released the blanket, and Mason spat the gag out, retching on himself.

Jairo pulled the blanket over Mason's head again and tightened the chokehold. His mocking, far-away voice said, "So, who is going to see who killed? You decide, Amelia, whether he ever writes another word." Jairo twisted the blanket ends tighter for emphasis. "If you're wondering where I learned this technique," he said to Mason, "the American military taught me." He looked at Amelia. "I hope you told him everything," he said. "That I'm an expert at information extraction. If not, that was irresponsible of you to involve this civilian. So, Mr. Writer, let's end your final chapter."

Mason descended into semi-conscious shock when the terrible pain resumed with more rounds of torture. After each near-drowning, Jairo removed the blanket from Mason's face to show Amelia. Mason was like a rag doll, his head lolling on his chest, too weak to respond when taunted, spat at, and ridiculed. Jairo had Amelia's gag removed. "I want to hear you beg me for his life." He grabbed a fistful of Mason's hair and lifted his face. "Your boyfriend's not so adorable now, is he?"

"Please, stop, I'm begging you, Jairo," pleaded Amelia immediately, but there was no mercy in that room. She screamed over the generators, "I'll tell you whatever you want to know. Leave him alone. I know about the thumb drive. Just stop hurting him. Please…"

"But we've just started."

Evidence of the torture smeared over his face and chest; Mason knew he was going to die. His eyes swollen to slits, he groaned out his response, "Not a word."

23. **Jail Sex**

The mine manager rushed into the room, shouting, "Stop this at once. Are you insane?" Uniformed men followed, bringing with them scuffling and confusion. Jairo let the towel sink in the tub.

A different man with an authoritative voice and brandishing a handgun said, "Line up against wall." Jairo released his grip on Mason and took a step back.

Desperately depleted, Mason still had enough strength to turn his eyes. Men wearing police uniforms trained their guns on Jairo and his thugs, ordering them to face a wall. The police kicked the goons' feet back, making them lean with their arms extended above their heads and against the wall. Uniformed policemen roughly frisked the NEWCorp thugs standing with their heads bowed.

The man wearing a gray Naval Captain's hat tipped back on his head issued orders. "Free these two. Keep those covered. If one moves, shoot them all in leg."

A cop cut Mason free from the chair. Another freed Amelia. While she peeled the tape strips from her legs and arms, Amelia spoke directly to the grizzled Captain, nodding toward Jairo. "That one has the keys."

The Captain raised his gun muzzle and held it to the side of Jairo's face. He said, "Hands higher." The Captain took Amelia's Grach from Jairo, searched his pockets, found the key, freed Amelia from her handcuffs and used them to restrain Jairo. "In Kazakhstan," said the Captain in deep and threatening undertones, "kidnap and torture is hanging crime."

Jairo said, "We were teaching these trespassers a Russian lesson."

"American? If you move, we shoot in head. With Russian bullet, if you like."

Amelia stood up, rubbing her wrists and hands vigorously while flexing and rolling her shoulders to encourage circulation.

"What kind of animal are you?" yelled the enraged mine manager at Jairo. "We are not torturers." Jairo remained stoic and aloof.

Amelia came to Mason's side. "Can you stand?" She bent down to lift one of his arms over her shoulder and help him up. Mason's knees started to buckle, but he fought the collapse and stiffened his legs. "I can't believe we do that to people in the name of a free world," he said, his voice croaking. "How many times did I die?"

"They had you for fourteen minutes. I've heard of guys lasting an hour."

Amelia looked at the Captain, then at his gun, then at Jairo. Amelia accepted a cop's help to hold Mason up, and then she moved to stand in front of Jairo. She lashed out viciously, kicking him sharply in the testicles. He grunted and staggered but stayed on his feet. One of the guards moved to intervene, but the Captain raised his hand and shook his head.

"You obviously have no balls, Jairo. Then again, you never did." She eyed the water tub. "Thirsty?"

Amelia slashed him in the throat with the rigid side of her right hand. Jairo gagged. She hacked at the back of his neck with her elbow when he bent forward from the blow to his throat, then used his forward momentum to frog-march him two steps to the tub, where she shoved and held his head and shoulders under the water. It took two cops some time to pull Amelia off Jairo. Mason proclaimed proudly to the approving Captain, "My girlfriend is one *deadly bitch*." When they pried her off, Jairo collapsed backwards, thrashing and twitching on the floor, gulping for air between spasms. He suffered a grand mal seizure, soiling himself as bubbly spittle foamed from his mouth.

"Fun time is over," said the Captain, *blasé,* despite the violence. "You two are under arrest. Follow me." The Captain, the manager, and a cop led Mason and Amelia outside.

Amelia said, "Under arrest? For what?"

The mine manager said, "Trespassing."

The Captain lowered his voice to a growl. "I'm Matvey. You carry false identification. You are not British. You are spy; you go to prison after judge finds you guilty."

"What about that bastard? You're not arresting him?"

Matvey looked at her with disbelief on his face and explained, "No. He has American dollars." Matvey turned to the cop, asserted his final orders in his native tongue and sent him back inside.

Amelia draped Mason's arm over her shoulders. Mason said, "Let it go. Any way out of that room alive is a good exit."

140

Matvey held his hand toward his ancient Land Rover and said, "We go now."

*

"Jail only place safe tonight. We don't take them prisoner; hold here." Matvey, Mason, and Amelia sat in Captain Matvey's truck. They listened passively, watching Jairo and his men file out of the generator building in a single line. Captain Matvey lit a smoke.

Mason said, "Kazakhstan is a complicated country."

Matvey drove them through the mine gate, taking Mason and Amelia to the Shieli jail, but he left them unrestrained during the quiet drive. They parked behind the jail. Matvey unlocked the side door and walked into the office. "Guards gone now. I wait... all doors locked. Tomorrow, bus comes, you go to Nursultan prison." His office was rundown and poorly lit, but Matvey produced a bottle of Russian Vodka from the top drawer of his shambles of a desk, exchanging it for Amelia's gun. He closed the drawer, looking at Amelia, who watched him closely. "Only thing Russian is good," he said to her. Matvey took a gulp and passed it to Mason. "You need."

Mason shook his head. "Drink," ordered Matvey. Mason's throat burned as if he had swallowed gasoline, but he took a second, small sip and then took more, forcing it down. He offered the bottle to Amelia, but she shook her head. Mason handed the bottle back to Matvey.

He said, "I don't change what is tomorrow." He patted his revolver. "The other, the bad one, will come for you." Matvey took a swig and passed the bottle back to Mason, who showed signs of recovery; the vodka fired a warming glow in his belly, and his cheeks flushed red.

Amelia said, "Captain, why can't you let us go? We'll disappear, and you'll never see us again."

"Mine owns police and courts. You go to prison."

Mason asked, "How much time will we do?"

"Tonight." Then Matvey processed the meaning of Mason's question. "Ten years each. Judge strict on crime when foreigners make the trouble."

"Ten fucking years?" This time Mason swallowed a bigger gulp of vodka, coughing but keeping it down.

Misunderstanding Mason again, the laconic captain said, "No. Jail sex not legal. Good lawyer and bribe judge will make two years each. We send hard case like you to Nursultan. Bus comes every day." He offered Mason the vodka again. Mason slugged back another mouthful and then put the bottle down on Matvey's desk. "Thank you, sir."

"Now lock up." Matvey stepped over to a tape deck and pushed the play button. Roy Orbison's *Crying* filled the room, playing over a tinny loudspeaker system. The song echoed in the hallway between the cells.

Amelia said, "Captain, am I out of it, or is that Roy Orbison?"

"This like hotel for miners for sleep, to sober for work. Music makes everyone asleep."

Both Amelia and Mason nodded. They were foreigners, with status, but still prisoners. Matvey had Amelia's Grach, so he separated them from their ID, money, shoelaces, and belts. The sympathetic captain gave them each an extra blanket and walked them down a dimly lit hallway to the last cell. The whimsical opening bars of *Blue Bayou* soothed the incarcerated of Shieli sleeping off the alcohol. Matvey stopped in front of an open steel door, solid except for the waist-height, small, rectangular food tray slot. Matvey motioned they were to enter the dark cell. Matvey shoved the heavy jail door closed behind them, its rusty hinges groaning until the lock snapped shut with a metallic, echoed finality. His face appeared in the food tray hole. "Guard bring tea at six."

Light from the single lamppost outside filtered in through a horizontal window slit eight feet up on the outside wall. Mason rooted around one corner of the cell. "What are you looking for?"

"Spiders… or maybe a Cold War corpse or two forgotten in a corner." Gradually Mason's eyes adjusted to the twilight, vaguely defining the shapes of a bed, a toilet, and a small shelf attached to the opposite cement wall. A single speaker mounted high on the ceiling piped in Blue Bayou. Mason tried to be glib. "I think he likes us, but…"

She caught him before he fell to the cement floor. "Sit." Amelia helped Mason to the bed, where she leaned against him to place her arm around his back.

"Did they hurt your arms?" he whispered. "That looked horrible."

"You were so brave," she whispered back.

"Haven't we had enough strong language for tonight?"

She held up the folded wool blankets. "We'll probably have to be sheep-dipped when we leave."

"That's probably considered a luxury where we're headed. I'm not looking forward to years in any fucking prison without you, I mean."

"We're not going to any Kazakh prison. Lay back. Let me hold you; you're shivering."

Roy Orbison and the rest of the Travelling Wilburys started *Handle Me with Care.* Amelia curled up beside Mason and arranged the blankets to cover them. They snuggled together, her arm across his chest held him tight. The fingers of her other hand combed lightly through his hair.

"Would Jairo have killed us?"

"We're safe, for now. Matvey may be the single cop in this town not on NEWCorp's payroll. I made a stupid mistake thinking we could walk in and unravel the truth."

"*We* made that mistake." Mason cleared his throat after every whispered sentence, but the vodka had given him some strength, and his thoughts were clearing. "Jairo will go after Ivan now."

"I won't let you down, but let's not worry about tomorrow. We still have each other—right now." She kissed his cheek tenderly and stroked his chest.

He responded, leaning in perceptively to accept her affection. "My ex did dump me, and I took it badly. And I only ever sold seventy-three copies. I'm no writer."

"Hey, you, don't disappoint me now. I always wanted to date a writer."

"Would you look at me—I'm emaciated. Have you always been this lucky in love?"

"You're not emaciated; you're strong, and I can prove it." Amelia kissed him again.

"But we're olives and onions, you said…" She moved her hand under the blanket. "Oh…oh. We're going to be in more trouble now…"

Amelia was alarmed. "Did you hear something?"

"No, but I think we're about to break a Kazakh jail sex law."

"Then, the time must be right."

"The worst day of my life, sick, tortured, facing years in

prison, and you're telling me…"

"Yeah, okay, you had a tough day, but," Amelia persisted with her hand and her kisses, "let's end it better than it started. You know I love you."

"I love you, too. But…?" He needed them to be kind in their intimacy.

She touched his chest lightly, kissing his neck, nibbled his ear. "You're so…"

"Tough…manly?"

"Vulnerable."

"Like a newborn kitten, if that's what works." Mason rolled on his side to hold her waist, pulling her into him. "How weird is it that a week ago, we didn't even know each other?"

They kissed. "I knew you—from your novel."

"When I asked you before if I scared you, you said I reminded you of someone you used to know… was it another boyfriend?"

"No, silly," she said, placing an index finger across his lips. "I meant me. We'll find a way—together. Kiss me."

"Do you know how demanding you are?"

"I know this—I pick 'em just fine."

While *You Got It* rang down the sad, darkened Shieli jail hallway, they made the sweetest love. Until those moments, Mason imagined their lovemaking would be a magnificent contest, a hungry dance of epic proportions played out in a dramatic setting greater than Michelangelo himself could portray. Instead, their intimacy was revitalizing, caring, touching. Still under Amelia's trance, he kissed her tenderly for long moments, shutting out the world and all his doubts. When their song ended, she held his face with her hands and snuggled him under her body. When they made love again, they both released more physical, selfish compelling urges. Mason fell into an exhausted sleep; his last thought was *Today was the best day together—so far.*

*

A commotion in the hallway startled Mason awake. It was pitch black in the cell, and Amelia was gone. The music had stopped. Disoriented, he lay on his back. He struggled, but his mind and body had seized up as if he'd been knocked out in the twelfth round of a prizefight. His entire left arm was numb. Eventually, he made out Amelia standing at the door, bending to peer through the tray slot. He said, "I think my arm may be paralyzed."

"From the waterboarding?"

"From you sleeping on it. I'm going to jail for ten years with only one good arm."

"I didn't sleep. Quiet. Us locked in here might be Jairo's best chance."

Footsteps approached. It was too early for their transfer and the other prisoners' release, so they were still asleep in their cells. Steps echoed in the hall, coming closer until they stopped outside the door. A key scraped in the lock. The metallic latch snapped, reverberating like a gunshot. Amelia moved to the side of the door with a blanket, ready to throw it over the intruder and then strike. When the door opened a crack, it ground on its rusty hinges as if in pain. A triangle of pale light from the hallway sliced through the dark cell. Then the intruder pushed it farther open, then wide open. A thin man, his features shadowed, stood in the door. Mason held his breath, waiting for the next version of Hell to descend.

"You kids up for some eggs and coffee?"

"Daddy. What took you so long?"

Mason was half right.

Amelia threw herself at Alacrán. Mason watched him hold her in a warm, father-daughter embrace. "Are you okay?"

"I'm good, but Jairo washed Mason's face."

"For how long?"

"Fifteen minutes," said Amelia.

"Oh, well, that was his first time, right?"

"And his arm is paralyzed," said Amelia quickly.

"That bastard." Alacrán came to the bed, deep concern in his voice. He loomed over Mason like the harbinger of relationship Death. "How are you holding up, buddy?"

Holding back how he sustained the injury, Mason said, "My arm is a little numb, is all."

"You don't have to be brave to impress me." Alacrán turned back to Amelia. "I'm springin' you two. We have to talk to Matvey first." He scanned the jail cell. "Are you about ready to move out?"

Mason jumped up, but a wave of nausea proved he was still affected by his torture. He was blacking out and collapsing, but Alacrán grabbed him with steel-talon hands and kept him from falling to the floor. "Easy there, tiger." Alacrán stood him up, and then Amelia filled in under Mason's other arm to walk him out. Alacrán said, "Whoever did this to you, they'll pay."

Amelia asked Mason, "Can you make it?"

"Twice, if I recall," he gasped.

She smiled, then brandished a fist. "If you weren't so sore..."

By the time they reached the door at the end of the hallway and stood in the pale yellow office light cast over them by the naked bulb, Mason's nausea had subsided, and he could stand by himself. Still, Amelia stayed close. In the better light, Mason saw Alacrán wore full camouflage clothing; his green and black face paint mottled in a swamp pattern made him appear fierce. Belts of ammunition crisscrossed over his chest. He had the biggest knife Mason had ever seen tucked into the front of his waist belt, which also holstered a 9 MM pistol. Alacrán looked like a combination of Che Guevara, GI Joe, and Dirty Harry Callahan.

"Are you expecting the Russian army?" Mason asked.

"Just NEWCorp security."

They walked into the jailhouse office, the last hurdle between them and freedom.

Matvey waited with another man, also dressed in camouflage and armed similarly to Alacrán. Mason recognized him from the compound in Pennsylvania. "How long have you been in Kazakhstan?" asked Mason.

"Amelia called from Jakarta, so we came right over. I'm also a concerned father, so when you failed to bring my daughter home before midnight..."

"Sir, I assure you my intentions are honourable." Mason was sincere.

"Then I'm sorry to hear that, daughter," said Alacrán, winking at Amelia. She smiled wide, enjoying Mason's awkward adolescent moment with her dad. Alacrán said to his backup man in the office, "Yuri, fix Mason up. He needs it."

Yuri unzipped a black leather pouch on his belt, pulled out a short syringe, and removed the protective cap over the needle. Mason did not resist. Jabbing Mason's deltoid muscle, Yuri squeezed the plastic bubble, forcing the liquid into Mason's arm, and said, "Welcome back to Mardi Gras, buddy." Within seconds, Mason felt the release from the anxiety that accompanies physical agony and parental intervention. Then, the physical pain melted away. Dr. Feel Good had made his cameo appearance in Kazakhstan. Mason flexed his legs, his hands, rolled his shoulders and neck. "Whatever the hell that stuff is," he said with relief and enthusiasm, "I like it."

Captain Matvey was unshaven and looked exhausted. He rocked back in his chair, his feet crossed on his desk. Smoke from his cigarette drifted lazily upward to the bare overhead bulb. His neutral expression remained unchanged when he waved his hand at the personal belongings on his desk. Mason was alarmed when he saw their passports were missing. Amelia checked the clip and loaded her gun. Alacrán tossed the ring of jail keys onto the desk. They rattled loudly in the subdued office. Matvey frowned. Alacrán tossed a stack of US currency on the desk. Matvey smiled.

"Me and Captain Matvey worked out a financial arrangement. You're free to go," said Alacrán.

"Ya, go. Take that stinking Inkai with you," said Matvey. "Since mine, there is sickness here. We trade prisoners for money for medicine, and Americans make money to go to Disneyland." Matvey tucked the cash inside his tunic before rising from his chair. He walked to the sink on the back wall and turned the tap. He flashed his lighter under the spout, and a blue-green flame ignited from the fumes. The wavering flame petered out and disappeared when he shut off the tap. He turned the tap again so the gasses could blow out the pipes before brown goo poured from the faucet. "One day, we all blow up. This Inkai poison. Before the mine comes, this is water. Now, who can say?"

Mason said, "Captain Matvey, have you asked the mine manager why the water is so bad?"

"He say my memory is no good. Is all. I am first son of Kazakh farmer. I don't say bad against rich Russian mine." He grunted. "Or Russian bullet."

"Can we get some of that water to take with us?" Matvey shrugged his shoulders.

Alacrán said, "Yuri, give your canteen to the kid."

The kid? Mason bristled; he had at least four years on Yuri, who handed his metal canteen to Mason. He emptied it in the sink, then filled it with the sickening sludge choking the water system.

"Time to go," said Alacrán. "I want to be out of here before that prison bus shows up. Captain, thank you." Matvey stood, and Alacrán shook his hand with affection. Then Alacrán punched Matvey hard in the mouth. "Now it looks like local thugs kidnapped the Americans for the ransom, right?"

"If he ask," said Matvey, spitting blood.

Outside the jail, another of Alacrán's men guarded two rented SUVs. Alacrán nodded to one of them and said, "That one's yours. There's water and food inside." Alacrán stayed to thank Matvey while Amelia opened an envelope left on the front seat and found new passports. Alacrán joined them. "Oh, we're Canadians. Thanks, dad."

"Well, the Inkai mine is half Canadian," he said before he left to speak with Yuri.

Mason said, "You knew your father was coming here."

"We set this up while you went toe-to-toe with *Montezuma's Revenge* in the hotel."

When Alacrán returned, he was all business. "NEWCorp will still be coming after you. That bastard Jairo is dangerous." Alacrán looked at Mason. "You're lucky to be alive. Time to head home."

Amelia looked at Mason, then Alacrán. "We're going to CERN."

"That's highly predictable and tactically unsound. They'll be there."

Mason looked Alacrán in the eyes and said, "We're going. Alone." Alacrán was about to respond, but Mason said, "If we all show up, they'll think we want to start a war. We'll call you if we need help."

Amelia said, "They won't expect us."

Alacrán looked at Amelia, then at Mason with new respect. "Your new ID will get you to their front door; the rest is up to you two. The border guards here will honour those exit visas." An ominous, gray prison bus with thick bars welded over the windows lumbered past them on the highway. Mason shuddered. "We'll separate at Shymkent, before Nursultan; you two turn south," said Alacrán. "You can make it from there to Samarkand and the International airport. When can I expect to see you stateside?"

Amelia was confident. "A week."

*

148

Their extraction was on. The sun broached the mountainous eastern horizon moments after they left the Shieli jail. The soft dawn helped Mason forget his torture as the rising sun turned the desert into a palette of subtle grays, revealing the morning as an exotic bloom. Distant snow-capped mountains ringed the enchanting landscape. "You know," he said, "it's weird, but, somehow, I feel free here. These people have every right to expect this world to stay the way it was for them in the past. It's their land."

Alacrán drove ahead of Mason and Amelia until they separated on the main road. They drove for several more hours, quietly eating and drinking from their water bottles. Mason became homesick for his dog, the Pacific Northwest coast; he even felt nostalgic for his lunatic fringe podcast audience. Amelia, too, looked sad. He asked, "Homesick?"

"It's silly..."

"Try me."

"I miss my Glock."

Mason nodded. "That was a good gun. There are others, and we'll get you another good one." He squeezed Amelia's hand, giving her a reassuring nod.

They still faced a long day. If they could get across the border, they would fly out of Uzbekistan. Mason flipped through both passports. "There aren't any exit visas." He flipped to his photograph in his passport. "Not too bad, I guess." He showed Amelia the photo—Mason's doctored headshot taken when they were still in bed in Alacrán's Pennsylvania stronghold.

"You're way thinner than that now. Our names... we're not married anymore."

"That honeymoon didn't last long." The highway turned south for the run to the border.

Their eyes met. "We'll definitely have another," she said.

"I'll try to call Ivan from Samarkand. NEWCorp can't be monitoring CERN's switchboard."

"Are you sure about that? Jairo is still out there."

They stopped behind a truck transporting a load of complaining sheep at the end of a long line of vehicles at the border crossing. Amelia waved a guard over and said, "We're a bit late to a hockey game... do you mind if we jump this line?"

He didn't after he found the four hundred-dollar bills slipped inside her passport. The guard's eyes popped wide, and he said, "Montreal Canadians." While the guard forced the truck driver to pull out of their way, Mason said, "Exit visas?" Amelia smiled at him. "You could get good at this."

When they drove through, the last border guard bowed at them as both Amelia and Mason smiled wide and yelled, "Montreal Canadians."

*

Mason called Ivan from the Samarkand airport. The CERN switchboard operator, a perceptible hint of Austrian in his accent, said, "I'm sorry, sir, Mr. Sobriev is on-site but is only accepting messages."

"Can you tell me where he's staying?"

"I'm sorry, sir, that's against CERN's privacy policy."

When Mason tried a North American call to Lena, no one picked up. He was frustrated but could not leave her or Ivan a voicemail message warning him about a pending attack by a determined death squad assassin. Mason compromised when he called CERN again and left Ivan the message: The extra baggage you brought to Europe is way too heavy. Get rid of it; it's not worth the freight.

*

They were on a first-class flight to Rome. Amelia said, "We'll hop a commuter flight to Switzerland."

"He beat us to Inkai, didn't he?"

They flew at five hundred miles an hour toward Italy on an Aeroflot passenger jet and their transfer point to Switzerland, worried they might be too late.

*

When they landed worn out and dishevelled at Leonardo De Vinci Airport in Rome, the distracted customs agent made a cursory, uninterested investigation of their bags and passports. Inside the airport, they hurried to purchase tickets to Geneva. The delay until the next direct flight required they wait exposed in the terminal for three more hours for the Geneva connector. "That won't do," Amelia said to the ticket agent.

"If you're in that much of a hurry," said the Alitalia ticket agent, "perhaps you would consider Swiss Air to Zurich and drive to Geneva. It would be less convenient but faster."

They needed to avoid sitting in the airport lounge for

150

three long hours, so they rushed to the Swiss Air counter and bought two tickets to Zurich.

Mason waited impatiently for their boarding call in the busy passenger lounge. Amelia was visiting the lavatory. He went back and forth from sipping a *latte,* scanning the crowd, hiding behind his newspaper, and watching Italian TV. When their mugshots appeared, the excited Italian news anchor made it abundantly clear they were still celebrity gangsters at large and were wanted for the double murder in New York.

Two *carabinieri* entered the lounge, moving slow, watching everything and everyone. Mason buried his face behind his *L'espresso* newspaper, waiting out what felt like an eternity. The *carabinieri* approached, scrutinizing every passenger, asking some for their passports. Mason crouched behind his pages, but a hand slowly pushed the top of his crinkling paper down.

"Have you seen the TV?" Amelia spoke over the paper. She had her back turned to the police and blocked him from their view. She wore onyx-black Sophia Loren sunglasses.

"That's all I've been looking at."

Amelia sat down after the *carabinieri* passed by harmlessly.

"Where's the sample," he asked. "We'll never get it through Swiss customs."

"This is one of those what-you-don't-know-can't-hurt-you things."

Ten agonizing minutes later, Swiss Air called their flight, and an attendant ushered Mason and Amelia into first class. The flight attendant had a delightful accent and large, gorgeous eyes. She spoke with flawless English when she said, "May I offer you champagne," pouring the bubbly into long-stem crystal glasses.

*

Jairo spoke into his phone. "I lost them, but they are not important. I am in Switzerland for the scientist."

Senator Victor said, "You must be successful on all accounts."

"Their friend is the honey trap."

"The vote is days away. They cannot get their hands on that thumb drive. What if they escape again?"

"Then lock your doors, Senator. They will be coming

for you."

*

Delaci read the text, then slammed his fist down on the boardroom table. Furious, he picked up the phone, speed-dialled a number, and waited.

"I expected your call," answered Jairo.

24. **The Good Cop**

The Swiss customs agent evaluating Mason in the Zurich airport was a young, officious man with a shaved head, white eyebrows, and piercing Albino eyes. The agent's eyes flicked between Mason and his passport. "John Hopkins? That is also the name of a world-famous university, a professional school of medicine." His accent sounded vaguely Germanic.

Mason said, "They have a famous lacrosse team, too."

"Never heard of it. What is the purpose of your visit to Switzerland, and how long do you intend to stay?"

"We want to see the Eiger. My girlfriend and I are hoping to stay about a week or so."

"You travel with her?" He tossed a glance toward Amelia. She balked at Mason's albino, recovered quickly, then flashed a radiant smile even as she explained to her agent why she had a bag of wet underwear with her. "Like I said, I washed it in the hotel room... it's in bags because I didn't want it to soak my other clothes."

Mason's agent asked, "She is not your wife?"

"My girlfriend. We want to see the Eiger."

"So you said."

The two agents conferred away from the counter. Nervous, Mason saw cameras and computer screens at every station. When he looked at Amelia, she appeared confident, flashing another dazzling smile at him.

Seconds later, both customs inspectors returned. Mason's agent flipped through his passport again, snapping the pages slowly through his fingers. "We Swiss can appear lenient toward foreigners seeking temporary asylum, but we are not a safe haven for international criminals." A stern woman in uniform patrolled slowly behind the agent but did not stop. "If you're not trying to surrender to my supervisor, I would appreciate you not looking at her and keeping your face down."

Mason turned his head back to look in the agent's eyes, then looked at the counter. "As I was saying, the Swiss cannot offer asylum, but my coworker and I agree, if you tell us the truth, to issuing you each a five-day visitor's visa. What is your real destination, and why are you here?"

"CERN. To meet a friend, a research scientist."

"My family lost our life savings when our broker

153

invested in Wall Street."

"We don't want trouble with the Swiss." Mason was about to thank the man, but he interjected, "On the morning of the sixth day, you will be arrested and handed over to the Americans." The slightest flicker of a smile twitched at the corner of the agent's mouth. He stamped Mason's passport. When the agent returned it, he flashed his eyes downward to a tablet, displaying the Interpol bulletin on the full-screen, including high definition headshots of both Amelia and Mason. "It's all I can do. Welcome to Switzerland. Next, please."

*

They retrieved their luggage and exited through the glazed double doors that separated them from the free Swiss mountain air. Mason stopped walking. "Why *is* your underwear wet?"

Amelia kept up her pace, so he sped up to catch her. "I told the truth. I washed it, but I used the water sample we brought from Shieli. The residue on the clothing should be enough for Ivan to analyze. I mean, Jesus, they claimed they found a few threads to analyze and wrote a set of encyclopedias and made documentaries about the Shroud of Turin."

"I knew it. Everybody has at least one pet conspiracy. Hold on, are you comparing your underwear to a religious icon?"

"My underwear is the genuine article, unlike the *Scam of Turin*." She dropped her latest burner cellphone in a trash can. "I arranged for our car rental." The human stream of passengers from several arrivals mixed and branched off into tributary channels within the sprawling concourse. Amelia and Mason carried on, side by side, past the domestic luggage carousels, to the farthest counter and their car rental agency. She said, "I hate entering countries through customs. It can get messy."

Amelia showed her passport to the gracious agent at the rental counter. She handed over the insurance papers, the keys, and the key card for the security gate then directed them toward the appropriate parkade. Outside, Amelia steered them toward a vendor and his sausage and coffee cart.

"We need two coffees, please," she said, "and can you double cup them for us?"

When she handed Mason his drink, he said, "Thanks, but I don't want a coffee."

"Keep the cups." They walked briskly toward the car rental logo across the expansive parking lot, following the series of glowing, bright yellow signs.

"It was clever of you to soak the clothing in the water from the mine."

"The plastic bag is melting. My custom's guy wouldn't touch it." Amelia swiped the key card at the security gate, the lock buzzed open, and they walked onto the business class lot. "There's our ride." Amelia walked to a compact Mazda.

Mason stopped beside a sleek metallic-blue Mercedes parked beside the Mazda. "What about this one instead?"

"But... I rented a family car so we would blend in."

"Yours is cute, but mine looks faster and more fun."

Amelia scanned the lot and stared; Mason followed her gaze. She liked the red Audi. "They're like 280 klicks off the production line." They walked over to appraise it.

"Won't it have a sophisticated security system?"

Amelia handed Mason her coffee, so he waited by the Audi. She walked back to the Mazda family car, took a quick look around, and then kicked the driver-side mirror off. It dangled on wires at the side of the vehicle. The assault activated its alarm system. Amelia walked back to Mason.

"It's a nice evening. Some fresh air won't kill us, will it?" With another powerful kick, she shattered the driver's window of the Audi, setting off its alarm. Mason picked up their suitcases and hurried around the complaining Audi, tossing the luggage in the back seat before jumping in, laughing.

"I've lost count... is this our eighth or ninth stolen car?"

Amelia worked calmly on the bottom side panel of the steering column. She studied the wires briefly before ducking under the dash on the driver's side. She removed the fuse box cover and unplugged a tiny black chip. The Audi car alarm stopped blaring, and the lights ceased flashing. She sat up again, calm and serene, and fiddled with the wiring. Two airport security guards approached the main gate.

"They're getting close, but they're running to the Mazda."

The Audi engine turned over. Amelia drove them slowly across the parking lot. The guards milling around the chirping Mazda never looked at them. Amelia punched in the security code for the Mazda rental at the locked gate, which swung open, and they drove away from the airport.

"My God," she said, "look at the Alps."

They pulled onto the A1 autobahn as the sunset blazed orange and purple behind the towering peaks. Amelia averaged two hundred kilometres an hour, quite legally. The roar of the wind from the broken driver's window was loud, but their stereo was louder. A mileage sign read, "Geneva 255 kms." They would arrive in a little over an hour. Mason settled back and took Amelia's hand in his. Her hair flew straight back in the wind. She looked amazingly vibrant, even joyful, speeding in a stolen car toward a life and death confrontation with possible global implications. When Abba came on, Amelia turned up the volume, and they sang along to *Waterloo*.

Halfway to Geneva, they stopped at a traveller's convenience stop. Amelia said, "I need your cups."

She stacked her empty cups into his and then reached into the back seat to open her suitcase. A rank smell permeated the car. Amelia took the coffee cups, scooped her soaked lingerie into two of the cups, and then crushed those into the other two. She zipped the suitcase closed. "That crap could probably burn right through to China. You owe me some shopping time when this is over." She accelerated onto the autobahn, merging smoothly at 170 kmh.

*

In a meeting room in Geneva, at Interpol headquarters, Chief Inspector Descartes shared the video report with five other detectives seated around a conference table. They watched images of Mason and Amelia leave the gruesome murder scene on Wall Street. An American voice-over warned, "We believe these two armed and highly dangerous American murderers are in Switzerland."

Descartes paused the video, stood, and turned to his staff. "Please note the accusations omit the legality—*alleged* murderers. I want them arrested for questioning, not shot." Everyone acknowledged his order. Inspector Descartes spotted the projected image with his laser pointer. "The NSA labelled the Wall Street shootings a possible terrorist attack, but I have my doubts. They want to imprison anyone these days for disagreeing with their president." He flipped to the next slides of profiles and headshots of both Amelia and Mason. "Our customs agency reported less than an hour ago that these two suspects are headed for CERN. We will intercept them there, using a wishbone roadblock on the Route de Meyrin. Heinrich, you will see to that." Heinrich nodded. "Our suspects are driving a stolen red Audi. You have the details in your folders. Look now, please." The team studied their dossiers.

Stephan spilled his folder's contents on the floor. Inspector Descartes suppressed a sigh as the nervous young man on his first big case ducked under the table to retrieve his papers. Descartes paused until Stephan reappeared with the mess of documents in both hands, apologizing silently. "I will alert airport security," said Descartes, rolling his eyes back to the others, "so they are aware of our operation. Until we know more, consider these two suspects highly dangerous. Stephan," Descartes addressed his rookie, "I will need your assistance throughout this night. You and I will take the advanced observation position nearer the airport and watch for this Bonny and Clyde." When Stephan nodded, Descartes widened his scope to the other officers in the room. "Any questions?" None were forthcoming, so the detectives stood and put on their bulletproof vests.

Heinrich left first to liaise with the Geneva detachment of highway police. Stephan asked, "Inspector, are we calling out our tactical squad?"

"We are not quelling a riot," answered Descartes, "and neither do we want to instigate a massacre. These two will drive into our quiet trap, and we will capture them. Then we can sort out what it is that has riled the American authorities." There were no high fives or rowdy, aggressive displays. Except for Stephan, each was a seasoned professional, a team member who had confidence in himself, his partners, and Inspector Descartes. "Go now. Remember, vigilance is safety."

The team established the roadblock twenty-five minutes later. Beyond the crest of a slight rise in the road and between large drainage ditches on either side of the roadway, they arranged the unmarked cars in an inverted herringbone pattern. Any vehicle entering or leaving CERN would have to wind slowly through the police vehicles, so there was no possibility a driver could avoid the roadblock. Inspector Descartes had every reason to believe the capture would be both uneventful and successful. For Mason and Amelia, Meyrin Way had become a vice-like trap.

25. **Cleanup on Aisle One**

Minutes from CERN, a car slammed into Amelia and Mason, rear-ending them near the Geneva airport interchange. Mason turned to look at the idiot who hit them. "Guess who else isn't rotting in a Kazakhstan jail?" he shouted. "Wouldn't this be an official *time of stress?*"

"And me without my gun. We'll have to inform Jairo you're anti-violence and have a strong sense of social values."

"I'm reconsidering my position." Jairo slammed his car into them again. Alarmed, Mason said, "That maniac is going to kill us."

"That his MO."

She dumped the accelerator and cranked the Audi into the exit lane at the airport's northern boundary. Swerving off the autobahn, they heeled over dramatically through the cloverleaf turn, racing toward the tunnel under the airport runways, toward the French border. Amelia pulled a crazy, high-speed turn across all four lanes at the last intersection before the tunnel. They raced between private hangars and the main runway, with Jairo gaining on them. Buildings flew past in a blur as they approached the end of the road. Amelia cranked the Audi into a dangerous right turn. They slid off the pavement and onto the grass, picking up speed and spraying sod and gravel. They smashed through the ten-foot, chain-link security fence, blowing out their windshield. Amelia straightened the car, sped up, and raced alongside the main runway. Jairo was gaining on them. They sped under the wing of a taxiing 767, swerved to avoid its monstrous jet engines. Their tires screamed as they slid onto another broad access road that looped out to the end of the main runway. Jairo's headlights were still full on them when they pulled onto the main runway.

"No! A plane is landing."

"Tell me when it's close."

Coming up fast behind them was a monster of a plane hovering over the runway. Its landing lights blinded Mason like a murderous Cyclops about to pound them into the cement. "It's already close."

"Closer, I meant."

Seconds before the plane crushed them, Mason yelled,

and Amelia swerved to the left. The aircraft roared over them, sounding like a dozen freight trains. They were caught at the edge of the hurricane-strength vortex swirls formed by the engines, but Amelia kept them on four wheels. Behind them, the corkscrew tailwind sucked in Jairo's Mercedes. His car flipped twice, spinning off the runway on its roof, across a grass border, and back onto the pavement, where he slammed into a wall inside an open hangar.

"That's the end of his rental deposit."

Amelia slowed down after they passed the passenger terminal and the last hangar on their left. "Car," said Amelia, "get us out of the airport on the west side." The map screen lit up immediately and produced a yellow line indicating the route on the map. She drove onto another access road that curved around the south end of the airport, past the same passenger liner that had almost taken them out. They followed the service road halfway along the length of an alternate runway, veering into an ungated access service road. Eventually, they parked on a quiet, treed street of middle-class homes.

Mason said, "Now let's see where this mapping software says to go. Car, where are we?" The map zeroed in on the west side of the airport.

Amelia said, "*Auto. Rue de Violet, s'il vous plait.*"

Mason said, watching Amelia, "Show off. Car. Speak English." The car responded to Mason's request. "Good evening, this is your roadside assistant…"

"Violet Street, car," said Amelia.

The car said, "Make your next left turn to *Route Forestier.* Proceed to *Avenue du Mategnin.* Veer left onto *Avenue Sainte-Cecile* and proceed to *Violet.*"

They looked at the highlighted route on the screen, connecting to *Avenue Sainte-Cecile.* Amelia said, "We'll be at CERN's gates in minutes." Emergency vehicles and sirens shattered the silence of the Geneva night. "Did you see where Jairo ended up?" Mason shook his head and then agreed when Amelia said, "We assume Jairo is still in the picture."

"The guy does come back like crabgrass. Let's go find Ivan."

*

A security car's dome lights revolved inside the hangar, causing the moving spotlight to illuminate the walls. The police radio chatter filled the hangar. Two security guards inspected the accident scene. One guard spoke to Jairo, "Sir, please remain at the security car." The other security guard had his ticket book out. "We have called an ambulance for you. In the meantime," he began methodically writing out a moving violation ticket. "I wonder, sir, whether you are a lucky drunk driver or simply suicidal?"

His partner searched Jairo's car and found a portable radio monitoring the police channels. Suspicious and alarmed, she searched further and found the loaded magazine in the front of the over-turned Mercedes. Thoroughly alarmed, the guard meant to warn her partner, but he fell and sprawled on the pavement, shot in the forehead. Jairo stood over the dead security officer. The unarmed policewoman hesitated, allowing Jairo time to aim and fire. The woman raised a hand to ward off the three bullets that took her life. Like her partner, she was dead before hitting the ground.

Jairo took the dead guard's hat and then sat in the security car. The keys were in the ignition, so he started the car, turned off the overhead emergency lights, and adjusted the two-way radio volume. He drove the patrol car out of the hangar and then the main gate. Because of the emergency on the runway, no one took second notice of the security man driving slowly away from the airport.

Jairo made a right turn onto the *Route de Meyrin*, toward CERN.

*

Inspector Descartes and Stephan waited patiently in the Land Cruiser. The Inspector scanned the road. Stephan snapped his Swiss Army knife blade open and closed. A ten-foot hedge of landscaped Norwegian Cedars partially concealed their vehicle. They both watched the light traffic for the appearance of the Audi.

The Chief Inspector furrowed his brow and checked his wristwatch. "Does it seem to you, Stephan, that the highway officers should have reported the suspects exiting the A1 by now?" Stephan stopped twitching with the knife and slipped it into his pocket. "*Oui*, I do, sir." Descartes rechecked his watch.

Heinrich checked in from the roadblock, his voice tense over the police radio. "Still no sign of the suspects."

"Remember, *mes amies*," said Descartes, broadcasting his

concern to all the detectives over the police radio, "be vigilant." He released the mic, then wondered aloud, "Where have you two gone?"

Descartes and Stephan watched the airport security Fiat drive slowly past. The driver stared at their Land Cruiser. Descartes radioed Heinrich, "Airport security is approaching." More distracted and thinking aloud than conversing, he said, "That is odd too, isn't it? Airport security agreed to stand down."

"We see it," reported Heinrich.

"Wait here," said Descartes, "and remain on guard. I am going to check the roadblock. Call my cellphone the minute you see the red Audi."

"Yes, sir."

Descartes exited the Land Cruiser, stepped out from behind the hedge, navigated the yawning ditch, and strode onto the *Route de Meyrin*.

*

Amelia parked in the road across from the deserted gate at CERN's main entrance and shut off the engine. They exited the Audi and walked alone through the expansive CERN complex, bringing the last of their money and the Shieli sludge. Amelia said, "These cups are almost finished. We need to find Ivan." Around them were nuclear research labs and offices and administration, maintenance, and service buildings.

"That was a good car," said Mason.

"That thing hauled the mail."

"It was always Ivan's dream to come here. He joked that nerds do better with a hobby." The Large Hadron Collider, CERN's ongoing flagship project, ran twenty-seven kilometres through France and the Geneva countryside. He was thoughtful. "Trillions of dollars have been spent here since 1959. Ivan tells me the crowning achievement, the nano-second observation of a Higgs bosun is the so-called God particle. But I think the Big Bang, at best, is a whimsical way for theoretical physicists to collect a paycheque, make bombs, and not have to admit they don't have a clue how life began. And all that still hasn't cleared up the water for half the houses in the states." He looked around; most of the windows were dark. Only a few dedicated souls still worked this late. "Finding Ivan in this place will be the real trick."

They read the sign at the gate, which notified them that CERN was closed to the public, and all access was restricted to authorized persons after 10:00p.m.

"He's here," said Mason. "It takes years to book accelerator time and weeks to set up experiments. But how do we get inside?"

*

One hundred yards closer to the roadblock, Descartes stopped. He saw the airport security car parked at the roadblock, its emergency lights flashing bright yellow and blue. One man waited there, and Descartes saw it was not one of his team. Walking steadily forward, the Chief Inspector phoned his rookie. "Stephan, slowly proceed to the roadblock with your headlights out but do not exit your vehicle until I order you to do so."

Descartes exchanged his cellphone for his pistol but held it behind his back. When he was close enough, he stopped and asked, "You are NSA?"

Jairo shot Inspector Descartes three times in the chest with his Glock automatic. Descartes grunted, wheeled backwards with the impact, and staggered off the roadway where he tumbled into the drainage ditch, rolling on top of five of his dead inspectors, sinking into the swampy muck. Jairo calmly walked to the last unmarked police car in the roadblock, stole it, and drove past the CERN gates, the battered red Audi parked there, and into the night.

*

Stephan crept up to the roadblock in the Land Cruiser. The headlights on the airport security car lit up the eerily deserted scene. He turned on his headlights and waited. He opened his door, stepping outside and calling, "Chief Inspector?" He listened but heard nothing. He squatted to get a backlit perspective of the roadblock against the CERN streetlights; there were no human silhouettes near the cars. He stood and took brave steps into his headlights. He heard a moan from the ditch. Stephan ran toward the muffled cry for help. Scanning the horrific scene in the ditch with his flashlight, he saw Descartes's upturned face floating amongst the bodies of the dead detectives.

"The killer is getting away."

The kevlar vest saved the Inspector's life, but not

162

before Jairo had shot each of his team members once, fatally, in the forehead.

*

After negotiating a twisted labyrinth of country roads that rewound to Geneva's outskirts, Jairo parked the police car in the Bohemian quarter. He texted Victor and then Delaci. Satisfied with their responses, Jairo went inside a rundown hotel, where he asked the wary night clerk, "You have WI-FI?" The clerk nodded. "A single room, one night." In the dark, sparse room, stretched out on the single bed, Jairo lit a cigarette, turned on the TV, and changed the channel to GNN.

26. **Nerds Need Hobbies**

Mason and Amelia watched five people in long, white smocks exit a nearby building, all of them talking animatedly and lighting cigarettes. They shadowed the scientists until they stopped in *the garden,* the outdoor smoking quad.

Amelia hissed, "You'd think with all their brains, they'd know better." She had the paper cups in one hand.

They lingered, waiting for the smokers to return to their labs, and followed them as if they owned the place, right into a building. Hanging back and stopping inside the doors, they pretended to be in a discussion as the researchers vanished up the stairs. Mason handed Amelia a visitor radiation badge from the self-serve rack, keeping one for himself.

Amelia sat down at the small vestibule desk in front of the computer monitor, mouse, and keyboard, placing the cups beside her on the floor. She typed Ivan's last name in the search request in the electronic directory. The computer presented a list of four names beginning with 'SOBR' on the screen. "And here he is." Amelia clicked Ivan's name, but the computer returned his status as *In Attendance.*

"Try Van Schleger," said Mason. "She's collaborated with Ivan before."

"Van what?"

"S-c-h-l-e-g-e-r, maybe?"

Three variations of the spelling produced frustrating 'Name not found' messages. Amelia typed in 'TRIGA.' They both sighed with relief when "Dr. Van Shlegher, TRIGA" appeared. Amelia clicked the name, and a local phone extension popped up. She looked at Mason. "It's your move."

Mason picked up the handset and entered the local. "He better not be dead, or I'll kill him." A woman answered the phone, speaking German. Mason said, "Hello, this is Mason Stone. Can I speak with Ivan Sobriev, please?"

She switched to English. "One moment."

Almost immediately, Ivan said in a monotone, "Sobriev."

"It's me, Mason."

"What the hell are you doing here?" he burst out,

overjoyed to hear his friend's voice.

"Just dropped by. Trillions poured into a black hole, but did CERN buy you guys a beer fridge?"

"Of course. What time is it? Jesus, I've been at it since 5:00 a.m. Where are you?"

"We don't have a clue."

"It's 'we'? Get the other part of the 'we' to look over the door outside the building." When Amelia returned, Mason said, "We're at building 596 on Route A Einstein."

"That's near the smoke pit. Wait there."

They met Ivan outside. He looked exhausted but happy, and he was smoking. "Finally, someone normal to drink with." They shook hands, and Mason introduced Amelia. "How'd you end up here? With this guy?"

Amelia said, "It's a long story."

"Is there ever a short version?"

*

They sat at a bench under a tall Maple tree at the smoke pit. Ivan lit another cigarette. "Your message was pretty damn ominous. I haven't left the building since I got it." Ivan listened as Mason told him about the firefight in his apartment, the attack in Lehi, and the Wall Street murders. When Mason finished, Ivan smoked quietly for a full minute. The news about Jairo and the violent crash at the airport tipped the scales for him. "This airport? Here? So, why did you lead this psycho here?"

Amelia said, "He was here. NEWCorp is..."

"A bunch of crooks and murderers?" said Ivan caustically.

Mason was urgent. "Come with us."

Ivan looked at Mason with kindness and understanding. "You know," said Ivan, "I still do research because I can, it means something, and I love it."

"If you won't come, promise me…"

"I'll stay in the lab."

Mason was about to answer when Amelia held the coffee cups out to Ivan. "It would help if you could analyze this goop for us. Maybe we can slow NEWCorp down or even stop them."

Ivan nudged her hand away. "I'll get us inside; you two bring the goop." He held up his cigarette. "And I thought these things were going to kill me."

Ivan led them to his second-floor lab. Dozens of high-definition computer screens glowed in the cold, subdued shades of the dimmed lighting until motion sensors activated the overhead lights.

"I guess Marta went home."

"Marta?" asked Mason.

"A physics theorist. She answered the phone when you called."

The lab was expansive, sterile, and impressive. Three wide workbenches ran the length of the middle section of the room, complete with orderly sections of Bunsen burners, sinks, and hoses. A complex and expensive array of glass paraphernalia and connected tubes and beakers in dizzying configurations defined each workspace. Glass-walled office cubicles lined the interior wall's length so that natural light would filter through the exterior office windows during the day.

"You can put that goop on that tray, for now," said Ivan, indicating a ceramic dish at a workstation bench.

Water and air hoses hung from the ceiling beside three impossibly huge aluminum fume hoods at one end of the room. Ivan's workbench was across from glass-encased cabinets below the fume hoods. Limp black rubber arm-length gloves attached to the plexiglass hung inside each case.

He filled a beaker with ice cubes, handed out coffee mugs, and produced a bottle of single malt scotch from his desk, then he poured the drinks. "A Mass-Spec analysis will tell us a lot. In the meantime, I'll phone security about this Jairo maniac. If I tell them he's a persistent salesman, he'll never get in. They hate that here."

When Ivan ended his call with security, Mason said, "How's Lena? Anything weird going on?"

Ivan cut a tiny square from the underwear sample and delicately mounted it on a slide. "Other than she dyed her hair pink—nothing unusual." He slid the sample into a tray on the machine and then pressed a power button. The tray slid into the spectrometer. Ivan adjusted the magnification. "I don't usually run this gizmo, but I have a notion of what needs doing to get a sample running," he said. He studied the first images of the analysis on the computer screen. "Your goop's exothermic reaction qualifies as potent and weird. Where'd it come from?"

"Water taps in a jail forty miles south of a uranium fracking site in Kazakhstan."

Ivan looked at Amelia and smiled. "Fun date?" Then he turned serious. "A water tap?" He turned to Mason. "NEWCorp, I presume?" He asked, but Mason's confirmation nod was unnecessary. Ivan used stainless steel tongs to place their sample's remains inside one of the glass cabinets and then turned on the powerful vacuum pumps. The rubber sleeves popped up. Ivan slipped his arms into the sleeves up to his armpits. "This stuff, which is laced with radon, should be encased in lead, not in a water pipe. I'll need a few minutes..."

Amelia poured more drinks. "Who else needs ice?"

"In the staff room fridge. If samples are lying around, don't touch them or shake them. Almost everything in a bottle around here can expand rapidly if disturbed, and by *expand*, I mean explode." Amelia looked dubious but went to refill the ice beaker.

Ivan pulled his arms out of the rubber gloves. He picked up a wand attached to a portable Geiger counter, waving it over Mason's hands and torso while looking at the digital display. "Your radiation levels are elevated but not dangerous. Wash your hands—thoroughly. Get under the nails. Where did you find her?"

"We met on Skype."

Ivan raised his eyebrows. "And suddenly you're touring Europe together? She seems nice."

"Nice? Yes," Mason exhaled, knowing Ivan deserved a better explanation, "but the first time I met her, she pissed me off. The second time, she saved my life."

"What about now?"

Mason looked past Ivan. He smiled back when he saw Amelia, radiant, leaning against the staff room door frame, holding the beaker full of ice, watching and smiling at him. Ivan looked at Mason, turned to look at Amelia, then back at Mason when he said, "Third time's the charm."

When Amelia joined them, Ivan scanned her for residual uranium poisoning. She held her gaze on Ivan, even smiling when he said, "You're mildly elevated too, so scrub."

"Besides the radon particles, this is a sulfuric acid solution, commercial-grade. Too much of it's not water," said Ivan, adopting a professional demeanour and studying the graphs on the screen.

"What does that mean?" asked Mason.

"It could probably run your car's battery, and it is definitely consistent with the effluent from a commercial fracking process." Ivan returned to the analysis. "This is interesting." He showed them an X-Y graph with an exaggerated spike off the baseline. There were ranges of numbers on the page as well. Ivan ran an app on his cellphone, typing in the numbers from the printout. He tested the sodden cups for radiation a second time. The wand crackled. He whistled. "I know one thing for sure…"

"What's that," asked Mason, instantly intrigued.

"You're still alive, so you didn't drink from these cups. This sample came from NEWCorp's In Situ leaching process?"

"Household taps, way downstream, but yes."

"Exposure to this stuff is a bad thing."

Amelia said, "We know they're fracking for uranium at Inkai, and that's close to Shieli."

"The kicker is the radon release. Hard rock miners inhale the dust, and the radon is in the dust. It varies, but it takes twenty years to destroy their lungs. The radon does eventually kill them as it would anyone downstream of the mine vents. I'm surprised we didn't set off any alarms. I can't let this leave here; I'll process it as waste with our samples."

Amelia said, "Can we take the Mass-Spec print out?"

"You didn't get it here, right?"

Mason said, "If we can't convince you to leave with us, at least give us the thumb drive. We'll figure out a way to let NEWCorp know we have it. That way, they should leave you alone."

"I still can't read the files." He looked saddened. He went to his office, returned with the thumb drive, and gave it to Mason. "I guess I started all this. Where are you heading to now?"

Amelia and Mason looked at each other. Mason said, "To find hotel rooms and showers. Stay in the lab; we'll call when it's safe. We can find our own way out and come back in the morning. It was great to see you again, my friend." Mason held out his hand, but Ivan gave him a Russian bear hug and a slap on the back.

"Amelia, you can do better."

Mason and Amelia shared a genuine laugh. "I'm doing fine," she said, warmly hugging Ivan. "Thanks for all your help."

They left Ivan peering at the spectrometer screen, sipping scotch, waiting for the final analysis to complete.

On the stairs, Mason nodded when Amelia said, "We'll set up outside." They walked out of the lobby into the dark night.

Two men stepped from the shadows, holding guns on them. Steely wrath in his voice, the older of the two said, "Do not move, or by God, I'll shoot you both right here."

27. A Good Man Down

Descartes held his gun at Amelia's solar plexus. His grey eyes were piercing. The younger man jamming his gun into Mason's lower spine had shaky hands.

Amelia said, "We're cool. We want you to arrest us."

The intense man said, "I am Chief Inspector Descartes, Interpol. Prove what you say is true and handcuff yourself behind your back." He passed Amelia a set of handcuffs, careful to keep the gun tight to her body. She complied.

"Stephan, do the same." Stephan fumbled for his handcuffs. "Quickly, please," said Descartes, patting Amelia down for weapons but finding none.

Eventually, Stephan stopped fidgeting. Mason peeked over his shoulder and saw the rookie detective had inadvertently hooked his handcuffs through a loop on his belt. He made efforts to untangle the handcuffs, but then his flashlight fell to the cement, shattering the lens with a whimsical tinkle. Embarrassed, Stephan looked to his senior for assurance.

"It is a small piece of glass, Stephan," said his understanding senior, "so, please, calm yourself." Descartes reassumed the role of mentor, visibly calmed himself, and explained to Mason, "You are his first arrest. He was only supposed to drive a vehicle and observe."

Stephan seemed overwhelmed by the moment. He asked Mason, "*Monsieur, s'il vous plait,* could you assist?" Mason looked at Descartes, who sighed. Mason lowered his hands slightly, cocked his head sideways at Descartes, and gestured that he would help Stephan. Descartes nodded his resignation, so Stephan handed Mason the gun to pass to Descartes. The Chief Inspector's eyes widened with disbelief at the transaction as he accepted the weapon from Mason.

Amelia watched the interchange and said, "Sir, do you mind if I sit down?"

"Please do; in fact, I will join you." The two most dangerous participants in the arrest sat it out. Descartes lit a cigarette and smoked quietly but never took his eyes entirely off Amelia.

Mason assisted Stephan. "Here, let's start by untangling these things from your belt."

"*Merci, monsieur.* I am sorry, but my nerves..."

"I can only imagine. See? Your belt is tangled."

While Stephan and Mason fumbled with the law enforcement detritus confounded on Stephan's belt, Descartes said to Amelia, "Your names, *Mademoiselle*, for the record?"

Amelia calmly replied, "We're Susan and Henry Haywood. Scientists with TRIGA. Whatever this is about, Inspector, you have the wrong people."

The Inspector sighed. "You are Amelia, and he is Mason Stone. You are fugitives, alleged murderers eluding the American authorities, running around the world, causing havoc. People die wherever you go."

They broke their stare to look up when Mason said, "It would be easier to cut the string on your whistle."

Stephan implored Descartes with his eyes. "Go ahead, Stephan; it will be dawn soon." Stephan fumbled in his pocket to produce his Swiss Army knife.

"You guys really use these?"

"It was a graduation gift from the *Académie*." Mason cut at the string. "Oh, sorry."

Stephan said, "You have cut my pants."

Descartes rolled his eyes. "Mademoiselle?" She declined his offer of a cigarette. The Inspector inhaled deeply, then allowed the smoke to waft out between his teeth. "Where were you two between nine and ten-thirty tonight?"

"Here… in the lab."

"What brings you to the most important experimental physics laboratory in the world hiding your identities? And please, do me the honour of no more lies." Amelia might have answered, but Stephan and Mason had managed to free the handcuffs. Stephan smiled and held them high in triumph, "*Monsieur*, I have freed them." Descartes looked at his rookie with baleful eyes, still holding his gun on Amelia. "And so the scales of Justice are again in balance. Stephan, we will bring our prisoners to the detention center. You can change your pants there. *Monsieur et Mademoiselle,* I apologize for the impression you may have of us, but *s'il vous plaît…*"

"Mason," said Amelia as Stephan finally restrained his prisoner, "tell them everything."

Descartes marched the group away from Ivan's building into the complications of international law enforcement.

*

Mason was chained to the steel desk bolted solidly to the cement floor in interrogation room B. A plain shade hung from the ceiling—a bright cone of light formed over the desk but failed to illuminate the gloom in the corners. Mason waited nervously, unsure what to say or what not to say. Across the table, Stephan fidgeted, absorbed with reorganizing his belt.

*

In Interrogation Room A, Inspector Descartes held his kevlar vest in one hand. A thick dossier was in front of him on the table. When Amelia's guard finished chaining her to the table, he nodded once at the guard, excusing her. Amelia sat with her hands clasped, watching Descartes.

When they were alone, Descartes smiled at Amelia fleetingly and remained standing. "I know you are not responsible for killing the two security guards at the airport. We have copies of the videos from their body cameras."

"Murder? What guards?"

"*Mademoiselle*, your dangerous chase launched a serious investigation to determine how two cars could access our international runways—while a flight was trying to land. One of those vehicles, a black Mercedes, crashed upside down at high speed into a garage at the airport. We recovered the other car, the Audi you stole from the rental lot at Zurich, at CERN." Descartes leaned into the cone of light, pausing to let her process the words. Then, with anger tainting his professional demeanour, he said, "The two first responders arriving at the airport accident scene are dead—murdered. The killer shot each officer once in the forehead."

"We didn't know," she said quietly, looking him in the eyes.

Descartes visibly calmed himself but remained impervious. "Then you admit you stole the Audi recovered at the CERN gates?"

"Of course."

He lit a cigarette. "Four of my detectives were murdered at a roadblock I set to arrest you tonight. My preliminary investigation suggests strongly each officer also died from a single gunshot to the forehead." Descartes slid Amelia enlarged colour photos of the gruesome murder scene, including a dreadful image of the corpses in the ditch. Descartes dropped his kevlar vest onto the table. Three black bullet punctures were grouped at the chest. He sat down, opening the dossier between them.

"I'm so sorry," whispered Amelia to Descartes, shaking her head.

"Our dashboard camera films captured the alleged killer shooting me three times—in the chest. We recovered the bullets. I believe our analysis will prove they match the bullets extracted from my detectives. I want to know why this carnage erupted in my city." The Inspector shoved the vest onto the floor. He took several pages from the dossier, including the computer printout, placing them on the table for Amelia to examine. "Are you terrorists?"

Her chains rattled when she picked up the documents. "We're running from a known assassin, Jairo. He's trying to kill us."

Descartes was unmoved. "And yet you're both still alive."

Amelia looked steadily at the Inspector. "I'd never work with scum like him." She looked down again to flip through the dossier pages. The heading at the top of the second page read: Informant: Victor-NEWCorp. It was clear the Inspector wanted Amelia to have this information, so they shared the silence, but a flash of her eyes over the photo confirmed she recognized Victor's name.

"This man, Victor, wants Jairo to kill you?"

"I guess Jairo works for Victor now. Jairo trained in US Special Forces. I knew about him when I was still on the inside… he's a murderer and a maniac."

"Agreed."

"Why are you so sure we didn't kill your men?"

"A security film from CERN shows you entered the grounds before my men were killed. Neither you nor Mr. Stone has black powder residue on your person, so neither of you is implicated in the shootings. I believe this man, Jairo, would kill you."

"You believe Jairo killed your detectives and left you alive to make you angry enough to shoot us on sight."

"*Oui.*"

"Then you believe…"

Descartes stared at Amelia with piercing eyes.

"*Oui.*"

"I, we, are so deeply sorry for your men and their families. Jairo does his work for a paycheque—he's a predator who enjoys killing. I will gladly share all the information we have. Will you please let us go?"

"There is still the stolen Audi. My team is eager to dust for fingerprints and swab for DNA. Grand theft auto, what you call it in America, carries a mandatory five-year sentence in Switzerland, with no possibility of parole. After your incarceration, we would have no choice but to extradite you to the United States."

"I don't have much to bargain with, Inspector." Her chains rattled when she reached for his hand. "We meant for none of this to happen."

He removed her hand, but Amelia levelling with him quelled Descartes' distancing. "What did you expect to happen?"

"Mason's friend is a target, and he needs protection. He's a scientist at CERN."

"Ivan Sobriev. He is cooperating. I posted guards to protect him."

"Thank you. We brought a water sample from Kazakhstan to have analyzed. Somehow, Victor is involved. We want Ivan to leave with us, but he refuses. We think Jairo will try to kill Ivan to retrieve stolen data."

Descartes pulled a plastic evidence bag from his jacket pocket and unfurled it to reveal the thumb drive inside, then he dropped it on the table. His eyes were fiery again. "Is this why two security guards…? I lost five of my team tonight."

"That information and the printout implicate NEWCorp in a massive corporate conspiracy. They're dumping nuclear poison into a public water source in Afghanistan."

"My officers were murdered because of pollution?"

"And maybe millions more sick and dying in the future from contamination. We know this is just the beginning, but we don't know the details yet. That printout and that thumb drive are all we've got—so far."

"I fail to see how this," he swept a casual hand over the printout and thumb drive, "proves what you say is true. It is, how do you say it in America, 'a smoking gun'?"

"Maybe, but that evidence leads us to NEWCorp. Captain Matvey, at the Shieli police station, will verify all of it."

174

There was a knock on the door, and then a woman in an unbuttoned white lab coat interrupted the interview. During their brief, whispered discussion, the woman handed Descartes a large photograph. He shook his head several times, "*Non, non. Une moment.*" The woman glowered at Amelia before she left.

"My people are angry. They want you charged." Descartes placed the photo on the desk. "Can you identify this man?" The angle was difficult, shot from the ceiling inside the garage at the airport.

Amelia glanced quickly at the photograph. "That's Jairo," she said, looking up at Descartes. "He's your killer. We need to get the bastard who set Jairo on us."

"Victor."

"Yes. Please tell me you have Jairo in custody..."

"Not yet, I'm afraid, but we've alerted all our border crossings."

"He may still be in Geneva."

The Inspector raised his eyebrows, "So?" Amelia told the Inspector about the breach at NEWCorp, the break-in at Ivan's Seattle home, how they were framed for the murders on Wall Street, the assassination attempts on Mason, his torture— the works, right up to their moment of arrest.

*

In interrogation room B, Stephan wept quietly in his chair across the steel desk from Mason. They were looking at pictures Stephan had taken from his wallet of his young wife and new baby.

*

When Amelia finished their story, the Inspector said, "We'll see if anyone is playing games." He left the room to make a long-distance telephone call to Kazakhstan's small, out-of-the-way police station.

*

Stephan jumped up when Amelia and Inspector Descartes entered the room minutes later. The Inspector sighed, looked at his rookie with disbelief, then back at his prisoners, then back to Stephan. "You may remove Mason's restraints."

Stephan freed Mason, then quickly gathered up his photos. The Inspector said, "*Monsieur*, we suffer the loss of our comrades tonight. Stephan is emotional, but I assure you I feel the same." Amelia stood beside Mason, putting a hand on his shoulder; he held it there. The Inspector said to his rookie, "You have done nothing wrong, Stephan, but I must ask you to leave the room to gather yourself."

Nodding, Stephan left. When the door closed, the Inspector lit a cigarette, sat down, and said, "I am going to release you. But you will do something for me."

Mason looked up at Amelia, who said, "Anything." She squeezed Mason's hand lightly. They both looked at Descartes.

"When we arrest Jairo, you will testify. You will volunteer to return to Switzerland for the trial. If you both give me your word, I will not process the car until you leave Switzerland, and the results will remain on my desk."

Amelia said, "I'll do you one better. I'll give you my New York contact information."

Mason confirmed with a nod to Descartes. "We will both testify for you," he said.

Descartes studied them briefly, then said, "Now we have to get you out of my country. Your passports are forgeries. Another felony. Your tourist visas will expire in three days. I cannot be a party to any illegal activity. Any ideas?"

*

Laying on his bed in his hotel room, watching TV, Jairo was perplexed. He had set it up perfectly. Two armed American fugitives had murdered policemen and security guards and then shot the Chief Detective. The story should have been white-hot, but none of the news channels carried it—not anywhere. He checked his weapon for one in the chamber and a full clip before he left the sanctuary of the hotel room—a brooding, determined killer.

Forty minutes later, dead eyes stared back at Jairo. The officer lay at the foot of the stairs in Ivan's building. Jairo had already surprised and killed the officer stationed outside, leaving him behind the building's hedge. He pulled the second dead man by his jacket collar into the janitor's closet. Jairo ascended the stairs, brazenly unconcerned about the security cameras, as he neared the door to Ivan's lab. *Plácido Domingo's* sublime tenor increased in volume, bringing Verdi to life on intensifying crescendos.

Jairo slipped inside the door. Ivan worked alone in the lab, so Jairo turned off all the overhead lights and locked the door from the inside. Ivan was disposing of the sample in the glass booth. His back was to the door; his arms and hands were constrained in the rubber gloves, so he could not turn to see Jairo. "Hello. I'm working," Ivan called out. "Could you please turn the lights back on?"

"This lab is even more impressive than at NEWCorp," said Jairo after he muted the opera on the player. "Time for a break, Doctor Sobriev."

Ivan, his arms still in the gloves, craned his neck toward the voice. "How did you get past security?"

"Stay as you are." Ivan froze, intimidated by the menacing voice and the gun in Jairo's steady hand. "Your former employer wants me to reacquire their property. They compensated you generously—but you betrayed them. Why?"

"They doctored my reports. I know what they're doing with the nuclear waste. I know what the LA Project is... I left proof with a lawyer."

Jairo scoffed. "You were angry because NEWCorp used your reputation like a sailor buys a whore." Jairo's face was a killer's mask and his voice a low growl. "What did you tell Amelia? Where did they go?"

"They never told me."

Jairo fired once at Ivan's left knee. The bullet smashed through Ivan's femur, the smooth articular cartilage, the lateral meniscus, then exited, dislodging the tibia. He screamed in agony, but the sound was muffled because Jairo had clamped his hand over Ivan's mouth. Ivan's knees buckled, but his arms, caught inside the twisted rubber sleeves, kept him from collapsing to the floor.

Jairo waited several seconds for Ivan's pain to gain momentum. "I don't apologize for my methods," he said calmly. "My next shot will destroy your other knee. After that, it will be your testicles, then your elbows, and if that doesn't work, I will use the Bunsen burner to blind you one eye at a time. Talk now or after. It is your choice."

Ivan wavered between crescendos of pain. Blood from his wound ran down his leg, pooling on the floor. He tried to stand but slipped in the blood, gasping in agony, "What... what do you want to know?"

Jairo calmly removed the cap from the bottle of scotch still on the workbench and drank. "Not bad," he said. "Did you really think you could play God with uranium your whole life and not suffer the consequences?"

Ivan choked out the words, "What? What do you...? I'm just a chemist."

"So you're innocent?"

Jairo scoffed and pushed on Ivan's wound with his shoe. Ivan screamed in agony, then breathed through gritted teeth, "You're insane."

Jairo pressed hard on Ivan's wound again, causing him to scream with more intensity. Jairo sipped his scotch until Ivan's pain levelled, then Jairo raised his foot again. Ivan begged for mercy with his eyes. His voice was weak with resignation. "I ran a Mass-Spec on a water sample from Kazakhstan. That's all."

"What were the results?" Sirens outside alerted Jairo that the police were closing in.

"Elevated radon gas emissions and a concentration of sulfuric acid." He grunted in agony. "Please... stop."

"What else?"

"They have the printout."

"You kept the sample? Is the data stored on these computers?"

He shook his head. "I destroyed it all. I... I wasn't supposed to do the tests."

"And the NEWCorp thumb drive?"

"They have it. They insisted. Please... call for help."

The sirens were close. Jairo fired two shots into Ivan's head, then holstered the pistol beneath his black leather jacket. Sneering at Ivan, he raised his eyebrows and said quietly, "Help."

Jairo searched Ivan's pockets for the thumb drive but found nothing. The sirens stopped, which meant the police had arrived.

He hurried to the storage room. The shelves were stocked with litres of various acids and alkaline solvents. He fired into the many bottles on the shelves, releasing a volatile mixture of gasses and chemicals. He ran out of the lab, down the stairs, and through a side door of the building. Three police cars had pulled up to the front curb. The deadly, potent flammable concoction in the storage room ignited when the lithium sparked, exploding out of the confined space with the force of a pound of C-4. The secondary bloom of gases ignited, charged by the initial explosion, and disintegrated everything inside the laboratory walls.

A block away, Jairo walked backwards, capturing a video of his work on his cellphone. Emergency sirens approached from several directions. The responders would fear the potential for radiation contamination, and CERN would warn them off the property until the building was declared safe. That could take days, perhaps even weeks.

*

Descartes stopped his Land Cruiser beside the steps up to the Swiss Air Force repurposed Boeing 737. A cold, persistent pre-dawn breeze gusted across the Reichenbach airfield. He turned sideways to speak to his passengers. "I called in this favour with the commanding general of this base. Your plane departs within the half-hour for Canada, to a place called Goose Bay." Descartes seemed amused.

Both Amelia and Mason enthusiastically thanked Descartes, knowing that the right people can still accomplish minor miracles through back channels. "I gather Captain Matvey is your friend now," said Descartes. "We will continue with our vigilance at every Swiss border crossing, and we will protect Sobriev until he leaves Switzerland." Descartes flashed a warning look at his two new confederates. "Until we arrest this savage Jairo, travel with caution, *mes amies*." Descartes held his hand out to Mason. "Stephan wanted you to have this. He said you were *empathique*." Descartes handed Mason the swiss army knife, adding, "Do not forget your promises. *À bientôt*."

*

Descartes was returning to Geneva when he stopped the car to take a phone call. "Inspector," said Stephan, "there has been a major explosion at Doctor Sobriev's lab." Descartes closed his eyes to massage them before speeding to CERN.

*

The ageing Scot with a prolific, grey mustache, glasses, and muttonchop sideburns crossed the Swiss-French border near the Geneva airport. He looked directly at the customs agent. The woman compared the driver with Jairo's photo, which Interpol had dispersed to every border crossing. "Enjoy your stay in France, sir," said the border agent.

"Aye."

Jairo removed his disguise at a rest stop sixty kilometres

inside the country. It was a risky exit route but seeing the hanging glaciers and soaring crags in his rearview mirror released him from such petty concerns. He made the call from his stolen car. "Did you get my video?"

"Yes." Delaci's voice was neutral. "Where are you going next?"

"New York. The trail is cold here. I'll tie up any loose ends in the US. Where else can they go to hide?"

28. **The Recruits**

They were alone in the cavernous cargo hold of the converted passenger jet, where just three rows of first-class seats remained for the occasional passengers. Before retreating behind the closed cockpit door, the copilot handed them a package of K-rations and two litres of water each. "And I'll bet you thought this was a 'no frills' flight," he said. "We'll be landing a little late; there's turbulence ahead."

The jet punched through the gloom of the jagged, dark clouds layers, where Dawn painted the eastern horizon's uplifting radiance. The jet flew them away from Descartes' protection, but the Edelweiss still bloomed in the high alpine valleys below them, and people drove to work or got the kids to school or had reasons to carry on with their lives. They were thirty-five thousand feet above the French-Belgian border when they levelled off, about to cross the English Channel's northern reaches, traversing the globe on the polar route. However, soaring above the daily grind's security and comfort, Mason grew aware that meeting with Ivan had caused something fundamental to change for him. He turned to Amelia, away from the crags of the sky-scraping Alps and said, "Back at the lab, what were you smiling at when I saw you at the door?"

"Two good friends meeting again and sharing a scotch. It was nice."

"No one wants to end Jairo's rampage more than me," he said, "but… we have to quit killing people. Promise me, no more."

"I do."

Mason paused, then said, "Jairo murdered people in Geneva and New York because of us."

"Because of who they are," she snapped, and then mellowed, "and because they don't care how they get what they want."

"We've been hunted since Seattle. The printout has to lead us to NEWCorp, and then the justice system can take over." Mason crossed his arms and snapped a questioning look at Amelia. "I wanted to figure this out, but if this is what revenge feels like, I don't like it, and I won't keep going. I mean, six dead cops?"

Amelia took his hand. "We never meant that to happen;

we needed to save our lives—and Ivan's. Except, maybe I took a little advantage with my ex in Seattle..."

"You blew up his helicopter—when he was in it."

"Yeah, but, no, it sounds bad when you say it like that."

Mason's exasperation deflated to melancholy. "I hate the guns, the killing, and I'm no fan of torture."

"I do too. It's never easy, but if it puts a stop to more killing..."

"Enough! Killing just starts another revenge killing cycle."

"I think of America every day. It's all a terrible loss of dignity and humanity," said Amelia. "Just tell me, how?"

"Stop shooting, burning and stabbing—for starters. Then try listening instead of telling."

Amelia crossed her heart. "We will find another way."

He kissed her with welling affection. "You set my heart free, but because of you, I may go to death row. I love you. Or, maybe this is a new form of hate."

"You love me even though I have killed people?"

"That's different; it *was* them or us."

She undid her seat belt, raised both his armrests and straddled him. "That is the sweetest thing to say." Amelia wrapped her arms around his neck. Clasping her fingers, she leaned forward and kissed him, sending it special delivery: warm, sensuous, soft, hungry, and giving. She said in a passionate whisper, "I'm as surprised as you are."

"We haven't had much time to ourselves since we were in jail."

They spent the next twenty minutes joining the mile-high club in the bathroom, unleashing their demanding sexual passion. When they were both satisfied, Amelia took a blanket and fell asleep on a row of three seats across the aisle from Mason, who was already asleep.

*

"Are you awake?" Amelia's voice cut through the droning airplane engines.

Mason opened one eye. "No."

"Brace yourself; Descartes called. There was an explosion. They found Ivan in his lab."

Mason asked with his eyes, and Amelia shook her head once.

"Oh, no." Mason choked up.

"Descartes couldn't say too much, but he did say, 'the wolf is still in the meadow.' Jairo is out there. I'm so sorry." Tears welled in her eyes. She tried to place her head on his shoulder, but he slipped away to the bathroom—alone. He cried for his friend, for Lena, and their children, and everyone else in the world who feels powerless against corrupt politicians and serial killer corporations.

After some time, he gathered himself, washed his face, and returned to Amelia, fury smouldering in his eyes. "They won't stop. We're next; maybe Normy is already dead, then Lena, where does it end?" His eyes were lost in the angry question. "This changes everything. If I ever see Jairo again…"

Amelia responded to his urgency. "We need to draw him into the open—Victor, too. We have to come up with a plan, but he's too much for you."

"We'll see about that." Mason's eyes teared up again; he swiped them away with the back of his hand and pushed past it. "Have you talked with Alacrán?"

"The copilot patched me through."

"We have to get inside NEWCorp." He looked at her for assurance, but she was worried. "What?" he asked.

"NEWCorp put a dead or alive bounty on us."

"Do we know who, exactly, did that?"

"Dad thinks it has to be their CEO, a real peach of a guy, Delaci."

"Then that's where I'm going."

*

They landed at the Armed Forces base in Goose Bay, Labrador, an outpost in the Canadian Shield barrens. They skipped through customs because they arrived on a military flight at a military base and with Canadian passports. They hired a taxi to take them to the nearby civilian airport and used all but the last $600 of their cash to purchase business class tickets to foggy Pierre Elliott Trudeau International airport near Montreal. Early that afternoon, they arrived in a taxi at the inconspicuous *Mont-Royal* district safe house. Amelia did something magical with a credit card to unlock the door. She said, "Locks are only meant to keep salesmen or honest people out."

They ascended the stairs to the second-floor landing. Amelia knocked on a door; her effort returned dead silence.

She knocked again and said, "It's Amelia and Mason. Open up." Still nothing. "I promise we won't hurt you."

They heard a muffled curse, then footsteps, and then the metal lock clacked, the knob turned, the door opened, the security chain tightened, and Normy's scared, little-boy face appeared. "What do you want?" Amelia pushed through the door, snapping Normy's face with the chain. "Ow. Why'd you do that?"

Mason followed her in, quietly closing the door. Amelia shoved Normy back in one swift motion, his hair combed, his boxer shorts, a T-shirt, and knee socks all white, across the room, and slamming him into the bureau against the opposite wall. She held him there with her hand flat on his chest, their eyes locked. Amelia said, "Where's our money?"

Normy's eyes rolled to the bed, so Amelia let him go. He hastily pulled a shoulder pack from under the bed and handed it to Amelia. While they discussed finances, Mason went to the open laptop on the table, where their host had been nibbling at a stack of buttery rye toast. The bachelor suite was stuffy and cramped. A small widescreen TV sat on the dresser.

"It's here," said Normy, afraid and jabbering. "Your dad FedEx'd it."

Amelia locked her eyes on his. She raised and lowered the pack once. "It feels light."

"I spent some of the money..."

"Do you mind if I check my email?" said Mason, displaying belated manners because he'd already commandeered Normy's laptop. Mason disabled the WI-FI to ensure local privacy, plugged the network cable into the modem and changed the interface to a *wired connection*. Doing that disabled the universal Socket 7 privacy breach built into every cellphone on the planet. He said to Normy, "Give Amelia your cellphone." Normy grumbled but followed orders and surrendered his phone.

Amelia removed and destroyed the SIM chip, rinsing it down the sink. "We're in the big kid's sandbox now, Normy. Your mommy will have to wait a while before your next call."

"How did you know?"

"Just a hunch. Mason, who are you contacting?"

Mason typed furiously. "For once, I know the guy. He's a kid, a hacker, who likes his privacy protected." Mason opened an operating system command shell window, typed in the command and IP address required to side-slip the standard vendor interface, and launched the VPN request to the hacker's private server. "When he was twelve, he hacked the university database and put his mother at the top of the hip replacement list. He's a bit of a legend in our crowd." Mason logged on using his ID and password, called up a chat session, and typed in another password.

IBM, the kid, replied:

u r all over the web dude did u do it?

no it's a setup how secure is this site?

512-bit encrypt behind my hybrid algorithm

k I need your help

sorry no can do 2 weird now i work 4 the man

this will be fun right up your alley u still a video guy?

can't I got NDAs the works…

Mason looked at the blinking cursor on the screen. He waited, then typed: this is bigger than that. He said aloud, "Come on, IBM, this one's made for you."

In the background, Amelia was distracting Normy. "This place reeks. Have you considered opening a window?" She scoffed at his purple velvet loveseat, the only furniture in the room other than the unkempt bed and the messy kitchen table. Normy was about to flop on the settee, but Amelia said, "At the table." Normy looked peeved and about to protest, but, instead, he relented and then sat across from Mason as directed.

IBM returned a text: what do u have in mind?

"I got him, I think." Mason typed out the skeleton version of their plan and why they needed a teenaged hacker in Montreal to join their team.

dude u r nuts that's totally hi end tough 2 do

insane 2 try…

so you're in?

man…

Normy watched Amelia search the loveseat. She pulled out a German luger pistol from behind the seat cushion. "Really, Normy?"

"It was here when I moved in. It's for whatever."

Amelia snapped the clip out of the gun, checking it for a full load and its functionality, replaced the clip, and then slipped the weapon inside her jacket on her waist belt. "You had one in the chamber. You could have blown hot lead through your boys."

Normy huffed, looking out the window. Then said, "Take your money and go. I don't want anything to do with you."

Mason continued with IBM: it could be dangerous
u promise?
u'll be even more famous...
BS when?
3-4 days u up 4 it?
i can b, but it has to go down at 16:00 i have trumpet lessons at 17:30 if i skip i b grounded if mom finds out I will use the u hospital fibre connection
the u?
my new gig i know peeps there.
Ok, u pull the strings in the background, I'll tell you when watch for my next login that's your signal we'll get ready for u then it's a go
i'm erasing all records of this session peace out

Mason said, "It's unfair of me to take advantage of his authority issues, but we can rely on him."

Normy said, "Who is this hacker kid, anyway?"

"I met him online when I was at college. His father is a math prof, and his mother's a linguist. The first two words out of his mouth were, 'I pad.' He's one of the most sought-after Internet securities experts in Canada. He's already taking advanced courses at McGill University. But he's still a minor, so he's also one of their best secrets."

"Normy," asked Amelia, "do you remember how we saved your life and helped you get away from the New York mafia?"

"Yes." Normy's voice dripped with resigned dread.

"Then come with us. You know we can save your life again, right?"

"My life—again?"

"If we leave you here, the professional killer stalking us will find you. And Matty won't stop until he gets his money back, all of it—plus interest." Normy blanched at the Mafioso's name. "But we have a plan. Mason and I need your help."

"I don't know; maybe I'll stay here. Don't worry, I won't rat you out."

Amelia shook her head. "Let me repeat… a killer is stalking you. All of us. He's why we need to move."

"Normy," said Mason, "don't you want to go get the bad guys, shoot 'em all up and the horses they rode in on?"

"What does that mean about the horses?"

"It means we get even with every last one of them. It's a common expression."

Amelia looked at Mason doubtfully.

Normy said, "Not in Queens, it's not."

"Normy," asked Amelia, "did you happen to buy a car?"

*

They left the apartment and drove Normy's metallic blue, five-year-old Fiesta east, away from Mont-Royal. They made two stops, one to a Radio Shack to buy a cellular modem for the laptop and the other to fill up the gas tank and buy coffees and more plastic gas station food. Mason set Normy's laptop back to WI-FI and scanned the Internet for news about CERN.

Amelia said to Normy, "Border crossings are out for us. We'll take our chances on the terrorist highway."

Mason plugged the cellular modem into the laptop's USB port, and, after he initiated the account, they were online. They followed the GPS map route to twenty miles south of Saint Stephen in New Brunswick, where a remote railway bridge crossed the St. Croix River. Three hours after dark, they abandoned Normy's car, Amelia slung the pack over her shoulder, and they walked out of the forest toward the river and the unguarded railway bridge. Fifteen minutes later, on the bridge, Mason tossed the laptop into the river. They were back in the United States.

Mason asked Amelia, "What about drones and infra-red heat sensors?"

"We're temporary blips on a screen, disappearing into a population of over three hundred million. By the time they dispatch someone to track us down, if they can even wake anyone up and make them look for us, we'll just be people in a car in America."

Amelia drove them through the night. Normy said, "So, we steal cars too?"

Mason said, "Technically, we bought this dated Civic from an outdoor lot…"

"Someone's driveway."

"… driveway, and we left $11,000 in a paper bag on the front doorstep, grossly over-compensating the previous owner."

"That still gets us charged, technically, with grand theft auto."

Amelia flashed her eyes in the rearview mirror and kept driving.

In Bangor, Amelia excused herself while Normy and Mason sipped a beer in a honky-tonk. She caused a sensation when she came back into the bar, so they left immediately, and this time took a silver family sedan. Like one of the millions of silver salmon schooling to get upstream in the fall, it would be impossible for a cop to isolate their van at night on New England's highways.

Even at that late hour, Boston traffic escalated around them. Normy slept in the back seat as they bypassed Boston, stopping at a truck stop on Hwy 95, bought take away coffees, refilled the gas tank, then continued straight through to New York City. When the glow from the skyline appeared on their horizon, Amelia said, "I hope our idea works, or we'll be in a world of shit."

Normy piped up from the back seat. "Are you ever going to tell me what's going on?"

"How 'bout some pizza?"

"Dumb idea."

Mason caught Amelia watching him, so she offered him the money bag and the vial of Mr. Feel Good. Mason shook his head but rolled a meaningful glance over his shoulder. Amelia began distracting Normy by reminiscing about their days at university.

29. Family Business

When it was apparent their destination was Queens, Normy became alarmed. "Are you shittin' me? Let me out!"

"We need to talk with Matteo."

"Oh no. Don't take me there. The moment he knows we're short, he'll hack me to death with an ice pick. I owe them $800,000. Amelia..."

"Coincidentally, we all do. We're taking Matty a deal he can't refuse. We're almost family; he'll meet with me." Unconvinced, Normy tried to open the sliding door—he was going to jump. "Damnit. Get his arm."

Mason wrestled Normy's fleshy arm into the front seat. She jabbed his hand with the needle while somehow managing to keep the van on the road. Normy fought back until the wonder drug kicked in, then he sagged back in the rear seat, sighing. "Not the drugs again..." Normy's voice was airy, even whimsical. His eyes turned from terrified to glassy when he slipped sideways to lay down on the bench seat.

"Music helps." Mason turned the car stereo to a soft rock station. "Believe me, Normy," he said, "if there was any other way..."

Amelia said, "I can get us inside, Normy, but you're our ticket out if we can make all the pieces fit."

Mason sighed, took her hand in his, looked at her, and said, "That sounds pretty crazy, but whatever happens, you and me."

Deeply worried, Amelia looked back at Mason. "You and me."

*

They parked illegally on Grand Avenue and left the keys in the ignition. "Hopefully," said Amelia, "someone will steal it."

They walked three blocks to a pizza joint on Mulberry Street, close to the Ravenite. The restaurant's neon *OPEN* sign still glowed red, white, and blue in the street window, which felt to Mason more of a sinister warning than an invitation. He looked at Amelia. "Ready?"

She nodded.

Normy, still high as a kite, had become the group's optimist. "Oh boy. Pizza."

They turned into a narrow, poorly lit, rusty red brick-lined passage between the restaurant and ancient brownstone. Halfway down the gauntlet, a mountain of a man stepped out of a receded doorway below a single overhead bulb. He stopped them with a giant hand; the other he kept tucked inside his New York Giants jacket. "*No permesso.*"

Mason, unfamiliar with Italian, easily translated that warning into "family only."

Amelia said, "*Mi scusi. Il mio italiano è orribile. Parla Inglese?*" She looked at the camera over the door. "Matty, I need to talk. Alacrán and I both ask for this favour."

Seconds later, the muscle and bone mountain received a text, read it, stepped aside, and held the door open. It wasn't an invitation. The giant followed them inside, closing the door on the trap.

Amelia led them through the brightly lit kitchen. Trilling accordion music played in the background. Mason glanced back and saw the goon escorting them had suffered from childhood chickenpox. Since then, he appeared to have survived on slabs of hot fat, white-bread mayonnaise sandwiches, and whiskey chasers. Mason smiled; stoic, the man hurried him forward.

A bouquet of pungent fresh parmesan cheese, garlic, and pepperoni filled the air. The thin, olive-skinned cook still made pies in the stifling heat but ignored them as if they were ghosts. Mason nudged Normy, distracted by the aromas, to keep him moving. Their escort herded them through swinging doors at the back of the poorly-lit restaurant. They walked to a secluded banquet table covered with a red and white checkered tablecloth. Two stocky, iron-hard, double-tough Sicilian hitmen, zips, stood behind the angry man seated in the single cone of light

Matteo Indurito was a huge man in his seventies who filled a baggy, dark suit jacket over a white T-shirt. His clean-shaven face was pasty, but his eyes glistened like wet black coal under intense, bushy black eyebrows. He still had an impressive mop of black hair greased straight back from his receding hairline and deeply creased forehead. Heavy smoke curled upwards from the cigar he held in the crooked fingers of a meaty hand. A single glass of red wine, a handgun, and a cellphone was on the table in front of him. At his side, a monitor displayed the live CCTV shot of the alley entrance to the restaurant. One of the intimidating zips moved without orders to stand behind Normy, and he remained there.

The mafia capo motioned for his three visitors to take seats. When Amelia tried to lift the moneybag to place it on the table, their escort grabbed her arm and held it. She looked at the thug, then at his stone-faced boss, and then dropped the bag. Matteo Indurito nodded at the thug, so he released Amelia's arm. She clasped both her hands in front of her at her waist and said, "Matteo, thank you for seeing us. It is good to see you again. I hope all is well with your family."

Mason thought her voice impressively formal.

Matteo's eyes never left her face, reading her for any hint of betrayal.

Amelia continued, "It's our obligation to return what is yours to you." She nodded toward the bag.

"Georgio…" Indurito's voice was a raspy huff from his barrel chest. The alley thug, Georgio, took the bag to the opposite end of the table and unzipped it to count the cash. The chef delivered two pies, placing them in front of Matteo, and then bent to speak in quiet Italian tones with solemn deference. Matteo nodded and said, "Thank you for your work. Lock up on your way out."

"It is always at your pleasure, Don Matteo," said the chef. He left the table to secure the front door and then extinguish the lights behind the bar.

Matty growled, "And turn that shit off."

The cook ejected the DVD, ending the background music.

Georgio continued counting. Don Matteo was silent, watching the chef hurry down the outside alley on the video screen. The intimidating Mafia capo looked at Amelia and broke the silence, "I know you and him," he nodded at Normy, then looked toward Mason, "but who is dis?" Mason shivered involuntarily; Matteo's attention felt like the pronouncement of a death sentence.

"This is my friend, Mason. I vouch for him."

Matteo Indurito's stare lowered the full weight of a century of New York *Omertà* on Mason when he said, "He looks tired."

"We've been travelling. Don Matteo," her voice was confident but not aggressive, "we're short. We have a way to make it up to you—today. Will you listen?"

His husky whisper was deliberate. "You were never family to me. I have daughters. I don't need another. Double for the pain you caused me." He nodded at Normy. "And the courier is mine."

"Please, Don Matteo, our families have a long history. Normy leaves with us—alive and unharmed." Matteo bore down his stare at Amelia's counter offer. She changed from bargaining to imploring. "This man and I, and my friend, can hand you any amount of bond certificates you want from Meister-Fleisher-Fuchs. As you know, these bonds are untraceable and instantly negotiable anywhere along Wall Street."

Matteo weighed Amelia's words. Finally, he said, "How much?"

A hint of relief in her voice, Amelia said, "Street value? Tens of millions to a powerful man like you."

Normy was out of it—his navel totally engaged his attention. Mason nudged him with his elbow. He giggled at Mason, "What?"

Matty nodded at Normy, then asked Amelia, "What's wid him?"

"I hit him with some fancy G-Man stuff."

Matteo reached down beside his chair and retrieved a portable butane burner. "We use dis."

"Normy," said Amelia quickly, "how many dollars worth of negotiable and untraceable bond certificates are at Meister-Fleisher-Fuchs?"

"Millions—billions."

"Can you take us?"

"Sure. It's in the vaults."

Matty locked his eyes on Amelia's. He took a slice of pizza. "Sit. Eat. Tell me more." Matty poured glasses of fine Italian red.

Giorgio said, "They're a hunnert eighty short."

"You eat, too." Giorgio's face lit up. He took two slices of pizza and sat beside the Sicilian *zips* at the table. Amelia laid out the plan while they ate. When she finished, she looked at Matteo and said, "Are we on?"

"Your father told me you would pay me a visit. You're smart, Amelia. What is it you really want?"

"All I ask is we three walk out of that bank free of our

obligation to you."

Amelia looked at Matteo, and then she looked at Mason. He looked at Normy and then at Matteo. Everyone smiled at each other. Giorgio reached for the last slice of pizza.

"We'll take my cars." Matteo looked at Normy. "He comes with me."

Mason said, "Don Matteo, with your permission, I need to step out for a minute."

"Giorgio, you take him. Amelia, you and the space pilot stay here."

When Mason used the facilities, he heard murmuring in the restaurant but not specifics.

*

At 9:10 a.m., Matty's zip stopped and parked the black limousine in front of the Meister-Fleisher-Fuchs tower. First Mason, then Amelia, got out from the back seat. The zip drove their car away as Mason scanned the height of the intimidating building. "It's all too easy," he said. Amelia's cautioning eyes fell on him, and her lips tightened. But just then, Normy, Giorgio, and Matty pulled up in the black Lincoln Town Car.

"We're on," said Amelia.

When Georgio held the door open, Normy exited first. Mafia protocol dictated the highest ranked members in the entourage appear last. Everyone followed Matty inside. Matty walked through the security guards, speaking briefly and quietly with their captain. He nodded and guided the entourage around the security portal, across the foyer, and over to the public elevators.

Mason shared a wry smile with Amelia.

Normy, swaying slightly in front of the private elevator that went straight up to the CEO offices, walked up to stand beside Matty. The captain used his own card to call the elevator. Matty took the guard's card from him after he swiped it. "I will return dis in twenty minutes."

"Of course, Don Matteo."

After the doors closed and they had crowded inside the elevator, Matty pressed the down button twice, paused, then pushed it three more times. "Hey," said Normy, playfully, "I was gonna do that." Elevator music played while dings signified they were descending closer to their destination—the subterranean depths of the murky world of Wall Street and government finances.

When the doors opened, they stepped out to a foyer that was not much more than a linoleum-surfaced, gated tunnel entrance. Two grim, armed guards blocked their progress, shotguns crossed on their arms. The first guard, an olive-skinned man, shouldered his shotgun and said, "Mr. Indurito. I'm honoured." Matteo swayed his head to acknowledge the respect. The other guard, a stern black man in his forties, said nothing but walked toward the massive, circular Meister-Fleisher-Fuchs entrance, his weapon also shouldered.

The primary door resembled a massive safe. Open wide, it revealed a floor-to-ceiling set of two-inch-thick, gleaming, carbonite steel bars. The second guard thumb-printed a screen on the wall and said, "Will you need a cart today, Mr. Indurito?" Motors hummed, and the steel bars slowly retracted into the floor and ceiling.

Again, Amelia and Mason looked at each other.

Matty, a man renowned for murder, racketeering and extortion, said politely, "Do you have a bag?"

The guard hastily produced the leather bag for his honoured guest. Matty indicated Georgio should carry the satchel.

Mason and Amelia followed Matty and Georgio into the tunnel linking the Federal Reserve Bank of New York and the adjacent investment bank beneath Liberty Street. *This,* thought Mason, *is the tunnel my lunatic fringe listeners call "the Holy Trail of gold conspiracies."* Each step they took disproved the official denial of its existence. It felt dangerous to Mason when a stern man in uniform observed them from a cell protected behind thick bars and bullet-proof glass at the far end of the tunnel. When they were closer, the guard's face formed a smile of recognition. He said, "Please, come on in."

The guard inside the cage swiped his card and then, with his gun drawn and pointed through the window at Normy, hurried across the room to place his thumbprint on the wall-mounted scanner. This procedure was unlikely to prevent someone from surprising the guard, killing him, swiping his card, and then using the guard's severed thumb for the fingerprint confirmation. The added precaution of implementing facial recognition software would certainly record any thief in the act and put the cage in lockdown. But this guard's theatre was for the benefit of the cameras and anyone interested in viewing the security film—they would see the guard acted as dictated by their stringent security protocols. In general, these precautions were highly effective. However, Matty Indurito stuffed pockets with cash, so all doors opened wide for him. Even if a guard resisted corruption, Matty's infamous historical savagery was likely convincing enough to persuade all opposition to seriously consider the offer of "the silver or the lead."

More motors hummed. The heavy steel barrier bolts slid open until they clanged in the receded position, allowing the massive door to swing wide. The guard smiled wanly and asked, "Will you folks need any assistance today?"

Normy said, "We have a bag."

"What room will it be then?"

"The usual; vault 167, please."

The guard returned to his computer console and clicked his mouse. Farther along the 200-foot hallway, there was a loud bang, and a steel door scraped open. "Georgio," said Matteo, "you wait here."

They passed a series of cells on either side of the hall and a bank of elevators on their left. Some doors were solid with a small wire mesh window; others, like jail cell doors, had bars. Mason looked inside each cell and was disappointed to see so few gold bars. Most of the rooms were full of empty pallets and shelves. Mason whispered in Amelia's ear, "It's not at Fort Knox, and it's not here, so where's all the gold?"

She whispered back, "I don't know, south pole, bloody battlefields, China, Space Force…"

Walking through the pocket door to vault 167, he said, "You're kidding, right?"

There was no gold in the room, but there were filing cabinets. Matteo walked over to the first cabinet. Normy said, "Not that one—here." Normy opened the top drawer of another cabinet. It was chock full of bearer bonds. Normy said, "Each sheet is worth $100,000. These all belong to NEWCorp."

Mason could have been knocked over with a feather. He stuffed the leather bag with $50 million worth of untraceable Wall Street certificates, leaving tens of millions more untraceable, untaxable bonds in each of the dozens of folders. Matteo inspected one of the bonds and then held it up to Amelia. He smiled and said, "Family."

Unexpectedly, Giorgio appeared at the cell door.

Amelia pulled a cellphone out of her pocket, dialling the same number that Hawke answered when he was alive.

Victor answered. "Yes?"

"We're in your vault. Because of NEWCorp, we owe a friend some money, so you're paying." Victor raged, "You listen here..." Amelia cut him off. "You can consider this fifty million dollar withdrawal our fee."

"You don't have a clue who you're dealing with or what he's capable of..."

"We want to meet your boss—today. We're coming for him."

"I doubt that."

Too late, Amelia spun around and froze when she saw Giorgio held a weapon pointed at Mason. Matteo turned his gun on Amelia. Mason tried to rush Matteo, but Giorgio stepped forward, clubbing him on the head. As he went down, Mason heard three shots fired. Amelia screamed once but was dead before she hit the floor. Blacking out, Mason heard Matteo say, "Now we're even. Georgio, bring them."

*

Mason struggled against his nausea and darkness. His vision was blurry; at first, he could not understand the red and white of the tablecloth. His head pounded. He squeezed his eyes tight shut to fight his nausea. When he opened them again, he knew he was slumped over the table in Matty's restaurant. Normy sat across the table. When Normy reached out for Mason, the zip standing resolute behind him stopped Normy, forcing him to sit back in his chair. Matteo waited patiently, seated and smoking a fresh cigar at the head of the table. Giorgio sat down beside Mason and propped him up by holding his arm. The third Sicilian thug, his eyes intense slits, scrutinized Mason from behind Matteo.

"If you're wonderin' why she's dead, it's because NEWCorp pays well," said Matteo. "Three million cash bounty, and we deal strictly in cash." The guard behind Matty shifted his hand across his waist, flashing his gun. "Besides, she had to pay for stealing from me. We knew it wasn't the space pilot who set us up. Now you and him," Matty nodded toward

Normy but kept his eyes on Mason, "are nothing to us." He looked at Normy. "She cleared your debt." He looked back at Mason. "You made that happen, so you're free to go."

"You fuckin' animal," growled Mason. Giorgio punched Mason hard on the side of his mouth. The massive blow blacked Mason out again.

*

When Mason regained consciousness, Matteo said, "Amelia lived by the gun, ever since I knew her. When she and you… she chose the wrong guy, that's all."

"Is that Mafia dating advice?"

"Boss," Giorgio's face flared red, "lemme shut him up for good. He's trouble."

"Not yet. Mason, that's your name, right? Think about this… we can disappear you two right now—and it's over. Or you can go live your life. You make the choice, but you make it for both of you. It makes no difference to me either way. You get one chance. What'll it be?"

"She said you were family."

"You forget all this. You don't fit in here."

Mason looked at Normy's pleading eyes. Matteo, a bonafide killer, had forced that decision on Mason. "Where's her body?"

"She's gone." Matteo threw a stack of bills on the table. "We see you again; we put you both with the fishes."

Norm picked up the cash, wrapped Mason's arm over his shoulders. "Come on, buddy," Norm said, "there's nothing for us here." Norm helped Mason up, and together they escaped from the mafia's jaws.

30. The Safest Place In New York City

Norm and Mason stumbled back into an overcast morning on bustling Mulberry Street.

"I can't... my head..."

"Yes, you can. We can make it." Norm grimaced at the oozing lump on Mason's head. "In the real world, I'd take you to a hospital, but we can't take the chance. I know a place. It's safe. C'mon, the van's not far if it's still there."

"They'll find us."

"Not where I'm taking you."

Norm looked back through the crowd and saw that the two zips followed them, maintaining a half-a-block separation. Mason blacked in and out, vomiting once. Their struggle was a trial of desperate but wasted effort—the van was gone. Norm hailed a taxi. The cabbie slowed, looked at them, then sped off. "Try to stand straighter." When the second taxi stopped, the older driver warned them through the open passenger window, "I don't take no gunshot guys anymore. What's up with him?"

"Headache."

In a bored monotone, the cabbie said, "It's an extra fifty if he pukes. Show me the money." Normy pulled the wad of cash out of his pocket and waved it at the cabbie. "That'll do. Get in."

Mason, his eyelids like granulated cement, said, "You go. Save yourself; leave me at a hotel."

Norm looked through the side window of the taxi at the zips. They stood on the adjacent curb, apparently satisfied Norm and Mason had understood Matty's message. "That's crazy—they'd get to you before the weekend." Norm was right; they were still hot as hell in the US and especially in New York.

The cabbie was impatient, "What'll it be, guys? I gotta make a livin' here."

Before Mason blacked out, Normy said, "Take us to the Village."

*

Norm shook Mason gently when their cab jerked to a stop in front of a pawnshop displaying a yellowing "Discount Handguns" sign in the barred window. The storefronts on this block laid a peculiar tourist trap. The neighbourhood store displays touted everything from tall, bulbous hookahs to

198

designer perfume, used musical equipment, advertised on-site tattooing, frilly women's lingerie, second-hand book, and sex toy shops.

The driver said, "You're sure about this?"

Norm paid the driver, handing him an extra hundred. "You dropped us in Jersey, right?"

The cabbie said, "You wouldn't believe how many half-dead guys I take there."

Norm walked Mason a block further down Fourth Street, wrestling him up the creaking back stairs to the second floor of a dilapidated tenement building. He knocked frantically, peeling red paint chips off the door with his knuckles.

Deadbolts rattled. A thin, bald man answered, wearing a loose, silky ebony and scarlet Japanese dragon robe. He wore heavy, black eyeliner and long black eyelashes, which accented his eyes when his plucked eyebrows lifted into exaggerated surprise. His mouth turned down in a silent accusation, then he smiled doubtfully. He called over his bare shoulders, "Terry, look, Normy's here, who we haven't seen for ages, and he has an almost-dead man with him."

Terry called out, "If he's not all dead, they can both come in." Both men giggled.

Norm said, "Thanks, Malcolm. Hi, Terry. I have nowhere else to go. My mother would kill me if I brought my friend to her house in this condition. Does Terry still work at the hospital?"

Terry, also thin, drifted into the room like a diva in scarlet, coiffed wig, long bangles for earrings, gold necklaces, sparkling lime eye shadow, and Chantilly lace. "Six years." He showed genuine concern for Mason. "I hope your mom is doing better than this one. I haven't seen her in ages…God, is this one still breathing?"

Malcolm said, "Like that ever stopped you before."

"You're scandalizing me. Don't set him down yet. Get a blanket." Malcolm rushed to bring a blanket to the couch. "Oh God, he's cute. Thank you, Normy."

Norm said, "He needs to rest."

Terry said, "Malcolm, get a cold cloth." Terry spread out the blanket. "Put him on the couch." Together, they struggled to lay Mason down without jarring him.

Malcolm returned from the bathroom and gently placed the soft cloth on Mason's brow. Terry said, "Take off his shoes. Unbutton his shirt; he needs to breathe."

Malcolm said, "We should take off his pants."

Norm asked, "How would that help him?"

Terry said, "Malcolm, you're such a whore. This beautiful man needs our help, not our affection, not yet anyway."

"I'll get a pillow. The poor thing."

Seconds later, Mason watched a fuzzy frame of three worried faces looking down at him fade to black.

*

Over the first days, Norm had to help Mason off the couch to the bathroom and back. Waves of pain rolled up from behind Mason's eyes, circling and tightening around his scalp like a rope garrote. "Man," he said, "Giorgio laid a number on me." The lump on the back of his head oozed blood for two days, but the swelling gradually subsided.

Terry and Malcolm constantly nattered at each other over nursing Mason. Still, they changed his cold cloth, cleaned his vomit off the floor, made him chicken soup, and fed it to him if he drifted back into the world. Norm had parked himself in the chair opposite the couch. There was nowhere else for him to go.

Over the next days, Mason recovered from his severe concussion. He saved his tears for the bathroom, unable to accept Amelia's murder. He heard her first words, again and again, remembering her kisses, their lovemaking, her eyes closing after Indurito shot her. Mason wore it all. "We thought we were doing something to try to change the world," he said to Norm, adding the brutal, self-evident truth, "but I couldn't protect her."

*

At a private table in the plush dining room of an exclusive Florida golf club, the most powerful man in the world watched the young waitress place cocktails in front of several senior members of his entourage. The president answered a cellphone call. "I'm golfing today. Why are you calling me?"

The man phoning the president fidgeted with his Skull and Crossbones ring. He spoke loudly, so the president held the phone an inch from his ear. "What? I'm returning your call."

Both sides of the conversation were clearly audible to everyone at the table. "I'm offering you the same deal we agreed to last month. Why are you changing the agreement now?"

"I need more jam on my bread," said the president. "And what about my daughter? What does she get out of this deal?"

There was a lengthy silence from the caller, during which time the server waited to be paid. The president smiled weakly at several eavesdropping foreign patrons at nearby tables, then looked across the table at his guests. "This one's on one of you, isn't it? I'll be another minute with this joker."

From the cellphone came Dealci's acidic reply, "I can hear you. I will call you back at a less delicate time."

The president looked at his phone and said, "Hm." He put it back in his pocket without actually ending the call. "Now, what are we going to do about those damn illegals crawling over our borders?"

*

On July 3, days after Mason's life changed again in the tunnels, he and Norm turned to CSPAN to watch the Senate vote. They passed the NEWCorp contract into law, seventeen Democrats voted with the President, but he was stalling. The Senate had been called back in for a highly irregular summer session and, to a person, appeared silently furious with the tactic. To avoid a filibuster, the Republican Senate had even invoked cloture, formally driving the same bill at the same time through to the President's desk. But he was going it alone, again, by insisting on a more significant personal cut of the proceeds, so the goalposts for the deal had moved substantially.

"The president balked at signing the Nuclear Waste Bill into law," editorialized a journalist on Al Jazeera's channel, "because there was no quid pro quo for him. I remind you all the senate pushed to legalize 'special interest' income for elected officials after they refused to impeach the president."

On GNN, the talking head cut to a national broadcast, catching the president in another of his chopper talks. "Today," his voice resonating in a strained and unseemly tenor, "my lawyers will go over the contract fine print one last time. Tomorrow is… uh, tomorrow is the fourth, right?" he asked a nearby aide. The aide nodded. "Right, so tomorrow, if everything looks really good, I'm going to make the best history, perfect history, like no other president, better than any of them…"

Both Mason and Norm suffered another moment of deep bitterness. NEWCorp won—and it won big.

*

Mason sat at the kitchen table on the evening of the last day. He was using the laptop and downloading songs. Sipping a glass of wine, he selected every Roy Orbison song, filling the apartment with his magnificent, tortured voice. Malcolm and Terry ran out of their bedroom. Norm woke up in the living room chair. Mason cried at the console, his head down and his heart broken. Norm went to him, put his arm around his friend, and said, "She was so fucking awesome." Malcolm and Terry joined their hug, all of them crying to Roy Orbison and their own fallibility.

When the song ended, Mason looked at Terry's makeup running down his face and said, "Christ, you look like Tammy Fay Baker during a pledge drive." Their laughing softened the grief. Mere weeks ago, Mason would have thought himself insane if he saw his future framed and wanted for murder, hiding out in the Village, hugging two gay guys and a deposed Wall Street broker, crying with a broken heart after watching a Mafia capo murder his soulmate.

That was the last time Mason went into the bathroom to cry. "No more," he vowed in the mirror. He had lost Amelia. That was a fact. The heart-wrenching emptiness inside would last forever, but he was replacing sorrow with anger. The empowering rage grew with more clarity and purpose every hour until his thoughts and emotions had merged completely. "Amelia taught me that survival is the art of adaptation," he told Norm. "So if I'm going to be hunted down as a killer, then it's time I earned the reputation."

*

On the last morning, Mason woke without a headache but was weak and drained. He outlasted the dizziness when he sat up and waved Norm off, rising to his feet without help. Mason made it to the bathroom and showered until the hot water ran out. He lingered under the cold stream until his mind cleared.

When he stepped out of the shower, the vanity mirror confirmed that it was misnamed in Mason's case. "An Adonis," he said sarcastically and aloud. His eyes were dark and hollow;

he was thin and had grown a dirty beard. He borrowed a pink plastic razor left on the sink and began methodically cleaning himself up. When Mason returned to the kitchen, Norm silently motioned at him to sit down. Norm placed a trucker's breakfast he had prepared for Mason in front of him. Mason gulped down the mug of percolated coffee.

Mason ravenously inhaled the aromas, but he waited to see if he would experience more nausea. When none came, Mason asked, "Is all this for me?" Norm nodded, and Mason ate like a starving wolf. Their hosts had left their drug paraphernalia on the kitchen table, having indulged the previous night in Columbia's popular export product. Norm refilled Mason's coffee mug. "There's no cream or milk. Malcolm and Terry... Of all the things they do to their bodies, they can't handle dairy."

"Where are they?"

"They don't get up 'til two."

Mason lifted a curly red Jill St. John wig and a black bra off the other chair. Norm shrugged his shoulders with a smile. Mason chased the meal with the painkillers Norm placed on the table after pouring Mason a third coffee.

Norm said, "We can't do anything about Matteo." He crossed his arms over his chest, looking out the small, grimy window over the kitchen sink. When he turned back, he said, "Damn it. Why are you going to make us do this?"

"It doesn't have to be *us*."

"*How* are we going to do this?"

"Get me inside one more time."

"Matty, the cops, probably that Jairo guy, they'll all be waiting."

Mason looked at the powdery mirror on the table. "How much money do we have?"

*

Norm had kicked Malcolm and Terry eleven hundred dollars for putting them up and keeping quiet about it. That left them with a few hundred dollars in their bankroll. This was New York City, so, with Norm's ID and the last of their cash, they bought a handgun and ammunition from a pawn shop and then another burner phone.

"Being off the grid for a while works in our favour," said Mason, at the digital café, where they had espressos and rented time on a terminal. An hour later, they were back at the apartment to strategize. At noon, Mason knocked on the bedroom door to wake their hosts.

Malcolm said, from their bed, "You want to know something, Mr. Writer?"

"What's that?"

"When you go butch, I can see why Amelia had the hots for you."

Terry agreed. "Um-hm. Do let us know if there is any little thing we can do for you."

"Fellas, there is something..."

*

By 2:00 p.m., the boys had Mason pimped out like he was RuPaul's Vegas dream date. They thanked Malcolm and Terry for their hospitality and left their apartment forever.

31. **Wizards Behind Curtains**

Mason and Norm exited the cab at the car park entrance to the Meister-Fleisher-Fuchs building. Inside, the same unsmiling attendant sat in the booth.

"Smile for the camera, Norm," said Mason.

Seconds after Norm looked up, the door locks snapped open, and they walked into the small foyer. The guard glanced at them once but briefly. The metal door closed behind them. The elevator door was open. Jairo stood inside, holding a gun on them.

When the elevator door closed behind Norm and Mason, Jairo said, "Turn around, spread your legs, hands against the wall." Norm was clean. When Jairo found Mason's gun and cellphone, he tucked them both in his pocket. Jairo tore off Mason's wig and threw it on the elevator floor. "You thought you were going to fool us with this?"

"I thought I took care of you in Inkai."

"We own Inkai—all of it and everyone."

"Matvey might have something to say about that."

"Especially the dirty cops."

Mason swung at Jairo, but he quickly sidestepped the attack and smashed Mason in the jaw, driving him to the floor with a vicious elbow to the back of his neck. "I should end this right now," said Jairo, "but someone wants to meet you."

Norm helped Mason to his feet while the elevator rocketed upward. When they decelerated to an imperceptible stop at the seventieth floor, a bell chimed, and the doors opened. Jairo kept Norm and Mason at gunpoint, herding them through the deserted reception area and the security doors to the CEO's office's lavish furnishings.

A fragile, rather disappointing man gazed out the tall windows at the western Manhattan skyline. Without turning to look at them, the man said, "Mason Stone. I'm glad to finally meet you."

"That makes one of us."

The man's slightly bent frame was a silhouette against the glare of the sun. Silently, Jairo forced Mason and Norm to sit on the leather couch opposite the oversized desk. Mason folded his arms across his chest as Jairo moved closer.

"It was unfortunate about Amelia." Mason stiffened at

the mention of her name. The man at the window still had his back to the room. "But it was her decision to meddle in our affairs, and, unfortunately, it ended badly." He turned to face Mason, recoiling at him in drag.

Mason said, "Not your colour?"

The man standing before Mason was past his prime, balding and prematurely grey. There was a vestige of vigour, but the dark shadows under sunken eyes and the liver spots on his face underscored his obvious physical decline.

"I'll remind you, that gun Jairo has levelled at the back of your head never fails to hit the mark. I think it's time for introductions. I am United States Senator Victor, incumbent..."

"Do you even recall what state you represent?"

Victor lashed out at Mason. "I could have Jairo kill you with a single snap of my fingers. Or," he said more calmly, "would you rather survive?"

"Come on, I know you don't call the shots; you're a mop-and-pail flunky for NEWCorp but, go ahead, enjoy your fantasy."

Victor walked to the front of his desk, closer to the captives, leaned against it and looked at Mason with a curious stare. "Why are you here? To kill me and Jairo because Amelia is dead?"

"If that's a two-for-one offer, I'm in." Norm nodded as if considering the deal.

Behind Victor, a white light on the desk phone blinked, signalling an incoming call, but Victor failed to notice it. Instead, he glared at Mason, tapped his fingertips together, and processed Mason's insolence. "Mr. Indurito returned our bonds to us. The $3,000,000 bounty we placed on you and Amelia satisfied him."

"If Matty Indurito does your dirty work for you, then why would you hire lame-ass killers like Jairo?"

Jairo jabbed the gun muzzle hard into the back of Mason's neck. "Careful," he said.

"You're still angry about your interview in Inkai." Victor paused thoughtfully. "Mr. Stone, the world no longer cares about the afflictions of little men. Corporations have seized the day. People forget—the world forgets. No one cares today that we took Amelia's life yesterday or that Jairo murdered Daniels and his manager weeks ago."

"That last bit… it was Delaci who called that."

Victor paused for effect. "Do you think even the machinations of the Rockefellers and JP Morgans compare against NEWCorp's achievements?"

"Nice speech, Senator. How'd that one play to your constituents?"

"Tasteless sarcasm, Mr. Stone?"

"You've inspired me."

"Our base will always give us their loyalty. That's all they need, and they thrive on it. It's ours to use as we see fit… even to our personal advantage."

The white light on the phone stopped blinking; the caller had disconnected.

"A proposition… If you flush Alacrán out for us…"

"He was almost my father-in-law."

"Jairo, place your gun to Mr. Garfinkle's head. Kill him on my count of three." Jairo pointed the gun at Norm, whose eyes bulged in panic. "One… two…"

"Wait… Jairo! Wait. Don't shoot. I'll do it." Victor waved Jairo off Norm. Mason said, "You're sick, Victor. Do you know that?"

Jairo jabbed Mason in the neck again with his gun and said, "That's not nice."

Victor said, "You're in awe of power and control." Mason scoffed. Victor said, "You think we want you dead because your friend knew about Inkai."

"You couldn't turn Ivan, so you killed him."

"He died because he threatened our project. You see? We'll have the uranium…" Jairo dug the muzzle of his gun harder into Mason's neck. The light on the desk phone began blinking again. "We encourage fracking in all our member countries," said Victor, gloating. "Even our Americans accept it. All we have to do is pull 'socialist' triggers in the media, and the people come running to us like dogs. Mr. Stone, do I amuse you?"

Mason smiled, despite knowing the more this man told them, the greater the odds stacked against them leaving the office alive.

"How amused will you be when the LA Project is in place? We will control…"

Jairo's cellphone buzzed in his coat pocket. Victor

looked at Jairo, who looked at the caller's text. "It's Delaci."

Mason's eyes shot to the phone, then returned to Victor, staring into the eyes of the real lunatic fringe. "What I know is," said Mason, "that NEWCorp murders people, it's polluting drinking water to mine uranium, and your monkey has a gun pointed at my head."

"Then you know nothing." Jairo nodded at the blinking light on the desk. His insistence irritated Victor, but he picked up the handset anyway.

"Before you answer that call," said Mason, "I have something for you. Call your dog off me." Victor was intrigued. Mason looked sideways at Jairo, who watched him closely after turning his gun on Norm. Mason slowly unbuttoned his blouse, exposing the cellphone taped to his chest. He put the cellphone on speaker. "The decoy phone worked. Did you get all that?"

"Listen to the quality of the playback," said IBM. The men in the plush office high above Wall Street clearly heard Victor confess to Ivan's murder. IBM said, "I'm streaming it to the NEWCorp boardroom. Anything happens to you or Norm, and I'll send it all to cable TV."

Jairo tore the phone from Mason's chest, removed the SIM card, dropped both pieces, and stomped his heel several times to grind them into the carpet.

Victor raged at Jairo. "You absolute incompetent." Victor looked at the handset, lifted it to his ear, his face a portrait of dread.

Jairo, his gun pointed between Mason's eyes, said, "I've been waiting for this."

Victor snapped his fingers at Jairo and put the phone on speaker.

Delaci's sinister voice said, "Bravo, Mr. Stone. I'm inviting you to meet me in Washington. I make this offer once—negotiate with me, or Jairo helps you leap off the top of your building."

"Why should we trust you?"

"You have something I want."

*

Minutes later, on the roof, Jairo handcuffed Norm and Mason, duct-taped their mouths and blindfolded them, and then forced them through the wall of rotor wash into the helicopter where Mason wondered, *Was it enough?*

32. **Freedom Plaza**

Strong hands shoved Mason out of the helicopter when they landed, then held him by his collar. The noise and the downdraft subsided when the helicopter lifted off. Their steps crunched across roof gravel; a rush of wind made Mason wonder if he was about to be thrown off the roof, but then they entered a quiet room. He bounced when he stopped walking, so Mason knew they were in an elevator. No one spoke a word.

When the doors opened, someone jerked on Mason's arm, so he started walking again. Footsteps echoed in the corridor until a door opened, and he was shoved from behind. Mason collided with another falling body, and they tumbled over each other into a heap on the floor. A blade slipped under the duct tape over Mason's mouth, cutting his gag. The cold steel then slipped under his blindfold and cut it off his face. He blinked at the blinding fluorescent lights in the windowless room.

Norm was lying on his belly on the floor, similarly bound and gagged. Jairo knelt on Mason, one knee in the center of his back, and then he grabbed a fist full of Mason's hair, slipping his long blade around the front of his throat, the razor edge lingering in his flesh. But then a minimal tweak of the razor-sharp blade sliced his zip-tie handcuffs.

"Get changed. Three minutes. Don't bother yelling for help. The day staff are gone, and the night cleaning staff are not due in for three hours."

Mason pulled the last of the tape from his mouth, finally able to breathe a deep gulp. He said, "The mafia don't make killing personal—why do you?"

"I enjoy my job." Jairo cut Norm's bindings in quick movements, then instructed the guards at the door, "If they make trouble, do what you have to, but don't kill them." Jairo closed the door, leaving Norm and Mason alone in the room.

Mason helped Norm remove his gag and cuffs, then hurried to change out of the dress, borrowing a set of coveralls from a locker. Mason washed his face at the sink. "I never thought we'd survive New York," said Mason to a surprised Norm, "much less get past streaming the confession to IBM. From here on, it's uncharted territory."

"Yeah, way to look ahead, partner," said Norm.

Jairo returned with armed guards and signalled to Mason and Norm to follow him. They marched along a lengthy, deserted service hallway into a luxurious reception area, stopping before tall, solid mahogany double doors. Guards inside the room swung the doors open. Jairo shoved Mason and Norm forward at gunpoint, halting them in front of the polished mahogany table. Four dour, silent men flanked the vacant throne chair at the centre of the table. Victor was the fifth man sitting at the table, although he occupied a chair at one end. The centrepiece was a carved miniature of the world, and beside it was a miniature gavel. The men in the room were silent, waiting for Delaci's entrance. The natural light from the window drew Mason's attention. He saw, a mile in the distance, the sunlight reflecting off the Congress Dome.

Delaci strode into the room from a side door. He drew Mason's attention back to the room, which became electric with tension. Delaci stood still for a brief instance, looming over the miniatures in front of his place at the table, then took the empty chair, adjusting the crease in his pants before cupping the globe, leaving his hand to linger there. He was acute and vital, staring eye-to-eye at Mason with studied interest. Behind Mason, Jairo sneered while Norm's handler snapped to rigid attention.

Victor said with a flourish, "And so gentlemen, I deliver to you our nuisance." He placed Mason's cellphone on the table.

His stare still locked on Mason, Delaci demanded with a firm voice, "Did I ask you to speak?"

Victor blanched and submitted to silence. The double doors behind Mason and Norm opened, and four more guards entered. They marched two-by-two over to Jairo with automatics drawn, efficiently stripping the surprised assassin of his weapons.

Jairo said to Delaci, "What is this?"

One of the new guards slapped Jairo's face, silencing his protest. They clasped Jairo's hands behind his back and zip-tied his wrists. Shocked and incensed at the cold betrayal, Jairo yelled again, "I demand to know."

Delaci raised one hand, silencing Jairo, then turned to Victor. His voice calculated and atonal, Delaci said, "I've tolerated enough incompetence."

"I delivered these to you."

"You broadcast the LA Project across the internet after creating a trail of murder and chaos that leads back to here? To me?" Delaci waved a hand across the table. "And now I have to deal with this repellant street trash."

Mason shifted perceptively toward Norm. "I hope you mean Jairo… 'cause I like to think of Norm and myself as adorable street trash."

Mason's guard moved to club him with the butt of his Kalashnikov, waiting for permission from Delaci to administer the blow. Delaci paused, allowing his presence to re-collect the room. He spoke, but barely above a whisper, looking at Mason. "Another word, and I'll have that man cut your friend's throat." The guard lowered his rifle and half-pulled his black Delta Force knife half out of its sheath.

The room was quiet and under his control again. Delaci focussed his attention on Victor. As one, the board members followed Delaci's gaze. Obviously, Victor's usefulness to Delaci had expired; the unspoken judgement final, Victor was a dead Senator walking. Delaci and the Inner Circle turned as one back to Norm and Mason.

Delaci said, "You make bad jokes, but you have no allies of consequence. And we have him, our ex-employee…"

Norm defied Delaci. "I never worked for you."

"If you worked at Meister-Fleisher-Fuchs, you served, as we all do, at the pleasure of this corporation." Delaci slapped his hands down on the table. "However, some of us serve at higher levels than others." He leaned forward on both arms and yelled at Norm with the unrestrained rage of a defied Cesar. "Interrupt me again, and I will personally cut your tongue out." Norm wisely shrunk back into silence. Delaci took a moment to adjust his tie knot before continuing. "We are already campaigning in the media to denigrate your video as a hoax. You are still alive because we want the specific whereabouts of the internet hacker and Alacrán. Mr. Stone, if you convince the urchin to surrender the original recording and reveal her father's current location to us, I can offer you a trade."

"If you can't bring Amelia back—not interested."

"I can prevent your deaths."

"We have NEWCorp by the balls right now, and you

know it. You sent this jerk around the world to torture me and murder my friend and the Swiss cops, and then you had my girl murdered. Now you want to make a deal because it suits *you*? What do you think, Norm, is that gonna happen?"

"Not a chance in beggar's hell."

"But if I add $10 million to the deal," said Delaci, "it's no longer a beggar's hell. Take it; go away forever and forget about NEWCorp and Amelia and the scientist."

"What about the people you're screwing out of a future?" said Mason. "Theirs is not mine or yours to barter with just because you can. Take your sick, cynical offer and go fuck yourself."

"Bravo on your commitment to anti-establishment rhetoric," said Delaci, his voice thick with sarcasm, "but we will still have the uranium."

That bombshell landed, and Mason realized how naïve he had been. "And we still have the exposure card," he said weakly.

"I assure you, by tonight, there will be no trace left of your accomplice or that video," said Delaci. "And which of us has the knife at his throat?" He shrugged off the consideration. "If you are unwilling to work with us…"

"I'm sure you understood 'go fuck yourself.'"

Mason looked at Norm. He nodded agreement, looked at Delaci, and said, "And the horse you rode in on." Delaci looked at Norm, momentarily confused. Norm said, "What? It's a common expression."

Delaci took a quick visual census with his board members. They disagreed with Norm. "Not in this boardroom, it's not," sighed Delaci. "So, we are at the impasse where the righteous choose to sacrifice their lives. Joans-of-Arc, both of you, but your willingness to burn at the stake is duly noted, granted, and pointless." Strong hands took hold of their arms. "Victor, my dear friend," said Delaci, nodding at him before turning to the Inner Circle, "you and these esteemed members will accompany these condemned men to the King George landfill to witness Jairo execute, dismember, and scatter their remains." The board members looked at Delaci, the doubt on their faces turning to alarm. Delaci addressed Jairo, "Free Jairo's hands and feet." The guards followed his orders. "You vindicate yourself with NEWCorp as soon as you complete this task. This meeting is adjourned." Delaci tapped his gavel once on the table.

"I don't get it," shouted Mason. "What's so important that you, that NEWCorp would risk all this. What more could be in it for you?"

Delaci looked at Mason. He reached out to pull the globe toward him, folding his hands over the alabaster globe. He spoke in a matter-of-fact monotone. "I'll spell it out, then. I want exactly what you want—freedom. But I know that's an illusion, except at the top of the world, with total control. You? Well, you want freedom through… what? Decency and common respect? That's the road to martyrdom and, Mr. Stone, martyrs, by definition, must die."

"That's all bullshit, and you know it."

Delaci laughed sardonically. "Well, the money's good too, if that's what you're asking me. My wealth is a perk, and I'm entitled to it. NEWCorp, by proxy, is how I will have it all." He raked his ring across the globe statuette. "But how could you know? Squandering wealth, or simply having it, is plebian. That is only one legacy I will create in this world." He banged the gavel again.

The silent board members stood and began filing toward the doors, but they seemed less stoic after the speech. Delaci briefly pondered the globe on the table and then summoned Jairo to his side with a nod. Delaci whispered in deliberate tones, "Kill them all."

In the resounding silence, armed thugs were following orders, mindlessly marching others to their executions. While enjoying his reinstatement, Jairo joined the waiting group in the hallway and said to Victor, "I want my guns back."

"Not a chance. You two," Victor spoke to the guards, "keep your guns on these two."

Mason said, "What's next, Victor? After you get the uranium, what's next?"

"Why? Weren't you listening? We rule the world. Within a few years, we will own the Chinese too. The Russians and Americans are ours now." Victor menaced Mason with his gun. "Move. Into the service elevator at the end of the hallway."

"You think you can get away with this?"

Victor ignored him and spoke to a guard. "One word

from either of them, shoot them. They can die here."

When they arrived at the parking level, they found the carpool booth deserted, locked, and the lights out. The limo keys were inside the booth. Victor tried his cellphone but had poor reception in the underground. He said, "I'll call for a car from the alley." An orderly crowd had filled the lane and were walking toward the front of the building. Victor said, "What the fuck is going on out there, anyway?"

One of Mason's guards said, "Give me a reason." The guards holstered their weapons but held Norm and Mason by twisting new ties on their wrists. They marched through the near-empty parking garage and down the exit ramp.

When they entered the alley, it was plugged by a horde of hundreds that spilled out at the end of the block. Victor waded into the young crowd and was immediately swept away toward Pennsylvania Avenue. Jairo stopped, turned, and was also swept away with the unrelenting tide. The guards hurried Mason and Norm into the crowd to catch up. The board members tried to hold back, but their guards pushed them into the mob, and they were scattered and lost quickly in the sea of faces.

Mason and Norm spilled out onto the sidewalk across from Freedom Plaza with their two guards. Victor, panic on his face, swam through the expanding crowd until he was able to latch onto a dumpster, where one guard found him. "Don't let that happen again," hissed Victor. Mason's guard waved over the heads of the crowd to Victor. He nodded and pointed to the far end of the alley, where Norm and his guard struggled to hold their position. "We'll go back," said Victor. "Where's Jairo?"

A confrontation building on the street had heightened the tensions in the crowd. Victor raised his cellphone to his ear to order a limo, but a long-haired protestor was shoved into him, and he knocked the phone out of Victor's hand. The jostling increased, and a sense of anxiety raced through the crowd. Victor literally disappeared when he bent over to retrieve his phone.

Students Without Debt protestors waved signs on their side of the street. Across from them, decidedly angry men and women waved American flags and shouted insults and 'white is right' into bullhorns, taunting the student debt protesters. On the near sidewalk, a mixed group of younger and older veterans in vigil, some in Army gear, some with peace symbols and long hair, most with medals pinned to their coats, a few in wheelchairs, held and waved small American flags in the restless crowd swarming around them.

Dozens of armed and helmeted riot police, joined by a troop on horseback on the curb, muscled their way through the protesters on the sidewalk, forcing some onto the street. Police behind shields warned them to move off the road, grappling with those afraid of the mounted police. A longhaired veteran in a wheelchair joined the fray. A barely legible cardboard "Affordable Care for All" sign tied with simple English twine hung on his chest. He rolled into the street and shouted his slogan, "ACA now," into his bullhorn.

Victor was still anchored to the dumpster in the alley, talking on his cellphone. The crowd around Mason and Norm crushed together but separated them momentarily from their struggling guards. Mason yelled at Norm, "Back down the alley. Go." Echoes of competing slogans echoed off buildings along Pennsylvania Avenue as Mason and Norm tried to swim against the tide of agitated humanity. The police on horseback moved in as one, clearing the blocked sidewalk, swinging truncheons, escalating their aggressive campaign, cutting the guards off from Mason and Norm.

Victor tried to intervene, but the pandemonium surged against him. The Medicare for All veteran pushed his wheelchair across the avenue, where rabid dissenters fingered, yelled, and shook their fists at him. They doubled their vitriolic abuse, chanting, "Save our borders—save our country." The cadence and their intensity rose with each repetition. In the wheelchair, the veteran yelled something into his bullhorn, was mobbed, and both men and women wearing MAGA hats spat on him.

In the chaos, Mason lost sight of Norm. The Pennsylvania Avenue traffic had stopped, replaced by rows of riot police blocking both ends of Freedom Plaza. Mother Liberty and her sister, Freedom of Speech, were about to take a supremacist-era kick in the teeth. Mason's guard fought back against the human tide in the jostling crowd and was again within arm's length. Victor and his guard were unable to move and had been joined by one of the board members; the rest of their original group were nowhere in sight. The guard close to Mason had one hand on his earpiece, the other inside his vest.

The air was smoky with tear gas and stung with pepper spray. The chant, "Four more years," rose above the din and echoed down the alley. All hell broke loose. Riot cops tramped in formation and violently dragged students through their ranks and into police vans at either end of the plaza. The crowd surged back into the alley to escape the police.

Mason and Norm ran with them, but another phalanx of nameless, faceless riot cops wielded batons at students trying to escape the violence. Victor and the guard reappeared with the board member in tow. They grabbed Norm and separated from Mason. Victor yelled over the crowd, "Everyone back down the alley—go." They flowed with the crowd toward the advancing but overwhelmed riot police in the alley to escape onto 14th Street.

In the crush, Jairo appeared from the car park ramp. He surprised Mason's guard, turned the gun on him, and shot the guard in the ribs. As the surprised, wounded guard dropped, Jairo wrestled his handgun from him, then shot, hitting the board member in the throat. The man fell, pulling at the red gushing from his wound. The gunfire ignited panic in the crowd. Norm appeared in the chaos. "Run." Mason shoved him. Jairo lunged but missed Norm, who worked through the crowd and down the alley.

The terror-stricken, debt-ravaged students ran for their lives, engulfing Victor, sweeping him away too. They surged past Mason through the breached police riot line, pouring out of the far end of the alley.

Jairo appeared in front of Mason, his gun pointed at Mason's heart. "You may be lucky," he said, "but you aren't bulletproof."

Mason heard three rapid-fire gunshots and recoiled against the impact. He looked down at himself, but there was no blood. Jairo had disappeared into the mob. A hand on his shoulder spun Mason around.

Amelia stood there, holding a smoking gun in her hand. "I guess this is our second date?" she said, staring into his eyes.

He shook off his disbelief and took her in his arms, hugging her so hard he let go because he thought he would hurt her. "How? Is it really you?"

"Kiss me and see…"

They kissed for a long moment, separated but as one in the swell of humanity, insulated from the madness around them. Together again, they were centred in the pandemonium that had defined their lives together.

"Jairo…?" asked Mason.

"Gone. I'm against killing now." She tucked the gun in her belt. "You taught me that."

"Wait a minute… If you're alive, then that means you dumped me in New York."

"No. I protected you in New York. I did that for you."

"But Matty said this was always about the money."

Amelia grabbed his hand, "He lied. That's what he does, but he's a good bad guy, so he doesn't kill—family. It's complicated." She tried to pull him through the crowd toward the far end of the alley. Mason held back, pulled her aside, and made her turn toward him.

"I need you to promise me there was no dumping."

"There wasn't."

"Promise, and you have to mean it."

"I promise I only wanted to protect you."

"Then you have to promise me you won't… no, promise me you will never protect me again."

Amelia stopped, and Mason's world stopped with hers. They embraced. "Mason, I could never… hold that thought." Amelia slipped out of their embrace, kicked a guard looming out of the crowd in the groin and then smashed his knee with a devastating sideways kick. He screamed, fell back, and was swallowed by the mob. She slipped back into Mason's arms. "Now, where were we?"

"You were promising to never protect me again."

"I do promise, never again, except for that guy."

"Yeah, that guy was okay, but never again, right?"

Her lips curled into her best Mona Lisa smile. "Never."

"Then I'll stand by you."

They held the moment to cement their vows until Amelia said, "Now, let's get the hell out of here."

Mason looked around quickly, "What about Norm?"

"We have him. Quick, this way." She jerked on his arm to get him moving, but Mason refused to move. Amelia curled her body into his, her mouth at his ear. "You're right. I'm sorry, really sorry. I needed some room to make things happen. Matty had blanks in his gun."

"Matty might have fired blanks, but Giorgio didn't."

"You have a right to be angry, but you needed to be free from me... and us. And then you did this dangerous, stupid, courageous thing."

"Delaci called me stupid too."

"Jesus... you're adorable when you pout. I'll never leave again if that's what you want."

"That's what I want."

"Then come on." She pulled Mason by the arm. He let Amelia lead them through the crowd, down the alley. They ducked through the breached lines of riot police and rushed toward an unmarked black van.

Yuri was behind the wheel. He and Alacrán had on police riot helmets. Alacrán slid the side door open and said, "How've you been, Mason? Nice work in New York." Amelia and Mason crouched to climb inside. Alacrán slammed the side door shut.

Norm was in the van. He said excitedly, "We made it out and fuck all their horses!"

Alacrán looked at Norm, then at Mason, and then back to Norm. "Did he take a headshot?"

Amelia said, "It's in common use in Canada, Dad." She pulled Mason onto the rear bench seat beside her.

Alacrán had his doubts but said, "This ain't over yet. All three of you still need to clear your names."

Norm seconded, "You're preaching to the choir." He put on a police riot helmet.

"What about Victor and Jairo?" asked Mason.

Alacrán took the front passenger seat. "They slithered back into some sewer. Put these on... we want to look like cops." Alacrán tossed Mason and Amelia police riot gear helmets. "Yuri, get us the hell out of Dodge."

"Dodge?" asked Norm.

"It's very common vernacular," said Alacrán.

"Really? I've never heard that expression before."

"Right. Well, it's nice to have you all back anyway."
After cursory looks, the cops ignored them as they drove out of the alley and away from D.C.

Alacrán played the Eagles reunion DVD, popped the

top off water bottles for Yuri and Norm, and relaxed in the shotgun seat. Mason and Amelia commandeered the back seat. He held her hand, unable to look away from her, unable to believe they were together until he believed it again. Mason looked at Amelia. "So, what do we do now?"

"We have a choice… you and I can go get Brooke and then disappear."

"I want a life with you, not a life on the run with you." He was thoughtful. "I hear the desert sunsets over Los Alamos are beautiful this time of year."

Alacrán interrupted them. "We think Delaci's plan is bigger than cornering the global uranium market."

Mason whispered in Amelia's ear. "On one condition—we stop bringing your dad on all our dates." On the outskirts of Washington, they tossed the police riot helmets out the window.

They chanced travelling on I-95 all the way to Richmond. Alacrán sat in the front passenger seat. They cut over to I-85 to head farther southwest through West Virginia. As a tribute, Alacrán played a Goose Creek Symphony DVD. While the upbeat music played, Amelia had to be satisfied holding Mason and being beside him because Giorgio's crushing blow mixed with the excitement made Mason drowsy. He took painkillers, sleeping when they passed by Greensboro, famous as the Ku Klux Klan's birthplace and their spawning of 2,500 anti-government militia hate groups throughout the US.

33. The Hydrogen Event

When Mason woke, it was days past the deadline for
NEWCorp lobbyists to place the nuclear waste bill before the
president. They were through Atlanta, heading west on Hwy 20.
Mason ate a plastic convenience store burrito and finished a
coffee watching the landscape race past, south of Neshoba
County in Mississippi. Mason shivered at the kind of trouble a
flat tire could still bring an unarmed coloured man or woman
on a lonely stretch of road, or a grid-locked highway for that
matter, anywhere in America. They faced another marathon day
of travel before they would arrive in New Mexico.

Amelia said, "We're too hot for the airports, and they'll
be watching for us at Dad's bunker."

Yuri drove the van over a series of intersecting
highways that resulted in them heading due west. Mason put
Alacrán's iPad down. He was baffled. "Any news on the video
yet?"

"Not a single replay."

Mason looked out the window, checked the map, then
the highway identifier. "I thought we were going to Los
Alamos?"

"Change of plans," said Alacrán. "We're going to where
NEWCorp is most vulnerable. A few months ago, the WPIF
facility leaked a radiation plume across three states. We want to
know what went wrong."

Amelia said, "Their press statement downplayed it as 'a
hydrogen event.'"

"I read about it… from what I understand, that was like
calling the crash of '29 a market adjustment."

Amelia continued, "Greenpeace traced the source to a
scramble at the plant. They shut the whole $14 billion facility
down until further notice. Five years later, it's just up and
running again."

"Let me guess, fat government contracts are up for
grabs."

Norm said, "Some things never change." Yuri nodded
his agreement.

"NEWCorp is importing nuclear waste, mountains of
it," said Amelia, "and supposedly disposing of it—at WPIF."

"My conspiracy loonies would go nuts, but is it a

scam?"

"We're going to find out."

*

Twenty-seven hours later, the sun was low on the western horizon, setting behind the isolation plant buildings. They were thirty-five miles east of Carlsbad and had turned south off Hobbs Highway onto a lonely, dry stretch of gravel road. They might have missed the turnoff entirely without their digital mapping app. When they stopped at the intersection to look for the road sign, they found it shot full of holes and lying in the ditch. Twelve miles of high-plains desert and dust later, they stopped the van on a cactus-cluttered rise to look over the facility. Norm tuned in to a news station and listened for their names. Alacrán and Yuri were absent and scouting the layout of the plant.

Amelia and Mason, leaning on the front of the van, drank bottled water. She laid her head on his shoulder. "There's your setting desert sun."

"Too bad it's behind the glow of the leaking radiation plume."

"We're close to Roswell. It's on the route from here to Los Alamos."

"Will they ever leave those poor people alone?"

"Roswell might be the biggest red herring ever concocted, but if it's fake, what are they hiding from us? It's as big as JFK."

"Maybe it's the same thing."

Mason told Amelia about an idea he had during the drive to Arizona. They talked about it together and turned his idea into a plan.

Alacrán and Yuri returned from scouting the site, so they rehydrated and ate military-grade rations in the van, preparing to break into the facility. "We can get in over the fence between the power grid and the powerhouse. That's where we want to be... Norm, you chill here. Watch the van. We'll go when it's dark."

*

It was full-on night under a fantastic cloak of stars. "Mason," said Alacrán, "bring that cover from the spare tire, will you?"

The hum and crackle generated by the power grid's high-voltage wires grew louder as they approached the chain-link fence. They slipped single file through the night, crossed the dirt road, and squatted in the long shadow cast by the industrial yard lights blocked by the tallest building. Their first obstacle was the 10-foot fence and three strands of barbed wire at the top. Alacrán unravelled a length of rope and twirled the weighted end around his head like it was a bolero before he flung it over the fence and around a light standard. The heavy end came back down on their side. Alacrán tied a climber's knot on the rope's end, attached a carabiner to the loop, and then pulled it tight around the pole. Yuri handed Alacrán the spare tire cover, which he draped over his shoulders, and then Alacrán used the rope to scale the outside of the fence. Holding onto the rope with one hand, he fixed the heavy tire cover across the barbed wire strands, then barrel-rolled over the protective cover. Alacrán dropped silently to the gravel inside the compound.

Mason was next to go over. Yuri boosted him onto his shoulders, and Mason used the rope to clamber across the top. Mason bear-hugged the light standard and slid down the metal pole. Amelia came over next, and then Yuri dropped down silently behind her, pulling the rope over and coiling it at the base of the pole. He left the tire cover in place should they need a fast escape.

Still in the shadow cast by the power station, each of them turned their attention to familiarizing themselves with the layout. The facility lighting illuminated the entire perimeter road, except for a failed overhead light causing a shadow at the base of one of the buildings. On Alacrán's word, they risked brief exposure, sprinting into the light where, for an instant, their elongated shadows stretched across the wall of the building that contained howling exhaust blowers. When they were covered by the deep shadow thrown across the compound, Amelia said, "These must be how they vented the radioactive contamination."

Mason said, "This is way too easy."

"Feels like a trap," said Amelia, "right?" She was enjoying the moment.

Mason felt a cold shiver run down his spine. "Let's get what we need and get the hell out of here."

He watched Alacrán and Yuri scale the raised loading dock platform and then disappear among the containers.

Mason counted eleven huge cans by the time he and Amelia joined up with them at the far end of the warehouse dock. He separated from the group, inspecting the rows, looking at the NEWCorp radioactive logos on each container. Amelia found him. "This one's from Los Alamos, that one's Oak Ridge, this whole row is from Hanford."

"Noted." She motioned they should follow Alacrán and Yuri, who waited impatiently near the set of massive, open doors.

Alacrán stood up, relaxed his body, pointed at the cameras, and said, "They know we're here." He shrugged his shoulders, holstered his pistol, and walked into the light.

Two security guards appeared from inside the doors of the cluttered loading bay. One of them pointed his AK-47 at Yuri and Mason. The other guard had his weapon trained on Amelia. "Guns and knives. Just drop them on the ground. Walk over here backwards, one at a time. You first, little girl."

First Amelia, then Yuri and Alacrán dropped pistols and knives to comply with the orders. Mason raised his hands and said, "I'm unarmed."

One guard patted each of them down while the other held his automatic on Mason. Satisfied they were disarmed, the guards marched everyone inside the warehouse.

The building was cavernous. A grid of industrial sodium vapour lights mounted sixty feet overhead cast a sulphurous hue onto everything. Cranes mounted on rails dangled unmoving cables with massive metal hooks from the grid of steel girders welded like mesh into the ceiling. Dwarfed by the building's extent, forklifts as large as the flatbed trucks sat idle behind six white, parked pickup trucks with NEWCorp logos on the doors. Rows of more containers crowded the inside of each of the three docking bays. The guards motioned them to cross the extensive, eerily quiet warehouse floor, over the train rails, toward the steel mesh that encased the bellowing, winding mineshaft winches. They slowed, and the bright yellow elevator cage dangling on a cable arrived from the tunnels far below them. It was empty.

They waited at the head of the mineshaft, outside the open cage of the elevator. One of the guards looked skyward, so the captives followed his line of sight to the skywalk, where a man held his hand up, indicating they should wait there.

Unhurried, the man walked down the steps to the plant floor to join a group of six more security guards, each in paramilitary gear and armed to the teeth.

Mason said to Amelia, "We've got him right where we want him. Now what?"

"Let's hear his confession."

Not deigning to look at his prisoners, Victor walked past them and waited on the elevator. He motioned with a wave of his hand, then the guards forced everyone to follow the senator. Victor turned and looked at Alacrán, still standing in defiance. Victor said, "We've been looking for you for some time. Join me, will you?"

"This is where NEWCorp exiles the losers, senator?" said Mason, unable to help himself, but Victor ignored him.

A guard closed the wire mesh gate behind them, another pushed a green button on the sparse console, a loud buzzer echoed in the plant, and they plummeted downward at sixty miles an hour. Mason felt his lungs push into his throat. His heart pounded in his chest until, seconds later, metal squealing indicated the brakes were being applied. Amelia looked at Mason to reassure him, but the confines of the shaft were decidedly unnerving. The elevator decelerated rapidly, making his legs feel like they were filling with cement until they lurched to a bouncing stop. A guard opened the gate, and they walked off the elevator to the entrance of miles of tunnel shafts gouged out of the deep salt deposits.

Victor said, "This is what you came to see, isn't it, Amelia?"

"What I want to see is you and the rest of your crew in jail for murder."

Victor scoffed. He ordered the guards, "You four can return to your duties on the surface." So far below the winches, the elevator whisked them upwards as if on a silent whoosh of air.

Victor took a pistol from under his suit jacket and then addressed the remaining group, "Just follow the yellow line." The line Victor indicated led down one of several lighted tunnels. The floor was cemented, and the opening was tall and wide enough for two forklifts to pass each other easily. They walked past another parked pickup truck. Two hundred yards further on, they still had not encountered any employees. It struck Mason as eerie that so much industry was left this deserted. He looked at the tunnel walls. *If this is a salt cavern,* he thought, *it's not table salt.*

Amelia stayed behind Mason as they marched along silently for another five hundred yards, passing five more dark openings to subsidiary tunnels. Finally, they arrived at a large, lighted cavern, hollowed out enough to park a Boeing 737. Three tiers of yellow containers filled the cavern to the ceiling. Victor ordered two of the guards to wait at the entrance.

"We'll carry on…" On a nod from Victor to a guard, he stepped up to Yuri from behind, striking him viciously on the head with the butt of his rifle. Yuri fell to the cavern floor.

Incensed at Victor, Alacrán said, "There was no call for that. You could have killed him."

Smiling, Victor pointed his pistol at Amelia. Alacrán made a move to rush Victor, but the second guard stepped in to hammer Alacrán on the back of his neck with the butt of his rifle. The blow knocked Alacrán down.

Victor said, "Anyone else up for some false heroics? Look at the novelist—he cowers like a little girl." Amelia tensed, glaring at Victor. He shrunk back a step. "Think about it. The salt," said Victor, his threat crystal clear, "dehydrates the body slowly… it could take days to die down here." Amelia considered the guard and his weapon aimed at her. She backed down.

Ignoring Victor and the muzzle jammed into his ribs by his guard, Mason moved to Alacrán's side, lifting one of his arms over a shoulder. Amelia helped. She nodded at Mason, and together they lifted and held Alacrán up so he might regain his strength. Mason felt Alacrán's coiled power when he glared at Victor.

"I have something to show you, old man." Victor led them over to a row of containers. He looked at Mason. "Pick one."

Mason nodded at the closest container to humour him.

Victor shot into the bottom of the container. If there was a hydrogen buildup or volatile material inside, at the very least, the entire cavern would have erupted in a chain reaction explosion that might have equalled the toppling of WTC-7. Instead—nothing. Victor enjoyed himself. "You people are fools. There is nothing in these containers. Do you think I'd be here if there were?" He put a cigar in his mouth. "Now, in other tunnels, that's where we store our uranium—our future."

Mason was appalled. "Then, why all this?"

"These containers are filled with money, a lot of it. Each represents $30 million to NEWCorp annually, and we expect that will keep coming for generations. It's really quite beautiful." He took a moment to enjoy the silence. "No one can manage nuclear waste. Everything we tried as a country failed. The Russian's don't even bother trying; they dump their nuclear waste in the Barents Sea... been like that for decades. We took their lead."

"You dump radioactive waste in the ocean."

"Practically every day—there's no law that can touch us; it's pure profit to NEWCorp. And it's not like our customers give a shit, as long as they're not called on it." He looked shocked that Mason was outraged. "But we have our morals," said Victor, "we dump in international waters. The few containers we do bring here are chock full of radioactive material, but it's not waste or spent fuel. It's Kazakh uranium."

"You could never get it through customs."

"We give them the paperwork they want, and before we make port, our bookkeeping is in order. We control the gangs running the Los Angeles docks..." He stopped his boast to light his cigar. Two gunshots echoed from behind them, down the tunnel they had just walked. Victor rolled his eyes, looking through the cigar smoke, and waved his gun at Mason. "I suggest you two," he looked at Alacrán and Amelia, "remain calm, or I will kill him." Amelia and Alacrán looked at each other, and something passed between them, something dangerous and missed by Victor. He continued, "The $2 billion spent each year at Hanford is a smokescreen. That amounts to our assets you see in just this cavern alone."

Mason kept Victor talking. "You call nuclear waste an asset?"

"The socialist writer is outraged. Who would have guessed that?" He laughed.

"I think you're an asshole, and that makes me a leftist?"

Victor shook his head. "We move containers about for the satellites. It plays well in Washington, but nobody asks serious questions. Why would they? We provide senatorial oversight on a project that is designated national security. Soon, all these tunnels will be filled with our uranium."

Footsteps approached from down the otherwise silent tunnel, a single set of footprints. Pleased NEWCorp's betrayal of trust had hit home, Victor shrugged, then spun around to face Alacrán. "God," said Victor, "it's so much better when it's personal, isn't it?"

The guard joined the group, his gun drawn; he nodded at Victor. The senator's eyes were wide, crazed, flushed with the power the guard murdering Yuri gave him. He commanded Alacrán's guard, "Take this one over there, behind the second row of containers. Be quick about it." The guard followed orders, and Alacrán led them out of sight. From behind the containers, two shots boomed in the cavern.

Victor laughed like a maniac. He shot another container, then another, before turning on the closest guard and shooting him in the face. He crumpled and died on the floor. At that moment, Alacrán raced out from behind the containers toward Victor. In the blood frenzy of the moment, Victor aimed at Amelia and fired. Alacrán leapt in at the last possible instant as the bullet smashed into his femur, shattering it. Alacrán fell to the ground, releasing an involuntary, guttural growl; he dropped the gun in his hand.

Victor still had his gun on Amelia, but she had her cellphone out and threw it at his face, hitting him in the left eye, deeply cutting his brow. Victor screamed, his cut bleeding profusely. He discharged a harmless shot into the ceiling. Amelia kicked the gun from his hand. Mason watched the pistol arc away from the two combatants and ran to retrieve it. Victor fell to his knees, holding his face, blood pouring from between his fingers. "You blinded me."

Calmly, Amelia said, "It's only the one eye."

Mason ran to the gun, picked it up and fired, hitting Victor in the ass. He yelped and grabbed at his wound. Mason shot Victor in the ass again. Victor fell, rolling onto the floor, grabbing his wounds, screaming in pain.

Amelia said, "Good shot."

"I should plug him again."

"You've done enough *plugging*." She tried to take the weapon, but Mason held onto it, pulling it back and pointing it at Victor.

"Get the hell out of my way… I'm gonna kill this

bastard. He murdered Yuri, and he was going to kill us." At that moment, Mason was capable of firing the killing shot.

Victor begged for his life. "I never wanted you dead. That was Jairo. He went too far."

"You hired him." A fine rage burned inside Mason. His finger was on the trigger, aimed at Victor's face.

"Mason," said Amelia, her voice calm, "give me the gun,"

"You're rubbing off on me. I want to kill this sick bastard and make it stop, right here, right now." His finger curled on the trigger.

Amelia's voice was tender. "But you're not a killer. I love you because you are who you are, not who I am."

He looked at her, surprised, then her words reached him, filtering through his crimson rage. He regained control, but his gun-hand was still steady. Victor flopped across the dead guard—one bloody hand holding his ass, the other stretched out from his twisted torso. He beseeched Mason like an untouchable begging for alms from a gutter in a Mumbai ghetto.

"Have you got your cellphone?" Amelia found it quickly and nodded. "Take a picture of that. It'll make a great Christmas card."

Amelia snapped three photos of Victor begging for his life in front of the containers. The guard he murdered was lying prone beneath him.

"I don't want him to forget. I should shoot him in the ass again."

"You don't think he'll remember every time he changes his colostomy bag?"

After staring long and hard at Victor shuddering on the ground, Mason reluctantly handed Amelia the gun. They stopped the bleeding wound by binding Victor's suit jacket around Alacrán's leg, stripping Victor of his belt, and using it to secure the coat.

Alacrán groaned. "Mason, help me up." Alacrán was in excruciating pain but was able to stand on his other leg. "Give me Victor's gun. Daughter, find us a ride out of here." Amelia handed Alacrán the gun and then ran off to find transportation. She returned minutes later with the pickup truck they saw parked near the bottom of the elevator shaft.

Alacrán could not bend his leg, so they dropped the tailgate, loaded him onto the truck deck. Next, they loaded Victor at gunpoint. "Sorry about the company," said Mason to Alacran, "but it's a short trip." He and Amelia carried Yuri's body to the truck. Mason drove to the elevator while Amelia rode the tailgate staying close to comfort her father and monitor his shock while keeping an eye on Victor. Mason opened the elevator gate then drove the truck onto the platform. Amelia looked coldly at Victor. "How many are we going to run into up there?"

"Only a skeleton security shift," he groaned, defeated. "Everyone else is off duty."

Satisfied he was telling the truth, she punched the green button, and the elevator lifted them to the warehouse floor.

Exiting the elevator, they saw the facility was still deserted, so they did not have to blast their way out. They drove out of the main gates, surprising the sleepy overnight guard, and went to get Norm. They transferred Yuri's body, Victor, and Alacrán from the stolen pickup to the stolen van.

Norm peppered them with excited, non-stop questions. "How'd you get a broken leg? How'd you get a gunshot wound? Where'd you find this guy? Where's Yuri? How'd Alacrán get shot?" Norm's worry turned to admiration when Mason admitted he shot Victor in the ass—twice.

"I wish I'd done that."

"Keep working at it... Maybe you'll get your turn."

Victor was humiliated. He said, "I'm dying. Get me to a hospital."

"Put a sock in it," said Norm.

Amelia upgraded Alacrán's bandage to a field dressing. Norm and Mason trussed up Victor with rope and bandages. Victor scowled at Norm. "Just in case he remains conscious," said Norm, and he stuffed the senator's mouth with a ball of gauze.

"Carlsbad airport is too close. Get us to El Paso," said Amelia to Mason. Travelling with gunshot wounds and a dead man would raise too many local authorities' questions, even in that state.

*

At the airport, they waited in the van while Amelia went to steal a car. She returned with an SUV. After they transferred Yuri and Alacrán over, Alacrán shook Mason's hand and held it. "You're officially an honorary member of the team."

Mason was genuinely proud of the promotion. "What about Norm?" Norm raised his eyebrows expectantly.

"He's still in training." Norm frowned. Alacrán looked at Amelia. "We can't travel as a group. See you in Pennsylvania?"

"Mason and I have a plan."

"Don't think this scratch means I'm not coming too."

"I know that, but we're going to recycle our trash first." Amelia hugged her dad lovingly. They left them waiting for the Pursuit's jet, which would arrive with a doctor within the hour.

Outside the airport, Mason asked, "We have a plan?"

Amelia smiled and said, "Not so much, but I know you want to be alone on our date, so I guess we'll have to come up with something, won't we?"

34. **Sunrise on a New Day**

Dawn was still two hours off. They backtracked on their trail, driving the van back toward Carlsbad. Under a moonless sky, the Milky Way sparkling over them was a limitless universe of possibilities.

Amelia said, "Do you think we're alone in the galaxy?"

Mason threw a glance over his shoulder. "Not yet."

Victor complained, "I'm bleeding out back here."

They both giggled like school kids. They retraced their trail at a leisurely pace, eventually turning north on 285. They deserted Victor in New Mexico. Dropping him in the small, sleepy, high-plains town on the dirty sidewalk in front of its famous UFO museum. Victor jeered bitterly at them.

"What's so entertaining, senator?"

"You have nothing on me except the pictures of me begging for my life. I'm a gunshot victim, and you're leaving me behind to die in the dirt... But I'm still an American senator."

"Amelia, is it too late to finish the job?"

Victor didn't back down. "You're both still wanted for murder."

Mason said, "I'm telling him." Amelia nodded. "We hacked into NEWCorp. We have it all—financials, the names, your entire global operation—the LA Project is dead."

"That's a bluff."

Mason said, "Oh yeah? Where'd NEWCorp buy that security software?"

Before he could stop himself, Victor blurted out, "Canada. The ..." It hit him then.

"Right, from our guy... Hawke cleared him to do the work. Who'd think a fifteen-year-old computer whiz-kid would leave himself a back door to his own computer system, eh?"

"We'll suppress the information."

"Maybe, but the public is always hungry for a political corruption story."

"Don't leave me here. I can pay you—make you rich beyond your dreams."

"That's your ideal, not mine," said Mason.

"You're leaving me to die."

"Yeah, maybe, if our luck finally changes..."

*

Mason drove them away from Roswell across a high desert plateau. Ridges of grey rock and white sand formed a lunar moonscape, but the hint of the sunrise was changing the pre-dawn monochrome into colours by the minute. "Even if I take some solace," said Mason, "in the image of Victor left destitute on those streets, that was unsightly." He was taken by a moment of despair, then sadness. "I shot a man. Worse... I wanted to kill him."

"You were caught up in the moment, but you didn't pull the trigger. You're not a killer."

"I'm worried that I'm becoming..."

"Me?"

He looked at Amelia, then back to the road. "It's that lately, the moral boundaries seem blurred... They've been running us."

They waited for the hurt between them to dissipate in the silence before Amelia said, in a soft voice, "But you went back to Wall Street. That was brave and your own decision."

He replied with more than a hint of bitterness, "And I found the moral majority had surrendered to the bad guys. I never thought giving a shit would be so hard."

The orange sun crested the horizon in front of them. The entire desert sky was a marvellous swirl of wispy morning clouds vibrant on a blue sky. Mason stopped the van and turned off the engine on top of a lonely, cactus-covered mesa.

"Why are we stopping?"

"Look at this beautiful new day." He unwound his window to gulp in the cool, fresh air.

"Hold me," said Amelia, "and kiss me."

*

They paid cash for the flight to Dulles International. At that hour, airport security was lax and going through the motions. Mason texted IBM on a burner cellphone, setting in motion the new plan. In the Men's room, he removed the SIM chip and flushed it. He stomped on the cellphone and tossed it into a garbage can. When he rejoined Amelia, he said, "Destroying that phone was uplifting."

"Technology ain't all it's cracked up to be."

"And I told Peabody the truth. We made it to New Mexico."

35. **The Reveal**

They took a suite in the Watergate Hotel. Mason had insisted.
"Why not start at Nixon's Waterloo. And something else..."
"Anything, darling."
"When your dad shows up, he has to have his own room. I'm tired of him catching me in bed with you."

*

They were finishing the meeting in Mason and Amelia's rooms, agreeing on what would transpire the next day. While leaving, Norm said, "This will be the first real bed I've slept in since Canada."

Alacrán said, "Let's hope the next won't be in prison." Alacrán left on crutches.

Frowning, Norm followed Alacrán out. "It's always pleasant being around you, you know that?"

"I'm just sayin'..." They left bickering along the hall like a long-married couple.

In reality, if Mason followed his first self-survival instinct, he would take Amelia away, disappear fast, and then try to clear their names. They had the data and confession videos they needed to expose the scam, but there was no way to use the evidence if they were captured or killed. After all, they were still in D.C., the heart of Delaci country, and they were vulnerable. When the door closed and his eyes met Amelia's, he was worried. She had started running the shower when Mason said, "I'll be back in a few minutes."

"What's so important?"

"Don't bother getting dressed after your shower," he said suggestively. "You know, I love you."

"Mason Stone, don't ever stop." She waved him over to kiss his cheek, squeezing his hand lightly before he left.

*

Twenty minutes later, Mason finished his mission and was back in the elevator in the lobby, waiting for the doors to close. A bellhop squeezed through the gap at the last second. Mason stared straight ahead, absent-mindedly watching the light ascend the brass button panel. Then he saw in the panel reflections the bellhop staring at him. Their eyes met, setting off his taxi-driver gut reaction. The bellhop punched in a low floor number, then got off the elevator.

Holy shit, thought Mason, *he made me.*

*

Victor received the text from NEWCorp security services at his home. The last of the funeral services staff were departing, offering rehearsed condolences. His wife had succumbed to her illness while he was murdering Yuri in New Mexico.

The text read: watergate room 745

*

When Mason unlocked the door, Amelia was lying on the bed, naked and sensational. He said, "Give me a minute." She looked disappointed, but he moved with precision. He decided against telling her about the bellhop. He showered and shaved.

Amelia called out, "Should I order room service? I'm starved." Mason exited the steamy bathroom, tossing her a white fleece robe. She said, "Come to bed. I want to make love."

"That's the best offer I've had since Norm and I bunked in with the two gay guys in New York."

"Is it ever not the good-looking ones?"

Mason told Amelia about the bellhop, but before they had time to discuss the significance, they froze at the knock on their door. Amelia hurriedly pulled the white robe over her body, reaching under her pillow for her new Glock.

Mason said, "Easy… I've got this."

When he swung the door open, three effervescent black women rushed in, and Mason stepped aside. One woman wheeled in the spa-on-wheels cart. The other two graciously introduced themselves. "I'm Danielle, nails and manicure," and then, "I'm Sharica, massage, and Dante is shiatsu and pedicure." Amelia threw Mason a wicked, twisted-lip reproach that was all play and no bite. They enjoyed the pandering massage and hot towel treatments for the next forty minutes, lying beside each other on the bed.

Sharica had magic hands. Dante was finishing with Amelia when they heard another knock on the door.

"Time to switch it up, ladies." Mason tipped their retreating spa-on-wheels trio each an extra $100 while the new waiter set the table. The blending aroma in the room was intoxicating—buttery garlic Escabeche of Sea Scallops, the Napoleon of marinated organic salmon and an amazing Cesar

234

salad. The accompanying wine was a simple, chilled French *Sauvignon Blanc*. The flavours danced an amazing ballet, complementing Mason's hunger for his lover.

Amelia was delighted. When the waiter left, she teased Mason. "You're going to pay for this."

"Not to worry, darling. I charged this to Alacrán's room."

"You know what I mean."

"Your earrings are beautiful. I've never seen you wear jewelry before."

"They were my mother's wedding earrings. I asked Dad to bring them."

"Will we see dad again tonight?"

"I promised to knee-cap him if he disturbed us."

"In that case, I'd like to toast to a loving daughter and a hot date." They touched glasses, ringing the crystal. They dined to Mozart sonatas playing in the background. After satisfying their demanding passions, they rested and then made love again before falling asleep, exhausted, and in each other's arms.

*

The next morning, they ate leftovers with their fingers, showered, and dressed for the day. Amelia cleaned her gun while Mason sipped fresh hot coffee and skipped back and forth on the television between cable news outlets. No one mentioned them. Gossip columnists and news anchors disregarded Lady Ga Ga's talents, sniped at her addictions and then worried about who would wear what gown to the Oscars.

There was a knock on the door.

"That'll be dad." Amelia bounced across the carpet and pulled the door wide open. She backed away slowly from the door. BK stepped into the room, brandishing a gun. "Keep going," he said, "and very slowly..."

Without looking back, BK tried to kick the door closed with his foot, but another foot stopped it. Norm shoved open the door, saying, "Here's the burner phone you wanted." Norm inadvertently knocked BK off-balance into the centre of the room. BK stumbled and discharged the gun, lodging the bullet in the door jamb.

Alacrán leapt out of the way, uttering a surprised oath, hooking his cast on a chair, twisting it horribly before falling awkwardly to the carpet. The plaster cast broke on a diagonal line, and his leg produced a sickening crack. Alacrán rolled on his side in agony.

Amelia threw a lamp at BK's head, and Mason pounced on BK, subduing him and taking his gun away. Mason struggled briefly with BK before pinning him to the floor.

Norm kneeled to help Alacrán. Amelia ran to help her dad. He gruffly waved them both off, gasping at the waves of pain before crooking an arm over his eyes. Alacrán said, "Get me into a chair."

Mason said. "Norm, gun." He tossed the weapon to Norm. Amelia was lifting Alacrán to his feet. At the same instant, BK lunged upward to attack Mason from behind.

Amelia shouted, "Mason."

Norm caught the gun and tossed it back to Mason, who, still on his feet, grabbed it out of mid-air, twisted, pistol-whipped BK with it, and then held it to his head. Mason's face was contorted into a crimson killer's mask.

Amelia appeared at Mason's side. "This is so not you."

"Maybe it is now. Why not do this fucker here? Seems like he wants it."

"You know why not."

Mason was about to say something, but then his eyes mellowed; his shoulders relaxed—she had gotten through to him again. "Yeah, maybe I still do." He handed Amelia the gun.

She aimed the gun at BK's eyes. "Both legs under the couch, hands on the cushions. If you move, I shoot." BK collapsed silently into submission and assumed the position.

Amelia turned back to Alacrán. His ashen face was drawn, his jaw tight. He flinched violently, sucking air when Norm poked the break in the cast. Norm looked at Amelia. "Definitely broken again."

"That's settled then," she said. "We're sending you two back to Pennsylvania."

"Forget that idea. You kids need me here."

"We don't need to worry about you two," said Mason. "We'll see you in a few days."

Norm tended to Alacrán, who griped about taking care of himself and made bold, claiming, "Quit fussing... It's a mosquito bite. Hell, in 'Nam, we'd put a band-aid on this and keep going..."

Mason interrupted Alacrán before he could get wound

up about past glories, patted Norm on the shoulders, and said, "He's asking for your help."

"Yeah, I got it. Sounds fun. What about you? Are you going to be alright?"

Mason rolled his eyes toward Amelia, still guarding BK. She loaded a full clip into her Glock, then cranked a shell into the chamber. She saw them watching and said, "What?"

Mason looked at Norm, who said, "Right."

Mason took the Swiss Army knife out of his pocket and handed it to Norm. "This goes with our two coffee mugs. Alacrán knows where they are."

Norm pocketed the knife with a quizzical look on his face. "You got it, buddy."

"Now," said Mason, "it's time we got the real party started."

Father and daughter quickly hugged each other. Amelia handed Alacrán his crutch, then Norm boosted Alacrán's arm over his shoulder to steady him. Norm said, "Okay, peg leg, lean on me, and we'll have you home in no time to have someone look at that *mosquito bite*. In the meantime, I find war history fascinating, so you can tell me all about your escapades in '*Nam*.'" Norm gave Mason a sardonic thanks-for-nothing smile on the way out.

When Amelia closed the door, Mason said, "We actually had to break his leg before he would leave. That man has staying power."

Amelia rechecked her Glock for the bullet in the chamber, looked at BK, and said, "My guess is you don't make it past sundown alive."

They taped BK's mouth shut. Mason snuck him outside in a commandeered laundry cart, plopping him down between two dumpsters in the hotel service alley. Three dishevelled and miserable dumpster divers watched them. "Maybe one of these people will help you," said Mason. "After all, your masters helped put them here." He walked away. The three homeless people approached BK slowly and with interest.

*

In the hotel room, Mason said, "I think that nightmare of a man has finally found his true station in life. Let's get out of here."

"How far are we going?"

"All the way."

*

Later that evening, they sat on a park bench, talking over a casual burger and fries take-out meal, when it hit Mason like a truckload. He stopped eating and said, "There has to be more."

"Not for me; I'm already stuffed."

He was not amused. "People, friends of mine, have died... Everything happened so fast... I think I've become them."

"We hurt them. We won."

"Bullshit." Mason's outburst drew attention from an elderly couple strolling past. He lowered his voice. "We're not even hitch-hikers on their road to Hell. None of us are. That's why they're letting us walk. Delaci even sacrificed Victor to dismiss us."

She reached for his hand. "They did not dismiss us."

He pulled his hand away. "They did. And they win if we leave Washington. Don't you see?"

She whispered sadly, "They'll kill us." She implored him, "We have a future..."

"I can't... there's nothing there for me."

"I'll be there."

"I'm done running."

"Are you giving up on us...?"

"We're not important if the NEWCorps in the world win." He paused as the dark realization hit him. "We won't be enough. I need time—to think." Mason stood. Amelia reached out to him, and he took her hand. He said, "It was never going to be you leaving me, was it?" and then he walked away from her.

He paced crowded Washington's sidewalks for hours, confused, mulling and heartbroken, obsessed with the thought, *There must be a way...*

*

Mason knocked on the door. Amelia opened it, pointing the gun at his belly. He froze. In her other hand was a tablespoon full of ice cream. Her hair was askew, her eyes red from crying, and Elle was lamenting love on the stereo.

"I need you," he said.

"I know. I need you too."

238

Mason put the parts together and came to the correct conclusion. "You think I dumped you."

"No...I...well, didn't you?"

He took her in his arms and hugged her and kissed her tears away, and hugged her again.

"Not in a million years. Not, like, intentionally."

Amelia's weak smile was reassuring but not yet full strength. "Then I hate you," she said.

"I know. But I never...I have a plan... interested?"

"Intrigued." Amelia dropped her spoon, tossed the gun onto the couch, reached up to clasp her hands together behind his neck and walked him back into the suite and her life. His hands fell on her hips. As the door gently swung shut, Amelia said, "Tell me, darling, everything."

*

Late the next morning, Mason called IBM. No answer—no surprise. IBM was too smart to accept a call from an unknown number, so Mason sent a long text message. He placed the phone down on the table, this time unconcerned about being tracked.

Sitting across from him, brushing her hair, Amelia said, "I hope IBM's trumpet lesson doesn't land us on death row."

"We'll be okay," he said, but they both knew winning or losing big depended on the outcome of the next few hours. "Let's order in lunch."

At 2:00 p.m., Mason switched the channel to C-SPAN. The member from Vermont finished eloquently and logically slamming the Republican House leader for stifling another universal health care bill. He yielded to the member from Arizona, who lavishly praised the president for building a scant few but insanely expensive miles of his proposed southern border wall. Mason looked at Amelia's gun and holster lying on the bed, then at her. Amelia shook her head, holding up her latest phone. Leaving the suite, they walked along the same hallways Richard Nixon's White House "plumbers" had tarnished so many presidents ago. Mason wondered idly if they, too, might be walking into history.

Outside the hotel entrance, Amelia said, "Look up."

Alarmed, he looked up and involuntarily staggered a step to his right. "Why? Clones?"

"It's all still free..."

"Is it?"

"In about an hour, maybe not."

"No matter what they do to us, we'll always have me shooting Victor in the ass."

"Twice," she said, bursting into laughter. The first taxi in line pulled up. "Take us to the House of Representatives, please."

*

Just minutes later, they arrived. Mason was humbled. "It's breathtaking every time."

The taxi driver said, "Even more, from the inside. I bring my daughters here every year, so they remember who built our government. Did you know most of the men that built the White House were slaves? It seems like folks nowadays forget that."

Mason tipped him a hundred dollars. "Buy your daughters some ice cream."

"Thanks to you folks, but they gets lots of Ben and Jerry's already. I'll split this between them for their college funds."

*

Inside the magnificent Halls of Congress, the security guards were professional, attentive, and armed. Amelia and Mason breezed through the security portal. They passed armed marines standing at ease in dress blues and a gauntlet of eager-eyed ushers directing the stream of visitors into the various galleries.

The iconic Capitol dome rivalled even Louis XVI's magnificent palace in Versailles for grandeur. The scale dwarfed any single person before the primary symbol of a free and democratic nation.

"Washington," said Mason in awe, "commissioned this for a purpose." However, Mason's cynicism returned when he stood at the first president's self-portrayal, which radiated a distinct aura of the aristocracy. Mason did a double-take. "There really is a ladder leading up to a spaceship in his portrait." Then Amelia drew his attention to the dome painting. "All hail the emperor."

A fawning retiree usher directed them to the Visitors' gallery overlooking the floor of the House. They approached a door labelled "RESTRICTED" and partially obscured by an obese white woman.

The guard was in her forties. Blonde Harpo Marx hair escaped from beneath her cap, and her white, short-sleeve shirt bulged too, filled to capacity. Amelia stopped to ask, "Is this the door to the public gallery?"

In a voice of controlled petulance born of repetition, the guard said, "No, ma'am, this is the member's private entrance." She slid to the side, fully revealing the sign over her shoulder. "The public gallery is farther along this hall, to your right. That way. Have a nice day." They thanked her, continued along the hallway toward the public gallery entrance, and went inside.

Expanding below them was the epicentre of American Democracy. The Arizona member was still at the podium but had changed topics to praising the NRA propaganda that every citizen, even children, should own guns.

Just three other members attended, and they lounged in the first few rows, texting or otherwise distracted by their cellphones. Congress was in session for two more days, but it was also happy hour. Many members were out for dinner, vying for tables and drinks at joints like Bull Feathers, hoping for a mention in a local gossip column or for the unlikely event they might meet someone they could seduce.

Two cameras pointed at the speaking member. Another camera, hanging from the sturdy ceiling mount, pointed almost straight down to the podium. A lone camerawoman operated the floor TV camera from behind the tripod ten feet off to the politician's side. Mason and Amelia sat in the balcony, joining the few listeners blasted by the vitriolic member punishing them with her hating monologue. A clerk recorded the member's address to the nation from beside the vacated Speaker's chair. Everyone had better things to do than listen to more orchestrated twisting of the constitution's intention and her willful unravelling of hundreds of years of democracy.

Mason dialled the number he had found in the phone book in their hotel room. "Are you ready?"

Amelia nodded. "It's now or never."

Mason spoke intensely and clearly to the person who answered his call. "There's some kind of disruption inside the House of Representatives, on the floor… I'm sure I heard gunshots. You'd better send a camera crew down here right now." They left the balcony, quickly retracing their steps back to the door at the top of the stairwell. The cop was gone.

Amelia said, "What do we do?"

"We could try this..." He knocked on the door and waited. He knocked again, this time louder and more insistent. The door opened.

A waft of cigarette smoke emanated from the open door. The same guard said, "I'm sorry, folks, only representatives and their staff are allowed." Amelia moved in, punching the guard decisively in the solar plexus. The guard huffed. Amelia helped the surprised and collapsing woman back into the stairwell to sit her down on the steps. To any casual observer, the guard had simply opened the door and ushered them inside. Mason closed the door.

"We don't mean you or anyone any harm, and I'm pretty sure we're not crazy," he said.

Amelia punched Mason in the arm. "I don't know; he might be a little nuts. He made us come here unarmed. But we need access to the floor." Amelia stuck the guard with the Dr. Feel Good pin. The gasping guard tried to hold Mason's leg, but her fingers slipped off when the familiar glaze fogged her eyes. A sly smile formed, and she tilted her hat back. "Thanks," she said.

They left her humming a Shania Twain tune to herself. Skipping down the stairs two at a time, Amelia emptied the guard's weapon. The bullets rattled in the stairwell when they fell to the floor. They left the gun, her radio, and her whistle at the bottom of the stairs. Racing across the lobby, they pushed open both doors at the top of one of the aisles, surprising two pages—a young man and a young woman—when they rushed past them. "Can we help you?" the young man said, trying to hold them back.

"Pay attention. Maybe you can learn to help yourself."

Protesting, they followed Mason and Amelia for a few steps, but both pages stopped in the aisle, unsure of themselves. Mason and Amelia continued sprinting down the long stretch of blue carpet to the floor in front of the Speaker's benches. They made so little commotion, the member from Arizona continued to justify gun violence to the near-empty theatre. The recording clerk was startled when Amelia walked onto the floor. Mason followed, just steps behind her, hoping he was streaming the audio and video through his phone to IBM. The member stopped talking when Amelia stepped in front of the cameras.

Amelia said, "You're done. I have to table something important."

The member said, "Well, I never..."

"We know." The member retreated in a huff.

At that moment, a blur of action began with yelling, a gunshot, then a scream echoing in the foyer. Jairo rushed through the doors at the top of the aisle. He ran toward them, aiming his handgun. The clerk screamed, "He has a gun." Then there was another scream at the top of the aisle, and BK appeared in the doorway.

The stoned guard, her hat askew, followed him inside and promptly fell down. "Shittin' Jesus, that god damned trick knee again."

"Jairo. She's mine," yelled BK. Mason threw himself in front of Amelia, but Jairo had turned to face the intruder. BK, shooting with his left hand, placed a bullet in the center of Jairo's forehead. He crumbled—dead. BK fired three quick shots into the ceiling and yelled, "This isn't over, Amelia." He turned and vanished back through the swinging doors. Both pages screamed long and loud.

Mason looked at Amelia. "Talk about the serpent eating its own tail."

Amelia looked into the television camera and then looked back at the cowering clerk. The politician had pancaked on the floor at the first sound of gunfire. Amelia turned to Mason and said, "See? That's why I have always..."

"Cameras, babe," cautioned Mason, "don't finish that sentence."

Amelia gathered herself and spoke to the stunned attendees. "We mean you no harm. We are unarmed."

The doors swung wide again. Two SWAT teams of six heavily armed men and women rushed in, performing a choreographed military exercise down both aisles. Between the rows of empty seats, they shouted authoritative orders to each other. A TV camera crew followed on their heels. The security guard saw the camera and said, "Well, if I'm going to be on TV..." and sat in an aisle seat, rearranging her hair under her hat. The members of the flanking security squad had drawn their weapons and trained them on Mason and Amelia. The red light on the floor camera went out. Whatever was about to happen would not be broadcast on C-SPAN.

"On the floor, on the floor," threatened the two SWAT team captains, meaning business.

Amelia looked at Mason and said, "You have my back?"

"Always."

Her hands in the air, Amelia spoke calmly and clearly. "We're not here to hurt or shoot anyone. We're here to expose American voters to one of the largest lies ever perpetrated on US citizens. This is the proof."

Amelia waved the Mass-Spec printout. Laser pointers on the SWAT team guns circulated on Amelia and Mason. The members waited for shoot-to-kill orders from their commander. He evaluated the confrontation by remote camera.

"Mason, stand beside me."

He looked at the film crew from Al Jazeera. The camera operator gave Mason a thumbs up. The journalist said, "Our feed's live; keep talking." The sound man aimed a remote mic.

Mason and Amelia stood together. Whatever was going to happen would happen to both of them. He raised his hand over his head, and they clasped their hands together.

The double doors at the top of both aisles blew open. More people yelled as footsteps thundered down the aisle. Their confusion of voices disarmed the extreme tension. The security guard turned to see what the commotion was about and inadvertently threw a leg into the aisle. The blonde running down the aisle with a microphone tripped over the guard's leg, face-planting in the aisle, yelling, "Fuck!" A lighting man energized the third string of portable lights—cable news was on the scene. The security cop sheepishly retracted her leg. The blonde stood herself up, wiped her imperfect hair off her face, glared once at the security cop, turned to face the camera and said, "This is Kirsty Goodlove live for GNN. Terrorists have taken over the House of Representatives. There is no official body count yet, but it's chaos here. Security has the terrorists surrounded. It's a tense stand-off..."

Mason said, "Please tell me you're getting this?"

IBM, on speaker, said, "That faceplant is going to go viral. I cut the GNN remote feed. You're online and live all over the internet world. Take it viral, dude."

Mason said, "Hey, chairman Delaci, this one's for you. The Nuclear Energy World Corporation is a multi-national crime syndicate operating on American soil, backed by corrupt US senators and a complicit President. Their crimes are murder, bribery, extortion, theft of US citizens' rights, the rights of world citizens, and the futures of our children. They are conspiring to dump nuclear waste in our oceans. A man is lying dead, shot, in the aisle in front of us, an assassin hired by the alleged criminals to kill us." He paused to look at Amelia. She smiled at him, squeezing his hand.

"Besides this video you are watching now, we have data and video of confessions. The perpetrators admit they are guilty of the Wall Street murders of which we are unjustly accused."

Two SWAT members stood next to the Al Jazeera camera crew but allowed them to continue filming. Behind them, the confused GNN team yelled at each other, unable to establish a live feed. Their producer urged them to continue filming.

The SWAT lieutenant appeared sympathetic. "Are you done?" he asked. "We're not in a real hurry, but I'm supposed to ask you to desist."

"We're giving ourselves up, but first, we ask the American people to examine this evidence as proof. Once you do that, we believe you will bring the real criminals to justice."

*

In the basement of the hospital in Montreal, IBM confirmed he was feeding Mason and Amelia live to GNN and that Al Jazeera had copies of the decrypted and now legible NEWCorp files. The mainstream media had picked up the feed. "You're still live and kickin' it," he said to Mason. "I'm sharing the raw video around the world."

*

Amelia and Mason kissed each other and then surrendered— their duty satisfied.

Amelia and Mason marched proudly up the aisles of Democracy at gunpoint and handcuffed, escorted by armed SWAT members. At the doors at the top of the aisle, the female security guard stood aside for them. She smiled crookedly, her hat askew again. She saluted and said, "Let 'em through; they're great. Just what we need." She spotted a camera lens. "My left side, cutie," she said to the dubious Al

Jazeera cameraman, "is my most photogenic." Mason tried to apologize to her, but she shook her head, "Forget it, honey, let's all do shots tonight. Hey, everybody, I got dibs on the cute camera guy."

Before the crush of journalists swarmed them, Mason said to Amelia, "See, you didn't have to, you know… pop anyone." They answered as many questions from rabid journalists as they could while SWAT officers escorted them through the crowd as if Mason and Amelia were rock stars. Finally, though, the police ushered them onto a service elevator that transported them to the subdued basement carpark. There, they were quietly marched into a police van. The SWAT teams deployed to disarm and probably kill them saluted them before closing and locking the SWAT van doors.

Amelia and Mason sat in silence on opposite benches between serious officers. Mason asked the guard handcuffing him to the bench, "What happens now?" The officer quoted Jim Morrison in a monotone voice, "The future's uncertain, and the end is always near."

The black, unmarked police van drove away from underground parking. Amelia sent Mason another of those enigmatic looks that would have so cleverly seduced Leonardo—if he had let her.

*

Delaci waited until she entered the boardroom. He said, "I knew you would come. This is for the best. We have much to accomplish."

"Of course. I'm ready to start now."

"Wonderful. I have a daughter again. Cessily, your boyfriend, I…"

"Don't."

For an instant, Delaci saw something dangerous flash in her eyes. "Well, then, let me bring you up to speed on our next project." Delaci texted security while Cessily poured coffees and brought them on a tray.

He texted: weapons?

Security replied: she is unarmed.

Cessily hesitated briefly behind Delaci. He froze. She lightly dragged her fingertips across his neck and one shoulder, then slipped into a chair beside him and offered him a coffee.

Delaci pocketed the phone and looked at her. "Thank

246

you. I know you've had a rough time of it, Cessily, but that's all behind us now. You've found your way back to me. That's what matters. I can make the rest up to you—how does 'ruling the world' sound for starters?"

"Did you really think I would come here armed?"

"Cessily, you know I trust you completely."

"That might be your last mistake."

"But I trust you."

In the silence, the room seemed immense. "Nice view," she said. She tapped her nose stud, deep in thought. "What are you going to do about them?"

"Did you read what I sent to you?"

"Everything. You're not concerned with the optics?"

*

In a room off the oval office, the most powerful man in the world sat below an American flag under the watchful eyes of John Kennedy's portrait. The President was playing Tetris on his cellphone. A pile of white, glossy folders had been stacked on his desk. The fussy makeup artist finished with the president's hair and powdered down his glistening face before stepping away.

The press secretary whispered, "Mr. President. The cameras are recording." The president looked up, sighed, and asked, "How do I save this?" The press secretary exchanged the phone for a pen. Under the watchful eyes of several men in expensive suits, the president opened the first folder. He signed the blank page inside with a flourish. Several bulbs flashed from cameras, the onlookers approved. The President smiled once, condescendingly, then closed the folder and opened the next.

He was about to sign, but a meticulously manicured male hand with a Skull and Crossbones ring on one finger nudged the pen aside and closed the folder. The president looked upwards and to his right. Delaci leaned in to whisper into his ear, "Not this one," he said, his voice silky and slithery. "the optics… it's not quite time yet." No cameras flashed.

The president became testy and said aloud, "Can't you people make up your minds." He opened the next folder and smiled for the cameras.

*

Even under house arrest, Mason watched television and talked on the phone with Amelia. There were still no formal charges against them, but they were pending. Mason received a call from an anonymous source two weeks into their house arrest, instructing him to watch the informal press conference.

The President flippantly responded to reasonable questions from the press on the tenth tee on his golf course. "You fake news people, you're always so rude, so negative. A film can lie."

One persistent and daring journalist shouted, "Does that mean you think Mason and Amelia are innocent of the Wall Street murders?"

"Oh no," said the President, "that one looks like, well, we saw it, and I...make America great again, it is great, we're great, doing great." He glared at his press secretary for unforthcoming answers and said, "Didn't I ask you what I saw on TV?" The president's open-neck golf shirt underscored his lack of concern over the event in congress or the accusations he was integral to the scam. "I have no comment," said the President. "Besides, all that stuff is national security." He then sliced his drive into the middle of the lake bordering the first fairway. "Looks like that one stayed on the grass," he said. "Let's go find it."

The press secretary smiled on cue at the President's moral nonchalance. The President joined his golfing buddies slipping away from the cameras, eluding responsibility to the scorecard and the nation, and dumped it squarely on his underling.

One journalist shouted, "Can you comment on the president's distancing himself from NEWCorp? The polls show..."

Over the next ten minutes, the press secretary defrayed the uncomfortable questions about NEWCorp and the shelved, historic uranium waste bill by insulting the press. Then he added, "No one pays attention to the damn fake polls. The people voted our president into office because he declared war on the swamp. No more questions."

Mason turned off the TV. He called Amelia. "Did you watch that? Not a word about the scam."

"I saw it. Have you talked to IBM today?"

"His trumpet lessons are going good, and his prime minister sent him a thank you text."

"And we got our pardons. The paperwork will be done

soon, then we can see each other."

"I had hopes Victor would serve his state from inside a federal prison, but that's not going to happen. And BK and Delaci are still out there."

"I have to ask... after everything, would you do it again?"

"Just try me."

36. **Honeymoon Redux**

Though NEWCorp tried to hack him, IBM replayed the video on a continuous loop for weeks through a cryptocurrency server in Reykjavik. Many Icelanders had been defrauded of their futures during the crash of 2008 and were sympathetic.

After a superficial investigation, the US Attorney General dropped all the charges on Mason and Amelia due to insufficient evidence. They caught a break when a civil attorney offered to represent them on a Pro Bono basis. Even so, they languished for another month before finalizing the court paperwork.

During that time, Norm moved back home with his parents, where he endured loose talk from his father about the virtues of becoming a rabbi. Alacrán rehabilitated his leg, enjoying arguments with his crew over the attributes of various sidearms and the merits of knuckleballer pitchers in baseball. The dog days of August had descended on the Eastern seaboard, so the Yankees and the Red Sox floundered while the Astros supporters taunted everyone with World Series jibes.

Alacrán called Mason. "Matvey says there are almost no convoys of ore passing through Shieli now. INTERPOL is investigating NEWCorp for international trade, environmental law, and combines violations." The Times reported that the NYSE and Chicago Futures exchanges had suspended all NEWCorp stock trading, setting NEWCorp adrift in financial waters. "Matvey told me," said Alacrán, "their video clips were almost better than old Baywatch episodes." The crime for Victor conspiring to have Amelia and Mason murdered, even as a wealthy criminal, was still twenty-five years to life on each count. "But slime like him, a guy who knows where the bodies are buried," said Alacrán, "is looking at house arrest and pardon. At least the D.C. AG ordered a forensic audit on NEWCorp, at its expense. That should keep it busy in court and drain funds into the US legal system for decades."

Every day, GNN reported more NEWCorp assets seized and frozen around the world. "It won't be long," said Mason, "before the lawyers have all the money. The Inner Circle will be eating watery macaroni in jail until their teeth fall out." The Senate ousted seven lobbyists. They left Washington in shame and with dates to face bribery, extortion, and obstruction charges in Federal court, alongside four congressional representatives and six senators. The member from Arizona never saw the wall finished or the inside of Congress after the election.

"It looks like Victor will avoid Federal Prison for the rest of his life." Mason was video conferencing Amelia.

"They have connected lawyers. Do you miss me?"

"So much it hurts."

"Me too. We'll be together soon."

*

On the cellphone, Delaci was infuriated, "Matteo, you gutter trash, you failed."

Matty was unimpressed. "Family loyalty comes first. You ever come down to my street again, you better hope we don't see you..."

*

When Mason and Amelia were freed from house arrest, they visited Lena in Seattle—at Ivan's graveside. Lena said, "He was diagnosed with third-stage cancer before he left for CERN."

"Why didn't he tell me?"

"He wanted his friends to remember him as he was during his life—not at the end. The radiation treatments weren't enough, and he refused chemo. It's so sad… he was a good man." Lena's eyes grew misty. "He loved his children and saw them grow. He always had that, and he left us financially healthy. I miss him every day, but he told me he had no regrets."

*

The Federal Bank paid them an unexpected reward of $150,000 for the returned bonds.

Julie was attending a conference out of town, so they visited Peabody for a weekend. It was pure, simple joy for Mason to have his devoted Brooke back again. To thank Peabody for babysitting, they bought him a new Yaris, throwing in enough money for gas, insurance, and maintenance to cover a few years. "You can write that second book now," said Peabody.

"I have the chapters titled and the summary

finished, but I'm looking for an editor." Peabody and Mason shook hands. "I'd be delighted," said Peabody.

"Not so fast, you two," said Amelia, "first we're taking a holiday."

"Since everyone is feeling so good," said Peabody, "why don't we celebrate? What's your pleasure?"

"Martinis," said Mason and Amelia together. "I'm olives; he's onions," added Amelia.

"But the magic is in the vermouth," said Mason, smiling with her, like lovers do.

*

It was a moonless night. A strong breeze blew Amelia's curls over her shoulders. She and Mason held each other in a strong arm-in-arm grip when Mason shouted over the wind, "As much as I love the mountains around Seattle, this view ain't bad."

"Do you remember our suite in Jakarta? Which is better?"

"Right here, right now."

His Bluetooth earpiece buzzed. "Hey, it's a text from Descartes. He says, 'Bonjour and congratulations on your freedom.' Hey, look who joined our party." Below and behind them, BK had parked under a light in the lot down and behind their position. Leaning on the hood of his Mercedes, he trained a rifle on them, but a string of police cars raced into the parking lot, sliding to stops beside BK's car.

"Wait, there's more... 'thumb drive contents clear you both in SW. I will hold it for your protection."

"The moon is rising, darling. It's time to leave."

A powerful spotlight zeroed in on them, and a man was yelling in Portuguese through a bullhorn. BK stood his ground, looking at Mason and Amelia, but he had ditched his rifle. The man with the bullhorn demanded in broken English they come down at once.

"They seem a little peevish," said Mason. "We should do what they say."

Far below, Norm and Brooke waited, outside the barrio, in a new BMW convertible Amelia had borrowed at the airport. "One second..." Mason pressed a button on his headset, and both their headphones filled beneath the star-filled skies with *Handle Me with Care*. Amelia and Mason leapt from the shoulders of the Christ the Redeemer statue high above Rio de Janeiro.

B.A.S.E. jumping above the city's spectacular night skyline, soaring as free as eagles, they sailed away.

www.ingramcontent.com/pod-product-compliance
Lightning Source LLC
Chambersburg PA
CBHW060912250626
47159CB00008B/2977